John Wilson

Index to the Acts and Proceedings of the General Assembly of the Church of Scotland

SALZWASSER
VERLAG

John Wilson

Index to the Acts and Proceedings of the General Assembly of the Church of Scotland

Reprint of the original, first published in 1863.

1st Edition 2022 | ISBN: 978-3-37500-089-9

Verlag (Publisher): Salzwasser Verlag GmbH, Zeilweg 44, 60439 Frankfurt, Deutschland
Vertretungsberechtigt (Authorized to represent): E. Roepke, Zeilweg 44, 60439 Frankfurt, Deutschland
Druck (Print): Books on Demand GmbH, In de Tarpen 42, 22848 Norderstedt, Deutschland

INDEX

TO THE

ACTS AND PROCEEDINGS

OF THE

GENERAL ASSEMBLY

OF

THE CHURCH OF SCOTLAND

INDEX

TO THE

ACTS AND PROCEEDINGS

OF THE

GENERAL ASSEMBLY

OF

THE CHURCH OF SCOTLAND

BY THE

REV. JOHN WILSON

MINISTER OF DUNNING

MDCCCLXIII

PREFACE.

THIS work is intended to supply a want which has been long felt by those engaged in the business of the Church Courts. It aspires to be something more than a mere Index. The analysis of the Acts is so full, and the Digest of the Proceedings and Decisions so particular, that, for ordinary practice, it will of itself be sufficient, it is hoped, as a convenient book of reference; while to those who wish for fuller information in regard to any ecclesiastical matter, it indicates where that information may be found, without the trouble of, what is at present necessary, a long and laborious search.

It was intended to have given a digest of the cases of disputed settlements that have come under the review of the Assembly, but these were found to be so numerous as to require a much larger volume than the present to make them intelligible; the idea was therefore abandoned, but a list has been given of the cases in alphabetical order.

In such an Index, referring to the Enactments and Decisions of the Assembly for more than a century and a half, many things have probably been omitted; but the compiler has been careful to verify his references, and hopes they will be found correct so far as they go.

The Roman numerals have been employed to denote the Acts, and the small figures the Sessions of Assembly: for example—1847. viii., means Act viii. of Assembly 1847; and 1847. 8, means Assembly 1847, Session 8.

Grateful acknowledgments are due to the late Dr Simpson, Clerk of Assembly, and William Young, Esq., W.S., Agent for the Church, and their successors in office, for their advice and assistance, and for kindly allowing access to the documents connected with the different cases decided by the Assembly, without which it would, in many instances, have been impossible to state the grounds on which the decisions were given, these not being always reported in the abridgment annually appended to the printed Acts.

CONTENTS.

ERRATUM.

Page 5, line 3 from bottom, *for* **" Edmonston "** *read* **" Cairncross."**

INDEX

TO THE

ACTS AND PROCEEDINGS

OF

THE GENERAL ASSEMBLY OF THE CHURCH OF SCOTLAND.

A

Absolution. Rules to be observed in absolving persons who have been excommunicated. Form of sentence of absolution prescribed. 1707. xi. chap. ix.

Accession. The solemn engagement that His Majesty came under upon his first accession to the crown, to maintain inviolably the doctrine, worship, discipline, and government, rights and privileges, of the Church of Scotland, read and recorded. 1715. iv.

Accounts. The public accounts of the Church ordered to be balanced every year on the 15th of April, audited, and reported to the Assembly, and a general abstract of the whole printed and circulated along with the Acts of Assembly. 1840. 9.

——— A full report as to the state of the several accounts given. 1841, *Appendix*.

——— *See* FINANCE.

Acts. Enacted that no Act rescissory of any standing Act of the General Assembly shall be passed until such Act be first transmitted to the several presbyteries of this Church, and their general opinion had for rescinding the same. 1736. viii.

Acts of Assembly. Enacted that before any Acts can be passed relating to the doctrine, worship, government, or discipline of the Church, which are to be binding rules and constitutions of the Church, they must first be transmitted as overtures to the several presbyteries of the Church, and obtain the sanction of a majority of said presbyteries. 1697. ix.

——— Anent the method of making overtures and Acts of the General Assembly. Anything of public concern and great weight, after the first reading, to lie on the table till next day, for the consideration of the members. 1700. xvi.

——— Every minister and kirk-session enjoined to have a copy of all the printed Acts of Assembly. Presbyteries to inquire into this. 1700. xvi.

——— The agent for the Church to transmit to every presbytery as many copies of the printed Acts as will serve for them and for the several parishes within their bounds, at the expense of the kirk-sessions and presbyteries. Presbyteries and sessions, at their first meeting after receiving said Acts, to cause read the same. Synods to see that this Act is observed. 1705. xviii.

Acts of Assembly. The Acts 1700, xvi., and 1705, xviii., recommending kirk-sessions to buy the printed Acts of Assembly, revived and re-enacted. 1773. vii.

——— A copy of the printed Acts to be sent annually to the Advocates' Library; a copy for each synod and university; and a copy for the moderator and clerk of each presbytery. 1779. xii.; 1762, ult.

——— Complaint from the printers to the Church, that, of 500 copies of the Acts printed yearly for twenty years past, scarcely one-half were disposed of. 1744, ult.

——— A petition from the clerk anent reprinting in a small volume all the Acts of Assembly already printed, with an abridgment and alphabetical index for the use of the Church, referred to the Commission. 1704, ult.

——— **Printing**. The Assembly authorise the sum of £15 to be paid annually to Mr Hill, in time coming, for printing the Acts of Assembly, in lieu of the £10 formerly allowed him. 1804. 8.

——— Presbyteries recommended to send for copies of the printed Acts as soon as notice is given in the newspapers that they are ready for delivery. 1816. 7.

——— Committee appointed to consider and report on any alterations which it may be advisable to make on the printing and publishing the Acts of Assembly, and also on the republishing such as are out of print. 1832. 9; 1833, ult.

——— The Assembly authorise the procurator to pay £5 additional to Mr Waugh, for printing the Acts of Assembly 1831; but when the Acts do not exceed 60 pages in length, the old allowance for printing to be resumed. 1832. 9.

——— A motion to print the Acts of the General Assembly previous to the year 1638, referred to the Commission. 1741, ult.

——— Proposal to consolidate Acts relative to the election and admission of members of Assembly, referred to a committee. 1790. 4. Report of committee rejected *simpliciter*. 1790, ult.

Acts of Parliament. Committee appointed to excerpt the Acts of Parliament that concern the Church, and that are against profanity, that the same may be printed. Kirk-sessions recommended to procure said Acts. 1696. 6.

Adultery. The Commission ordained to apply to Government for the more effectual suppressing and punishing of adultery. 1706. 12.

——— In a process for adultery, kirk-sessions are not to proceed further than to deal with the parties accused to confess—which done, they are to refer the case, and send an extract of their procedure thereanent to the presbytery. 1707. xi. chap. vi. 1.

Advocates. The General Assembly, considering that they have a title to the assistance of all their members as judges, in all causes brought before them, enact and declare, that in time coming none who are constituent members of court shall act as counsel or procurators in any causes which shall come before the Assembly, or Commission thereof. 1751. iv.

Advocates' Bar. The keeper of the advocates' bar in the Court of Session allowed a salary of four guineas per annum, in consideration of his admitting all ministers of the Church, and those concerned in the Assembly clerk's office, to enter said bar. 1749. 9.

Agents. Remitted to the Commission, to prevent insults by agents in inferior judicatories. 1708. 10.

——— A kirk-session having refused to allow a party the assistance of a law-agent in a process before them, the party appealed to the presbytery and synod, and Assembly. The Assembly, after reasoning, unanimously dismissed the appeal, and affirmed the judgment of the inferior judicatories (Synod of Glasgow and Ayr). 1827. 9.

Agent for the Church. John Blair allowed "£50 sterling for agenting the Church's affairs, and £5 to his servant yearly." 1699. 17.

——— Reference to the Commission to nominate one to be conjunct agent for the Church with John Blair, and to give them instructions. 1706. 14.

——— Act declaring Nicol Spence, who was conjunct agent with the deceased John Blair, to be now sole agent for the Church. 1722. 11.

——— Mr Robert M'Intosh appointed conjunct agent and sub-clerk with Mr Nicol Spence; and, in the event of his surviving Mr Spence, to be sole agent and sub-clerk. 1738. 9.

——— On the death of Mr Spence, the Assembly found, by a

majority, that there was "a vacancy in the half of said offices;" and appointed a committee to consider and report as to how it should be supplied. 1743. 5.

Agent for the Church. On the report of said committee, Mr M'Intosh having judicially resigned the half of said offices, to which he had been found entitled, the Assembly appointed him and Mr John Baillie, W.S., conjunct agents for the Church, and sub-clerks to the General Assembly, with equal right to the stated salaries thereof. Mr M'Intosh to exercise the office of sub-clerk and clerk to the Royal Bounty, with right to the casual emoluments thereof; and Mr Baillie to exercise the office of agent, with right to its emoluments; and the survivancy of both offices to be in the longest liver of the two solely. 1743. 7.

——— Mr M'Intosh having died previous to the meeting of Assembly 1753, Mr Baillie gave in a letter to the Assembly proposing to resign the offices held by him, on condition that either Mr James Edmonston or Mr William Alston should be joined with him in said offices, "upon the same plan that Mr M'Intosh and he were joined in these offices;" which proposal the Assembly, by a great majority, agreed to (Professor Cumming and many others dissenting). Mr Edmonston to perform the duties and enjoy the emoluments formerly performed and enjoyed by Mr M'Intosh. 1753. 3.

——— On the death of Mr Baillie the Assembly found that the sole right to the foresaid offices had devolved upon Mr James Edmonston, and he was appointed to exercise them accordingly. 1754. 3.

——— Mr Edmonston being confined by sickness, requested the Assembly to allow Mr George Cairncross, Writer, Edinburgh, to officiate for him, which was agreed to. 1768. 1; 1775. 1; 1780, ult.

——— Mr Edmonston having died before the meeting of Assembly 1781, the offices aforesaid were disjoined, Dr William Gloag, one of the ministers of Edinburgh, being appointed sub-clerk, and Mr George Cairncross, agent for the Church. 1781. 1.

——— Mr Edmonston being indisposed, the Assembly, at his request, appointed Mr William Murray, junior, to officiate in his place. 1785. 1.

Agent for the Church. Mr Edmonston having resigned the office of agent for the Church, Mr William Murray was unanimously appointed to that office. 1795. 4.

——— Mr William Murray resigns; and he and Mr John Murray appointed joint-agents, with survivancy to the longest liver. 1809. 1.

——— On the death of Mr William Murray, Mr William Young, W.S., was appointed agent. Other two candidates were proposed—viz., Mr Harry M. Inglis, W.S., and Mr James Crawford, W.S. Before the candidates were proposed two motions were submitted as to the mode of election. The first being in effect, that in conformity with the invariable practice of the Church, only one vote should be taken on all the candidates, and that the candidate having the greatest number of votes should be declared duly elected; and the second being, that a vote should first be taken on all the candidates, and that the candidate having the smallest number of votes should be struck off the list; that this process should be repeated till the number of candidates was reduced to two, when the decision of the Assembly should be taken between these two, and the candidate having the greatest number of votes to be declared duly elected. The first motion was carried by a majority of 171 to 158. It was agreed that any member might demand a scrutiny, and, with a view to this, every member's vote was marked. A committee was appointed to inquire and report what are or ought to be the duties of the several office-bearers, and also to regulate their fees and emoluments. 1831. 1, and ult.

——— Mr John Beatson Bell, W.S., appointed agent, in the room of Mr William Young, deceased. 1855. 6.

Agent in London. William Gordon, Esq., D.C.L., appointed permanent agent for the Church in London, to give timeous intimation concerning such affairs there as may concern the Church or its members. 1766, ult.

Agent in London. Mr John Spottiswood appointed Solicitor for the Church in London in room of Dr Gordon, retired from business. 1770. 6.

——— Mr John Spottiswood appointed Solicitor for the Church in London in room of his father, deceased. 1805. 5.

Agents. All persons who are constituent members of Assembly prohibited from acting as agents, counsel, or procurators in any causes which come before the Assembly or Commissions thereof. 1751. iv.

Algiers. Money collected for the redemption of William Dowell, a Scotsman, captive in Algiers, and said to be dead, to be paid over to the Treasurer of the Christian Knowledge Society. 1738. 11.

Alison, Colin. Recommendation in favour of his book, entitled 'The Hierarchical Bishops' Claim tried at the Scripture Bar,' with a reference to the committee anent libraries in the Highlands. 1705. 15.

America. A committee appointed to consider a letter received from the Presbyterian Church in the United States of America, recommended that, owing to the peculiar circumstances of the case, it would be prudent not to notice the letter further. 1839, ult.

——— Another letter received with the highest gratification, and a committee appointed to answer it. 1842. 3.

America, British. *See* Colonies.

Anger. Indulging in a sinful excess of anger admitted as a relevant charge in a libel against a minister. 1749.

Angus and Mearns. The Synod of Angus and Mearns disjoined from the Synod of Aberdeen, and the two distinct synods appointed to meet in their usual places of meeting, according to the Act of Assembly 1638. 1701. vii.

Annan. The presbyteries of Annan and Langholm erected out of certain parishes disjoined from the presbyteries of Middlebie, Lochmaben, and Jedburgh. 1743. v.

Annexation. A reference relating to the annexation of the parishes of Broughton, Glenholm, and Kilbucho, remitted to the procurator and agent, with instructions to take such steps, at the public expense, as might be necessary for obtaining redress. 1803. 8.

——— Resolved to oppose the suppression and annexation of the parishes of Broughton, Glenholm, Kilbucho, and Culter, in consideration of the ample funds for the maintenance of four ministers, the extent of the parishes, and the general disinclination of the people. 1793, ult.

Annuity-Tax. The Commission, without a vote, agreed to a series of resolutions strongly disapproving of an arrangement proposed by a Select Committee of the House of Commons with reference to the annuity-tax in the city of Edinburgh "as a confiscation of the patrimony of the Church inconsistent with the principles of an establishment, and highly injurious to the interests of religion." Com., Nov. 19, 1851.

Appeals. An appeal must be taken immediately when the sentence appealed from is pronounced, and reasons of appeal must be given in to the court appealed from, or to the moderator or clerk thereof, within ten days, and extracts produced to the superior court, otherwise they shall be rejected. Defenders to be summoned either *apud acta* or by separate citation. 1694. viii. ; 1707. xi. chap. v. 1.

——— Frivolous appeals to be dismissed.

——— If the superior court find that an appeal is unnecessary, litigious, or malicious, they may inflict such censure upon the appellant as they deem meet. 1707, xi. chap. v. 4.

——— An appeal sists the execution of the sentence appealed from while the case is being duly prosecuted. 1707. xi., chap. v. 10.

——— An appeal stops the settlement of a parish by an inferior court until the appeal be decided or fallen from. 1732. v.

——— Appeals on preliminary points do not sist procedure until the relevancy has been determined. 1835. xi.

——— In all cases, except those which involve error in doctrine, the presbytery, after the relevancy has been found proved, shall proceed, notwithstanding all appeals, to prepare the case for final judgment. 1851. ix.

——— All appeals to the Assembly to be lodged with the clerk on or before the second or third day of the Assembly's meeting, with certification. 1718. vii. ; 1819. v.

——— Appeals to the General Assembly, together with the record and evidence adduced, to be printed in sufficient numbers—viz., 450 at least—so as to afford a copy to every member of Assembly; which printed papers shall be lodged with the agent for the Church on or before the Monday preceding the meeting of Assembly, otherwise the appeal shall be held as fallen from. 1850. xiv. 17.

——— The same method to be followed in appeals from kirk-sessions to presbyteries, and from presbyteries to synods, and from synods to the General Assembly. 1707. xi. chap. v. 9.

——— An overture proposing that the members of the inferior court from which an appeal is brought should not be prohibited from judging in the superior courts, was transmitted to presbyteries in 1730, 1741, 1754, 1771, 1772, and 1773, but not passed.

Appeals. A party failing to compear at the hour of cause to insist in his appeal, the appeal was found to be deserted and fallen from, and declared null and void. 1743, ult., *and others.*

——— The Synod of Perth and Stirling censured for proceeding with the settlement of the parish of Dull in the face of an appeal. 1743. 8.

——— An overture proposing to allow presbyteries to proceed with the settlement of parishes in the face of appeals, when the opposition was small, referred to the Commission. 1759. 7.

——— The Presbytery of Arbroath having settled a minister in the church and parish of Arbroath in the face of an appeal taken to the Assembly, the Assembly waived the consideration of said appeal, and found that the ordination and settlement of Mr Gleig were good and valid, seeing that they had already taken place; but that the presbytery had acted irregularly, and were subject to censure. The presbytery were ordered to sist themselves at the bar of next General Assembly to answer for their conduct, which they did, and were severely censured for their "highly irregular and incompetent" procedure. 1789. 8; 1789. 9; 1790. 5.

——— Appeals found to be incompetent, because the reasons of appeal were not lodged with the clerk in due time. 1790. 6; 1807. 6; 1834. 5; 1846, ult.; Com., 1839, Aug. 15.

——— An appeal dismissed as incompetent because (in violation of Act of Assembly 1639, sess. 23) it had been taken directly from the presbytery to the Assembly, and not to the intervening meeting of synod. 1807. 4.

——— An appeal against a decision of the Presbytery of Brechin having been objected to on the ground that it had been taken directly to the General Assembly, though two meetings of the synod intervened, the Assembly, "considering the peculiar circumstances of the case, agreed to waive the question how far the appeal had been correctly taken, no such objection having been stated by the respondents, and resolved to hear the case on the merits." 1833, ult.

——— An appeal from the Presbytery of Irvine having been

objected to on the ground that it had been taken to the General Assembly, and not to the synod, which met six days after the judgment appealed from, the Assembly, by a majority of 50 to 41, resolved to waive consideration of the point of form, and proceed to hear the appellants—Principal Lee and several others dissenting. 1845. 14.

Appeals. In a case relating to the erection of a chapel of ease, the reasons of appeal had not been lodged in due time; but the appellants having assigned a special reason for the delay, and shown that it was undesigned on their part, the Assembly *ex gratia* agreed to pass from the objection and to hear the appellants. 1826. 8.

——— An appeal can be taken only by a party, and immediately after the sentence has been intimated. 1836. 9.

——— A party having at the time acquiesced in a sentence of the synod, afterwards refused to obtemper it on the plea that he had not understood it, and on being called to account at a subsequent meeting, he appealed to the Assembly. The Assembly found that the sentence of synod not having been appealed from had become final, and dismissed the appeal. 1839. 11.

——— Presbytery in prosecuting a cause not to be sisted in their procedure by intermediate complaints and appeals, but not to pronounce final judgment until such complaints and appeals have been fallen from or determined. 1829. 6.

——— A member of an inferior court, not being a party, cannot appeal from any sentence of that court to a superior judicatory, but may enter his dissent and protest for leave to complain. 1738, ult.

——— In an appeal against a sentence of the Synod of Angus and Mearns, the Assembly found that the synod had taken up the case upon the appeal of certain members of presbytery, who, not being parties, had no right to appeal, and that consequently the sentence of the synod was incompetent. 1812. 9.

——— A member of synod having appealed against a sentence which, as he alleged, affected his character, and the synod having refused to enter his appeal on the record, he brought the case before the Assembly by a *petition*. The Assembly referred the case to the Commission, who dismissed the petition as incompetent, on the ground that the petitioner should have come before them by a dissent and complaint. Com., June 3, 1845.

Appeals. Not competent to appeal from a presbytery to a superior Church court, in cases relating to manses, glebes, and churchyard walls, &c. 1826. 7.

——— Not competent for a presbytery to receive an appeal when obtempering an appointment of synod. 1849. 8.

——— A party protested against a sentence of a presbytery, but did not add that it was for "leave to appeal." Reasons of appeal, however, were given in in due time; but the presbytery refused them on the ground that, as no appeal had been taken at the proper time, no reasons of appeal could afterwards be received. He brought the case before the Assembly by petition. The Assembly found that, as no competent appeal had been taken at the time when the sentence complained of was intimated, said sentence had become final. They accordingly dismissed the petition, but disapproved of the conduct of the presbytery. 1837. 6.

Argyle. The Synod of Argyle authorised to meet alternately at Lochgilphead and Inveraray on the first Wednesday of September annually. 1842. xxiii.

——— The Synod of Argyle authorised to meet at Inveraray on the first Wednesday of September annually. 1846. xv.

Arminianism. The General Assembly discharges the venting any Arminian or Socinian errors, and ordains the respective Judicatories of the Church to advert to any who shall teach or vent such errors, and to proceed to censure them therefor, as shall be found just and requisite. 1704. xii.

Army. Ministers and kirk-sessions, where any of His Majesty's forces are quartered, enjoined to provide them with convenient seats for hearing the Word, and to inspect and notice them as they do other parishioners; and the Commission instructed to fall upon all expedient ways convenient for them, how the said forces may be provided with preachers, and, upon application, to settle ministers in regiments belonging to this kingdom. 1697. xiii.

Assembly, General. Act concerning the better attendance of members. Absentees to be reported to their presbyteries by the clerk. For the first fault to be censured by their presbytery; for the second by the synod; and for the third to be suspended conform to Act 1647, ult. 1709. vii.

Assembly. Act for the better despatching the business of the Assembly. All references, complaints, and appeals to be lodged with the clerk on or before the second or third day of the Assembly meeting. 1718. vii.

——— Foregoing act renewed, and additional regulations made. Papers connected with every private cause to be on the table on or before the first Saturday of the Assembly. Committee on Bills to meet on preceding Thursday, also on Friday evening, and again on Saturday morning. Appeals, references, and complaints not presented at or before the third meeting to be held as deserted or fallen from. This Act to be read on the first day of the meeting of every Assembly, and a copy thereof to be sent to every presbytery. 1819. v. *See* STANDING ORDERS, 1859.

——— Act regulating the election of members. Act v. 1694, Act vi. 1698, and Act vi. 1704 renewed. Presbyteries enjoined to choose such persons as probably can attend. No commission to an elder to be sustained unless it bear that he has signed the Formula. Commissions, after they are written out, to be read and attested by the presbytery. Commissions from royal burghs to be attested both by kirk-session and presbytery. The time limited for choosing commissioners from presbyteries and burghs to be the same. 1718. ix. 7; 1836. 8; 1790-4, ult. *See* COMMISSIONS TO ASSEMBLY.

Assembly Accommodation. Committee appointed to consider the proper means for the accommodation of the members of Assembly. 1801. 8.

——— Act respecting the arrangement of the Assembly House for the proper accommodation of the members, strangers, students of divinity, preachers, ministers not members, &c. 1802. iii.

——— Committee appointed to communicate with the Lord Provost concerning the state of the Assembly House, and the repairs necessary. 1811, ult.

——— Committee appointed to look after the interests of the Assembly in the accommodation to be provided as an Assembly House. 1819. 9.

Assembly Accommodation. Committee appointed to consider the means of providing better accommodation. 1785. 9; 1821. 8.

——— Committee empowered to apply to Government for a grant of money for completing the accommodation, plans of which had been approved by the Barons of Exchequer. 1828. 6.

——— The Assembly aisle having proved unsuitable, a committee appointed to apply to Government with a view to obtain a convenient and respectable place of permanent accommodation. 1834, ult.

——— The Assembly disapprove of the Castle Hill as a site for the proposed new Assembly Hall. 1839. 7; Com., 1839, Nov. 20.

——— The Assembly acceded to the proposal made for erecting and fitting up a new Assembly Hall on the Castle Hill, on condition that their suggestions in regard to the size and internal arrangements were carried into execution. 1840. 3.

——— Assembly meet for the first time in the new Assembly Hall. 1844. 1.

——— Resolved that all applications for admission into the body of the house from distinguished strangers shall be made to the committee for providing accommodation to the General Assembly, who shall confer with the Moderator on the subject. 1839. 3.

Assembly, Business of. A motion that a committee be appointed for arranging the business before the House, and the order in which it should be taken up, was, after discussion, withdrawn. 1834. 1.

——— In the following year a committee was appointed for said purpose, Dr Cook, who had for many years exclusively arranged the business of the Assembly, having expressed his conviction of the impropriety of laying on any one individual the burden and responsibility of so important a task. 1835. 1.

——— When a certain order of business has been sanctioned by the Assembly, no departure therefrom to be permitted. In cases of adjourned debates and dropped overtures, the order of the day to have precedence. 1853. 11.

——— Causes affecting the status of ministers to be taken up first, after reading the minutes, in such order as shall be fixed by the committee of business.

Assembly, Business of. Committee appointed to consider and suggest the fittest method for having the roll of business printed and circulated among the members daily. 1852. 6.

——— Arrangement in regard to the order in which the reports of the various schemes of the Church shall be taken up. 1852. viii. Said arrangement modified. 1853. 11.

——— *See* Standing Orders, 1859.

Assembly Committees. Committees to take the greatest care not to encroach, even for the shortest space, on the hours when the Assembly is convened. Officers of the House to give notice to all committees whenever the Moderator is about to take the chair. 1846. ix.

——— A separate record to be kept of the appointment of committees, and of the purpose of their appointment. A List to be prepared therefrom at the commencement of every Assembly of the committees from which reports are due; and, on the first Saturday of every Assembly, a time to be fixed for receiving the report of each committee. 1829, ult.

——— Members of a committee appointed to investigate a charge against a minister, admitted to sit as judges when the case came before the Assembly. 1717. 5.

Assembly Committee of Whole House. In the absence of the Lord High Commissioner from indisposition or otherwise, it was for some time the practice of the Assembly to resolve themselves into a committee of the whole House, and proceed with the business before them. At their next meeting, the Assembly called for the report of the committee, which was given in and read. For examples, see 1738. 6; 1768. 9; 1786. 5; 1789. 5; 1825. 6; and many others.

Assembly Galleries Cleared. The galleries ordered to be cleared on account of a noise during a debate, and all the strangers turned out *except the ladies.* 1801. 8.

Assembly Causes. A brief report of the more important causes decided by the Assembly ordered to be printed annually along with the Acts. 1825. 3.

Assembly Devotional Exercises. Resolved that the meetings of the Assembly be constituted each morning by the singing of praise and the reading of the Word of God in addition to the usual exercises of prayer. 1842. 3.

——— The Assembly resolved to meet for devotional exercises in St Andrew's Church in the Sabbath evenings during the sitting of the Assembly. 1844. 2.

Assembly Sabbath State Ceremonies. The Moderator having requested a conference with the Lord High Commissioner in regard to the evils resulting from the observance of certain state ceremonies on the Sabbath-day, His Grace intimated that he had brought the matter under the notice of His Majesty, who had been graciously pleased to approve of the discontinuance of the public dinners on the Lord's Day, and to leave it to His Grace to make such arrangements on the other subjects as might appear to him expedient, and most in accordance with the wishes of the Assembly. 1834. 4.

Assembly: Right of Admission. Declared that the public have a right of admission to the public gallery of the Assembly without charge; and that the beadle at the door of that gallery be immediately instructed that, in the opinion of the Assembly, he has no right to make such exaction. 1853, ult.

Assembly: Anent Time of Annual Meeting. A committee appointed to consult Her Majesty's High Commissioner, and endeavour to learn the views of members from all parts of the country as to the best time for the annual meetings of the Assembly. 1848. 9.

——— The committee reported that they were not prepared to recommend any change, either in regard to the season of the year in which the Assembly should be held, or the day of the week on which its sittings should commence. 1850. 14.

Assembly. All papers and processes to be delivered to the clerk in the interval between the diets, and not while the Assembly is sitting. 1694. vii.

——— The Register, and all papers belonging to the Assembly or its Commission, to be given up to the clerk. 1701. 21.

——— Two authentic copies of the Register to be kept for the better preservation thereof. 1703. xi.; 1799. ix.

——— The year appointed to be marked at the top of each page of the records. 1753. 8.

Assembly Attendance. No one to enter the Assembly House except members, persons of quality and note, and others in attendance on Her Majesty's Commissioner, ministers, ruling elders, probationers, and students of divinity. 1711. 3.

Assembly Attendance. Act for keeping order in the Assembly, and hindering persons from coming in who are not concerned to be there. 1718. 2.; 1723, ult.; 1724, ult.; 1727. 19

Assembly Sentences. Referred to the Commission to consider a method for securing the execution of sentences of the Assembly and its Commissions. 1750, ult.

——— Presbytery of Linlithgow censured for not implementing a sentence and order of the Assembly. 1751. 6.

——— Presbytery of Perth censured for a similar offence in the Methven case. 1750. 6.

Assembly Royal Commissioner. Anent the right of the Church to hold valid national assemblies, without the presence of the Sovereign or his Commissioner.

The King's commission to the Earl of Leven not having arrived on the day fixed for the meeting of the Assembly, the Assembly met, chose a moderator, appointed the usual committees, and adjourned for a week, until the arrival of the Commissioner. 1746. 3 and 4.

For a List of High Commissioners, *see* APPENDIX.

Assembly Vote. The Assembly unanimously ordered that, before the clerk begin to call the roll, the doors of the Assembly House shall be shut, and not be opened until the judgment of the Assembly shall be declared. 1789. 8.

Assembly Beadles. A collection made in the Assembly for the beadles, and referred to the Commission anent a suitable allowance to them. 1710. 9.

Assistant-Minister. A minister being laid aside from duty by indisposition, the Assembly found that the presbytery were not at liberty to appoint a substitute or assistant until a vacancy occurred ; and in the event of the continued indisposition of the minister rendering it necessary to make provision for the regular administration of ordinances, the presbytery were enjoined to proceed according to the rules of the Church. 1808. 4.

——— In a case regarding the appointment of an assistant, the Commission, finding that no adequate supply had been provided by the incumbent for the discharge of ministerial duty, empowered the presbytery, so long as he failed to provide the services of a resident assistant, themselves to do so, by the aid of such contributions as they might be able to raise. Com., June 2, 1842.

Assistant-Minister. On a reference from the Presbytery of Arbroath, the Commission recommended them to take the opinion of counsel as to whether the assistant-minister of Arbroath, in the event of his being admitted to the position of a colleague minister, with a seat in the Church courts, would still be entitled to the benefit of the mortification mentioned in the reference. Com., Nov. 16, 1842.

Assistant. A minister being incapacitated for the discharge of his duties, the presbytery ordained an assistant with power to hold sessions and exercise discipline; and there being no elders in the parish, the assistant announced the names of certain persons to the congregation, and no objections being offered he ordained said persons elders, and admitted them members of that kirk-session. The Assembly on a reference found that, as it appeared from the minutes and official documents produced that the persons specified as elders in the reference had not been ordained according to the rules and laws of the Church, their ordination was null and void. 1827. 6.

Assistant and Successor. An overture and interim Act was transmitted to presbyteries for four successive years, but not passed into a standing law, by which it was proposed that a minister and his ordained assistant and successor should both be constituent members of kirk-session; that in the presbytery and synod either of them who was present might deliberate and vote, but if both were present this privilege to belong only to the parish minister; and that either of them might be elected a member of the General Assembly, but not both in one year. 1784. vii.; 1787. ix.

——— An overture anent the right and power of ordained assistants and successors advising, voting, and determining in causes coming before presbyteries and synods, read and referred to the Commission. 1759. 7.

——— An overture to the effect that an ordained assistant and successor ought not to sit as an elder in a kirk-session, nor summon meetings of session, nor preside therein, was transmitted to presbyteries, but not passed. 1806. v.

——— A synod having found that an ordained assistant and successor was a constituent member of the kirk-session, the Assembly reversed the judgment, and found that an assistant and successor is not a constituent member of kirk-session, except in the absence of his principal. 1806. 8.

Assistant and Successor. An assistant and successor and his principal cannot both be members of presbytery at the same time. The assistant and successor may act in presence of his principal, but cannot act along with him. 1833. 4.

——— Declared to be not contrary to the principles and practice of the Church of Scotland to elect an assistant and successor a commissioner to the General Assembly, in the presence of his principal, whose name was entered on the sederunt when the election took place. 1834. 4.

——— An assistant and successor, as moderator of presbytery, attested the commissions from the presbytery to the General Assembly, when a complaint was taken against the attestation, on the ground that it was not competent for him to act as moderator in presence of his principal. The question came before the Assembly as to the validity of the commissions, which were sustained, on the ground that they were in themselves formal and regular, and that the mere *presence* of the principal did not incapacitate the assistant and successor from acting, *unless* the principal made a formal demand to be received as a member of court, and to have the name of the assistant and successor struck out of the sederunt, which, in the case before the House, it did not appear from the minutes that he had done. 1833. 3 and 4.

——— A motion for a committee to inquire into the status of assistants and successors rejected as unnecessary, the law on the subject being already as clear as it was possible to make it. 1834. 8.

——— A minister having, from infirmity of body and imbecility of mind, for several years been incapable of discharging the pastoral duties of his parish, and there being no prospect of his recovery, the presbytery, at the request of the heritors and elders, agreed to sustain a presentation in favour of an assistant and successor. Their judgment was brought under review of the Assembly on the ground that the consent of the incumbent had not been obtained. The Assembly affirmed the judgment of the presbytery, and instructed them to proceed to the settlement of an assistant and successor—declaring, however, that in the circumstances of the case no part of the stipend nor any of the emoluments could be allocated for his maintenance ; and that if it should please God to restore the incumbent to the sound exercise of his judgment, it would then instantly become incompetent for the assistant and successor to discharge any part of the pastoral duties of the parish, or to sit and vote in any Church court, without the explicit consent of the incumbent. 1813. 5.

Assistant and Successor. A civil action pending as to the right of a town-council to appoint an assistant and successor, the Assembly instructed the presbytery to proceed according to the rules of the Church, but not to complete the settlement till the decision of the civil court should be pronounced. 1830. 7.

——— A minister under a *fama* was enjoined by the presbytery and synod to consent to the appointment of an assistant and successor on certain conditions. The Assembly, on appeal, reversed the sentence of the inferior courts, and directed the presbytery to investigate the charges against the minister according to the rules of the Church. 1839. 11.

Note.—For a clear and comprehensive summary of the law and practice of the Church in regard to assistants and successors, see Lord Moncreiff's Note on the Tron Church case, December 24, 1831; see also the speeches of Dr Cook and Mr Dunlop on the Dunoon case, Assembly 1834, sessions 3 and 4.

Atheism. Ministers enjoined to warn and guard their people against the atheistical principles of those who go under the name of Deists. 1696. xxi.

Attendance of Members of Assembly. Commissioners not attending to be reported to their presbyteries—and for the first offence to be censured by the presbytery; for the second, by the synod; and for the third, to be suspended. 1709. vii.

Attestation. *See* COMMISSIONS.

Auchterarder. The Presbytery of Auchterarder censured for a certain proposition emitted by them, which, however orthodox in intention, was expressed in words very unwarrantable and exceptionable. 1718. viii.

Augmentation. An overture to apply to the Legislature for an augmentation of stipend to the ministers of the Church of Scotland, rejected by the casting-vote of the Moderator. 1748. 6.

——— Committee appointed with instructions to apply to Parliament for an augmentation of stipends—to get an account of the annual value of all the stipends in Scotland—how and by whom paid—the extent of glebes and the state of the tithes—and all other funds that may be applied for augmenting of stipends. 1749. 7.

——— Report of said Committee. The Assembly resolve to apply to Parliament. Committee appointed for that purpose. 1750. 4, 7, 10.

——— Report of Commissioners sent to London. 1752. 4. *See* STIPENDS.

B

Banning. Swearing and cursing found relevant as charges in a libel. 1746. 6.

Banns. Proclamation of banns to be made on three separate Sabbaths, immediately before divine worship in the forenoon, the names of the parties having previously been given up to the minister of the parish. 1690. vii.; 1699. v.

——— The precentors in the churches in Dundee enjoined to observe Act v. 1699. 1760. 9.

——— Session-clerk prohibited from proclaiming parties until he has intimated to the minister of the parish the names and residences of the parties. In case of a vacancy in the clerkship, this intimation to be made by two elders. 1784. viii.

——— Ministers enjoined not to marry parties residing in newly-erected parishes *quoad sacra*, without a certificate of their having been proclaimed in the church to which such parish shall have been attached. 1836, ult.

——— Proclamations to be made both in the church of the *quoad sacra* parish and of the original parish. Com., May 28, 1839.

——— Session-clerks advised and authorised to resume the practice with respect to the proclamation of banns which prevailed previous to 1836. Com., May 30, 1843.

Banns. Report of a committee in regard to the proclamation of banns in New Zealand remitted to the Colonial Committee, with powers to remedy the grievances complained of. 1854. 2.

——— Regulations enjoined. Ministers prohibited from marrying any parties without a certificate from session-clerk that they have been regularly proclaimed. If they reside in different parishes, they must be proclaimed in both. Not to be considered as residenters until they have resided six weeks within the parish. No session-clerk to grant a certificate of proclamation unless he can certify that the parties are residenters, that they are unmarried, and not within the forbidden degrees of consanguinity. A form of certificate prescribed. 1782, ult.

Baptism. Children of parents one or both of whom profess the Christian religion, have a right to be baptised. No other sponsors to be admitted unless the parents are dead, or absent, or grossly ignorant, or under scandal—in which case some one related to the child to be sponsor. Kirk-sessions to get foundlings or exposed children baptised and educated. Parents or sponsors to speak to the minister before baptism. 1712. iv.

——— The administration of baptism in private—that is, in any place or at any time when the congregation is not orderly called together to wait on the dispensing of the Word—strictly discharged and prohibited. 1690. x.

——— Ministers recommended to show all tenderness to persons educated in other Protestant Churches when they apply for the benefit of sealing ordinances. If free from scandal, their children are to be baptised. 1711. xiii.

Barbary. The Commission instructed to do what in them lies for relief of Alexander Stewart, shipmaster, and his crew, captives in Barbary. 1720. 10.

Barrier Act. Overture anent novations transmitted to presbyteries. 1696. xi.

——— Passed into a standing law—commonly called the Barrier Act—by which it is enacted and declared that before the General Assembly pass any Acts to be binding rules and constitutions of the Church, they must first be transmitted as overtures to the presbyteries for their consideration and consent. 1697. ix.

Barrier Act. Act vii. Assembly 1730, and Act viii. 1732, repealed, as having been passed in violation of the Barrier Act. 1734. v.

——— All Acts rescissory to be transmitted as overtures in terms of the Barrier Act. 1736. viii.

——— An Act having been passed by the Assembly in 1752 (Act vii.), entitled "An Act concerning Presbyteries neglecting to send up their opinions upon overtures transmitted to them," it was, in consequence of remonstrances, transmitted as an overture by the Assembly of 1753, and re-enacted in 1758 with the consent of a majority of the presbyteries of the Church, to the effect that when overtures have been twice transmitted, the General Assembly will, without further transmission, take them into consideration, and pass them into Acts or reject them as they shall see cause, although presbyteries have not sent up their opinions. 1758. v.

——— The Assembly of 1745 having enacted that the Rules of the Form of Process, chap. vii., with respect to informations against ministers, should be made applicable to probationers, the Assembly of 1746 found that this had been done in violation of the Barrier Act, and transmitted the proposal as an overture to presbyteries. 1746. xi.

——— Declaration of Assembly 1814, anent the union of offices, declared to have been passed in violation of the Barrier Act, and not to be regarded as a standing law, nor binding upon the Church. A new overture and interim Act for preventing the improper union of offices, transmitted to presbyteries. 1816. 6.

——— The Committee for classing returns to overtures having reported that twenty presbyteries had reported that year in favour of a particular overture, and twenty-three in former years, making in all a majority of one approving, the Assembly found that "in respect there are not *this year* returns from a majority of the presbyteries of the Church approving of the overture, the necessary consent of the Church has not been obtained," and therefore directed said overture to be retransmitted. 1849. 9.

Note.—For a full exposition of the nature and effects of the Barrier Act, see the debate on the subject in Assembly

1816, particularly the speech of Dr Cook. See also debate on the Regulations anent calling of Ministers, Assembly 1834. 10; and the debate on the Act as to Chapels of Ease, Assembly 1835. 6.

Beadles. A minister carrying on a process before the Court of Session regarding the right of a minister to dismiss his beadle, applied for aid from the funds of the Church to assist in defraying the expense of the process—the Assembly found that "their funds are in such a state that no aid can be given." 1809. 9.

Beggars. Presbyteries enjoined to apply to justices of the peace to put the laws in execution against vagrants and beggars, and provide work and maintenance for them. 1711. xi.

——— Ministers and kirk-sessions, presbyteries and synods, recommended to see that the laws against vagrant and sturdy beggars are put in vigorous execution, and not to give recommendations for charity (*i. e.*, passes for begging) to any without their own bounds. 1724. vii.; 1696. xix.

Bells. The Assembly found and declared that "the power of regulating the time and manner of ringing the bells of the parish church, as connected with ecclesiastical and religious purposes, belongs exclusively to the minister of the parish," and remitted to a committee to take such steps as might be considered proper for vindicating the rights of the Church. 1818. 6; 1823. 5.

——— The Assembly found that the conduct of a bellman, in refusing to ring the bell when expressly desired to do so by the parish minister, was highly reprehensible, and instructed the procurator and agent to give advice, if applied to, to the kirk-session for preserving the rights of the Church. 1823. 5.

Bibles. 3000 Irish or Gaelic Bibles, 1000 New Testaments, and 3000 Catechisms, sent down from London, and distributed among the Highland parishes. 1690. xi.

——— Presbyteries having Highland parishes to consider what may be done for getting a fund for a new impression of the Bible in the Irish language, and of the Psalms in metre, and of the Shorter Catechism. 1699. xvi.

——— Reference to the Commission anent do. 1709. 12; 1710. 14.

Bibles. Said Act of 1699 renewed, and the Commission instructed to make inquiry anent the Irish Bibles. 1705. 12.

—— Presbyteries to report to the Commission anent the receipt of their proportion of the Irish Bibles, and how they disposed of them. 1706. xviii.

—— The Commission to require a full account from the committee concerning the Irish Bibles, and from the agent anent the £120 sterling gifted by the Queen; the balance remaining to be a fund for promoting a new impression of said Bible. 1706, ult.

—— The Commission instructed to use their best endeavours to procure more copies of the Bible in the Irish language, because there are demands for them in several places of the Highlands. 1715. 12.

—— The Commission appointed to take care that the impressions of the Holy Scriptures, of the Confession of Faith, and Catechisms, and of all other books relating to the doctrine, worship, discipline, and government of the Church, be correct. 1718. 15.

—— A standing committee appointed to consider the means that have been employed for procuring the best version of the Sacred Scriptures in Gaelic, and whether any further means can be used for rendering it more perfect. Meanwhile the Assembly prohibits the use of any other Gaelic version of the Scriptures in churches, chapels, and schools, than the editions published by the Society for Propagating Christian Knowledge. 1816. vi.

—— The quarto edition of the Gaelic Bible, with the Psalms and Paraphrases attached, published by said Society, and no other, authorised to be used in the churches and chapels within the bounds of the Church, where public worship is conducted in Gaelic. 1826. iv.

—— The thanks of the Assembly conveyed to Mr Kerr, the King's printer, for his strenuous exertions that copies of the Bible should be correctly printed and furnished at the most moderate rate. 1794, ult.

Biblical Criticism. All practical efforts to be used for the establishment and endowment of a professorship of Biblical Criticism in every one of the universities of Scotland; and after such chairs are established, all divinity students to be required to give regular attendance on the lectures of the professor during two years of their course, without additional expense. 1839. ix.

Biblical Criticism. Preachers nominated professors of Biblical Criticism to be taken on trials by the presbytery of the bounds, and if found qualified, to be ordained previous to their induction as professors. 1838. xii.

Bigamy. A man who had married a woman in ignorance that she had a previous husband then alive, applied for baptism to a child born to him by her. The Assembly found that the said man, at the birth of his child, was in possession of his status of husband to the said woman, and legal father of said child, and did not discover anything in his conduct to deprive him of the Christian privilege of standing sponsor in baptism for the child, and remitted to the kirk-session to admit him as sponsor accordingly. 1803. 6.

——— In the case of a woman cohabiting with a man to whom it was alleged she had been married before a quorum of justices, while another man, to whom she had been lawfully married, was still alive, the Assembly instructed the procurator and agent to lay the reference, and all the circumstances of the case, before the Lord Advocate, for his advice. Further, they prohibited the cohabitation of said parties, and appointed them to be laid under the severest censures of the Church. 1805. 9.

Bills. A committee of bills to be appointed at the first sitting of the Assembly, whose duty shall be to consider the regularity of the different proposals in point of form, but not to determine whether they are worthy of the notice of the Assembly. 1850. xiv.; 1859. xii.

Blair. A deputation of the Assembly appointed to attend the funeral of Lord President Blair. 1811, ult.

——— His opinion as to the laws anent Sabbath profanation. 1823. x.

Blind Students. Ordained that, before any presbytery or synod take a blind man on trials for licence, they shall first consult the General Assembly. 1761. vi.

——— A student afflicted with blindness allowed to be taken on trials for licence, in consideration of the very ample testimonials borne to his character and talents. 1815. 5.

Blind Students. Leave refused to the Presbytery of Mull, "by a very great majority of the Assembly," to take a blind student on trial for licence. 1829. 9.

Blind. Mr John Alston, in name of the directors of the Glasgow Asylum for the Blind, presented to the library of the Assembly a copy of the New Testament, printed in embossed Roman characters, for the use of the blind. 1838. 2.

——— Do. do. The Book of Genesis and the Psalms in metre. 1839. 2.

——— Do. do. The Shorter Catechism. 1840. 8.

——— Do. do. The Bible, complete in 15 volumes. 1841. 2.

Bona fide. *See* ELDERS.

Books. Presbyteries enjoined to take special notice of books published by ministers, and to see that they contain nothing contrary to the doctrine or discipline of the Church. 1707. vii.

——— Some passages out of a book, entitled 'The Marrow of Modern Divinity,' declared contrary to Holy Scripture and the Confession of Faith. 1720. v.

——— The Act Assembly 1720. v., vindicated and confirmed; certain ministers who had censured it rebuked and admonished; and the received doctrine of the Church on the points referred to in said book, declared. 1722. vii.

——— Ministers earnestly recommended to preserve their flocks from the contagion of infidelity and immorality openly avowed in certain books recently published. 1755. iv.

——— The Commission of Assembly instructed to take care that the impressions of the Holy Scriptures, Confession of Faith, and Catechisms, and other books relating to the doctrine, discipline, and government of this Church, be correct. 1720. xi.

——— The Commission instructed to apply to Government for discharging the importing or printing for common sale any atheistical or blasphemous books or pamphlets, or such as contain tenets contrary to the fundamental principles of our religion contained in our Confession of Faith; or incorrect copies of the Holy Scriptures. 1706. 12.

——— Kirk-sessions recommended to buy copies of the book entitled 'Collections and Observations Methodised concerning the Doctrine, Worship, Discipline, and Government of this Church.' 1709. 11.

Books. A book written by the late Mr Gilbert Rule, Principal of the College of Edinburgh, entitled 'Catechetical Exercises,' recommended. 1709. 14.

——— Mr Thomas Blackwell's 'Methodus Evangelica' dedicated to the Assembly. 1712. 9.

Bourignionism. A book entitled 'An Apology for M. Antonia Bourignion' condemned as containing a mass of dangerous, impious, blasphemous, and damnable errors. 1701. x.

——— Dr George Garden of Aberdeen deposed for being tainted with said errors. 1701. xi.

——— Presbyteries earnestly recommended to use all effectual means to prevent the spreading of these and other errors. 1709. xii.

——— Ministers ordained to preach most particularly and faithfully against said errors; and professors of divinity recommended to make a full collection of the errors of Antonia Bourignion, and of such other errors as do reflect upon the nature, person, and offices of our Lord Jesus Christ, and to write a confutation of the same. 1710. ix.

Breslau. A general collection ordered for building and endowing a church and school for the Protestants of Breslau, the capital of Selesia. 1750. 9.

Bridals. Ordained that the Act of Assembly 1645 against penny bridals be read in all the churches and enforced; and that presbyteries have their thoughts upon what further may be necessary for suppressing and preventing abuses at such occasions. 1701. xx.

——— Presbyteries recommended to apply to the judges for putting the laws relating to penny bridals in execution. 1706. 14; 1719. x.

Bridge. A collection recommended to be made in all the churches within the bounds of the synods between the Moray Firth and the River Tay in aid of the funds for rebuilding a bridge over the river Dee. 1806. 5.

——— Earnestly recommended to all the parishes within the Synods of Fife, Perth, and Angus, to make a collection for building a bridge over the water that separates Lochlee from Navar. 1723. 11.

Broughton, &c. Resolved to oppose the suppression and annexation of the parishes of Broughton, Glenholm, Kilbucho, and Culter, on consideration of the ample funds for the maintenance of four ministers, the extent of the parishes, and the general disinclination of the people. 1793, ult.

Broughton, &c. The case remitted to the procurator and agent, with instructions to take such steps at the public expense as may be necessary to obtain redress. 1803. 8.

Brown. Ordered that Brown's 'History of the Church,' belonging to the Assembly, and lodged in the University of Edinburgh, be put into the clerk's hands. 1737. 8.

Buenos Ayres. The Rev. Dr William Brown from Buenos Ayres, with permission of the General Assembly, gave an interesting account of the state of the Presbyterian Church there. 1850. 4.

Burghs. Any city or town in which there are more congregations than one, to be held as one parish in so far as the Act anent the ordination of elders is concerned. 1816. x.

——— Found that the Presbytery of Dundee had acted contrary to the laws of the Church in prohibiting the Kirk-session of Dundee from appointing elders from among the members of their own congregation, although residing beyond the limits of the parishes respectively. Com., June 1, 1841.

——— A committee appointed to consider the claims of the new parliamentary burghs to be represented in the General Assembly. 1834. 9.

——— A proposal that certain new parliamentary burghs should be allowed to send representative elders to the General Assembly, negatived by a majority of 120 to 99. 1836. 7.

——— A motion having been made to the effect, that if the council of any burgh failed to elect an elder to the General Assembly before a certain specified day, it should be competent for the kirk-session or sessions within the said burgh, together with such members of the town-council as are members of the Church of Scotland, to meet and elect an elder to represent the said burgh in the General Assembly,—the Assembly approved of the general object, but considering that the instances of royal burghs declining to return members were very few, and in the hope that even in these cases a different view may be taken of the subject, they resolved to delay adopting any positive measure in regard to it. 1836. 7.

Burghs. A committee appointed to consider the right of royal burghs, as at present constituted, to elect representatives to the General Assembly. 1845. 3.

——— The Presbytery of Perth having declined jurisdiction over a body called the General Session of the Burgh (composed of all the parish ministers and elders of said burgh), on the ground that it was not an ecclesiastical judicatory, the Assembly, on appeal, affirmed the judgment of the Presbytery. 1852. 4.

——— *See* COMMISSIONS.

Bursars. Presbyteries enjoined to be careful to keep and maintain bursars of theology, conform to the ancient practice and the Acts of former Assemblies made thereanent. 1694. xvii.

——— Certain presbyteries enjoined to maintain bursars who have the Highland language, if they can be had. 1699. ix.

——— In consideration of the great scarcity of probationers having the Irish language, the Assembly recommend synods to maintain bursars of theology besides the usual presbytery bursars, allowing at least £10 sterling to each annually, to be continued for four years. 1701. viii.

——— Act viii., Assembly 1701, renewed, and appointed to be observed until the General Assembly see cause to recall the same. 1704. xiii.

——— An Act explanatory of the foresaid Acts. 1705. xi.

——— An Act enjoining inquiry to be made as to how the various Acts anent bursars were observed. 1707. xiv.

——— Act anent defaulting presbyteries and synods. 1709. xiv.

——— One half of the whole bursaries of all the presbyteries within Scotland to be applied for the education of such youths as have the Irish language—the respective synods to have the choice and presentation of said Irish bursars. 1710. x.

——— Bursaries under £10 to be united. Presbyteries to examine bursars at least once every year, and to be punctual in paying them. 1712. xii.

——— Bursaries to be withdrawn from students found unworthy of the encouragement, and conferred on those having the qualifications required by the Acts of Assembly. 1714. 7.

Bursars. Former Acts renewed, and ordered to be observed. 1715. vii.

——— Highland bursars to be examined upon their knowledge in the Irish language. 1717. 7.

——— The proceeds of four Highland bursaries provided by the Synod of Lothian and Tweeddale, to be appropriated for the maintenance of two Lithuanian students, to be educated in the University of Edinburgh. 1722. v.

——— The Assembly, considering the multitude of probationers in the Church, superseded the obligation upon synods and presbyteries to maintain as bursars students in divinity. 1737. vii.

——— The Assembly, considering the great scarcity of preachers and students in divinity having the Irish language, ordained that the former laudable practice of giving bursaries to such students should be revived ; and earnestly recommended every minister of the Church to pay to the clerk of his presbytery 3s. annually for that purpose. 1756. vii.

——— The Commission instructed to report on all the bursaries in Scotland. 1719, ult.

Business. Resolved that all affairs of public concern be taken up as they can be got prepared, preferable to any private cause. 1748. 3.

——— A committee appointed to draw up rules for regulating the method of procedure in causes before the General Assembly, and for this purpose to look over the standing Acts respecting this matter. 1752. 7; 1764. 9.

——— A proposal made that the Assembly should itself judge in all cases of importance, and not refer them to the Commission. 1765. 5.

——— A roll of the private causes, showing the order in which they should be brought before the Assembly, ordered to be made up and affixed upon the doors of the Assembly aisle. 1768. 3 and 4.

——— A motion that a committee be appointed for arranging the business before the House, and suggesting the order in which it should be taken up, was, after discussion, withdrawn; Assembly 1834. 1. But in the following year a committee was appointed for that purpose—Dr Cook, who had for many years arranged the business of the Assembly, having expressed his conviction of the impropriety of laying on any one individual the burden and responsibility of so important a task. 1835. l.

Business. Rolls of the order of causes, overtures, reports, and other matters of business, ordered to be printed for the use of the members of Assembly. 1832. vi.

——— Committee to be named for arranging the order of the business of the Assembly. 1850. xiv.; 1859. xii.

——— *See* ASSEMBLY.

Bute. The Assembly unanimously resolved to engross in their minutes a tribute to the memory of the most noble the Marquess of Bute, and to record the warm and grateful affection with which they are persuaded the Church of Scotland will ever cherish and regard his memory. 1848, ult.

C

Cairston. An Act erecting the Presbytery of Cairston. 1725. v.

Caithness. The presbyteries of Orkney and Shetland and Caithness erected into the Synod of Orkney. 1704. iv.

——— The Presbytery of Caithness disjoined from the Synod of Caithness and Orkney, and annexed to the Synod of Ross. 1725. vi.

——— The presbyteries of Dornoch, Caithness, and Tongue, erected into the Synod of Caithness, to meet at Dornoch and Thurso *per vices.* 1726. iv.

——— A commission appointed for visiting Caithness, Orkney, and Shetland, for the purpose of assisting the brethren of said presbyteries in their presbyterial work. 1700. xiii.

Calendar. Ordained that, in respect of a late Act of Parliament changing the calendar, synods, which usually meet on the first Tuesday of April or October, shall meet on the second Tuesday of those months, according to the new style; and so of the rest, advancing a week in the denomination of the days. 1752. viii.

——— A petition from the Synod of Lothian and Tweeddale anent the inconveniences which have arisen since the change of style, from the uncertainty of the time of payment of minister's stipend, referred to a committee to prepare an overture thereon. 1760. 6.

Call. Presbyteries instructed to think of an overture to prevent competing calls, and the giving of a call to a minister by any parish during the dependence of a prior call from another parish. 1708. 6.

——— An overture for regulating the calling of ministers, transmitted to presbyteries, but not passed. 1710. xiii.

——— Presbyteries discharged from putting the call from any parish into the hands of the probationer called, until his trials be completed, and the presbytery fully satisfied both as to his sufficiency and fitness for that parish. 1711. x.

——— An Act concerning the qualifications of persons claiming to vote in the calling of ministers to vacant parishes, enacts that no person shall be admitted to vote who refuses to make the following declaration—viz., "That they have not twice heard sermon or attended divine worship performed by a nonjurant minister, or preacher professing himself to be of the Episcopalian communion, in any meeting or congregation not allowed by the laws, or where His Majesty King George and the royal family were not prayed for in express words, within twelve calendar months immediately preceding the vacancy of the church to be supplied; and that they have not, during any part of the said calendar months, received the sacrament of the Lord's Supper, dispensed by such ministers, nor allowed their children to be baptised by them. 1748. 4.

——— A proposal for distinguishing the respect due in the calling of ministers to those who express a suitable regard for religion and gospel ordinances, and excluding those of a contrary character from voting in such elections, referred to the Commission. 1749, ult.

——— Declared that the moderation of a call in the settlement of a minister is agreeable to the immemorial and constitutional practice of this Church, and ought to be continued. 1782. vii.

——— The presentee to the parish of Glendevon rejected, the presbytery having found that there was no call before them in his favour, and that therefore they could not proceed to his settlement as minister. 1768. 4.

Call. The presentee to the parish of Gargunnock rejected for want of "a sufficient call." 1768. 5.

——— The proceedings of a presbytery found to be highly irregular and incompetent, in respect that they proceeded to take steps towards the settlement of a minister without having any call before them. 1790. 5.

——— Two competing calls ordered to be set aside, and the presbytery appointed to moderate in a new call, that the deliberate and free choice of the parish might more fully appear. 1708. 11; 1724. 11.

——— A synod having prohibited a presbytery from proceeding with the settlement of a minister on the ground that there was not a sufficient call, the Assembly reversed the sentence, and ordered the presbytery to proceed. 1815. 6.

——— An overture to the effect that if at the moderating of a call the major part of the male heads of families disapproved of the person in whose favour the call was proposed to be moderated in, such disapproval should be deemed sufficient ground for the presbytery to reject such person, rejected by a majority of 149 to 137. 1833. 8.

——— A similar overture carried by a majority of 184 to 139, and passed into an interim Act, and, along with regulations for carrying the same into effect, transmitted to presbyteries as an overture. 1834. 6, and ult.

Which overture having received the consent of a majority of presbyteries, was ordained to be held and acted upon in all time coming as a standing law of the Church, by a majority of 178 to 124. 1835. 9. ix.

——— This law, commonly denominated the Veto Act, repealed on the ground that it infringed civil and patrimonial rights with which the Church had often declared it was not competent for its judicatories to intermeddle; and presbyteries ordained to proceed in the settlement of parishes according to the practice which prevailed previous to the passing of said Act, keeping specially in view the undoubted privilege of parishioners to state any relevant objections to the induction of presentees. 1843. ix.

——— Declared to be the law of the Church that it is competent at moderating in a call for any male communicant to state objections, of whatever kind, without a libel, to the presentee, and that the presbytery are bound to receive and consider these objections. 1842. xxviii.

Call. A motion that immediately after the words "sustain the call," in the regulations anent calling of ministers, the following words be added—"Provided always that the same shall have been subscribed either by a majority of the whole said male heads of families, or at least by the major part of them who shall have convened in congregation at the moderating therein," negatived by a majority of 96 to 82. 1835, ult.

——— A similar motion made and withdrawn after discussion. 1836, ult.

——— Overture on the regulations to be observed in the induction of ministers, transmitted to presbyteries. 1843, ult.

——— The same, with various alterations and amendments, retransmitted every year till 1856, when, having obtained the consent of a majority of presbyteries, it was passed into a standing law of the Church. 1856. xii.

——— In a case of disputed settlement it having been objected that a compearance for callers was not competent under "The Scottish Benefices Act," the Assembly repelled the objection, and sustained the right of the callers to be heard. 1852. 11.

Calumny. Calumny found relevant as an article of charge in a libel. 1767. 9.

Campbell. An act and recommendation for preserving purity of doctrine, and concerning Mr Archibald Campbell, Professor of Divinity and Church History in the University of Aberdeen. 1736. x.; 1737. v.

Campvere. On the request of Sir Andrew Kennedy of Clowburn, conservator of the Scots privileges in the Netherlands, an extract was granted from the records of the Assembly of certain propositions recorded therein, and approved by the Assembly of 1642: From which it appeared that that Assembly, having joined the kirk of Campvere to this Kirk, directed the minister to observe thenceforth the same order in the outward worship of God and exercise of discipline as was here received by law and practice. 2dly, To send commissioners to the Assembly from that kirk as commodiously as they may, every third year at least. 3dly, To receive counsel and advice from the Presbytery of Edinburgh, or commissioners from the General Assembly, in any difficulties that might occur in the exercise of discipline; and, 4thly, That an act be made for payment of the expenses of the commissioners. Further, at the request of Sir Andrew Kennedy, the Assembly authorised all subsequent Commissions to determine in all affairs belonging to the said kirk that might be brought before them, as their immediate superior judicatory; but recommended the consistory of Campvere to pay the charges of their own commissioners out of their own stock, until this Church be in a better capacity to assist them. 1704. xxiv.

Campvere. Mr Thomas Hog allowed to demit his ministry at Campvere, and accept a call from the Scottish congregation at Rotterdam. 1699. 14.

——— The commissioners from Campvere publicly taken notice of by the Moderator, in name of the Assembly, and encouraged to continue to send commissioners, conform to Act of Assembly 1649. 1701. 2.

——— The Presbytery of Edinburgh authorised to proceed to the trial and settlement of any probationer that might be called to the Scots congregation of Campvere. 1722. 11.

——— The form of a commission from the consistory of Campvere approved of by the Presbytery of Edinburgh, and transmitted to the consistory. 1770, ult.

——— Mr John Chalmers transported from Campvere to the parish of Duffus, and letters sent to the magistrates of Campvere and the Scots consistory there. 1722. 3.

——— The sentence transporting Mr Chalmers, as aforesaid, taken off upon new emergent grounds, and he continued at Campvere. 1723. 7.

——— A petition from the minister of Campvere, praying to be admitted upon the Ministers' Widows' Scheme, referred to the trustees for their consideration. 1785. 9.

——— The Commission instructed to give their advice to the consistory of the Scots Church at Campvere in the case submitted by them to the Assembly. 1719. 9.

Canada. *See* Colonies.

Carsphairn. The parishes of Carsphairn and Dalry disjoined from the Presbytery of Kirkcudbright, and united to the Presbytery of Wigton. 1699. v.

Carsphairn. The foresaid parishes again disjoined from the Presbytery of Wigton, and reunited to the Presbytery of Kirkcudbright. 1703. xiii.

Carthagena. Congratulatory address to His Majesty upon occasion of taking the forts near Carthagena. 1741. vii.

Catechisms. 3000 Bibles, 1000 New Testaments, and 3000 Catechisms in the Irish language ordered, and the several synods having Highland parishes enjoined to appoint one of their number to receive their proportion of the same. 1690. xi.

——— The Assembly, understanding that in some parts of the Church the psalms are sung at the same diet in a different language, appointed that this incongruous way of worshipping God shall be hereafter forborne, and recommended all congregations and families who worship God in the Irish language to make use of a paraphrase of the Psalms in metre, together with a translation of the Shorter Catechism in Irish, bound up with the said Psalms in one volume, approven and emitted by the Synod of Argyle, as a uniform means of catechising the people. 1695. 20.

——— Recommended to the Synod of Argyle to translate the Confession of Faith of this Church, and the Larger Catechism, into the Irish language; the lesser Catechism and Psalms being already translated. 1699. xvi.

——— The Commission instructed to take care that the impressions of the Holy Scriptures, of the Confession of Faith, and Catechisms, and of all other books relating to the doctrine, worship, discipline, and government of this Church, be correct. 1718. 15.

——— Enacted that no minister shall presume to print or disperse in writing any catechism without the allowance of the presbytery of the bounds, and of the Commission. 1710. xii.

——— On an overture from the Synod of Perth and Stirling, the Assembly unanimously recommended the printer for the Church to cause a new impression of the Larger Catechism to be printed with all convenient speed. 1794. 8.

——— The General Assembly require and enjoin that the Shorter Catechism agreed upon by the Assembly of Divines at Westminster, and approved of by this Church, shall be taught in all parochial and other schools, and that the children be required to commit this Catechism to memory, and by frequent repetitions to fix it deep in their minds. 1794. x.

Catechisms. Ministers enjoined to exhort parents and masters of families to have the Confession of Faith, Catechisms, and other good books for the instruction of their households in faith and manners. 1708. 10.

Catechising. An overture anent the catechising of parishes dismissed, in respect the object was sufficiently provided for by the existing laws of the Church. 1800. 4.

Catechist. Alexander Buchan, catechist in St Kilda, allowed 400 merks out of the public money, and a letter ordered to be written to the Laird of Macleod to give him due encouragement. 1706. 12.

——— The Commission instructed to give advice and assistance for rendering effectual a mortification made by the deceased George, Earl of Cromarty, for maintaining catechists in Ross. 1718, ult.

——— Referred to the Commission to pitch upon fit persons to be employed as catechists and preachers in the bounds of the presbyteries of Strathbogie, Abernethy, and Lorn, to travel from house to house, and instruct the people in the principles of true religion; said preachers and catechists to be under the superintendence of the presbyteries of the bounds, who shall direct them as to their work. 1723. 8.

Catechetical Doctrine. Ministers recommended, besides their ordinary work of catechising, also to preach catechetical doctrine, at such times and in such manner as they may find most conducive to the edification of their flocks. 1696. xviii.

——— In said catechetical sermons, ministers recommended to insist on the great fundamental truths of religion, and to be earnest and instant in their prayers to God, that through His blessing their flocks may be preserved from the infection of dangerous errors. 1720. viii.

Catechetical Standards. Enacted and ordained that all students, previous to their first enrolment at the Divinity Hall, shall be examined by their respective presbyteries upon their knowledge of the Christian religion, as it is exhibited in the catechetical standards of the Church. 1837. ix.; 1849. xi.

Catholics, Roman. Petitions sent to both Houses of Parliament approving of religious toleration, and praying that, in the event of political privileges being conferred on Roman Catholics, securities should be provided against foreign influence. 1813. 7.

——— *See* POPERY.

Causes. A brief report of the more important causes decided by the Assembly ordered to be printed along with the Acts. 1825. 3.

Centessima. Recommendation anent a centessima of ministers' stipends for the relief of ministers' relicts and children in distress. 1698. 15.

——— Each minister desired to advance a quarter of a year's centessima of their stipend for one year for the suppression of Popery. 1707. viii.; 1715. 8.

——— A full account of the origin and nature of the fund given in a report by the committee on the public accounts of the Church. 1841, Appendix.

Certificates. Enacted that, when any young man comes to wait on the profession of divinity in any university, he shall bring along with him a testimonial from the minister of the parish from whence he comes; and when he leaves the profession, he shall also take with him, besides the professor's certificate, a testimonial from the minister of that parish in which he resided when he attended the profession. 1727. xii.; 1813. viii.

——— Enacted that no student shall be entered upon the roll of any professor, unless he shall produce a certificate from the minister of the parish in which he has his usual residence, or in his absence, or during a vacancy in said parish, from some neighbouring minister, that his character is suitable to his views, together with certificates from the several professors of philosophy under whom he had studied; and a certificate from the presbytery within whose bounds he chiefly resides, that he has, in a satisfactory manner, passed an examination upon his knowledge in the Christian religion, as it is exhibited in the catechetical standards of the Church. He shall also, at the commencement of every session of his course previous to being enrolled, produce to the professor a certificate from the presbytery of his having been examined by them on the progress made by him in his studies, and also a certificate of his good moral character from the minister of his parish.

Enacted, further, that no student shall be admitted to trials for licence unless he produces to the presbytery a certificate or certificates from the professors of divinity under whom he has studied, that he has prosecuted his studies and delivered his discourses in the manner prescribed by the laws of the Church, and that his conduct has been in every respect suitable to his views in life; which certificates the presbytery shall record in their minutes at full length, and transmit an extract thereof to the synod clerk to be laid before the synod. 1849. x.; 1827. vii.; 1837. ix.; 1837. 8; 1813. viii.

Certificates. The Assembly found that the certificate of a student's regular attendance at the Divinity Hall during the last session of his course not having been produced to the presbytery, ought to have been laid before the synod. 1815, ult.

Certificate. A presbytery having refused to take a student on trials because he had not produced a certificate of moral character from the minister of his parish, the student appealed, and the Assembly dismissed his appeal as inept and incompetent. 1832. 9.

——— Long delay having been occasioned in consequence of the serious indisposition of the presbytery clerk, the Assembly dispensed with the production of the student's certificates to the synod, and authorised the presbytery to proceed with his public trials. 1839. 5.

——— A minister having refused to give a student a certificate to qualify him for being admitted into the Divinity Hall, unless he signed a declaration of his opinions in regard to non-intrusion and the independent jurisdiction of the Church, the student brought the matter before the Assembly by petition and complaint, and the Assembly permitted the student to be enrolled without the certificate. 1841. 6.

——— The progress of a student's trials having been stopped, in consequence of his certificates not having been produced at the meeting of synod, the Assembly called for the required certificates; and being satisfied therewith, and that their non-production was not owing to any neglect on the part of the student, directed the presbytery to proceed with his trials according to the laws of the Church. 1853. 6.

Certificate. Students applying for licence required to produce certificates of attendance on classes of divinity, church history, and Hebrew, taught by professors in communion with the Church of Scotland—the existing indulgence allowed to students studying in foreign Protestant universities being continued. 1845. 14.

Certificate, Presbyterial. Every probationer on leaving the bounds of the presbytery by which he was licensed, and going to reside within the bounds of another presbytery, shall, within two months, report himself to the presbytery into which he has come, and lay before them a presbyterial certificate of his being a licentiate, and that his conduct is in every respect becoming his profession. 1736. ix.

——— A presbytery having refused a certificate to a presentee, in consequence of its being reported that, in a letter to the patron, he had stated it as his opinion that it was the duty of ministers to obey the laws as interpreted by the civil courts, or if their consciences were aggrieved by so doing, to resign their livings as ministers of the Established Church, the Assembly remitted the case to the presbytery, with instructions to refuse the certificate (1842. 10). But in the following year, on the case again coming before the Assembly, they instructed the presbytery to proceed with the settlement. 1843. 8.

——— In a case similar to the foregoing, the Assembly approved of the diligence of the presbytery in instituting an investigation, but found that, under the circumstances, there was no sufficient reason for refusing the certificate. 1842. 12.

——— The Assembly dismissed as unnecessary an overture anent presbyterial certificates, on the ground that sufficient provision was already made on the subject in the existing laws of the Church. 1848, ult.

——— A presbytery having sustained a presentation, and proceeded to the trials of a presentee without his producing a presbyterial certificate, the Assembly cassed and annulled all the proceedings of the presbytery from the time the presentation was laid on their table, and inhibited them from sustaining said presentation until a satisfactory presbyterial certificate in favour of the presentee was laid before them. 1849. 5.

Certificate, Presbyterial. A presbytery having refused a certificate to a probationer, who had for some time resided and acted as assistant to a member of presbytery, on the ground that he had not produced an extract of licence or presbyterial certificate, nor reported himself to said presbytery when he came to reside within their bounds, the Assembly, on petition, reversed the sentence of the presbytery, and found that they were not entitled, on the simple ground of the probationer's error in neglecting to report himself, to refuse him a certificate on his departure, inasmuch as they were bound to exercise superintendence over him as a preacher regularly officiating in one of the pulpits within their bounds; further, they declared that his status as a licentiate should not be affected by such refusal, and instructed the clerk to grant him a certificate to this effect. 1850. 13.

Certificate, Elder's. Enacted that, along with every commission to the Assembly in favour of a ruling elder, there shall be produced a certificate from the kirk-session of which he is a member, that he is *bonâ fide* an acting elder. 1839. xii.; 1841. xi.; 1850. xiv.

Chaldaic. Ordained that none be licensed to preach unless they give good proof of their understanding the Greek and Hebrew; and recommended to all candidates for the ministry to study also the other Oriental languages, especially the Chaldaic and Syriac, so far as they can. 1696. xxii.

Chapels of Ease. Regulations respecting the Chapel of Ease in Dunfermline. 1779. viii.

——— The Assembly declared the persons forming the congregation of a chapel of ease subject to the jurisdiction of the kirk-session of the parish; that the minister of the chapel should regularly intimate to the session-clerk the time of his administering the sacrament of the Lord's Supper three weeks before its celebration; that the session-clerk, within eight days thereafter, should transmit to the minister of the chapel a list of the parishioners under scandal; and that the minister should be at liberty to admit to the Lord's table such as he judged worthy, excepting only the persons contained in that last; and to baptise the children of any person belonging to his congregation who did not appear to be under scandal. 1782. 9.

Chapels of Ease. Ministers of chapels of ease, being in the habitual exercise of the functions of the ministerial office, declared to be thereby disqualified from sitting as lay elders in the judicatories of the Church. 1796. 4.

——— A chapel minister having brought a complaint against the minister of the parish for refusing certificates to members of the chapel of ease, for the purpose of their obtaining baptism to their children from the minister of said chapel, the Assembly dismissed the complaint as groundless. 1800. 5.

——— In a similar case the Assembly dismissed the appeal of the chapel minister, and enjoined him scrupulously to conform to the terms of the constitution of the chapel in relation to the authority of the kirk-session. 1831. 9.

——— The General Assembly, judging it expedient that no chapel of ease should be erected without the knowledge and approbation of the General Assembly, prescribed the steps necessary to be taken by the presbytery on a petition being laid before them for the erection of a chapel of ease; enjoined them to report the whole circumstances of the case to the Assembly, and not to pronounce any judgment on the petition until they had received the special directions of the Assembly thereon. 1798. v.

——— Regulations enacted to be observed in framing constitutions for chapels of ease. 1826. x.

——— Twenty-two chapels had received constitutions in the twenty-seven years preceding 1826. 1826. x.

——— A chapel minister having resigned his charge, the Assembly found that the presbytery ought not to have accepted his resignation without obtaining possession of the bond for his stipend, and taking some regular method to satisfy their minds with regard to the state of his health. 1815. 4.

——— No provision having been made by the constitution of a chapel for the election of a minister, the Assembly authorised the managers, elders, heads of families, and unmarried persons who were seatholders in the chapel at the death of the deceased incumbent, to proceed to elect a minister. 1823. 7.

——— An appeal having been taken on the ground that it

was not competent for a synod to pronounce a judgment with regard to proceedings under the constitution of a chapel of ease, the Assembly appointed a committee to examine into the question of jurisdiction, and report. 1831. 8.

Chapels of Ease. Found competent for a synod to review the proceedings of a presbytery in assigning boundaries to a new parish *quoad sacra*. Com., May 31, 1837.

—— Found that it was not competent for the Assembly to grant relief from the grievances under which ministers of chapels of ease laboured, in being excluded from the privilege of sitting and voting in the judicatories of the Church. 1830. 8.

—— Ministers of chapels of ease declared constituent members of presbyteries and synods, and eligible to sit in the General Assembly, and entitled to enjoy every privilege as fully and freely, and with equal powers, with parish ministers of this Church, by a majority of 153 to 103; and presbyteries enjoined to allot territorial districts to said ministers. 1834. ix.

—— A motion to rescind the foresaid Act, as having been passed in violation of the Barrier Act, negatived by a majority of 108 to 176. 1835. 6.

—— The heritors of a parish opposing its subdivision and the allocation of a territorial district to the minister of a chapel, and having obtained a note of suspension and interdict from the Court of Session against the presbytery, the Commission instructed the presbytery to proceed to assign a district *quoad spiritualia*, taking care so to construct their deliverance as not to have the appearance of affecting the civil rights of the heritors. Com., Aug. 14, 1840; June 2, 1841; Aug. 11, 1841. Ass. 1842. 9.

—— A minister under libel having protested that the whole proceedings in his case were vitiated and rendered null and void by the participation of a chapel minister as a member of presbytery, and having obtained a note of suspension and interdict against the presbytery, the Assembly found him liable to the highest censures of the Church, and summoned him to appear at their bar. Having appeared accordingly, he was sentenced to be deposed, and his church and parish declared vacant. 1842. 13 and 17.

Chapels of Ease: Declared that the principle on which the Act ix., 1834, is founded, is a fundamental principle of this Church, to which she is resolved, by the grace of God, at all hazards to adhere. 1842. 17.

——— An elder, in a case affecting his qualification, having declined the jurisdiction of the presbytery on the ground that several chapel ministers had been admitted as members of the court, the Commission found that he had acted in contempt of the authority of the Church, and declared him incapable of sitting and voting in any ecclesiastical judicatory, aye and until he should withdraw his declinature of the jurisdiction of the presbytery. Com., Aug. 10, 1842.

——— A motion not to enrol chapel ministers in the sederunt of the Commission, on the ground that it had been declared by the highest legal authority that the General Assembly could not by its own act give such ministers a valid and legal title to sit as members of the ecclesiastical judicatories of the Established Church, rejected by a majority of 115 to 23. Com., Jan. 31, 1843.

——— The Acts of Assembly, 1833, 1834, and 1839, by which ministers of chapels of ease became members of Church courts, rescinded, the same having been incompetently passed, and a special commission appointed to petition Her Majesty that measures might be taken to have the unendowed districts created legally and properly into parishes, and endowments provided for their ministers. 1843. x.

——— A committee appointed to consider what ought to be regarded as the status of chapel ministers, and the duties required of them. 1843. 8.

——— A committee appointed to give advice and assistance to presbyteries in their endeavour to retain the chapels of ease to the Establishment. 1844. 14.

——— The elders who had been ordained to chapels of ease, and continuing in the exercise of their duties therein in connection with the Establishment, declared to be elders of the Church of Scotland, and presbyteries instructed without delay to make such arrangements as might be found needful for the due exercise of discipline within the congregations of said chapels. 1843. 10.

——— A proposal having been transmitted from the Free

Church Assembly to refer to arbitration the questions which had arisen respecting the right to the property of the chapels of ease, the Assembly appointed a committee to draw up resolutions in answer thereto. 1847. 7.

Chapels of Ease. The thanks of the Assembly given to Dr Simpson and the Home Mission Committee for their calm, dignified, and irrefragable statement vindicating the just claims of the Church to the possession of the foresaid chapels. 1848. 11.

——— Committee appointed to devise such measures as might seem best calculated to obviate certain difficulties which had arisen relative to the extracting from the Records of Assembly the constitutions of the chapels about to be endowed and erected into parish churches. 1850. 14.

——— A presbytery found to have acted irregularly in sustaining a call in favour of the minister of a chapel situated within the bounds of another presbytery, and fixing a day for his induction, without any communication to the presbytery in which his chapel was situated. 1852. 6.

——— Ordained that in the event of the minister of a chapel of ease in one presbytery being presented to any charge within the bounds of another presbytery, notification shall be given by the latter presbytery to the former, of the different steps to be taken by them in order to his settlement, which notification shall be duly acknowledged. 1856. xii.

——— Election of a minister to a chapel objected to on the ground that, on the day of election, the congregation had not had a leet of three candidates to choose from, in terms of the constitution,—the objection sustained, and election declared null and void. Com., June 2, 1841.

——— Application from the managers of a chapel to be relieved from their obligation for the minister's stipend. 1843. 8.

——— The thanks of the Assembly transmitted to the Earl of Roseberry for his exertions in obtaining the passing of an Act of Parliament for enabling proprietors of entailed estates to grant conveyances of sites for churches and schools. 1841, ult.

——— A constitution to a chapel refused on account of the inadequacy of the proposed salary. 1847. 9.

Chaplains. Four chaplains sent out to the African and Indian Company's colony of Caledonia in America. A letter sent to them by the General Assembly. 1700. vi.

——— Presbyteries enjoined to take special, particular, and exact notice of all chaplains within their bounds, and to cause them sign the Confession of Faith. 1700. x.

——— A committee appointed to consider the most effectual means of providing for the regular administration of the ordinances of religion to the regiments on the Scotch establishment, when they serve in Scotland. 1806, ult.; 1807, ult.

——— Committee appointed to embrace every proper opportunity of stating the claims of this National Church to have it provided that some portion of the army chaplains should be Presbyterian clergymen, whose character shall be duly certified by the Moderator of the General Assembly. 1812. 4.

——— A petition to Parliament for the employment of licentiates of the Church of Scotland as chaplains in the Presbyterian regiments. 1839. 11.

——— A letter from the Chaplain-General of the Forces in regard to the employment of Presbyterian chaplains at colonial stations, laid before the Assembly. 1844. 6.

——— Reported to the Assembly that, by the new charter for the East India Company, the Church of Scotland was fairly established in India, the Government having made it imperative that there should be a minister of the Church of Scotland settled at each of the Presidencies,—remitted to the Committee on Indian Churches to accommodate the constitution of said churches accordingly. 1834. 4.

Charges, Unsubstantiated. A minister rebuked at the bar of the Assembly for having on various occasions thrown out unsubstantiated charges against ministers in the Synod of Orkney. 1788. 8.

Charity. Enacted that no minister, kirk-sessions, or elders give recommendations for charity (or licences to beg) to any without the bounds of their own parishes; nor presbyteries nor synods without their respective bounds. 1696. xix.

——— Enacted that in all time coming the General Assembly shall disregard all petitions for charity unless accompanied with a recommendation from the synod or presbytery of the bounds. 1710. viii.

Children. Ministers recommended to show all tenderness to persons educated in other Protestant Churches when they come to desire the benefit of sealing ordinances. If they are free of scandal, their children to be baptised. 1711. 13.

——— Exposed children or foundlings to be baptised and educated by the kirk-session. 1712. 4.

——— Children of parents one or both of whom profess the Christian religion, to be baptised. 1712. 4.

'Christian Instructor.' Certain passages in the 111th number of the 'Christian Instructor' declared to be highly offensive and calumnious, calculated to injure the character of many ministers, and to vilify and degrade the supreme judicatory of the Church; and the procurator instructed to take such steps as may appear to him to be competent for correcting the present, and preventing the repetition of similar offences. 1820, ult.

Christian Knowledge Society. A letter of thanks ordered to the Society in England for Propagating Christian Knowledge, for their assistance in erecting libraries in the Highlands. 1704. 17.

——— A committee appointed for propagating Christian knowledge, and suppressing Popery. 1708. 2. Said committee to meet on the last Thursday of every month, or oftener, as business may require. Com., April 28, 1708.

——— Constituted into a society or corporation by letters patent, and subscriptions ordered to be collected in every parish in aid of the funds. 1709. vi.

——— The northern synods enjoined to inquire into the state of the Highlands and Islands, in regard to churches, schools, catechists, Popery, &c., and to send in their reports to the secretary of the Society. 1710. xi.

——— A report of the proceedings of the Society given in to the Assembly. 1712. v.; 1713. v.; 1714. xiii.

——— A public collection ordered to be made at all the church doors of Scotland, for buying books to the Society's scholars, and settling more schools. 1715. xii.; 1716. iv.; 1717. iv.; 1747, ult.

——— Reported that the stock of the Society had increased to £7000, and that the Society had erected forty-two schools in the Highlands and Islands. 1719. 5.

Christian Knowledge Society. Reported that the Society had 105 schools, attended by 4146 scholars ; and that many thousands had been taught to read who formerly lived in gross ignorance and superstition. 1732. iv.

——— Thanks of the Assembly given to the Society for their zeal in publishing a translation of the Holy Scriptures into Gaelic ; and the use of any other Gaelic version prohibited in the churches, chapels, missions, and schools of the Church of Scotland. 1816. vi.

Church. The Commission instructed to consider the case of parishes not very large, where one church might well serve, and yet have more places than one for public worship, and what is proper to be done therein. 1724, ult.

——— Mr Samuel Semple, minister at Liberton, recommended to proceed with a compilation of the History of the Church, from the first planting of Christianity to the present time, and to be careful that the authorities founded on by him were of good credit. 1708. 5; 1710. 13.

——— The procurator and agents instructed to concur with synods and presbyteries in preserving the patrimony of the Church. 1708. 13.

——— Presbyteries to collect an account of the sufferings of the Church under the late prelacy, and to send in the same to the procurator. 1710. 11.

——— Strangers from other Protestant Churches to be cheerfully admitted into the communion of the Church, if they are free from scandal, and profess their faith in Christ, and obedience unto Him. 1711. xiii.

——— Commissioners appointed to repair to London and attend His Majesty anent the affairs of this Church. 1690. xviii.; 1712. 10.

——— Intimated by the Lord High Commissioner that Her Majesty had given new assurances of her resolution to protect this Church, and defend the ministers and judicatories thereof from insults, and to redress their just complaints. 1712. 10.

——— Resolved to represent to Her Majesty the grievances this Church lies under from the growth of Popery, insolence of Papists, and the illegal encroachments and intrusions of the Episcopal ministers and their adherents. 1714. 4.

Church. An Act for restoring and preserving the unity and peace of this Church. 1714. viii.; 1713. vi.; 1715. vi.

——— Recommended that every minister should give an annual contribution of 5s. in aid of the funds of the Church. 1816. xi.

——— Enacted that every student shall attend regularly two sessions on the class of Church History. 1813. ix.

——— The heritors of a parish, having agreed to erect a new parish church, resolved to dispose of the old church to an Episcopalian congregation for their use. Against this resolution the petitioners petitioned, and the Assembly found that this being entirely a civil question, it was not competent for the Church courts to interfere. 1827. 4.

Churches. Presbyteries prohibited from consenting to or conniving at the annexation or suppression of parishes without the consent of the Assembly or synod of the bounds. 1740. v.

——— Standing order in regard to applications for the erection of new churches. 1850. xiv.

——— Ordered that the drafts of the titles of new churches be submitted to the revising committee of the Assembly for their approval. 1842. xv.

——— *See* COLONIAL, INDIAN, EXTENSION, and ENDOWMENT.

Church Bell. Declared that the ringing of the bell of a parish church, in connection with ecclesiastical and religious purposes, belongs exclusively to the minister of the parish. 1818. 6; 1823. 5.

Church Keys. Declared to be the ecclesiastical right of the ministers of parishes to have free entrance to their churches for the purpose of divine worship and religious instruction, and that during vacancies or suspensions this right is vested in the presbytery of the bounds. 1828. 8.

Church Officers. The procurator instructed to appear in the civil court on behalf of the Church, respecting the rights and jurisdiction of the Church over inferior Church officers. 1809. 6.

——— A minister carrying on a process before the Court of Session regarding the right of the minister to dismiss his beadle, applied for aid from the funds of the Church. The

Assembly found their funds in such a state that no aid could be given. 1809. 9.

Church Officers. A session-clerk, having been dismissed by the kirk-session, appealed to the presbytery, who dismissed his appeal on the ground that he had not been appointed *ad vitam aut culpam.* The Assembly unanimously found that the subject-matter of the appeal resolved itself into a question of civil right, which could only be competently tried by the civil courts, and that the presbytery had acted incompetently in pronouncing any sentence on the merits of the case. 1819. 9.

Churches, Parliamentary. A report of the committee on additional churches, with an account of the population and extent of certain parishes relative to the want of additional churches, and a bill which had been brought into Parliament for making provision for supplying the said want, given in and read. 1819, ult.

——— A letter from the Lord Advocate on the subject of the Parliamentary churches, communicated to the Assembly. 1822, ult.

——— Committee appointed to thoroughly investigate and recommend such measures as may be necesssary for clearly ascertaining the nature of the relation which ought to be established between parochial and parliamentary ministers. 1830. 7.

——— Ministers of parliamentary churches declared constituent members of presbyteries and synods, and eligible to sit in the General Assembly. 1833. vi.

——— The foresaid Act, 1833. vi., rescinded. 1843. x.

Church Accommodation. An interdict having been granted by a sheriff, discharging the parishioners of a parish from entering their parish church without the authority of the heritors, the Assembly declared, that while they felt the deepest interest in the sufficient accommodation of the people of Scotland in their parish churches, this was a case in which they could not interfere, it being in dependence before, and to be decided by, a civil court. 1827. 8; 1828. 5.

——— A committee appointed to inquire into the evils resulting from the inadequate state of Church accommodation in many of the large towns, manufacturing villages, and populous parishes of Scotland. 1828. 4.

Church Accommodation. Declared that accommodation in parish churches cannot be made the subject of profit, or income of any sort, by the heritors. The surplus area, after accommodating themselves and tenants, falling to be appropriated for the accommodation of the other parishioners, the heritors having no right to let such surplus or to draw any income from the same, to whatever purpose it may be applied. 1830. 8.

——— The Court of Session having decided that the heritors could not be called on to enlarge a parish church unless it was ruinous, the Assembly recommended a general collection throughout the Church for ascertaining, by appeal to the House of Lords, the actual state of the law respecting church accommodation in parishes in which the population has so increased that the original fabric has become totally inadequate for the purpose of affording opportunity of attending divine ordinances dispensed by the ministers of the Church. 1832. 7.

——— Committee formed on the model of the Committee for Propagating the Gospel in Foreign Parts, with instructions to ascertain precisely, by communicating with the different presbyteries, the state of church accommodation throughout the country. 1834. 7.

Church Extension. The Church Extension Committee, formed by the union of the committees on church accommodation, church endowments, and the subdivision of parishes; Dr Chalmers, convener. 1835. 8.

——— Report of Church Extension Committee, and resolutions of Assembly relative to Religious Instruction Commission. 1837. 7; 1838. 5 and 8.

——— Two sub-committees appointed, one to sit in Edinburgh and the other in Glasgow. 1840. 9.

——— Church Extension Committee merged into the Home Mission Committee. 1842. xviii.

Circular Letters. Enacted that, before taking students on public probationary trials, presbyteries shall write circular letters to all the presbyteries within the bounds of their synod, acquainting them with their design at least two calendar months before the meeting of the synod. 1711. x.; 1782. viii.; 1788. viii.; 1813. viii.; 1849. xi.

Circular Letters. A synod having allowed a student to be taken on trials without circular letters having been written to presbyteries, the Assembly reversed the sentence of the synod. 1777. 9.

Citation of Parties. Citation of parties may be upon forty-eight hours' notice, if the parties reside within the bounds of the parish, before two or three witnesses. 1707. xi., chap. ii. 3.

——— All citations *apud acta* are peremptory, and, if instructed, infer contumacy if not obeyed. 1707. xi. chap. ii. 5.

——— Three citations to be given before the party be declared contumacious. 1707. xi. chap. ii. 6.

——— In the case of a minister, citation in writing, with a copy of the libel and list of witnesses to be served on the party accused, either personally or at his dwelling-house, at least ten days before the day of compearance. 1707. xi., chap. vii. 5.

——— In a case of translation, when a minister is called from one parish to another, to prevent rabbling of messengers and profanation of the Lord's day, it is ordered that he shall himself give citation from the pulpit to the defending party and parish to appear before the presbytery on the day of cause, to give in their objections to the translation, if they have any. 1704. vii.

——— A presbytery having granted warrant to their officer to cite a minister under libel "personally, and at his own church," the officer left a copy of the citation at the manse, the minister being absent, and affixed another copy to the church door, there being no divine service there. The presbytery held the minister to have been duly and regularly cited; but the Commission reversed the finding of the presbytery, leaving it to them to serve the libel anew if they saw cause. Com., June 2, 1846.

——— Appeal taken on the ground that the warrant of citation did not allow ten free days for the party to lodge answers to the relevancy of the libel, and other ten free days between the day of lodging answers and the day of compearance. The Commission dismissed the appeal, found the libel, with certain alterations, relevant, and instructed the presbytery to proceed with the case. Com., June 3, 1840.

Citation. *See* Form of Process.

Citation of Witnesses. Witnesses to be timeously cited. If they refuse after three citations, may be proceeded with as contumacious; or, if judged needful, application may be made to the civil magistrate that he may compel them to appear. 1707. xi. chap. ii. 9.

——— Committee appointed to consider and report on an overture anent the citation of witnesses. 1845. 11.

——— The Assembly, on the recommendation of said committee, instructed the procurator and agent to select a favourable case, if any such should occur, for having the question regarding the citation of witnesses tried at the expense of the Church. 1846. 13.

Claim of Right. Claim, declaration, and protest against the encroachments of the Court of Session. 1842. xix.

——— Address to the Queen on the subject of the Claim of Right. 1842. xx.

Principal Clerks of the General Assembly.

Clerk of Assembly. Mr John Spalding acted as clerk to the general meetings and the Assembly, 1690. 1698. 11.

——— Mr Robert Park, advocate, was clerk to Assembly 1694. 1695. iii.

——— Mr John Bannatyne, minister at Lanark, appointed to officiate as clerk until another was chosen, and Nicol Spence to assist in that office. Mr Bannatyne continued to be re-elected from year to year down to 1701, when Mr David Dundas was chosen clerk to the General Assembly and Commission thereof, and Nicol Spence continued sub-clerk *sicut ante*, which office he held until 1738, having also, in 1708, been conjoined with Mr Blair as agent. 1701. 1.

——— Mr John Dundas, advocate, chosen clerk to the General Assembly and the Commissioners thereof in the room of Mr David Dundas, deceased. 1703. 1. He was also, in 1706, appointed advocate in ordinary and procurator for the Church. 1706. 13.

——— Mr William Grant, advocate, elected procurator for

the Church, and principal clerk of the Assembly in place of Mr John Dundas of Philipston, who died during the sitting of the Assembly. 1731. 7.

Clerk of Assembly. Mr Grant allowed to depute Mr Andrew Macdonal, advocate, to officiate for him as clerk. 1745. 1; 1737, ult.

——— The offices of principal clerk and procurator not incompatible with the office of solicitor-general. 1738. 3.

——— Mr Grant having been appointed His Majesty's Advocate, deputed Mr George Buchan of Kelloe to officiate as clerk; but the Assembly found that the offices of procurator and principal clerk were at their disposal, and elected Mr DAVID DALRYMPLE, advocate, procurator, and Mr GEORGE WISHART, one of the ministers of Edinburgh, principal clerk, *during pleasure*. 1746. 8.

——— Mr Wishart having, in 1748, been elected moderator, was allowed to depute Mr Hamilton to officiate as clerk *pro tempore*, the Assembly, however, taking care to enter upon the minutes that by the power they had given him of deputing a clerk, it was not to be understood that he or any future clerk was to have such power without the previous allowance of the Assembly. 1748. 1.

——— Mr Wishart, after discharging the duties of the office for thirty-two years, resigned the clerkship into the hands of the Assembly, whereupon he and Dr JOHN DRYSDALE were elected conjunct clerks, the survivancy to be in the longest liver of the two. 1778. 8.

——— Dr Wishart died in 1785, Dr James Macknight having been appointed to act for him during Assembly 1784. 1784. 1.

——— Dr John Drysdale succeeded as sole principal clerk; and being in bad health during the meeting of Assembly 1787, Mr William Murray, junior, writer, was appointed to assist him *pro tempore*. 1787. 2; 1788. 2.

——— PROFESSOR DALZEL elected after a very keen contest. When the vote was taken, Dr Carlyle had an apparent majority; but a scrutiny having been demanded, it was found that "a majority of legal votes was in favour of Professor Dalzel," who was accordingly elected to hold the office during all the days of his natural life. 1789. 8.

Clerk of Assembly. Mr Andrew Duncan, minister at Ratho, elected by a considerable majority over Dr Robert Dickson of South Leith. 1807. 1.

——— Dr John Lee elected in room of Dr Duncan, deceased. 1828. 1.

——— Dr Alexander Lockhart Simpson, minister at Kirk-Newton, who had been sub-clerk since 1828, promoted to the principal clerkship in room of Dr Lee, deceased. 1859. 1.

——— Dr John Cook, minister at Haddington, who had succeeded Dr Simpson in the sub-clerkship, promoted to be principal clerk in room of Dr Simpson, deceased. 1862. 1.

Clerk, Sub. Mr Nicol Spence, who had for several years assisted the principal clerk, appointed sub-clerk to the Assembly and Commissions thereof. 1701. 1.

——— Mr Spence was conjoined with Mr John Blair as agent for the Church in 1708, which office he held, along with the sub-clerkship, until 1722, when, at Mr Blair's death, he was appointed sole agent and sub-clerk.

——— Mr Robert M'Intosh appointed colleague to Mr Spence as agent and sub-clerk, with the survivancy. 1738. 8.

——— Mr John Baillie, W.S., on the death of Mr Spence, appointed colleague to Mr M'Intosh in said offices. 1743. 7.

——— Mr James Edmonston, W.S., appointed colleague to Mr Baillie in room of Mr M'Intosh, deceased. Mr Edmonston to exercise the office of sub-clerk and clerk to the Royal Bounty, and Mr Baillie that of agent for the Church. 1753. 3.

Mr Baillie having died in 1754, Mr Edmonston held both offices alone until his death in 1781, when the offices of agent and sub-clerk were disjoined, and have ever since been distinct.

——— Dr William Gloag, one of the ministers of Edinburgh, appointed sub-clerk and clerk to the Royal Bounty in place of Mr James Edmonston, deceased. 1781. 1.

——— Mr Thomas M'Knight, Leith, and Mr David Ritchie, Edinburgh, appointed conjunct sub-clerks on the death of Dr Gloag. Dr Ritchie resigned in 1808. 1802. 1.

——— Dr John Lee elected conjunct sub-clerk with Dr M'Knight, reserving to Dr M'Knight the privileges, salary, and emoluments. 1826. 1.

Clerk, Sub. Mr Alexander Lockhart Simpson, minister at Kirk-Newton, elected conjunct sub-clerk in room of Dr Lee, promoted to be principal clerk. 1828. 1.

——— Dr John Cook, minister at Haddington, appointed sub-clerk in room of Dr Simpson, who succeeded Dr Lee in the principal clerkship. 1859. 8.

——— Dr John Tulloch, Principal of St Mary's College, St Andrews, appointed sub-clerk in room of Dr Cook, promoted to be principal clerk. 1862. 1.

Clerks of Synod. Ordained that the clerk at least shall subscribe every book before it come to the Assembly, and that every act be noted on the margin for a directory of expedition. 1642. 11.

——— Clerks of Synods ordered to transmit their books to the General Assembly, with certification that if they failed to give due obedience they should be summoned to the bar of the Assembly. 1804. 5; 1827. 4.

——— The clerk of the Synod of Perth and Stirling, and of the Presbytery of Perth, having been deposed by the Commission, the Assembly removed the sentence of deposition, and remitted to the presbytery and synod to do to him with respect of their clerkships as they might see meet. 1720. 3.

——— Synods recommended to take care that their registers are completely filled up, and that the proceedings of every synod be signed both by the moderator and clerk. 1698. xi.; 1700. ix.; 1713. iv.

——— Erasures to be marked on the margin, and signed by the moderator and clerk. Marginal additions and corrections to be signed by the clerk. 1706. ix.

——— The clerks of the several judicatories enjoined to transmit in due time to the clerk of Assembly all references made by their respective judicatories. 1718. vii.

Clerk of Presbytery. Found that a presbytery clerk was not entitled to withhold a commission to the General Assembly on the ground that the usual fee had not been paid. 1825. 3.

Clerks of Session. A session clerk, having been dismissed by the session, appealed to the presbytery, who gave judgment on the merits. The Assembly found that as the appeal referred to was a matter of civil right, it could only be competently tried by a civil court, and that it was incompetent for the presbytery to enter upon the merits. 1819. 9.

Clerical Errors. The omission of the surname of an elder in a commission held to be a valid objection to the commission. 1808. 3.

——— An erasure in the date of an election held to be a valid objection in a commission. 1821. 3.

——— In a case of erasure proof was allowed of the authenticity of the correction, and the commission sustained. 1847. 3.

——— Through an error of a clerk of presbytery the reasons of appeal in a case not having been transmitted until the last day of Assembly, the Assembly appointed the committee on bills to meet and receive said reasons. 1825, ult.

——— Errors in date of minute allowed to be corrected on production of original record. 1839. 3; 1834. 5; 1846. 3.

——— Errors and omissions as to dates held to be corrected by the contents of the documents. 1821. 3; 1836. 9; 1849. 2; 1850. 2.

Collections. Ordered for helping to build a church in Konigsberg for those of the Reformed religion there. 1698. 11.

——— For relief of the Christians taken captive by the Turks and detained in Barbary. 1698. 15; 1707. 7; 1722. 10.

——— To assist in building bridges at Lanark and Ancrum. 1699. 18.

——— Do. at Blackburn. 1720. 11.

——— Do. at Kelso. 1756. 9.

——— Do. at Montrose. 1773. 5.

——— Do. at Tulloch. 1726. 7.

——— For additional schools in the Highlands. 1704. xiv.

——— For John Maculloch, an old minister in great distress. 1704. 10.

——— For the harbour at Irvine. 1706. 6.

——— Do. at Eyemouth. 1753. 8.

——— Do. Crail harbour. 1760. 8.

——— For building the Tolbooth at Tain. 1706. 14.

Collections. For the Protestants at Lisbourne in Ireland, who had suffered from a great fire. 1709. 4.

——— For the Scots Presbyterian congregation of the city of New York in distressed circumstances. 1720. 3.

——— For the erection of new parishes in Lord Reay's country. 1725. 3.

——— For church at Enzie. 1728. 18.

——— For Edinburgh Infirmary. 1737. 5; 1785. 6.

——— For Edinburgh Surgeons' Hospital. 1737. 7.

——— For Christian Knowledge Society. 1715. 12, &c.

——— For church in Pennsylvania. 1752. 8; 1760. 8.

——— For Jersey College. 1754. 8.

——— For the Protestant congregation at Saarbruck. 1762, ult.

——— Ministers and presbyteries ordained to transmit an exact amount of all collections made by order of the Assembly to the clerks of Assembly, who shall keep a separate book for enrolling said collections. 1777. ix.

——— A collection recommended to be made at all the parish church-doors within Scotland for relief of Mr Francis Robertson, who had sustained a heavy loss by fire. 1737. 10.

——— The managers of a chapel having been interdicted from applying the collections at the church-door for the maintenance of the minister, the Assembly instructed the managers to continue the practice,—a motion by Lord Moncreiff to sist procedure till the question had been decided by the civil court having been lost by a majority of 101 to 52. 1837. 10.

——— Collections earnestly recommended to be made on behalf of the Schemes of the Church. 1836. xx., &c.

——— Synods to take cognisance and record in their minutes as to the collections made within their bounds for the Schemes of the Church; their omitting to do so to be noticed in the printed Acts of Assembly. 1850. xiv.

Colleges. *See* UNIVERSITIES.

Collegiate Charges. Collegiate kirks in which there use to be two or more ministers to be understood to be as many distinct parishes in so far as concerns the representation of presbyteries in General Assemblies. 1694. v.

Collegiate Charges. The Commission instructed to use all proper means for obtaining new erections in large and spacious parishes, or stipends to collegiate ministers in the same. 1708. ix.

Colonial Churches. Declaratory enactment and recommendation relative to colonial churches. Ordained ministers of the Church of Scotland, with fixed congregations in any of the British colonies, recommended to form themselves into presbyteries and synods; such presbyteries not to exercise the power of licensing probationers, but to ordain licentiates of the Church of Scotland. 1833. v.

——— A standing committee appointed to correspond with colonial churches, to be called "The General Assembly's Committee for Promoting the Religious Interests of Scottish Presbyterians in the British Colonies," and to meet statedly on the Tuesdays before the stated meetings of the Commission. Parochial collections recommended, and the Colonial Mission adopted as one of the Schemes of the Church. 1836. 9.

——— An extract of the proceedings of a committee of the Presbyterian Church in Montreal respecting the appointment of an assistant and successor to the minister of said church having been laid before the Assembly, the Assembly declared their satisfaction that the congregation desired to be considered in full communion with the Church of Scotland, and that, so long as the congregation continued to elect pastors licensed and ordained by this Church, they would be regarded as in full communion with the Church of Scotland. 1817. 8.

——— The Assembly, considering how very desirable it is that a close connection should be kept up with the ministers of this Church in the West Indies, British America, and other foreign parts, appointed a committee to receive communications from said ministers and their congregations, and to consider the best means of continuing an intimate connection with them. 1818. 5.

——— A petition respecting a Presbyterian church in Montreal referred to a committee. 1820. 9.

——— Colonial committee instructed to support, by all the means in their power, the claims of the Presbyterian ministers in Canada to a competent provision out of the Clergy Reserves. 1823. 9; 1824. 3; 1827. ult; 1828. ult.

Colonial Churches. Full report on the case of the Scottish settlers in Upper and Lower Canada, Nova Scotia, Cape Breton, New Brunswick, and other colonies, giving a detailed account of the proceedings of the committee from its first appointment, and recommending the Assembly to continue their inquiries, and in the strongest manner to urge the claims of the colonies upon His Majesty's Government. Com., June 1, 1830.

——— A communication from Lord Glenelg relative to the Clergy Reserves, to the effect that no fresh measures could, without inconvenience, be adopted in reference to that property at that time. Com., August 12, 1835.

——— A petition to Parliament on the subject of the endowments withheld from the Presbyterian Church in Canada. 1838, ult.

——— The Assembly recorded their heartfelt acknowledgments to Her Majesty's Government for supporting the ecclesiastical judicatory recognised by this Church in New South Wales, for sanctioning the endowment of a minister in Ceylon, and for admitting the right of this Church to participate in the proceeds of the Clergy Reserves in Canada. 1839. 9.

——— A pastoral letter transmitted to the ministers, elders, and people of the Presbyterian Church in New South Wales, with reference to certain divisive proceedings in that colony. Com., August 8, 1838.

——— A special committee appointed to confer with Dr Lang with reference to the aforesaid lamentable divisions. Com., August 15, 1839; 1840. 3.

——— A subscription recommended in aid of a college to be established at Kingston, Upper Canada, for the education of candidates for the ministry, to be called Queen's College. 1840. 3; Com., Nov. 18, 1840.

——— Principal Macfarlan resigned the convenership of the colonial committee, and Dr Walsh appointed in his stead. 1841. 8.

——— Principal Macfarlan reappointed convener, and Dr Grant vice-convener. 1843. 10.

——— Dr Clark appointed vice-convener, in room of Dr Grant, resigned. 1844. 14.

Colonial Churches. Dr Arnot appointed vice-convener, in room of Dr Clark, resigned. 1854. 13.

——— A licentiate of the Church of Scotland having been deposed by the Presbytery of St John's, New Brunswick, a question was raised as to the competency of reviewing a sentence pronounced by a church court in the colonies. The Assembly found that, while they do not review the sentences of colonial courts recognised by this Church, with reference to ministers subject to the jurisdiction of these courts; yet, when the connection of such ministers with such courts has been regularly brought to an end, said ministers revert under the cognisance and jurisdiction of the courts of this Church, by which they were licensed. 1841. 3.

——— Remitted to a presbytery to inquire into the truth of a report that a minister in Australia had withdrawn from all connection with the Church of Scotland, with instructions, if satisfied of the truth of said report, to find and declare accordingly. Com., May 30, 1843.

——— Resolution regarding seceding ministers in Australia. 1845. 15.

——— Certain proceedings of the Presbytery of Demerara highly disapproved of. 1846. 13; 1847. 1.

——— The Assembly heard with satisfaction that a very large majority of the Synod of Australia had resolved to maintain their connection with the Church of Scotland. 1847. 1.

——— The Assembly highly approved of the conduct of the colonial committee in regard to the Canada Clergy Reserves Bill; expressed their regret that the efforts made to oppose that bill had not been successful, and left the results of the measure with the Supreme Governor among the nations, who can overrule events, apparently the most adverse, for the advancement of His own cause and kingdom in the world. 1853. 2.

——— The Assembly expressed their regret at certain proceedings which had taken place in the Presbytery of Demerara and Essequibo, which had led to a suspension of friendly intercourse between said presbyteries and the colonial committee. 1851. ult.

——— The Presbytery of Demerara having petitioned the Assembly to recommend the colonial committee to renew friendly intercourse with said presbytery, the Assembly complied with the petition, leaving to the committee to carry it into effect as they should think best. 1853. 2.

Colonial Churches. A deputation, consisting of Dr Simpson, Dr John M'Leod, and Mr Norman M'Leod, appointed to visit the churches in British America in connection with the Church of Scotland, gave in their report. 1846. 11.

——— Another deputation, consisting of Messrs Fowler, Stevenson, and M'Intosh, gave in their report. 1848. 8.

——— A deputation, consisting of Messrs Irvine, Monro, Pearson, and M'Lean, appointed to make strict inquiry into the state of the Church of Scotland in British Guiana, and especially into the charges which have been mutually made by the members of the Presbytery of Berbice against one another, with power and authority to act as they shall see cause. 1860. 14.

——— Report of said deputation given in and approved of. 1861. 6.

Commemoration. An Address to His Majesty on the commemoration of the glorious Revolution. 1788. iv.

Commission, Royal. Appointed to visit the universities and colleges of Scotland; their report presented to the Assembly. 1832. 1.

——— Appointed for inquiring into the opportunities of religious worship, and means of religious instruction and pastoral superintendence, afforded to the people of Scotland, "respectfully but firmly declared to be not such as to entitle it to the confidence of the friends of the Church of Scotland." Com., August 13, 1835.

——— Reports of Church Extension Committee relative to the commission aforesaid. 1837. 7; 1838. 8.

Commission of Assembly. Resolved that there be appointed by the Assembly a delegated number of the most experienced ministers and elders, to take to their cognisance all references and appeals, and other things which, being stated before the Assembly, shall be by them specially referred to the said Commission. That this Commission do not take on them to meddle with anything not expressed in their commission, and to be in all their actings accountable to and censurable by the next ensuing General Assembly. 1690. xv.; 1694. xi.; 1711. viii.

Commission of Assembly. A commission appointed to meet monthly for the more expedite planting of ministers on the north side of the water of Tay. 1695. xii.

——— Commission appointed to meet the first day after the dissolution of the Assembly, and afterwards on the last Wednesday of October and first Wednesday of March, and oftener when and where they shall think needful, with power to choose their own moderator. Absentees to be noted, and their names read in the Assembly. The Presbytery of Edinburgh, and all other presbyteries within twelve miles thereof, prohibited from meeting on any of the days or weeks appointed for the meeting of Commission. Presbyteries having four or more members of Commission to take care that at least two of them attend. 1706. xvii.; 1711. viii.

——— Presbyteries recommended to supply the charges of their ministers who are members of Commission during their attendance thereon. 1699, ult.; 1704. xvi.; 1705. vi.

——— Commission empowered to choose their own moderator and clerk. 1698. xii.

——— Committee appointed of members of Assembly who were not members of Commission, to revise the proceedings of the Commission. 1699. viii.

——— The High Commissioner having represented the dangerous indisposition of His Majesty, the Assembly appointed a commission, consisting of all the old and experienced ministers that were ministers in 1661, together with those of most experience and ability, with instructions to provide for the maintenance of "a public and established course of discipline and order in the Church, whatever might fall out." 1702. iv.

——— An Act anent the better attendance of members on the Commission. 1703. vi.; 1705. xv.

——— Presbyteries enjoined to consider and report upon the means of securing a just and equal representation of the synods and presbyteries in the Commission. 1704. xvi.

——— All the Presbyteries to be equally represented in the Commission. Three out of each synod to be appointed a committee for naming the members. Expenses of commissioners to be paid, and their pulpits to be supplied. Absentees to be censured. 1705. vi.

Commission of Assembly. The same formula to be observed in the approbation of the registers of the Commission that is prescribed to be observed in the attestation of synod books. 1706. viii.

——— Full instructions given to the Commission in regard to their proceedings and powers. 1717. vi.

——— All the members of the Commission to be qualified in the same way as members of Assembly. 1719. vi.

——— Ordained that the same proportion be observed between ministers and elders as obtains in the Assembly, and that certain of the nobility, officers of state, lords of session, and barons of exchequer be superadded. Presbyteries failing to obey the sentences of the Commission, declared to be *ipso facto* sisted before the next General Assembly. 1736. xii.

——— Presbyteries to take account of the attendance of their members on the quarterly meetings of the Commission. 1742. v.

——— Commission to take care that the impressions of the Holy Scriptures, Confession of Faith, catechisms, and other books relating to the doctrine, worship, and government of this Church, be correct. 1720. xi.

——— Commission instructed, if a favourable opportunity occur, to apply to the King and Parliament for redress of the grievance of patronage. 1736. xi.

——— A similar instruction given annually until 1784, when it was discontinued. 1784. xii.

——— Found that an affair determined by the Commission should not be recognosced by the General Assembly. 1706. 4.

——— Certain proceedings of the Commission disapproved of by the Assembly, and Commissions enjoined in time coming strictly to observe their instructions, and not transgress them on any pretence whatsomever. 1708. 9; 1711. 7.

——— In an appeal case the Assembly found that, as the Commission had not exceeded their powers, their sentence could not be reversed. 1741. 4; 1813. 8; 1839, ult.

——— The Commission found to have exceeded their powers, and their proceedings disapproved. 1724. 10.

——— The Assembly disapproved of the proceedings of the Commission in the settlement of a minister, on the ground "that they had acted disagreeably to the injunctions of the preceding Assembly," but by a vote refused to rescind the Commission's sentence. 1726. 10.

Commission of Assembly. The Commission found to have exceeded their powers in disposing of money out of the funds of the Church, and their orders cancelled. 1761. 7.

——— A motion having been made that, in regard of the moderator living at a great distance from Edinburgh, the clerk should be empowered, on a requisition from the Presbytery of Edinburgh, or any ten ministers of the Church, to call an extraordinary meeting of the Commission—the Assembly, after reasoning at great length, rejected the motion. 1778. 7.

——— Several cases referred by the Commission to the Assembly. 1726. 10.

——— In a case that had been before the Commission, a question was raised as to those members of Assembly who were members of the Commission, when the sentence complained of was passed, being allowed to judge in the cause. After reasoning, parties consented to depart from the objection, "to which the Assembly agreed, without making a precedent on either side." 1737. 8.

——— A similar objection having been made, the Assembly unanimously overruled the objection, and called for the votes of all who were members of the Assembly then present, whether they had been members of the preceding Commission or not. 1813. 8.

——— Petition and complaint against a sentence of the Commission rejected by the Assembly, on the ground that the petitioner had no right to be heard on allegations which tended merely to show that, in his judgment, the Commission had passed an erroneous judgment. To hear him would be to place him on the footing of an appellant, to which standing he had no title. 1853. 11.

——— In a matter remitted to them by the Assembly, the Commission found that there was no case before them. The Assembly found that the Commission ought to have heard parties, and remitted the consideration of the case to the ensuing Commission. 1854. 11.

——— Committee appointed to revise the instructions given

to the Commission, for the purpose of removing certain doubts as to their nature and import. 1839. 10.

Commission of Assembly. The Commission, at an early part of a sederunt, having resolved to adjourn at the close of the diet to the following day at eleven o'clock, was afterwards counted out for want of a quorum. On their meeting next day the counsel for both parties called in question the competency of the Commission to take up any case, inasmuch as there had been no regular adjournment, the house at its rising not being sufficiently full to be entitled to exercise the choice of either adjourning or proceeding with the business. The Commission, without a vote, repelled the objection, and proceeded to business. Com., June 3, 1836.

——— Similar cases of adjournment. Com., Nov. 21, 1838; Com., Aug. 15, 1839.

——— The Commission having, at a meeting on the 20th November, adjourned to the 11th December following, met accordingly, when a protest was taken against the approbation of the minutes of the former meeting, in so far as that meeting had adjourned to a distant day, without having the power of so adjourning; and also against proceeding to any business at a meeting held in consequence of such illegal adjournment. Com., Dec. 11, 1839.

——— The foregoing matter having been brought before the following Assembly, the Assembly found that the Commission had not exceeded their powers. 1840. 5.

——— Dissent and complaint allowed from the Commission to the next General Assembly. Com., Dec. 11, 1839; Com., Mar. 4, 1840.

——— Questions regarding the powers of the Commission, and the obligation of its sentences on inferior Church courts, not allowed to be put to the moderator. Com., Dec. 11, 1839.

——— In a case of libel, the parties pled that the Commission, not being a court established or sanctioned by the law of the land, had no power to issue or try the libel served on them, declined the jurisdiction, and protested against the whole proceedings as illegal and unconstitutional. The Commission repelled the objection, and found the libel relevant. Com., Nov. 18, 1840.

Commission, Quorum. The Commission to consist of fifty ministers and twenty-five ruling elders; fifteen to be a *quorum*, of whom ten to be ministers. 1694. xi.

——— Fifteen declared to be a *quorum*, of whom nine to be ministers. 1696. xx.

——— Twenty-one declared to be a *quorum*, of whom fourteen to be ministers. 1703. iv.

——— Thirty-one declared to be a *quorum*, of whom twenty-one to be ministers. 1711. viii.

——— Counsel refused to plead before a court not consisting of a *quorum* of members. Com., June 3, 1841.

——— An appeal having been dismissed by a majority of fifteen to nine, the party protested against the judgment, on the ground that there was not a *quorum* of members. Com., June 2, 1841.

Commission, Special. A special Commission appointed to visit all the presbyteries on the south side of the river Tay, and another to visit all the presbyteries on the north side. 1690. xv. xvi.

——— A special Commission appointed to settle a minister at Denny. 1737. 6.

——— A special Commission appointed to lead proof in a case. 1787. 6.

——— A special Commission appointed to co-operate with the Presbytery of Strathbogie. 1840. xii.

——— A special Commission appointed to co-operate with certain presbyteries within whose bounds certain vacant parishes are situated. 1841. xv.

——— A special Commission appointed with reference to the difficulties of the Church. 1842. xxiv.

Commissioner, Lord High. Certain ministers appointed to preach before His Grace, with power to name others to succeed them. 1699. 1.

——— The Assembly met, but adjourned without proceeding to business, the Commissioner being indisposed. 1753. 7.

——— The Assembly met on the 21st May, but the Commissioner was not able to meet with them until the 26th, his commission not having been certified under the Great Seal, in consequence of a vacancy in the office of Lord Keeper. An express was despatched to London for a special warrant;

meanwhile the Assembly proceeded to appoint the usual committees and to other business. 1761. 1 and 5.

Commissioner, Lord High. The Commissioner, being indisposed, sent a letter to the Assembly informing them of his inability to attend, and desiring them to proceed to business in his absence if they thought proper. 1763. 6.

——— The Commissioner being prevented by sickness from being present at the opening of the Assembly, sent a written message to the Assembly along with the Royal Commission in his favour, and the King's letter to the Assembly. The Assembly appointed a committee to wait upon His Grace, and proceeded forthwith to business.

At the fourth diet the Commissioner appeared in the House, and made a most gracious speech; and the Moderator, at the Assembly's desire, assured him of "the high satisfaction they felt at seeing His Grace in his own place among them." 1776. 1 and 4.

Commissioners sent to London to wait upon His Majesty anent the affairs of the Church. 1690. xviii.

Commissions to Assembly. Commissions to be given in to the clerk the night at least before the first diet of Assembly, or in the intervals between the after diets, and nowise in presence of the Assembly while actually sitting. 1694. iv.; 1698. vi.

All commissions to be transmitted by the parties elected to the agent for the Church as soon as may be after the date of election, and not later than the second Thursday in the month of May in which such Assembly is to meet. Commissions lodged with the agent at any period during the sitting of Assembly, shall be by him submitted to the Assembly on the next day after that on which they have been so lodged. 1859. xii.

Form of commission prescribed, and presbyteries enjoined to keep a uniform method. 1695. viii.; 1698. vi.; 1720. iv.; 1723. vii.; 1724. iv. ix.; 1725. vii.; 1726. viii.

The Assembly, considering the disadvantage of having what belongs to the necessary forms of commissions and attestations lying in separate Acts, did appoint all to be brought together into one act, and instruct the agent for the Church to cause print the same, and transmit copies thereof

Commissions to Assembly—*continued.*

to the several presbyteries, universities, and burghs, ordaining that all such commissions and attestations as are not conceived and executed in the very words of the form prescribed shall be rejected. 1768. iv.; 1783. x.

Enacted that all commissions shall bear that the commissioners have subscribed the Confession of Faith of this Church according to Act xi. 1700; and that no minister or elder be commissioned to be a member of the General Assembly but such as usually reside in or have a relation to the presbytery, burgh, or university they are commissioned from. 1704. vi.; 1722. x.; 1720. iv.

Presbyteries discharged from giving commissions to missionary ministers, or ministers employed by managers of the Royal Bounty. 1753. iv.; 1789. 7; 1732. 3.

Enacted that all commissions, after they are written out and extracted, and before they are put into the hands of the commissioners, shall be first read in presence of the presbytery, and revised by them; and that it be attested by the moderator and clerk of the presbytery that this was done, according to a form of attestation prescribed. 1720. iv.; 1718. ix.; 1768. iv.

Ordained that no commissions from royal burghs to their representatives in the General Assembly shall be sustained but such as shall be consented to and approven, not only by the ministry and kirk-sessions of the burgh, but also by the presbytery of the bounds, and upon which it shall be attested that the persons therein named are elders lawfully ordained, and have signed the Formula, and likewise that they are either residenters in the burgh, or heritors in the burgh or in the bounds of the presbytery in which the burgh lies, or that they have formerly resided and officiated as elders in the said burgh or presbytery. 1718. ix.

Enacted that when a kirk-session or presbytery refuse their concurrence or attestation to a commission by a burgh or university, without assigning the reasons of their refusal, that commission shall be sustained as if duly attested. 1768. iv.; 1741. 3.

Declared that the attestation of any one kirk-session within the electing burgh shall be held as competent, and

Commissions to Assembly—*continued.*

sufficient to all purposes for which sessional attestations are required. 1788. ix.

Enacted that in future all commissions from presbyteries and burghs shall be printed by the printer of the Church, under the superintendence of the clerks of Assembly, agreeably to the authorised forms, and a sufficient number forwarded to all clerks of presbyteries and burghs, from time to time, as occasion may require. 1807. viii.

The procurator, the clerks, and agent appointed a committee to receive and revise all commissions reported by them as defective, to be remitted to a committee of nine appointed by the Assembly. 1850. xiv.; 1859. xii.; 1701. 1 and 3.

Along with every commission in favour of a ruling elder, there shall be transmitted to the agent a certificate that the commissioner is *bona fide* an acting elder. 1839. xii.; 1840, ult.; 1859. xii.

Standing orders in regard to commissions. 1859. xii.

Commissions.—*See* Elections.

A presbytery having refused to attest a commission from a burgh, the Assembly found that the conduct of the presbytery in so doing was unwarranted, and injurious both to the burgh and to their commissioner, sustained the commission, and ordered a copy of their judgment to be recorded in the presbytery book. 1772. 3.

Similar cases. 1772. 4; 1781. 4; 1782. 4; 1783. 4; 1749. 3.

A commission sustained, though not attested by the kirk-session or presbytery of the bounds, in respect their respective attestations were required under form of instrument taken in the hands of a notary-public. 1741. 3.

A commission from the burgh of Selkirk not having been attested by the presbytery, by reason that certain fees demanded by the clerk had not been paid, the Assembly sustained the commission, and ordered a letter to be sent to the presbytery inquiring how any fees came to be demanded for such attestation. 1743. 8.

Referred to the Commission to consider what shall be the effect of informalities in commissions to members of

Commissions to Assembly—*continued.*
Assembly, or the want of certain clauses respecting the qualifications of members. 1754. 9; 1755. 3.

A presbytery having found that, after election, one of the ministers chosen to represent them in the General Assembly had laid himself open to censure, elected another minister in his room. The Assembly, after hearing the charge against the minister first elected, suspended him for three months from the exercise of his ministry; finding him, however, to be the member duly elected, and that it was not competent for the presbytery, at an after meeting, to alter that election; but, in respect of his suspension, the Assembly declared him to be deprived of his privilege as a member. 1758. 6.

A presbytery having refused to admit upon their roll an elder bringing a commission from a kirk-session, but who was, on appeal, found by the Assembly to have been duly elected, the Assembly found that the election of commissioners to the Assembly having taken place when a constituent member of presbytery was excluded from voting in their election, the commission was null and void; and ordered the names of the commissioners to be scored out of the roll. 1766. 4.

Objected to the commission from the Church at Campvere that a minister had been commissioned instead of a ruling elder; the Assembly repelled the objection in the circumstances, and sustained the commission, but "without prejudice to their afterwards considering the general point whether clergymen can be elected as ruling elders, when it is brought regularly before them." 1769. 4.

A commission from a burgh having been presented to a presbytery for attestation at a *pro re nata* meeting, the presbytery refused to attest it. Principal Robertson justified the presbytery on the principle that a presbytery met *pro re nata* could take no other business under consideration but the *res* for which they had been called together. The commission, however, was sustained. 1776. 3.

Objected to a commission that the commissioner was only a *nominal* and *fictitious proprietor;* repelled, and the commission sustained. 1776. 3.

A presbytery having refused to attest a commission from a burgh, on the ground that the commissioner was an

Commissions to Assembly—*continued.*
entire stranger to them, and that they had no evidence of his character and qualifications, the Assembly, after a long discussion, sustained the commission. 1776. 3.

Report of committee appointed to inquire into the method of revising commissions, and amendments on that method adopted. 1781. 8.

A double return of representation from the Presbytery of Perth ; the last sustained, and the first rejected as being neither revised nor attested, and the election of the members therein named having been made by only seven ministers before the ordinary time of the presbytery meeting. 1789. 4.

A similar case. 1736. 3.

A presbytery having discovered that the person first elected to be their representative ruling elder was not an elder, did, at a meeting within forty days of the Assembly, elect another by the form of substitution prescribed by the laws of the Church. The Assembly declared such substitution to be null and void, and rejected the commission. 1789. 5 and 6.

A presbytery having dissolved without fixing a day for their next meeting became defunct ; but certain of the members met and attested the commission from the presbytery and burgh. The Assembly rejected the commission from the presbytery as not duly attested, but sustained the commission from the burgh, and appointed a day for the next meeting of presbytery. 1775. 3 and 4.

A minister laid aside from being a member of Assembly until he should sign the formula prescribed by Act 1711, or produce a voucher of his having formerly subscribed the same. 1732. 3.

Declared competent for an elder to purge the objection that he had not signed the formula by signing it at the bar of the Assembly. 1719. 4 and 7 ; 1788. 3 ; 1796. 3.

A commission having been objected to on the ground that it was dated on the *30th April*, and attested on the 27th of April, evidence was offered at the bar that the former of these dates was a clerical error, and that the election took place on the *30th of March.* The Assembly ordered the original record of presbytery to be produced as evidence, and declared that, in the meanwhile, the commissioners were

Commissions to Assembly—*continued.*

not to be considered members of the Assembly until it should be made to appear from said record that the election was made in proper time. 1791. 3.

It having been objected to a commission that it was made on the 28th of February, being nine days too soon, a member stated that the date was a mistake of the presbytery clerk, and that it was consistent with his knowledge that the election was made not on the 28th of February, but on the 28th of March, and the Presbytery Record having been produced in evidence, the commission was sustained. 1792. 3.

A similar case. 1793. 3; 1797. 3; 1846. 3.

It having been objected that the commissioner was not designed ruling elder, the Assembly, in respect the words "ruling elder" are found in one part of the commission, though omitted in the other, did repel the objection. 1797. 3.

Protestation by the Lord Provost of Edinburgh against admitting a commissioner from the University of Edinburgh without the Town Council's choice. 1719. 1.

A commission was dated the 8th day of April, and the Assembly met on the 18th May. The Assembly rejected the commission, on the ground that forty FREE days did not intervene between the day of election and the meeting of Assembly. 1848. 3.

In a similar case a different decision was given. A commission was dated the 11th of April, and the Assembly met on the 21st May, consequently forty FREE days did not intervene; but the Assembly found that the election took place *on* the fortieth day, if either the day of election or the day of the meeting of Assembly was counted, and sustained the commission. 1846. 3.

See also 1827. 3.

It was objected to a commission that *ten free* days did not intervene between the resolution to elect and the day of election; the resolution to elect having been on the 30th March, and the election on the 9th of April. The revising committee recommended that the commission should be sustained, in respect of the general rule, *that when the last day of a specified term has commenced it is held to have been completed.* The Assembly, however, rejected the commis-

Commissions to Assembly—*continued.*
sion, and found that the ten days must be *ten free days.* 1847. 3.

Similar cases decided differently. 1818. 3; 1832. 3.

A town council resolved to elect a representative elder at a meeting of council to be held on the 4th of April; but finding that that did not allow ten days to intervene between the resolution to elect and the day of election, the meeting was adjourned to the 6th, and a marginal note added to the commission to that effect. The Assembly found that ten days had not intervened, and that the marginal note was an irregularity, and rejected the commission. 1831. 3.

It was objected to a commission that the election took place seventy-one days before the meeting of Assembly, the election being on the 6th of March, and the Assembly meeting on the 16th of May; whereas, in the directions appended to the printed forms of commissions, it is prescribed that "the election must take place not less than forty and not more than seventy days before the meeting of the Assembly." The Assembly repelled the objection and sustained the commission, on the ground that the 6th of March is "within a month preceding the first of the forty days," as prescribed by Act x. 1783. 1833. 3.

Proposal to refer all disputed commissions to a committee of fifteen, whose decision should be final,—after discussion withdrawn. 1834, ult.

Agreed to refer all disputed commissions to a committee of nine; parties being allowed to add one member as nominee for their own particular case, with power of appeal to Assembly. 1836. 1.

All commissions which shall have been transmitted in time to admit of it, shall, before the meeting of Assembly, be submitted by the agent to a committee, consisting of the procurator, the clerks, and the agent, who shall consider the same in so far as relates to their regularity in point of form, and report thereupon to the Assembly. 1840, ult. Standing Orders. 1850. xiv.

Declared to be not competent for a synod to decide as to the validity of a commission to the General Assembly. Burgh of North Berwick, 1835. 3.

Commissions to Assembly—*continued.*

Clerical error in date of commission allowed to be corrected by production of presbytery record, and commission sustained. Presbytery of Stirling, 1834. 5; Presbytery of Selkirk, 1839. 3; Presbytery of Dalkeith, 1846. 3; Presbytery of Dornoch, 1847. 3.

Clerical error in spelling a name not a valid objection to a commission. Presbytery of Aberdeen, 1850. 2.

Nor in quoting an act. Burgh of Dundee, 1821. 3.

In counting the forty days required by Act x. Ass. 1783 to intervene between the day of election and the day of the meeting of Assembly, the Assembly found that it is not necessary they should be *free* days; either the day of election or the day of meeting may be counted. Burgh of Queensferry, 1827. 3; Burgh of Lauder, 1846. 3.

A contrary decision given, and forty *free days* held necessary. Burgh of Inverness, 1848. 3; Burgh of New Galloway, 1848. 3.

The non-election of an elder held not to invalidate the commission of the ministers. Church in India, 1847. 3.

The want of attestation by the presbytery allowed to be remedied by the production of the presbytery record, showing that the presbytery had ordered the commission to be attested. Presbytery of Ellon, 1848. 3; Presbytery of Islay and Jura, 1848. 3.

In case of an after-election, found necessary that the minute of the original election be produced. Burgh of Lochmaben, 1809. 6.

A day having been fixed for the election of an elder within ten days from the resolution to elect, the Assembly found it to be incompetent for the town council to remedy the irregularity by adjourning the election. Burgh of Perth, 1831. 3.

Declared to be not necessary that a commission should be written on stamped paper. Presbytery of Glasgow, 1806. 3.

The commission of an elder objected to on the ground that he was not resident in, and had no connection with, the presbytery. Objection overruled and commission sustained. Presbytery of Perth, 1835. 4.

Commissions to Assembly—*continued.*

A presbytery having rejected the commission of representative elders from kirk-sessions because the commissions did not in the preamble contain the names of the members, nor in the conclusion the name of the moderator; and further, that there was no evidence that the said elders had signed the Confession of Faith, or taken the oath of allegiance; the Commission found the conduct of the presbytery in rejecting the commission on these grounds highly improper and unjustifiable, and appointed this judgment to be recorded in the book of the presbytery. Presbytery of North Isles, Com., June 2, 1842.

A kirk-session having refused to grant a certificate of *bona fide* eldership to an elder who had been elected a commissioner to the General Assembly, on the ground that he had for several years ceased to attend public worship in his parish church, but attended the church of a neighbouring parish; the presbytery overruled the judgment of the kirk-session, and in place of the *bona fide* certificate, appended to the commission a brief statement of the circumstances of the case. The case came before the Assembly by dissent and complaint, when the following motion was carried by a majority of 72 to 49: "That the General Assembly sustain the dissent and complaint, reverse the sentence of the presbytery as irregular and incompetent, so far as it overrules the judgment of the kirk-session refusing the elder a certificate as a *bona fide* acting elder—that judgment not having been brought regularly before them: Find that the brief statement of circumstances referred to in that sentence of the presbytery cannot be received as a substitute for the *bona fide* certificate, and that the elder cannot *hoc statu* be entered in the roll of the Assembly. Presbytery of Auchterarder, 1854. 3.

The Assembly refused to discuss the validity of a commission which had passed the committee on disputed commissions after the report of the committee had been sustained, and the commissioner had taken his seat. Presbytery of Garioch, 1838. 3.

Found that, in order to render the resignation of the elder first elected valid, and to warrant the presbytery to elect a substitute at an after-election, the resignation must be

Commissions to Assembly—*continued.*
made either by a letter from the person resigning, or by him appearing personally to declare his resignation, or by some person having specific authority from him to tender his resignation, which must be entered on the record. Presbytery of Garioch, 1834. 3.

A kirk-session and presbytery having refused to attest a commission on the ground that there was no evidence that the commissioner was an heritor in the burgh; the Assembly found him duly qualified as an heritor, and no other objection having been stated to his commission, they held that there was no need of further attestation. Burgh of Linlithgow, 1834. 3.

A minister, after the date of his commission, and before the meeting of Assembly, resigned his charge. The Assembly rejected his commission on the ground that his connection with the constituency had been dissolved. Church in India, 1834. 3.

Commissions, Forms of. An alteration in the printed forms of commissions sanctioned, and the clerks of Assembly enjoined to see that the alteration proposed be made and transmitted to presbyteries and burghs. 1808, ult.; 1827, ult.

Universities allowed to print commissions for themselves, agreeably to the prescribed form, at their own expense. 1814. 9.

Committee appointed to consider and report on what improvements may be made on the form of commissions, and the mode of transmitting and disposing of the same. 1840, ult.

Committee appointed to consider what steps may be necessary for securing greater regularity in the observance of the rules of the Church in regard to commissions to representatives to General Assembly. 1846. 3.

Committee appointed to consider and report on the right of universities to send commissioners to the General Assembly. 1846. 13.

Committee appointed to draw up a scheme of representation and form of commission for the Presbyterian Churches in India. 1818, ult.

Declared that, alongst with every commission in favour of

Commissions, Forms of—*continued.*

a ruling elder as commissioner to the General Assembly, there be produced a certificate by the kirk-session of which he is a member, that the commissioner is *bona fide* an acting elder of their congregation, otherwise the commission shall be rejected. 1836. 7, and ult.

The foregoing regulation to apply to retired ministers, not being professors of theology, in the same way as to other ruling elders. Burgh of Inverury, 1840. 3.

A form of certificate of *bona fide* eldership sanctioned by the Assembly. 1840, ult.

Enacted and declared that no certificate shall be hereafter sustained unless exactly agreeing with the form aforesaid. 1841, ult., and Act xi.

In the following among other instances, elders were not allowed to take their seats until they produced certificates of *bona fide* eldership. Presbytery of Aberdeen, &c., 1846. 3; Presbytery of Edinburgh, &c., 1847. 3; Presbytery of Perth, &c., 1849. 2.

Commissions rejected because an extract from the kirk-session record had been sent up instead of a certificate in the form prescribed. Presbytery of Peebles, &c., 1847. 3; Presbytery of Greenock, 1846. 3, &c.

Necessary that certificate be signed both by moderator and clerk. Presbytery of Haddington, 1846. 3; Burgh of Cullen, 1846. 3; Presbytery of Dunbar, 1847. 3; Burghs of Lauder, Peebles, &c., 1847. 3.

It was objected to a certificate that the words "*bona fide*" were omitted therein, the elder being certified merely as an acting elder. Objection overruled and commission sustained. Presbytery of Dornoch, 1847. 3.

Commissions rejected on account of irregularities in regard to the **date** of election. 1771. 3; 1775. 3; 1777. 3; 1784. 3; 1785. 3; 1786. 3; 1787. 3, 5; 1789. 5; 1789. 7; 1790. 3; 1794. 4.

Because the election was made *earlier* than the time prescribed by Act iv. Assembly 1768, and Act x. Assembly 1783—viz., "at least forty days before the meeting of Assembly, and within a month preceding the first of the said forty days." 1807. 3; 1810. 3; 1818. 3; 1818. 5; 1825. 3.

Commissions rejected—*continued.*

Because the election was made *later* than the time prescribed by Acts of Assembly. 1810. 3; 1811. 3; 1812. 4; 1814. 3; 1816. 3; 1818. 3; 1819. 3; 1826. 3; 1832. 4; 1839. 2; 1848. 3; 1850. 2.

Because ten free days did not intervene between the resolution to elect and the day of election, as prescribed by Act iv. Assembly 1768, and Act x. Assembly 1783, viz.: —1775. 3; 1777. 3; 1784. 3; 1785. 3; 1786. 3; 1791. 3; 1795. 3; 1797. 3; 1798. 3; 1802. 3; 1803. 3; 1804. 4; 1805. 3; 1808. 3; 1810. 3; 1811. 3; 1812. 3; 1814. 3; 1815. 3; 1817. 3; 1818. 3; 1820. 3; 1821. 3; 1825. 3; 1833. 3; 1847. 3; 1831. 3.

Because the election was not made between the hours of one and eight o'clock P.M., as prescribed by Act iv. Assembly 1768. 1787. 3; 1813. 3; 1819. 3; 1822. 3; 1827. 3.

Commissions rejected because not **attested.** 1788. 3; 1789. 7: 1807. 3; 1812. 3; 1817. 3; 1831. 3; 1834. 3; 1840. 3; 1850. 2.

Commissions rejected because of informalities or omissions in the **attestation.**

Because the kirk-session was not designed before which the commission was laid for attestation. 1784. 3.

Because the presbytery by which the commission was attested, was not specified. 1785. 3.

Because it was not certified that the elder resided or officiated in the burgh granting the commission, nor any of the alternatives stated which the Acts of Assembly prescribe. 1785. 3.

Because after the words "attested by," the following were added, "in terms of the evidence laid before us." 1786. 3.

Because of the omission of the words "conform to the directions of the Act ix. Assembly 1718, Act iv. Assembly 1720, and Act iv. Assembly 1724." 1801. 3.

Because of the omission of the place of the presbytery's meeting and the date of the attestation. 1808. 3.

Because the attestation wanted the qualification of the elder elected. 1808. 3.

Because the attestation was without date. 1811. 5.

Because the attestation was dated at a place not within

Commissions rejected—*continued.*
the bounds of the presbytery, at a time when the synod was not sitting. 1811. 5.

Because the attestation was by a kirk-session not within the burgh. 1806. 3.

Because the elder was not designed in the attestation. 1801. 3.

Commissions rejected for various Omissions and Informalities. Because of the omission of the words "and appoint." 1784. 3.

Because the minute of election was extracted by a person who did not add the word "clerk" to his name. 1784. 3; 1786. 3; 1794. 3; 1797. 3.

Because it is not agreeable to the Acts of Assembly and the practice of the Church that burghs should send ministers to represent them in the General Assembly. 1732. 3.

Because of the omission of the words "in order to elect their representatives to the ensuing Assembly." 1789. 6.

Because the person elected as elder was a missionary on the Royal Bounty, and designated minister of the gospel. 1789. 7.

Because the commission was not subscribed by any person whatever. 1789. 7.

Because the commissioner from a burgh had not been elected by a legal majority of the town council, and because his commission had neither been attested nor refused to be attested. 1789. 7.

Because the elder elected to represent a burgh had none of the qualifications required by law to entitle him to represent said burgh. 1784. 3; 1789. 7.

Because in an after-election the substitution was defective, being totally different from the prescribed form. 1793. 3.

Because of the omission of the name of the burgh after the words "town council of." 1786. 3.

Because of the omission of the word "eight." 1787. 3.

The following objections were held to be valid:—

That the words "according to the Word of God, the Confession of Faith, and agreeably to the constitution of this Church," were omitted. 1769. 3; 1791. 3; 1802. 3.

That the surname of the person elected was omitted. Burgh of Kintore. 1808. 3.

Commissions rejected, &c.—*continued.*

That the commissioner had ceased to be a minister of the Chŭrch in India. Church in India. 1834. 3.

That in an appeal from the presbytery refusing to attest commission, the reasons of appeal were not lodged in due time. Presbytery of Fordyce, 1834. 5 ; Presbytery of Skye, 1834. 5.

That a *quorum* of town-council not present at election. Burgh of Dunfermline. 1835. 3.

That there was an informality in the resolution to elect. Burgh of Haddington. 1837. 3.

That a *quorum* of senatus (or thirteen members) not present at election. University of Glasgow. 1840. 4.

That the commissioners had been suspended by the Commission of General Assembly. Presbytery of Strathbogie. 1841. 1.

That the commissioners had been deposed. Presbytery of Strathbogie. 1842. 1.

That the election took place on the tenth day after the resolution to elect, ten *free* days not intervening. Burgh of Dumfries. 1847. 3.

That forty *free* days did not intervene between the election and the meeting of Assembly. Burgh of Inverness, 1848. 3 ; Burgh of New Galloway, 1848. 3.

That the commission was not extracted by the clerk. Presbytery of Kirkcudbright. 1807. 3.

That there had been no previous resolution to elect minuted. Burgh of Perth. 1810. 3.

That the presbytery had returned more commissioners than it was entitled to do. Presbytery of Dunkeld. 1816. 3.

That the presbytery had made a double return at an irregular meeting. Presbytery of Zetland. 1817. 6.

That there was an erasure in the date of election. Presbytery of Turriff. 1821. 3 ; Presbytery of Dornoch. 1847. 3.

That the commission was not subscribed. Presbytery of Caithness. 1824. 4.

That the commissioner returned as representative ruling elder was an ordained minister of the Scottish National Chapel, London, and in the stated and regular exercise of his ministerial office. Burgh of Annan. 1829. 3.

That the election took place after the meeting of Assembly. Burgh of Dornoch. 1832. 4.

Commissions rejected, &c.—*continued.*

That the managers of a burgh had failed to produce the deed investing them with the powers assumed in the commission. Burgh of Kilrenny. 1833. 3 and 4.

After Elections.

The following objections were held valid, and the name of the substitute expunged :—

That the date of the after-election was subsequent to the date of attestation, and that the substitution was not attested. Presbytery of Abertarff, 1811. 3; Presbytery of Elgin, 1811. 3; Presbytery of Skye, 1822. 3; Presbytery of Chirnside, 1824. 4; Presbytery of Kirkcaldy, 1834. 3; Presbytery of Wigtown, 1835. 3; Presbytery of Cairston, 1839. 2.

That there was no evidence of the resignation of the representative in whose room the substitute was elected. Presbytery of Ellon. 1818. 3.

That the substitute was not described as minister of any parish. Presbytery of Strathbogie. 1827. 3.

That the original commission had been already sustained by the Assembly. 1836. 6.

Commissions disputed, but sustained. The following objections repelled, and the commissions objected to sustained :—

That the election did not take place within the time prescribed by the law of the Church—viz., "At least forty days before the meeting of Assembly, and within a month preceding the first of the said forty days." 1743. 7; 1750. 3; 1751. 3; 1753. 3; 1754. 3; 1791. 3.

The commission wanted the words "extracted by," and the subscription of the clerk. 1769. 3.

That the attestation had the word *minister* in place of *moderator* after the name of the attestor. 1786. 4.

A contrary decision given. 1793. 3.

That the date of the resolution to elect is not sufficiently explicit. 1789. 6 and 7.

That the word "*of*" is substituted for "*at*" in the designation of the ministers. 1789. 6.

That the elder is differently named in the commission and the attestation. 1789. 6.

Commissions disputed, but sustained—*continued.*

That the date of the attestation is in a different hand and ink from the body of it. 1789. 6.

That after Charles Hope, Esq., advocate, the words "*ruling elder*" are wanting. 1789. 6.

That the elder returned for a burgh wanted the necessary qualification, being only "a nominal and fictitious proprietor." 1776. 3.

The presbytery refused to attest a commission from a burgh, on the ground that the elder was an entire stranger to them, and that they had no evidence of his moral character, or of his being otherwise qualified to represent that burgh. 1776. 3.

That the minister chosen at an after-election is attested in the form prescribed for an elder, as well as in that prescribed for a minister. 1786. 3.

That the words "attested by" are awanting in the attestation by the kirk-session. 1786. 3.

That the commission has the words "between one and two o'clock," instead of "between one and eight o'clock." 1786. 3.

That the commission was blank as to the day of the sitting of the Assembly. 1786. 3.

That the resolution to elect was on the 29th of March, and the day of election on the 8th of April. 1788. 3.

That the extract minute of election is not subscribed. The commission was sustained on the ground that, though the commission was not signed, the attestation was both by moderator and clerk. 1795. 3.

That the attestation of the presbytery, though written on two pages, was not signed on the first page. 1789. 6 ; 1789. 7.

That commission contained a clerical error and misnomer. 1789. 7.

That the word "elder" on the margin in a different hand, and seemingly put in *ex post facto*, was not subscribed. 1789. 7.

That the resignation of the elder in whose room another had been substituted was informal. 1789. 7.

That the designation of the ruling elder is not sufficiently explicit. 1789. 7.

That in the case of an after-election the person originally elected was not attested either by the kirk-session or presbytery. 1789. 7.

Commissions disputed, but sustained—*continued.*

That "John Millar, Esq., advocate," should have been "John Millar, Esq., junior, advocate." 1789. 7.

That the commissioner was a minor, on the ground that the Assembly had no evidence in support of the objection. 1769. 4.

That the commissioner was a preacher. 1769. 4.

That the commissioner was no longer a constituent member of the presbytery from whom he had received his commission, having been translated to a parish within the bounds of another presbytery. 1769. 4.

The following objections were overruled, and the commissions sustained :—

Objections relative to "Time" of Election.

That the election took place on the 3d of April, and the resolution to elect on the 24th of March, leaving only nine *free* days. Burgh of Annan, 1818. 3, and burgh of Linlithgow, 1832. 3.

Note.—A contrary decision was given by Assembly 1847, when it was objected to the commission from the burgh of Dumfries, that the resolution to elect was on the 30th of March, and the election on the 9th of April. "The General Assembly, in respect there were *not ten free days* between the resolution to elect and the day of election, rejected the commission." 1847. 3.

That the election took place on the fortieth day before the meeting of Assembly, the election being on the 7th of April, and the Assembly meeting on the 17th of May. Burgh of Queensferry, 1827. 3; burgh of Lauder, 1846. 3.

Note.—A similar objection was sustained by Assembly 1848, and two commissions rejected because "forty *free* days did not intervene." Burgh of Inverness and burgh of New Galloway. 1848. 3.

That the election took place seventy-one days before the meeting of Assembly, the election being on the 6th of March and the Assembly meeting on the 16th May, where, as in the directions appended to the printed forms of commissions, it is stated that "the election must take place not less than forty

Commissions disputed, but sustained—*continued.*

days, and not more than seventy days, before the meeting of Assembly." The Assembly repelled the objection, and sustained the commission, on the ground that the 6th of March is within a month preceding the first of the forty days before the meeting of Assembly, as required by the Act of Assembly 1783. University of Edinburgh. 1833. 3.

That the day of the meeting of Assembly was left blank. Commission sustained on the ground that "the month of May next" was mentioned. City of Aberdeen, 1846. 3; burgh of Forfar, 1846. 3.

That there was an omission of the year in which presbytery entered on their minutes the resolution to elect. Commission sustained on the ground that the omission was substantially supplied by the narrative. Presbytery of Deer, 1849. 2; Presbytery of Chirnside, 1849. 2; Presbytery of Linlithgow, 1849. 2; Presbytery of Kelso, 1849. 2; Presbytery of Dunbar, 1849. 2; Presbytery of Greenock, 1849. 2.

That there was a mistake as to the day of the meeting of Assembly. Commission sustained on the ground it was stated alternatively, "or when and where it shall happen to sit." Presbyteries of Lochcarron and Nairn, 1849. 2; University of St Andrews, 1849. 2.

That the election took place within forty days of the Assembly. Commission sustained because "the burgh lies in the Northern Isles." Burgh of Kirkwall. 1811. 3.

That the election was stated to have been on the last Tuesday of "April," instead of "March." The Assembly allowed the presbytery record to be produced to show that it was a mere clerical error, and sustained the commission. Presbytery of Stirling. 1834. 5.

Informalities in Attestation.

That in the commission the elder is designed as "an heritor in the said burgh;" but in the attestation as "an heritor" simply. Burgh of Whithorn. 1825. 3.

That the commission was not attested, because the elder elected had not produced a certificate of character to the presbytery. The Assembly found that, though the elder had been attested in a former year, the presbytery were entitled

Commissions disputed, but sustained—*continued.*
to a renewed certificate ; but in respect that this demand was not usually made, they sustained the commission. Burgh of Culross. 1826. 3.

That the attestation wants the words "Act 4, Ass. 1720." Burgh of Wigtown. 1801. 3.

That the words "according to the Acts of Assembly" are omitted. Burgh of Stranraer. 1804. 4.

That the words "Assembly 1820" were inserted, instead of "Assembly 1720." Burgh of Dundee. 1821. 3.

That the attestation did not expressly bear that the commissioner was an heritor. Burgh of Dornoch. 1827. 3.

That the commission was not attested by kirk-session or presbytery. The Assembly found their reason for refusal irrelevant and inconclusive, and sustained the commission. Burgh of Irvine, 1827. 3 ; 1840. 4.

That the words "in the said burgh" are omitted. Burgh of Forfar. 1827. 3.

Informalities in Commission.

The following objections were overruled :—

That the words "enjoined by the 10th Act of Assembly 1711" are omitted. Presbytery of North Isles. 1802. 3.

That the words "the 10th Act of" are omitted. Presbytery of Tongue. 1804. 4.

That the commission was not written on stamped paper. Presbytery of Glasgow. 1806. 3.

That in a case of after-election the minute of former election was not produced. Former minute called for and produced, and commission sustained. Burgh of Lochmaben. 1809. 3 and 6.

That the elder was designed as "an heritor" simply, and not as an heritor within the burgh or presbytery. Burgh of Forfar. 1814. 3.

A similar objection. Burgh of Kirkwall. 1814. 3.

A similar objection. Presbytery of Lanark. 1830. 3.

That in a case of after-election within forty days of the Assembly, the elders first elected were not attested as duly qualified. Commission of substitutes sustained, on the ground that they were duly attested, and "such commissions had been sustained on various occasions." City of Aberdeen, 1846. 3 ;

Commissions disputed, but sustained—*continued.*

Burgh of Anstruther, Easter, 1846. 3; Burgh of Dornoch, 1816. 3; Burgh of Lauder, 1830. 3.

That the commission was irregular. Commission sustained because of difficulties connected with the judgment of Assembly 1814, empowering the Church in India to send representatives. Church in India, 1821. 5; 1818. 3.

That the person elected representative ruling elder is not designed as such. Presbytery of Abertarff. 1823. 3.

That the elder was not qualified as an heritor within the burgh. Proof allowed, and commission sustained. Presbytery of Linlithgow. 1834. 3.

That the fees of the presbytery clerk had not been paid. Burgh of New Galloway. 1825. 3.

That it is contrary to the principles and practice of the Church of Scotland to elect an assistant and successor a commissioner to the General Assembly in the presence of his constituent, the name of the constituent being entered on the sederunt where the election took place. Presbytery of Dumfries. 1833. 4.

That the elder did not reside within the bounds, and had no relation to the presbytery. Presbytery of Perth. 1835. 4.

That there was no evidence the elder maintained family worship daily. Burgh of North Berwick. 1835. 3.

That the resolution to elect was not entered in the jottings on the day when said resolution was come to. Commission sustained because it was duly entered in the extended minute, which was read and approved at subsequent meeting. Presbytery of Biggar. 1839. 3.

That a retired minister was returned as "a teaching elder." Commission sustained on the ground that that was the first year of the operation of the new Act requiring a certificate of *bonâ fide* eldership; but the Assembly resolved that in future retired ministers, not being professors of theology, should be subject to the same regulations as other ruling elders. Burgh of Inverury. 1840. 3.

That the commissioner was designed as "an officiating elder in the presbytery," and that this designation did not fulfil the requirements of the Act. It having been explained

Commissions disputed, but sustained—*continued.*
that the commissioner was an elder within the royalty, the commission was sustained. City of Glasgow. 1846. 3.

That the place and date of election were written upon *erasures.* The Assembly allowed proof that the date as altered was the true date, and sustained the commission. Presbytery of Dornoch. 1847. 3.

That the after-election was written on a separate commission from that containing the original election. Presbytery of Abertarff, 1847. 3; Presbytery of Uist, 1847. 3.

That the words "*bonâ fide*" were awanting in certificate, and the commissioner designed simply "an acting elder." Presbytery of Dornoch. 1847. 3.

That the commission was signed by elder as session-clerk. Commission sustained, "because this had frequently happened without objection." Burgh of Ayr. 1849. 2.

That the name of the presbytery was not in the commission. Commission sustained, because the name was in the attestation. Presbytery of Mull. 1850. 2.

That the elder's name was differently spelled in the commission and the certificate. Presbytery of Aberdeen. 1850. 2.

That the election was by a minority of the town-council, the majority refusing to elect. Burgh of Dunbar. 1850. 2.

Commissioners not certified to have signed the formula called upon to do so at the bar of the Assembly before their commissions were sustained, in terms of Act iv. Assembly 1720. Burgh of Culross, 1801. 3; Presbytery of North Isles, 1802. 3; Presbytery of Dundee, 1808. 3; Presbytery of Cupar, 1809. 3; Presbytery of Cupar, 1830. 3; Church in India, 1833. 3; Presbytery of Perth, 1833. 3.

Commissions to Presbyteries. Committee appointed to prepare a form of commission for elders to presbyteries and synods as representatives of kirk-sessions. 1834. 9.

Committee appointed for nominating ministers to preach before His Grace the Lord High Commissioner, and for supplying the pulpits of the ministers of Edinburgh and the West Church, who are members of Assembly. 1695. 6.

——— Act and certification against ministers who attend not committees. 1695. 6.

——— See ASSEMBLY and ROYAL BOUNTY.

Commonty. Aid granted from the funds of the Church to enable a minister to defend his rights to a common, and prevent the shutting up of public roads. 1810. 9.

Communicants. Concerning the admitting of persons to the Lord's table, enacted that greater uniformity be kept in this Kirk in the practice and observation of the Directory of Public Worship, and of Act Feb. 7, 1645, § 12. 1727. viii.

Communion. Strangers educated in other Protestant Churches to be received into communion, and admitted to Church privileges, if free from scandal. 1711. xiii.

Communion, Ministerial. Enacted that no minister shall hold ministerial communion with, or admit into his pulpit, any person not duly qualified to receive a presentation. 1799. v.

——— The Act v. 1799, rescinded. 1842. ix.

——— The Rescissory Act, ix. 1842, rescinded, and a committee appointed to take the whole subject into consideration. 1843. xv.

——— Overture and interim Act anent ministerial communion, enacting that the admission of ministers of other communions to the pulpits of the Establishment should not be left to the discretion of individual ministers, but that in every case permission be asked and received from the presbytery of the bounds or a standing committee of their number. 1844. vi.; 1845. xvi.

——— Declared that there was no ground or occasion for introducing any change into the law and practice of the Church in regard to ministerial communion, and the committee discharged. 1847. 11.

——— A committee appointed to consider and report whether any Act can be passed in consistency with the laws and practice of this Church, whereby the Church of Scotland may hold ministerial communion with other evangelical churches, and under what provisions the same may be safely guarded. 1860. 8.

Complaint. A complaint having been taken direct to the General Assembly, and not to an intervening meeting of synod, the Assembly dismissed the same as incompetent. 1807. 4.

——— A complaint by the minority of an inferior court brings all the parties and the whole case before the court of review, who may dispose of the sentence complained of, in the same manner as if it had been brought before them by an appeal. 1815. 5; 1817. 7.

Complaint. A complaint sists procedure in the court which pronounced the judgment complained of. In one case, where a presbytery proceeded to the ordination of a minister in the face of a dissent and complaint, the Assembly, "under all the circumstances of the case," overlooked the irregularity, and approved of the proceedings of the presbytery. 1828. 7.

——— Complaint dismissed as fallen from, in respect a full extract of the record and of the preliminary papers was not produced in court nor printed, in terms of the standing orders. Com., June 4, 1835.

——— Complaint dismissed because the complainer had not produced a certified copy of his reasons of complaint. Com., June 1, 1841.

Confession of Faith. Enacted that all probationers, entrants into the ministry, and all ministers and elders received into the communion of the Church, shall be obliged to subscribe their approbation of the Confession of Faith, approven by former General Assemblies of this Church, and ratified by Parliament. 1690. vii.; 1700. xi.

——— Enacted that such of the late conforming ministers as have qualified themselves according to law may be received into ministerial communion upon their subscribing the Confession of Faith according to a prescribed formula. 1694. xi.

——— All ministers and members of the Church discharged and prohibited from speaking, writing, printing, teaching, or preaching, any doctrine or tenet contrary to or inconsistent with the Confession of Faith. Gainsayers to be censured according to their demerit. 1696. xxi.

——— A new impression of the Confession of Faith ordered, in folio, for receiving the subscriptions of ministers, probationers, and schoolmasters. 1699. xiii.

——— The Synod of Argyle recommended to translate the Confession of Faith, &c. into the Irish language. 1699. xvi.; 1708, ult.; 1713. 8.

——— All schoolmasters, chaplains, governors, and pedagogues, required to sign the Confession of Faith. 1700. x.

——— Ordained that all commissions to ministers and ruling elders to subsequent Assemblies shall bear that they have subscribed the Confession of Faith of this Church according to Act xi. Ass. 1700. 1704. vi.; 1720. iv.; 1768. iv.

Confession of Faith. Found that the conduct of a presbytery was unjustifiable, and deserving the censure of the Assembly, in proceeding to settle a minister without requiring him to sign the Confession of Faith and Formula. 1790. 5.

Consanguinity. A reference relative to proclamation of banns between two parties supposed to be within the prohibited degrees of consanguinity referred to a committee. 1822. 5 and 7.

Conspiracy. An address to the King on occasion of the happy discovery of a horrid conspiracy. 1723. iv.

Consistorial Court. The procurator instructed to resist all attempts on the part of the consistorial court to interfere with the regular exercise of discipline by the judicatories of the Church. 1809. 8.

Contempt. Act and sentence concerning Mr Ebenezer Erskine, and some other ministers adhering to his protest, for their contempt of the authority of the General Assembly. 1733. vii.

Contribution. Act anent schools in every parish, and a general contribution ordered for that purpose. 1707. v.

Contumacy. Presbyteries to send in to the General Assembly the names of scandalous persons contumacious to discipline, with a full extract of the process, that they may be dealt with as the Assembly shall see cause. 1700. xv.

Corn-Laws. A committee appointed to watch over any proposed alterations in the corn-laws, and to petition Parliament, in name of the Church, against such alterations if they see cause. 1825, ult.

Corresponding Members. Declared incompetent and unconstitutional for a synod to appoint corresponding members to act with any presbytery within their bounds. 1812. 7.

——— Declared to be inconsistent with the order of this Church to send an elder as corresponding member to the synod within the bounds of which he exercises the office of the eldership, inasmuch as he is already represented in that synod, while the synod by which he is commissioned has no jurisdiction over him. 1836. 10.

Court of Session. Claim, declaration, and protest anent the encroachments of the Court of Session. 1842. xix.

D

Defamation. A process against a preacher for defamation. 1726. 3.

Delay. A presbytery found highly censurable for undue delay in the prosecution of a case, and ordered to proceed therein without further loss of time. 1849. 11; 1787. 4.

Delinquents. Committee appointed to draw up an overture anent delinquents where they should make satisfaction. 1771. 4.

——— An overture anent trying delinquents who are ministers, considered and dismissed. 1786. 6.

Demission. A letter from a minister given in to the Assembly, and accepted of as his demission of his ministerial charge, and ordered to be recorded in the book of the presbytery of the bounds. 1755, ult.; 1766. 7.

——— Mr Thomas Boston having demitted his charge, declared no longer a minister of this Church. 1758. iv.

——— Deed of Demission and Act of Separation given in by certain ministers and elders who withdrew from the Assembly on the 18th May 1843, and formed themselves into the Free Church, with the deliverance of the Assembly thereon. 1843. xi.

——— A minister having demitted his charge, the presbytery accepted his demission, although considering the reasons thereof to be insufficient, declared the parish vacant, and intimated the vacancy to the patron, who thereupon issued a presentation; and the presbytery took the necessary steps for the settlement of the presentee without challenge up to the day of admission, when the old minister appeared, withdrew his resignation, and protested against the presbytery proceeding with the settlement of the presentee. The Assembly, on appeal, found that the presbytery had acted irregularly and precipitately in accepting the demission of the minister before they had taken means to ascertain the state of his mind, and before they had called the people to appear for their interest. The Assembly, therefore, set aside the whole proceedings of the presbytery in the matter, declared him still minister of the parish, and instructed the presbytery to do what in them lay to contribute to his comfort and his usefulness. Presbytery of Dornoch, Ass. 1820. 5.

——— *See* Ass. 1856, ult., and 1858. 3.

Deposition. Dr George Garden deposed for being tainted with the dangerous and blasphemous opinions of M. Antonia Bourignion. 1701. xi.

——— Mr John Hepburn deposed for following divisive courses. 1705. vii.

——— Enacted that, before a deposed minister can be restored to the exercise of the ministry, the wound the scandal gave must be worn out and healed by an exemplary humble walk and edifying conversation. 1707. xi., chap. vii. 13.

——— Declared to be almost impossible that a deposed minister can ever again be useful in the same parish. 1707. xi., chap. vii. 14.

——— Sentence of deposition to be intimated in the congregation of the deposed minister. (*ib.*)

——— Synods and presbyteries enjoined to send accounts of all ministers who are or shall be deposed or suspended, and probationers who are or shall be silenced by them, to the clerk of Assembly, to be by him laid before the House. 1709. xv.

——— Sentence of deposition pronounced against Mr Thomas Elder by Ass. 1711 taken off, and he reponed to the exercise of the office of the holy ministry. 1715. 9.

——— Enacted that deposed ministers who continue to exercise the ministry shall be prosecuted as intruders. 1716. 10.

——— A minister deposed for his compliance in the rebellion of 1715. 1716, ult.

——— A minister having been deposed, appealed to the Assembly, and died. The Assembly referred to the Commission to judge how far the appeal subsisted, notwithstanding his death, and empowered them to determine in the cause itself, if they found that the appeal did subsist. 1730. 15.

——— Referred to the Commission to hear what a deposed minister had to say for his being admitted to sealing ordinances. 1730. 15.

——— Sentence of deposition pronounced against Mr John Glass removed, and he restored to the character of a minister of the gospel of Christ. 1739, ult.; *see also* 1813, ult.

——— Mr Ebenezer Erskine, and seven other seceding ministers, deposed. 1740. iv.

——— Mr Thomas Gillespie, minister at Carnock, deposed. 1752. iv.

Deposition. An overture anent varying the form of the sentence of deposition, in cases where the judicatories shall find reason to dismiss any of their members from the ministry of this Church in questions relating to her national establishment, dropped. 1754. 8.

——— Mr Thomas Boston having demitted his charge, declared no longer a minister of this Church. 1758. 4.

——— Sentence of deposition pronounced in 1740 against Mr Thomas Nairn, one of the seceding ministers, taken off, and he reponed to the office of the holy ministry. 1758, ult.

——— In a case of deposition, the sentence was declared to take effect from the day on which the judgment of the presbytery was affirmed by the Assembly. 1763. 7.

——— Found and declared that a sentence of deposition from the ministry includes also deposition from the office of elder, and that the person deposed is incapable of sitting as a member of Assembly, or of any other judicatory of the Church. 1770. 3.

——— Sentence of deposition removed, the minister restored to his charge, and admonished to be more circumspect in his conversation in time coming. 1722. 4.

——— Proceeding of the Commission disapproved in reponing a minister to his charge against a sentence of deposition. 1723. 7.

——— The Commission authorised to take off the sentence of deposition pronounced against a minister, and to repone him to his ministry if they shall see cause. 1723. 11.

——— Found that a presbytery acted irregularly and improperly in suspending and threatening to depose a minister who had not been summoned before them, and against whom no regular process had been instituted. 1826. 4.

——— It was unanimously agreed that, for the purpose of guarding against the risk of attempts being made to admit any of the ministers deposed by this or by the last General Assembly, either to permanent charges or to occasional ministrations in other parts of the world, notices of the sentences passed against them shall be sent as extensively as possible to synods and presbyteries, and congregations in communion with this Church beyond the bounds of Scotland, and particularly in the colonies, and that such notices shall contain a distinct account both of the presbytery from which they had severally received their licences, and of the stations which they had occupied before they forfeited the character of ministers of the gospel. 1851. 14.

Deputation. A deputation appointed to visit the churches in British America in connection with the Church of Scotland, consisting of Dr Simpson, Dr John M'Leod, and Mr Norman M'Leod, gave in their report. 1846. 11.

——— A second deputation, consisting of Messrs Fowler, Stevenson, and M'Intosh, gave in their report. 1848. 8.

——— Deputation appointed to visit the several parishes in the Presbyteries of Lewis, Uist, and Skye, with full power to call for the production of the records of presbyteries and sessions. Com., August 13, 1835; Report of Deputation, 1836, ult.; another deputation appointed, 1838, ult.

Destitution. Collection appointed in all the churches, in compliance with a letter from her Majesty recommending the poor and destitute to the pastoral care of the Church. 1842. 3.

——— A resolution expressive of deep sympathy with the working-classes and the poor generally, arising from the existing destitution, and a recommendation to presbyteries to use every effort for alleviating that distress. Com., Nov. 17, 1842.

Devotion. On a memorial from two of the chaplains of the Church of Scotland in India, expressing their desire to be furnished with such forms of devotion as might, with great advantage and edification, be used by many, and particularly by those who, in the course of Providence, are placed in situations in which they cannot have access to the public worship of God, the Assembly remitted the consideration of this memorial to a committee—Dr Robertson, convener. 1850. 15.

——— Dr Crawford, Convener of the Committee on Aids to Devotion, laid on the table a collection of forms of worship for the use of soldiers, sailors, colonists, sojourners in India and in foreign countries, and other parties who are destitute of a settled minister. 1858. 12.

——— Dr Crawford laid on the table a few copies of the 'Prayers for Social and Family Worship,' which the General

Assembly of last year allowed the Committee to publish if they should see cause. 1859. 13.

Devotion. The General Assembly rejoiced to learn that some progress had been made in the distribution of copies of Aids to Devotion among soldiers, and also of Bibles with psalms among sailors; and earnestly hoped that the Committee would ere long be able to succeed in providing a larger supply of Bibles among sailors, and copies of Aids to Devotion among Presbyterian soldiers and sailors. 1862. 5.

Dictionary. The design of Mr David M'Colm, minister at Duddingston, of printing an English and Irish dictionary, as tending to promote learning, remitted to the Committee for the Reformation of the Highlands and Islands. 1737. 8.

Digest. Committee appointed to consider anent the preparing a digest of the laws and decisions as to the jurisdiction and administrative powers of kirk-sessions in cases of pauperism. 1826. 5.

Directory. The due observance of the Directory for the Public Worship of God approved by the General Assembly held in the year 1645, sess. 10, recommended to ministers and all others within this national Church. 1705. x.

Discipline. Committee appointed to consider the overtures concerning Church discipline, with instructions to meet and continue together until they have concerted and agreed upon a form of process for regulating the procedure of Church judicatories. 1703. xii.; 1704. xxv.

——— *See* FORM OF PROCESS. 1707. xi.

——— Larger overtures concerning the discipline and method of procedure in ecclesiastical judicatories, transmitted to presbyteries. 1705. 15; 1707. xvii.; 1710. xvi.

——— The Acts of Assembly, 1707. xvii. and 1710. xvi., relative to the larger overtures anent discipline, revived 1718. x.

——— Act discharging prelatical preachers and separatists from exercising Church discipline. 1715. xiv.

——— An Act relative to cases of discipline. 1843. xiii.

Dispatch. Acts for the better dispatching the business of the General Assembly. 1718. vii.; 1819. v.

Dissents. Enacted that the reasons of dissent against the determinations of Church judicatories in causes brought before them shall not be entered on the register, but be kept *in retentis*, to be laid before the superior judicatories. 1730. vii.

Dissents. The above Act, 1730. vii., rescinded, as having been passed in violation of the Barrier Act. 1734. v.

——— The recording of dissents against a judgment of the Assembly in a particular case disallowed, as tending to disturb the peace of the Church. 1730. 14; 1732. 9.

——— Referred to the Commission to prepare an overture for determining whether dissents against decisions of Assembly in private causes should be admitted and recorded or not. 1737, ult.; 1738. 9.

——— Referred to the Commission to give advice how far members absent from one meeting of synod shall, upon hearing the minutes read at a subsequent meeting, be allowed to have their dissent marked. 1738, ult.

——— The Assembly disapproved of a synod allowing to be recorded in their books a protest and dissent by one of their members against a sentence of the Commission. 1741, ult.

——— An overture, proposing that the effect of dissents respecting the licensing of probationers should be to sist the actual licensing of such probationers till the complaint was considered, after discussion withdrawn. 1786. 9.

——— An overture for regulating the effect of dissents from judgments of superior courts, transmitted to presbyteries, but not passed into an Act. 1752, ult.

——— Certain members of Assembly dissenting from a resolution to proceed with the licensing of a probationer, the Assembly ordered them to attend on the day of the ordination, and to concur with their brethren, on pain of being summoned to appear at the bar of the next General Assembly. 1803. 5.

——— Reasons of dissent rejected as disrespectful to the Assembly, and injurious to the party in the case. 1803. 9; 1803, ult.

——— A presbytery having refused to receive and record a dissent as disrespectful, a complaint was taken to the Assembly, who dismissed the complaint, and affirmed the judgment of the presbytery. 1845. 11.

——— In a case where there had been no dissent or complaint

in the Inferior Court, the Assembly refused to hear parties, "in respect the said sentence revived a question affecting a private party, the decision of which had become final." 1811. 4; 1827. 5.

Dissents. A presbytery having, without a dissent or complaint, found that there was no ground for further proceedings in a cause, the synod disapproved of the proceedings of the presbytery, and remitted to them to re-consider the case. The Assembly reversed the sentence of the synod, and affirmed the judgment of the presbytery, on the ground that it had become final, in consequence of there having been no complaint or appeal. 1839. 5.

——— A member of synod, who had not dissented or complained against a decision of synod, craved to be heard in the General Assembly by the indulgence of the house. The Assembly decided that he could not be heard, save as a party in support of the synod's decision, without a departure from one of the most salutary rules of the Court. 1832. 4.

——— In a case brought before the Assembly by petition, although there had been no dissent taken against the judgment of the Inferior Court, the Assembly, in the exercise of its *nobile officium*, or general superintending power, ordered a special meeting of synod to revise the record of the presbytery. 1837, ult.

——— A presbytery having, in the face of a dissent and complaint, proceeded with the settlement of a minister, the Assembly, "under all the circumstances of the case," approved of their conduct. 1828. 7.

——— A dissent must be given in immediately after the judgment dissented from has been pronounced. The dissent of members not then present cannot be received at a subsequent diet. 1827. 5.

——— A synod having affirmed a sentence of presbytery allowing a member to enter a dissent and complaint against a judgment come to at a former meeting of synod, the Assembly reversed the sentence of the synod. 1819. 5.

——— A minister dissented from a deliverance of synod come to in his absence, and gave in reasons of dissent, which were recorded. The Assembly found that the minister, not having been present when the judgment complained of was come to, had no right to dissent, and ordered his reasons to be expunged from the synod record. 1813, ult.

Dissents. A committee appointed to consider whether those members who were not present at the decision of any cause before the Assembly, or who, being present, did not vote, should afterwards be permitted to enter their dissent against the judgment of the Assembly in the said cause. 1820. 6.

——— A committee appointed to search the records for precedents, and to report what they found to be the law and practice of the Church in regard to the entering of dissents; which committee reported that it was long the invariable practice that dissents were entered upon the day on which the sentences dissented from were pronounced, leave being given to members to adhere to the dissent on a subsequent day, but that in some recent instances dissents had been entered on a subsequent day. The Assembly, on the recommendation of the committee, enjoined that the ancient practice should be enforced, and uniformly observed. 1828. 9.

——— A dissent, without a protest for leave to complain, does not entitle the member dissenting to be heard as a party at the bar of a superior court. 1831. 8.

——— A presbytery who had appeared before a synod as respondents in an appeal against a sentence of the presbytery, dissented from the judgment of the synod, and protested for *leave to complain* to the General Assembly. The Assembly dismissed the dissent and complaint as incompetent, and found that the presbytery ought, as party respondents, to have brought up the case by *protest and appeal.* 1838. 8.

——— A reference from the Synod of Perth and Stirling anent the effect of a dissent and complaint. 1830. 9; 1831, ult.

——— A committee appointed to consider the subject. 1831, ult.; 1832, ult.

——— A separate register-book ordered to be kept by the clerk of Assembly for the insertion of reasons of dissent. 1831, ult.

——— Reasons of dissent from deliverances of Assembly given in and read on the last day of Assembly. 1834, ult.

——— Declared that any member of the house present at the vote may enter upon the minutes a dissent from the judgment or resolution of the house immediately after the vote, and lodge thereafter his reasons of dissent, to which any member present at the vote may adhere, either when such dissent is taken, or at the next diet of the Assembly thereafter; but not competent to enter a dissent at any diet after that at which the resolution dissented from was passed. 1859, xii. chap. v. 43.

Dissents. A member craved leave to adhere to a dissent entered against a judgment of the house passed in his absence, which the Assembly refused, in respect he had not been present at the vote. 1859. 12.

Dissenters. The admission of dissenting ministers or teachers to trials for becoming licentiates of the Church, declared to be a step of such magnitude that it should never be taken without the knowledge and authority of the supreme ecclesiastical judicatory. 1805. 9.

——— Presbyteries enjoined to use all care in the admission into the Church of ministers or licentiates of other denominations, and to apply to the General Assembly for its sanction. 1844. 14.

——— Regulations anent the admission of ministers and licentiates of dissenting bodies transmitted to presbyteries as an overture, 1845, xv.; and passed into a standing law of the Church. 1856. xiii.

——— Applications for admission into the Church, with all the necessary documents, to be lodged with the agent on or before the first Saturday of the Assembly, and none to be received after that day. 1846. xvi.; 1850. xiv.

——— A minister in connection with the synod of relief having applied for admission into the Church of Scotland, the Assembly, on the recommendation of a committee, resolved that he should not be taken on trials until he had been six years regular and exemplary in his adherence to the Established Church. 1805. 9.

——— A decision given in precisely the same terms in a similar case. 1824, ult.

——— In another case, the Assembly finding that the applicant had studied divinity regularly, and that he had been about six years in communion with the Church of Scotland, authorised a presbytery to examine him, and, if they found him qualified, to receive him as a probationer. Com., June 3, 1834.

Dissenters. A similar case. 1833. 7.

——— A minister in Jamaica having applied for admission, the Presbytery of Edinburgh were authorised to take such trial of his gifts and qualifications as they might deem necessary, and, on being satisfied therewith, to receive him as a minister in connection and communion with the Church of Scotland in the colonies, it being expressly understood and provided that he should not be considered as eligible for a charge in Scotland. 1848. 13.

——— A Presbyterian minister at New York having applied for admission, the Assembly found that they could not, consistently with the existing laws of the Church, comply with the prayer of the petition. 1835. 4.

——— Overture for reunion with the original Seceders adhering to the standards of the Church of Scotland passed into a standing law of the Church. 1839. viii.

——— See also 1856, ult.; 1858. 13; 1859, ult.; 1860. 12, 14; 1861. 13, ult.; 1862. 3, 14, *cum multis aliis.*

Dissenting Meeting-Houses. Declared that the performance of Divine service, or any part of public worship or service, by ministers of this Church, in meeting houses of Dissenters, is highly irregular and unconstitutional, and ought on no occasion to take place, except in cases in which, from the peculiar circumstances of a parish, its minister may find it occasionally necessary for conducting the ordinary religious instruction of his people. 1818. 9.

Distillation. Anent illicit distillation, the Assembly, fully aware of its fatal consequences, appointed a committee to devise and adopt every means for putting a stop to so great an evil. 1820. 9.

Divine Worship. *See* WORSHIP.

Divinity. Abstract of the Acts of Assembly in force in regard to the study of divinity, the licensing of students, and probationers, transmitted as an overture to presbyteries. 1856. x.; 1856. 14.

——— Professors of divinity recommended to use their best endeavours to have the students under their care made well acquainted with the true method of preaching the Gospel. 1736. 7.

Divinity. Enacted that if a preacher of the Gospel be nominated a professor of divinity or ecclesiastical history, or biblical criticism or Hebrew, he shall, previous to his induction, be taken on trials by the presbytery within the bounds of which the university lies, and, if found qualified, ordained. 1838. xii.

——— Committee appointed to consider and report anent the curriculum of divinity. 1862. 11.

——— The Commission instructed to take into their consideration a deed of the University of St Andrews, in admitting to the degree of doctor of divinity a person not of the communion of this Church. 1726. 11.

Divinity Hall. *See* STUDENTS.

Divisions. An Act for preventing division and promoting peace and unity in the Church. 1714. viii.; 1715. vi.

——— Committee appointed for considering representations from the south and west concerning some ministers who are alleged guilty of divisive courses. 1714. 4.

——— An Act for prosecuting some who, professing to be Presbyterians, do separate from this Church, and an appointment concerning papists and episcopal intruders. 1715. xv.

Division of Parishes. Committee appointed to consider what steps ought to be taken for removing the difficulties in regard to Act 7 and 8 Victoriæ, cap. 44, for facilitating the disjoining or dividing of extensive or populous parishes. 1858, ult. 1843. 6. Committee discharged. 1861, ult.

Doctrine. All persons discharged from disseminating erroneous doctrine, particularly from venting any Arminian or Socinian errors. 1704. 12.

——— An Act for preserving purity of doctrine: enacted that no minister shall print or disperse in writing any catechism without the allowance of the presbytery of the bounds and of the Commission. 1710. xii.

——— Professor Simpson of Glasgow charged with propagating erroneous doctrine. 1714. 8.

——— A committee of thirty ministers and six ruling elders, twenty-one being a quorum, appointed to meet in Edinburgh, with power to make inquiry into whatever may be necessary for preserving and maintaining the purity of the doctrine of this Church. 1715. viii.; 1717. ix.; 1727. x.; 1728. ix.; 1729. vi.

Doctrine. A probationer's licence declared null because of his errors in doctrine. 1714, ult.

——— An Act and recommendation for preserving unity and preventing error within the Church. 1735. vii.

——— Found to be incompetent to institute an inquiry into the soundness of a presentee's doctrine immediately after sustaining his presentation. 1830. 5.

——— Ministers recommended punctually to observe the Acts of former General Assemblies for preaching catechetical doctrine. 1720. viii.

——— An Act concerning preaching. 1736. vii.; 1737. v.

——— An Act concerning Mr William Leechman, professor of divinity in the College of Glasgow. 1744. ix.

——— The Commission instructed to notice any misrepresentations that may be made, either at home or abroad, of the doctrine, worship, or constitution of this Church, and to take all proper methods for the vindication thereof. 1709. x.

——— Recommended to all ministers and teachers of divinity to be cautious in their preaching, teaching, or writing, not to use doubtful expressions, or propositions, which may be construed in an erroneous sense, or lead the hearers or readers into error, however sound such words or propositions may be in themselves, or however well intended, but to hold fast the form of sound words. 1736. x.

Drunkenness. A committee appointed to inquire into the most effectual means for correcting the evil of intemperance. 1848. 12. Which committee gave in a very full report. 1849. 9.

——— A pastoral address on the subject of drunkenness issued, and ordered to be read from all the pulpits. 1850, ult.

Dundee. An Act joining the Presbytery of Dundee to the Synod of Fife, *pro tempore*. 1694. 2.

——— A committee appointed to consider and report on a petition from the Presbytery of Dundee regarding the position of the Church there, in consequence of the refusal of the town-council, as heritors, to provide suitable stipends to the ministers. The Assembly approved of the report of said committee, sympathised with the presbytery of

Dundee, and exhorted them to maintain, by all proper and constitutional measures, the rights and interests of the Church in Dundee, and the independence of its ministers there. 1851. 13.

Dundee. *See* ANNUAL REPORTS OF COMMITTEE.

Dunkeld. Certain parishes disjoined from the Presbytery of Dunkeld, and erected into the Presbytery of Weem. 1836. vii.

Dutch. Letter to the Dutch Churches read and approved. Com., May 31, 1838.

E

Edict. When a presentee has been appointed to preach in a vacant church, intimation of the days of such preaching to be given to the congregation on the Lord's Day preceding, by edictal notice under the authority of the presbytery. 1862. vii. 4.

——— In the admission of a minister, the presbytery shall in every case appoint one of their number to preach in the vacant church on a Lord's Day, at least ten free days from the day fixed for such admission, and to intimate the same from the pulpit, by reading an edict in the form prescribed. 1862. vii. 15.

——— When a presbytery have resolved to hold a presbyterial visitation in any parish, they shall cause an edict to be served from the pulpit intimating the same, at least ten free days preceding the visitation, and summoning the parties interested to attend. 1706. xvi.

——— In a case of complaint relative to informalities in serving the edict for the admission of a minister, the Assembly sustained the complaint, and remitted to the presbytery to serve the edict anew in due form, and proceed to the settlement with all convenient speed. 1834. 9.

——— In the ordination of elders, the edict was served on the 15th of May, and the ordination took place on the 22d of the same month. A complaint was taken on the ground that ten days had not intervened. The Assembly dismissed the appeal, and declared the ordination valid. 1843. 8.

Edict. *See* ELDERS.

Edinburgh. A special diet for prayer appointed to be kept by the members of Assembly, on account of the sad and astonishing conflagration that fell out on Saturday the 3d February 1700, in the Parliament Close. 1700. 5.

——— Enacted that the Presbytery of Edinburgh shall in time coming supply the churches of their commissioners to the General Assembly, and not trouble the Assembly therewith. 1709. 6.

Edinburgh Castle. A committee appointed to consider a reference from the Presbytery of Edinburgh for advice whether or not the minister of the Castle of Edinburgh should be received and admitted a member of said presbytery; having recommended that he should, he was, by a judgment of the presbytery, affirmed by the synod and approved by the Assembly; received and admitted accordingly. 1751. 7, 9; 1752. 7.

——— An overture from the Presbytery of Haddington anent the chaplain of the Castle of Edinburgh, dismissed. 1764. 8.

——— The garrison chaplain having claimed to be regarded as a parish minister, and as such entitled to enjoy and exercise all the rights and privileges of the office, on the ground that the Castle of Edinburgh had anciently been recognised as a separate parish, the Assembly appointed a committee to examine diligently into the whole matter and report. 1841, ult. Com., June 2, 1840.

Education. Recommended to presbyteries to take special notice what Papists are in their bounds, take pains to reclaim them, and advert how their children are educated. 1690. vii.

——— Presbyteries recommended to advert to the education of young noblemen, gentlemen, and others, children of Popish parents, and to put the laws thereanent in execution. 1695. ix.

——— Act anent erecting schools in the Highlands, appointing a voluntary contribution or subscription to be made throughout the Church for that purpose, and requiring presbyteries to send in an account of what parishes want schools, and the reason of their wanting them, and of what places most need, and are most convenient for erecting schools. 1704. xiv.; 1707. v.

Education. An Act and recommendation respecting the religious education of youth, appointing the Holy Bible to be read as a regular exercise in all schools—the Shorter Catechism to be committed and frequently repeated—ministers from time to time to visit and examine the schools in their respective parishes—presbyteries to examine all the schools within their bounds at least once every year—and a copy of the Act to be sent to every minister and parochial schoolmaster. 1794. ix.

——— Report regarding the state of education in Scotland ordered at the request of Henry Brougham, Esq. 1818. 6; 1818, ult.

——— Committee appointed to devise a plan for increasing the means of education and religious instruction throughout Scotland in general, particularly in the Highlands and Islands, and in large and populous towns. 1824. 7.

——— Report of the Education Committee adopted, and a general collection ordered throughout the Church for carrying it into effect. 1825, ult.

——— A very full and interesting report given in by Dr Baird. Ministers of presbytery seats appointed members of committee. 1826. 4.

——— A narrative of the rise and progress of the General Assembly's Education Scheme ordered to be prepared for preservation among the records of the Church. 1827. 8.

——— A full statistical report given in by Dr Baird. 1833, ult.

——— £6000 voted by Parliament towards the permanent endowment of a school in each of the forty-one parliamentary church districts. 1837. 8.

——— A committee appointed to guard against any attempts in reference to our educational system by which religion may be separated from science, and to use every constitutional means for strengthening the connection between the Church, the universities, and established seminaries of Scotland. 1837. 8.

——— £2800 sent from India and Berbice for the relief of destitution in the Highlands and Islands. If not needed for that purpose, to be applied in aid of the General Assembly's Education Scheme. 1838. 8.

Education. Address to Her Majesty and petition to Parliament against the Government plan of education by parliamentary grants under the superintendence of a Committee of the Privy Council, and a letter in reply from Lord John Russell. Com., Aug. 14, 1839; Nov. 20, 1839.

——— Resolved that there appear no grounds for rejecting the proposed grants by Government on the conditions explained in the communications received from the Privy Council Board. 1840. 8.

——— The Assembly record their grateful acknowledgment of the liberality of Government in promoting education in Scotland, and especially for the pledge given that no inspector of the schools which are in connection with the Church of Scotland shall be appointed without the concurrence and approbation of the General Assembly. 1841. 11.

——— Committee instructed to give encouragement to female schools. 1844. 16.

——— The conditions on which Government aid was offered, declared to be such as the Church might accept without any compromise of her right of superintendence, and teachers recommended to apply for that aid. 1849. 4.

——— Dr Muir resigns the convenership. 1849. 8 and 9.

——— A protest, declaration, and testimony on the subject of national education. 1849. ix.

——— Notes prepared by the Committee on Parochial Schools relative to education in Scotland, approved of by the Assembly. 1851. 3, 10.

——— A digest or abstract of the returns from presbyteries of the state of education within their bounds, ordered to be printed. 1851. 6.

——— The Committee instructed to communicate with Government with the view of obtaining such a legislative enactment as will meet the educational wants of the country. 1852. 9.

——— A department for the industrial instruction of male students, established in the Edinburgh Normal Schools. 1853. 3.

——— A memorial to Her Majesty, and petitions to Parliament, against a bill introduced by the Lords, entitled "A Bill to make further provision for the education of the people in Scotland, and to amend the laws relating thereto." Com., March 22, 1854.

Education. Resolved to petition Parliament against the Lord Advocate's Education Bill, and in favour of the bill introduced by Mr Stirling. 1855. 13.

——— Resolved to petition in the strongest manner against the Lord Advocate's Parochial Schools Bill. 1856. 3; 1862. 2.

——— Resolved to petition Parliament to institute an inquiry into the system pursued by the Committee of Council on Education in regard to the selection of lesson-books and text-books. Com., March 3, 1858.

——— Committee appointed to consider how, without interfering with the existing schemes of the Church, funds may be raised for enabling the Committee on Education to extend to all their schools the benefit of female industrial instruction. 1860. 6.

——— A committee appointed to represent the Church at a conference proposed to be held in Edinburgh by the Social Science Association, on the subject of National Education. 1861. 14.

——— Resolution relative to the Parochial and Burgh Schools Act, 24 & 25 Victoriæ, chap. 107. 1862. 8.

Elders. Ordained that all elders shall subscribe their approbation of the Confession of Faith. 1690. vii.

——— Recommended to ministers and kirk-sessions that none be admitted as ruling elders who do not make conscience of the necessary and unquestionable duty of family worship. 1694. xiii.; 1697. vii.

——— Enacted that all ministers and ruling elders belonging to this national Church subscribe the Confession of Faith as the confession of their faith, according to the Act vii. of Assembly 1690, and the Formula agreed upon in the Assembly 1694. 1700. xi.; 1704. vi.

——— Ordained that no minister or elder be commissioned to the General Assembly but such as usually reside in, or have a relation to, the presbytery, burgh, or university they are commissioned from. 1704. vi.

——— Elders enjoined to be faithful in the discharge of their offices, tender and circumspect in their walk, punctual in their attendance upon ordinances, strict in their observance of the Lord's Day, and in regularly keeping up the worship of God in their families. 1722. ix.

Elders. Ordained that in future all commissions given to ruling elders as members of Assembly shall bear that the said elders are qualified in every respect according to what is required by Act ix. Assembly 1722. 1724. ix.; 1737. viii.

——— Presbyteries enjoined to have a strict regard to the Acts of Assembly, especially in choosing of elders to represent them in the General Assembly, and in attesting commissions of such as are chosen either by themselves, by universities, or by royal burghs. 1727. vii.

——— Ordained that no person shall be ordained an elder unless he has attained the age of 21 years complete, is a communicant, and an inhabitant of the parish, residing therein at least six weeks annually, or an heritor, or heritor's apparent heir. If only an occasional resident, must produce a certificate, &c. Any city or town in which there are more congregations than one, to be held as one parish in so far as this Act is concerned. 1776. xii.; 1816. x.

——— Presbytery elders to be ordained within two months after the sitting of synod to attend the presbytery, and ensuing synod of the bounds. In case of a death or demission, a new election to be made within one month of the same. 1776. xii.

——— Enacted that no ruling elder shall be deemed qualified to sit as a commissioner in any presbytery, synod, or General Assembly who is not *bona fide* a ruling elder. Every commissioner to the General Assembly to produce a certificate to that effect from his kirk-session. 1839. xii.; 1840, ult.

——— Retired ministers, not being professors of theology, to be subject to the same regulation regarding a certificate as other elders. 1841. 3.

——— Act anent the election of elders. 1842. x.

——— Act x. Assembly 1842, rescinded. 1846. x.

——— The Assembly disapproved of a synod appointing their elderships to be changed, and condemning the continuing ruling elders for life. 1718. 15.

——— The Assembly disapproved of a synod excluding from their deliberations elders who were not constituent members of a presbytery, when a sentence appealed from was passed by that presbytery. 1730. 13.

Elders. A synod having refused to admit as members of synod certain elders of new chosen by their respective sessions to represent them in the presbytery and synod, the Assembly ordered the synod to be rebuked, which was done accordingly. 1742. 9.

——— An overture respecting the election of elders transmitted to presbyteries for many years, but not passed. 1784. x.

——— A minister found to have acted most unwarrantably and unconstitutionally in presuming to put to persons about to be ordained elders questions different from those implied in the Formula 1694, and by no means adequate to the spirit of that Formula. 1799. 8.

——— The same minister called to the bar of the Assembly, censured and admonished to testify greater respect in future for the Standards of the Church, and the fences wisely provided by our ecclesiastical constitution against dangerous innovations. 1800. 7.

——— Found competent for a kirk-session to select persons to be ordained elders from the congregation attending a chapel of ease within the parish. 1822. 5.

——— A presbytery having prohibited the kirk-session of a burgh from appointing elders from members of their own congregations, who resided beyond the limits of their respective parishes, the Assembly found that the decreet of the presbytery was contrary to the law of the Church, and instructed the presbytery to alter their decreet, in conformity with this judgment. Com., June 1, 1841.

——— An ordained assistant having ordained elders without the concurrence of his principal, the Assembly found that, as it appeared from the minutes and official documents produced, that the persons denominated elders had not been ordained according to the rules and laws of the Church, their ordination was null and void. 1827. 6.

——— Presbyteries enjoined to use their best and most prudent endeavours to have all the parishes within their bounds suitably supplied with elders, and to report the state of the kirk-sessions under their superintendence to next Assembly. 1825, ult.; 1827. 9.

Elders. Kirk-sessions ordered to return the names of the elders in each kirk-session, with the dates of their ordination or admission, and their usual places of residence, pointing out the alteration in regard to the number of members in the respective sessions, as compared with the return obtained in 1828. 1842. 5.

——— Committee appointed to inquire into the state of the eldership. 1843. 10.

——— A kirk-session having refused to allow an elder to vote on the ground that he did not reside within the bounds of the parish, the Assembly reversed the sentences of the Inferior Courts, and sustained his right to vote. 1806. 4.

——— Declared that, when a change of residence renders it impossible for an elder to discharge the duties of a member of the kirk-session of that parish in which he formerly resided, it is competent for the kirk-session to find that, if he does not, within the space of twelve months, return to reside, he can no longer continue one of their number, and to intimate to him by letter that they have come to this resolution. 1806. 7.

——— An elder having refused to sign the Confession of Faith without certain explanations and reservations, the Assembly declared that he was not legally qualified to take any part in the government of this Church, or to perform any other part of the duties of an elder, until he should have subscribed *simpliciter* the Confession of Faith and Formula. 1832. 4.

——— In a case of reference regarding the admission of a retired minister as member of the kirk-session of a parish in which he was neither resident, nor possessed any of the alternative qualifications of an elder prescribed in Act x., Ass. 1816; the Assembly remitted the matter to the presbytery of the bounds, with instructions to them to adjudicate therein according to the laws of the Church. 1841. 3.

——— An overture for substituting a more explicit attestation, in place of the *bona fide* certificate, transmitted to presbyteries for their consideration. 1854, ult.

——— Re-transmitted 1855, ult, and thrown out by a majority of 93 to 38. 1856, ult.

——— Presbyteries enjoined to inquire into the state of the

eldership within their bounds, and in case of deficiency in the numbers thereof, to report to next General Assembly the amount and cause thereof. 1858. 12.

Elders. A committee appointed to inquire into the state of the eldership, and report. 1860. 3.

——— An abstract of all the Acts in force relating to the eldership transmitted to presbyteries for their consideration, with a view to its being passed into a consolidated Act. 1861. 14.

——— An overture transmitted to presbyteries to the effect that, in addition to the qualifications specified in Act x., Ass. 1816, the following alternative qualification be added, "Or who is a member of the congregation, and a communicant of at least twelve months' standing." 1862. ix.

——— Found that it is unnecessary to transmit an overture anent the admission of an elder already ordained into another kirk-session. 1862. 14.

——— The Assembly refused to transmit to presbyteries an overture anent the ordination of elders for chapels-of-ease. 1862. 14.

——— The Assembly gratefully acknowledged the assistance they had received from the Elders' Wives and Daughters' Association. 1851. 6.

——— *See* BURGH, COMMISSION, ELECTION.

Election. In the election of a principal clerk, the Assembly resolved to proceed with the election at their first diet, under this proviso, that it should be competent to any member to demand a scrutiny of the legality of the votes; that for this purpose the names of all the members voting, and for whom they voted, should be taken down; and that, after the scrutiny, the Assembly should, at an after-diet, declare the election to have fallen on the person having the majority of legal votes on the roll as purged by the Assembly. 1789. 1.

——— A similar mode adopted in the election of the procurator for the Church. 1806. 1.

——— Also in the election of the principal clerk. 1807. 1.

——— Also in the election of a procurator. 1831. 1.

——— Also in the election of an agent for the Church. A motion to the effect that, after it had been ascertained by calling the roll how many voted for each candidate, the individual who had the smallest number of votes should then be struck off the list, and that this should be repeated till the number of candidates was reduced to two, when the decision of the Assembly, as between these two, should be finally taken, and the individual who, at such final vote, had the greatest number of suffrages, declared agent for the Church, having been lost by a majority of 171 to 158. 1837. I.

Election. Before proceeding to the election of an agent, the Assembly resolved, in the event of there being more than two candidates, that if, on calling the roll, the votes of a majority of the members present shall not be given in favour of any of the candidates, the name of the candidate having the smallest number of votes shall be struck off from the list, and the roll again called; and so on till the votes of a majority of the members present be recorded in support of some one of the candidates. 1855. 4.

——— Election of Mr Cook as joint procurator unanimous. 1856. 10.

——— In the election of a sub-clerk only two candidates proposed. 1859. 8.

——— In the election of a sub-clerk, there being four candidates proposed, the Assembly resolved to adopt a similar mode to that followed in the election of an agent in 1855. 1862. 1.

Election of Members of Assembly. Presbyteries enjoined to choose their commissioners for the General Assembly a competent time before the sitting thereof—at least forty days—and to choose such ruling elders as may attend. 1698. vi.

——— Election to be at least forty days before the meeting of Assembly, and within a month preceding the first of these forty days. The resolution to elect to be made and recorded at least ten days before the day of election. The election to take place on the day fixed, between the hours of one and eight P.M. 1738. vii.

——— Presbyteries enjoined not only to elect their full number of commissioners, but also to be careful to choose such persons as probably can attend. 1718. ix.

Election of Elders. A motion, to the effect that the congregations of this Church ought to exercise an elective voice in the choice of their elders, rejected as unconstitutional and inexpedient by a majority of 153 to 131. 1837. 5.

Election of Elders. A committee appointed to consider and report on the present state of the eldership, particularly as to what extent it may be advisable to allow greater influence to congregations in the choice of their elders. 1838. 9.

——— An overture transmitted to presbyteries to the effect that, when an addition to the number of elders in a kirk-session had been resolved upon, the whole male communicants of the congregation should be invited to give in lists of such members of the congregation, being communicants, and of full age, as they should choose for the office of the eldership—the number of names in such list being one half more than the number of elders required—and the kirk-session to select from those having the most votes the number proposed to be added to the session. 1841, ult.

——— The foresaid overture, having received the consent of a majority of presbyteries, passed into a law of the Church. 1842. x.

——— Committee appointed to inquire into the state of the eldership, and the working of Act x., Ass. 1842. 1843. 10.

——— Overture for rescinding Act x., Ass. 1842, transmitted to presbyteries. 1845. 14.

——— An overture and regulations anent the appointment of elders transmitted to presbyteries. 1845. 14.

——— Which overture, having received the consent of a majority of presbyteries, was passed into a law of the Church. 1846. x.

——— In the election of additional elders, only a week intervened between the serving the edict and the day of ordination, the synod, on a complaint, declared the proceeding of the kirk-session irregular, invalid, and inept. The Assembly reversed the sentence of the synod, and declared the ordination valid. 1843. 8.

Elocution. An overture, to the effect that the study of English literature and elocution should form part of the course of training for the ministry, and that every candidate, before receiving licence, should produce a certificate of his having attended such a class, dismissed as inexpedient. 1860, ult.

Emigration. The Colonial Committee instructed to pay special attention to the emigration at present taking place from this country, with the view of providing the emigrants in their new country with the ministrations of the gospel, and proper teachers, as speedily and extensively as possible. 1837. 5.

Endowment. A committee appointed to memorialise Government in order that such ministers as are or may be admitted to the status of parochial ministers may be fitly and adequately endowed. 1834. 9.

——— The Committee on Endowments, the Committee on Church Accommodation, and the Committee on the Subdivision of Parishes, united into one, as a Committee on Church Extension, with Dr Chalmers as convener. 1835. 8.

——— Committee appointed to employ all likely means for obtaining subscriptions, and making application in influential quarters, and sending deputations into the several districts of the Church, for relieving chapels-of-ease from the disadvantages under which they labour, so that they may as speedily as possible be raised to the full status of parish churches. 1846. 7.

——— In order to bring the objects of the Endowment Committee more fully and adequately under the view of the Church at large, the Assembly appoint this scheme to be put on the same footing with the other five Schemes of the Church, and thus to receive along with them the benefit of an annual general collection. 1849. 3.

——— *See* ANNUAL REPORTS OF ENDOWMENT COMMITTEE.

England. An overture anent ministers ordained in England or in foreign parts transmitted to presbyteries, but not passed. 1754. 7.

——— A committee appointed to consider a petition from the ministers and elders of the Scots Presbytery in London, and report to next Assembly. 1833. 9.

——— A committee appointed to consider a petition from the ministers and elders of the Scots Presbytery in London, and other similar bodies in England, having recommended that those presbyteries whose ministers were licentiates of the Church of Scotland should be admitted to the following privileges—viz., That the General Assembly should be their supreme ecclesiastical judicatory, to which they should have the power of reference and appeal, and to which they should be entitled to send one minister and one ruling elder as corresponding members, such corresponding members, however, to have no vote in the Assembly—on the motion of Lord Moncreiff, the Assembly unanimously rejected the proposal of the committee, as inconsistent with the principles and constitution of the Church of Scotland, and reappointed the committee, with instructions to reconsider what measures might be safely or expediently adopted for the purpose of extending to the members of presbyteries in England the most cordial support and countenance of this Church. 1834, ult.

England. The several presbyteries in England recommended to form themselves into one or more synods, as they may see fit, with the assurance that the Assembly would promote their interests by all legal means in their power. 1835, ult.

——— The Synod of Lancashire recognised as a branch of the Church of Scotland, to the effect of receiving their members into ministerial communion, and assured that the Assembly would gladly receive from said Synod, and make to them, as occasion offered, communications regarding the wellbeing of their respective Churches, and be ready to aid them with their counsel in matters wherein their advice might be required. 1836. 9.

——— A motion, to the effect of allowing the Synod of the Presbyterian Church in England to be represented in the General Assembly by two ministers and two elders, negatived by a majority of 199 to 57. The Assembly, however, resolved that the two Churches should mutually interchange friendly communications, by means of deputations to and from their respective judicatories. 1839. 5.

——— The Assembly expressed their gratification at receiving a deputation from the Presbyterian Synod in England, and resolved to maintain with that body the closest relation which the constitution of the Church allowed. 1840. 7.

——— A standing committee appointed for the purpose of corresponding with the Presbyterian Synod in England. 1841. 13.

——— The Synod of the Presbyterian Church in England having repudiated their connection with the Church of Scotland, the Assembly rescinded the resolution of 1836, by which said Synod was recognised as a branch of this Church, and appointed a committee to correspond with those ministers and congregations in England who maintain said connection. 1844. 16.

England. Dr Cumming and others declared to be the constituted members of the Scots Presbytery of London, in full communion with the Church of Scotland, and entitled to all the intercourse, correspondence, and encouragement heretofore afforded to Presbyteries or other church courts within the realm of England. 1845. xvii.

——— The Assembly advised the formation of a presbytery in the west and another in the north of England; said presbyteries, along with the Scots Presbytery in London, to constitute a Synod in communion with the Church of Scotland. 1850. 15.

——— The Assembly found that they had jurisdiction over a licentiate of this Church settled in England, against whom a *fama* had arisen, and appointed the presbytery of which he was a licentiate to proceed against him, and, if necessary, to send a deputation into England for the purpose of taking evidence. Com., June 4, 1840.

——— A doubt having been expressed as to the jurisdiction of the Church over an individual not resident within its bounds, the Assembly asserted its jurisdiction over a minister in England who had been licensed and ordained by a presbytery of this Church, and ordered the presbytery which had ordained him to proceed against him by libel for heresy. 1832, ult.; 1833, ult.

——— The Assembly resolved to record sentences of deposition or deprivation of licence pronounced against ministers or licentiates of this Church residing in England, by the Scots Presbyterian Synod in England, when reported. 1841, ult.

——— A minister officiating in England deprived of his licence, and declared incapable of receiving a presentation or call to be a minister of any parish or congregation in connection with the Church of Scotland. Com., August 11, 1841.

Enzie. Committee named to consider the state of the fund collected for a meeting-house in the Enzie, with instructions to apply £20 of the interest of that fund in repairing a house given by her Grace the Duchess of Gordon to the itinerant preacher in the Enzie, and making it a comfortable place for public worship. 1755. 8.

Enzie. All the funds to be accumulated into one sum, and lent out on bond. 1758, ult.

——— The committee instructed to make the best bargain they can anent obtaining the lease of a house for the missionary. 1759. 5.

——— A general collection in aid of the funds. 1767. 6.

——— The committee empowered to conclude a bargain, in consequence of a treaty entered into between the Duke of Gordon and the Presbytery of Fordyce with regard to the lands belonging to the fund. 1778. 1; 1779. 6.

——— The committee authorised to build a proper church. 1784. 9.

——— Found that the committee had exceeded their powers in the appointment of a missionary, and his appointment declared void. 1794. 9.

——— The procurator authorised to grant such conveyance of the lands belonging to the fund as might be found necessary in reference to the disjunction and erection of the church and parish of Enzie under the Act 7 and 8 Vict., cap. 44. 1849, ult.

——— An account of the origin and nature of the fund given in a report by the committee on the funds of the Church, printed along with the Acts. 1841, *Appendix.*

Episcopalians. The Commission instructed to receive into ministerial communion such of the late conform ministers, having qualified themselves according to law, as should apply personally to them, duly and orderly, and should acknowledge, engage, and subscribe upon the end of the Confession of Faith, according to a prescribed formula. 1694. xi.

——— Presbyteries seriously recommended to proceed in processes against ministers with all due circumspection and prudence, and not to censure any minister for not having qualified himself in terms of the Act of Parliament entitled "Act for Settling the Quiet and Peace of the Church." 1694. 12.

——— The Lord High Commissioner intimated to the Assembly that it "was evidently convenient, and likewise expected, that if good men applied to them to be assumed, they should receive their application with all charity and moderation." 1695. vii.

Episcopalians. A similar course strongly recommended in his Majesty's letter to the Assembly—"You know it is our inclination, and we do recommend to you to assume the Episcopal ministers whose lives and doctrine do render them useful to the Church." 1698. ii.

——— Presbyteries enjoined to be very delicate in their proceedings with any of the late conform ministers, in order to their reception into the government, on their applications in terms of the acknowledgment settled by the Assembly 1694. 1697. xvi.; 1706. xii.

——— The Commission empowered and recommended, when any of the ministers who served under the late Prelacy applied for reception, to receive them with readiness. 1698. xiii.

——— Mr John M'Calman, one of those that served under the late Prelacy, received into ministerial communion on his signing the Formula. 1699. 14.

——— A petition from certain ministers who served under the late Prelacy, craving to be received into ministerial communion, and a share of the government of the Church, referred to the Commission. 1698. 15.

——— Represented to her Majesty, "as a pregnant instance of moderation," that since the late happy establishment of the Church "there had been taken in and continued *hundreds* of dissenting ministers upon the easiest terms." 1712. x.

——— An Act anent irregularities committed by vagrant ministers. 1696. xxiii.

——— The Assembly complain to the Queen of the disorderly practices of some of the Episcopal clergy and their abettors. 1703. viii.; 1708. 5; 1714. 4; 1714. xii.

——— The Lord Advocate recommended to assist and concur with presbyteries in checking the irregularities and disorders of the Episcopal clergy according to law. 1706. 11.

——— An Act discharging them from exercising discipline. 1715. xiv.

——— Reference to the Commission anent preventing the Episcopal ministers from licensing probationers. 1710. 14.

Episcopalians. Commission empowered to grant all the assistance they can for removing the deposed Episcopal ministers from certain parishes in the Presbytery of Dunkeld. 1719. 3.

——— Presbyteries recommended to raise contributions for the relief of a late Episcopal minister. 1708. 5.

——— The minister of Kirriemuir allowed the expenses of his process for removing the intruder, and getting access to his church. 1716. 8.

——— An overture anent the removal of the restrictions which at present attach to Episcopal ministers in Scotland having been read, the Assembly, while fully alive to everything that might injuriously affect the interests of Protestantism, did not feel called on to take special action in the matter referred to, and dismissed the overture. 1857. 13.

Erasure. The judicatories of the Church recommended to take special care that the registers be correctly written, and that they allow no blottings or interlinings therein; and if there be anything blotted out as superfluous, to see that it be marked on the margin how many words or lines are blotted out, and signed by the moderator and clerk, by authority of the judicatory. 1706. 9.

——— A judgment of a synod reversed as incompetent and highly irregular, in so far as they appointed the minute of a preceding synod to be erased from the record. 1817. 7.

——— It having been objected to a commission that the place and date were written on an erasure, the Assembly allowed proof that the place and date as altered were correct, and sustained the commission. 1847. 3.

Erection of New Parishes. An overture anent the erection of new parishes in the Highlands and Islands referred to a committee, with power to apply to the Board of Trustees of Annexed Estates, and to take such other steps as they should think most effectual for obtaining the end proposed. 1778, ult.; 1782, ult.; 1784, ult.

——— The Assembly renewed their instructions to their committee to repeat their application for an appropriation of part of the money arising from the restoration of the forfeited estates, and to take every measure that may appear to them proper for attaining that valuable object. 1785. 9.

Erroneous Doctrine. All persons discharged from preaching or disseminating any erroneous doctrine opposite to any head or article of the Confession of Faith. 1704. xii.

Erroneous Doctrine. All ministers of the Church recommended to be careful to guard against the spreading of any errors contrary to our standards of doctrine, particularly such as strike against the fundamentals of our holy religion. 1731. viii.

——— An Act and recommendation for preserving unity and preventing error within the Church. 1736. vii.

Erskine. Act and sentence concerning Mr Ebenezer Erskine, and some other ministers adhering to his protest, for their contempt of the authority of the General Assembly. 1733. vii. 11; 1734. viii. 9; 1738. iv. 4; 1739. iv. 3; 1740. iv. 7.

Estates Forfeited. The Society for the Propagation of Christian Knowledge recommended to use their best endeavours for having the sum of £20,000 appointed by Act of Parliament, 4 Geo. I., entitled "Act for Vesting the Forfeited Estates in Trustees," &c., to be paid out of the forfeited estates, for maintaining schools in the Highlands and Islands of Scotland, made effectual. 1732. 8.

Examination. Order and injunction of the General Assembly to the presbyteries of the Church concerning the examination of schools. 1819. viii.

——— *See* STUDENTS.

Excommunication. Intimation of a sentence of excommunication ordered to be made throughout all the churches of the presbytery of the bounds; thereafter, if the party continue obstinate, in all the churches within the bounds of the synod; and finally, if need be, in all the churches of the kingdom: and in making such intimation, ministers are enjoined to hold forth the sad state of excommunicate persons, and inform their people how to carry themselves towards them. 1704. ix.

——— Concerning processes in order to excommunication, *see* FORM OF PROCESS. 1707. xi., chap. viii.

——— Sentence of the greater excommunication having been pronounced by the Presbytery of Edinburgh against two several parties, the Assembly ordered said sentences to be intimated from the pulpits of all the churches within Scotland. 1743, ult.

——— Similar cases: 1745. 9; 1719, ult.; 1723. 13, &c. &c.

Excommunication. A presbytery having pronounced a sentence of the lesser excommunication against a party, the Assembly, on appeal, disapproved of the conduct of the presbytery in pronouncing that severe sentence, and instructed them to proceed in the exercise of discipline with discretion and tenderness. Com., May 29, 1832.

——— In a similar case the Assembly annulled the whole proceedings in the kirk-session and presbytery, and ordered them to be expunged from the minutes as precipitate, irregular, and illegal. 1824. 9.

Exercise and Addition. Presbyteries earnestly recommended to set up the use of exercise and addition. 1694. xvii.

——— The mode of conducting the exercise and addition described in the larger overtures concerning the discipline and method of procedure in the ecclesiastical judicatories of the Church. 1705. Chap. iii. 12.

——— *See* STUDENTS.

Exculpation. An overture for repealing that part of the form of process relating to the exculpation offered by the defender in a cause transmitted to presbyteries for several years, but not passed. 1762, ult.

Expunging Minutes. Declared that when a minute is ordered to be expunged from the record by order of a superior court, it must be done so as to render it illegible. Com., May 31, 1837; 1819. 9.

Extension. *See* CHURCH EXTENSION.

Extracts. Found that a party is entitled to full extracts of everything on the record relating to his cause, but no partial extracts; and if he ask papers that lie *in retentis*, he may have attested copies thereof. 1783, ult.

——— On a reference for advice with respect to the giving a party extracts from the record, the Assembly unanimously appointed the presbytery to furnish him with extracts of all the proceedings relating to his case. 1818, ult.; 1828. 7; 1835. 10; 1822. 4.

——— A sentence of a presbytery refusing extracts to a party in a cause determined some years before, unanimously affirmed. 1808. 6.

——— A party having been excommunicated by a presbytery for contumacy, some weeks after the sentence was pronounced, applied, through a law agent, for extracts of the whole proceedings in his case; which having been refused, he applied to the sheriff to compel the presbytery to furnish him with said extracts. An order having been served on the presbytery to that effect, they lodged a formal declinature of the sheriff's jurisdiction, and referred the matter to the Assembly for advice. The Assembly approved of the conduct of the presbytery in declining the jurisdiction of the sheriff in this case, and remitted to them to grant the extracts. Com., June 2, 1842.

Extracts. In a process of libel the presbytery refused to the prosecutor extracts of certain documents in their possession, which he alleged were necessary for the prosecution of the libel, on the ground that a pledge had been given by the presbytery to the defender that said documents should not be used as evidence against him in the superior courts. The Assembly found the prosecutor entitled to extracts and attested copies of all the minutes and documents in the case, and ordered the presbytery to furnish them accordingly. 1845. 8.

——— A party in a cause refused to plead before a synod, on the ground that he had not received the extract minutes of presbytery in due time. The synod found that, as the summons, which had been served on the party ten days before the meeting of synod, bore that the clerk was instructed to furnish him with extracts on his applying for them, there was nothing in the objection to prevent them from taking up the case; which finding, on appeal, was affirmed by the Assembly. 1828. 6.

——— In an appeal case, a clerk of synod ordered to transmit extracts of the proceedings of presbytery in his possession, bearing upon the case before the Assembly. 1824. 6.

——— A complainant having produced no extracts of the proceedings in the Inferior Court, the Assembly found that there was no case before them. 1746. 10; 1833. 5.

——— An overture anent the printing of extracts referred to the committee on the form of process. 1831, ult.

——— Extracts from jottings signed by the clerk, but not attested by the moderator, held not to be of authority; and that the minutes must be extended, engrossed, revised, and signed by the moderator in name of the court before they can be considered the record. 1834. 4.

Extracts. The parties in a complaint having applied for the original jottings from which the minutes were made up to enable them to substantiate their complaints, and been refused by the presbytery, the Assembly found that they were entitled to be put in possession of said jottings. 1812. 9.

——— A party interested in a cause about to come before the Assembly, petitioned the Assembly to issue their warrant on the presbytery to furnish him with the jottings of said presbytery. The Assembly refused the prayer of the petition. 1823. 4.

——— Enacted that along with applications for transmission to the Assembly of appeals, or of dissents and complaints against the judgments of inferior courts, there shall be produced an extract of the judgment complained of, and an extract or certified copy of the reasons of appeal, or of dissent and complaint, with all documents or copies, certified by the clerk to be correct copies of all the documents forming part of the record in the Inferior Court: and that the record shall be held to consist of the entire minutes of the inferior courts in relation to the cause, and of the evidence, whether parole or documentary, adduced in the same, whether engrossed in the minutes or lodged in the Inferior Court, and kept *in retentis.* 1859. xii., chap. ii., 18, 19.

Evidence. Found that it is competent for ecclesiastical courts to receive the evidence of near relations of the parties, but that such evidence ought to be received *cum nota.* 1779. 8.

——— A presbytery authorised to grant commission to any presbytery of the Church to take the evidence of any witnesses residing in their respective bounds. 1785. 5.

——— In a reference respecting the admissibility of a witness, the Assembly found the objections against the admissibility irrelevant, but recommended the presbytery to receive the evidence of the witness *cum nota.* 1801. 4.

Evidence, Hearsay. A kirk-session having rejected the evidence of certain witnesses on account of its being *hearsay* evidence, the synod remitted the case to the kirk-session, with instructions to examine said witnesses; but the

Assembly, on appeal, reversed the sentence of the synod, and affirmed that of the kirk-session. 1805. 9.

Evidence, Extrajudicial. A presbytery having been petitioned to inquire into certain circumstances affecting the character of a minister, and as two individuals cognisant of these circumstances were about to leave the country, having been further petitioned to take the evidence of these parties, to seal it up and keep it *in retentis*, to be made available, if necessary, in the future proceedings in the case ; the presbytery granted the petition, and examined the witnesses. But the Assembly, on appeal, reversed their judgment, and found that they had acted irregularly in taking evidence in absence of any specific charge having been made, and before any libel had been served. 1834. 5.

Evidences of Religion. The Assembly approved of the report of the committee on the superintendence of the religious training of the youths connected with the Church of Scotland at the universities, recommending the establishment of lectureships on the evidences of religion. 1861, ult.

Eyemouth. The Assembly, on the report of a committee, approved of the principle of having the vicarage teinds of the parish of Eyemouth commuted on fair and equitable terms under the authority of an Act of Parliament, and authorised the committee to consent to any bill founded upon that principle. 1862. 12.

F

Falsehood as a charge in a libel found proven, the minister deposed, and his church declared vacant. 1746. 6; 1846. 6; 1851. 5.

Fama Clamosa. When a *fama* is clamant and the scandal great, a presbytery may begin a process without any accuser, but must first inquire into the rise, occasion, broachers, and grounds of the *fama*. 1707. xi., chap. vii., 3.

Family Worship. Ordained that the ministers and elders in each congregation take care that the worship of God be performed in the several families thereof, and that none be ruling elders who make not conscience of this necessary and unquestionable duty. 1694. xiii.

Family Worship. Ordained that elders and deacons who neglect to worship God in their families shall be seriously admonished to amend—if need be, rebuked; and if obstinate in their neglect, removed from their office. 1697. vii.

——— Presbyteries earnestly recommended to use their utmost endeavours that the worship of God be set up and performed in all its parts in the families within their bounds. 1711. vii.; 1819. vi.

——— A pastoral letter on the subject of family worship issued by the Assembly, and ordered to be read from all the pulpits of the Church. 1836, ult.

——— Private families recommended that, in their religious exercises in singing the praises of God, they go on without the intermission of reading each line. 1746. viii.

Family Visitation. All the families in a parish to be visited by the minister, accompanied by the district elder, once a-year; names of the several members of each family to be taken down, distinguishing those who can read, those who are examinable, and those who have recently come into the parish bringing certificates from other parishes. The minister to speak privately to the master and mistress; to exhort them to observe the worship of God in their family; to see that their children are properly educated, and that they and the servants attend public worship and observe the Lord's day; and to inquire who have communicated, and if any want Bibles. 1708. 10.

Fasts. A solemn national fast and humiliation appointed for the late and present defections of this Church and kingdom. The causes set forth at length. 1690. xii.

——— For the lamentable stroke of dearth and unseasonable weather in seed-time and harvest. 1699. vi.

——— For the continuance of the pinching dearth, the great and unusual sickness and mortality, the failure of the African and Indian Company's colony, a stupendous burning of great part of Edinburgh, and the woeful heart-plagues of impenitency and insincerity. 1700. v.; 1701. ix.

——— For the unseasonableness of the weather in seed-time, and many other weighty grounds. 1704. xxvi.

Fasts. For the long continuance of a wasting and desolating war, with special reference to the present state of affairs at home and abroad. 1705. xvii.

——— For the continuance of the bloody war, the increase of Popery and profaneness, and the decay of trade; and to pray for divine guidance to the commissioners appointed to treat of a union with England. 1706. xix.

——— For unseasonable weather in seed-time, and threatened dearth; mortality among flocks and cattle, and many spiritual plagues. 1709. viii.

——— On account of great and crying sins, errors, and dreadful delusions. 1710. vi.

——— For national defection and immorality. 1722. v.

——— On account of the war and famine. 1741. iv.

——— On the declaration of the war against France. 1756. vi.

——— For the prevailing sins of the land. 1835. xxi.

——— On account of the present circumstances of the Church. 1841. ix.; 1842. xxx.

——— On account of the distresses prevailing in this and in other nations. 1848. viii.

——— A call for humiliation and prayer on account of the fearful judgment of war. Com., March 1, 1854.

——— The Assembly appointed a fast to be observed in the month of March, and applied to the Privy Council for their civil sanction, leaving it to their lordships to name the day. 1699. vi.; 1700. v.

——— Fast appointed, and the day fixed by the Assembly. 1701. ix.

——— Fast appointed, but left to the several synods and presbyteries to fix the day to be observed within their respective bounds. 1704. xxvi.

——— Resolution of the General Assembly with respect to the keeping of a fast. 1783. vii.

——— Presbyteries recommended to take notice of all ministers within their bounds who do not observe fasts and thanksgivings indicated by the Church. 1690. vi.; 1710. vii.

——— Presbyteries ordained at their first meeting after every fast and thanksgiving, whether appointed by the Church or the supreme magistrate, to call the several brethren within their bounds to an account how they have observed the same. 1722. 3.

Fasts. The Commission instructed to apply to the Crown for the civil sanction to fasts and thanksgivings appointed by the Church. 1708. ix.

Fees. Declared that the dues which were in use to be paid ever since the Revolution to the clerks of the Assembly by the commissioners from presbyteries, &c., at delivering in their commissions, do belong to the clerks, and ought to be punctually paid. 1746. 6.

——— Remitted to the procurator and agent to select a case in which payment of the fees due to presbytery and synod clerks had been refused, and to obtain a decision thereon at the public expense. 1802. 4.

——— A reference respecting precentors' and session-clerks' fees remitted for consideration to the procurator and agent for the Church. 1805. 9.

——— Committee appointed to consider and report anent the fees payable to presbytery and synod clerks. 1815. 9; 1825, ult.; 1827. 9.

——— Found that a presbytery clerk was not entitled to withhold a commission to the General Assembly in favour of a burgh elder on the ground that said elder had not paid the usual fee. 1825. 3.

——— Ordained that no fees shall be exigible on presenting petitions to the Assembly on general subjects. 1842. xxvi.

——— The practice of ministers connected with this Church, in certain colonies, receiving fees for administering the sacrament of baptism declared to be inconsistent with the principles of the Church. 1840. 3.

——— An overture to do away with fees in theological classes as an infringement of the rights and privileges of the Church introduced, and, after discussion, dismissed. 1830. 9.

——— A committee appointed to consider what are or ought to be the duties of the several office-bearers of the Assembly, and also to regulate the fees to be paid for extracts, and all matters relating to the conduct of business. 1837. 1.

——— Report of committee aforesaid. 1837, ult.

——— Committee appointed to consider the nature of the

duties which have hitherto been discharged by the clerks of Assembly with the assistance of the agent for the Church, with the emoluments received by them, and how far any change should be made on one or other of them. 1859. 1.

Fees. Report of committee aforesaid. 1859, page 43.

Fellowship Meetings. A sentence of the Synod of Sutherland and Caithness discharging fellowship meetings of the ministers and people that had been usually held in that corner of the Church reversed, and every minister allowed to attend said meetings or not as he might see cause. Com., June 6, 1758.

Fiars. Committee appointed, with instructions to take such steps as to them might seem proper, for obtaining an equitable mode of striking the fiars, either by a new Act of Sederunt or by legislative enactment. 1807. 9.

——— Committee appointed to communicate with the Lord Advocate for the purpose of obtaining some legislative measure for fixing the method of striking the fiars of grain and meal. 1808. 8.

——— Procurator instructed to select a proper case respecting the mode of striking the fiars of grain to be tried before the competent court. 1813, ult.

——— Appointed that the Fiars Committee shall be an open committee. 1822, ult.

——— Committee instructed to consult with the proper authorities with a view to arrive at a mode of payment of stipend which might do away with the inconveniences attending the annual computations of the fiars prices, either by making the average fiars of Linlithgow a general average for all Scotland, or by taking a general average every twenty-one years, to be held as the rule of payment for the succeeding twenty-one years. 1832, ult.

——— Committee instructed to prepare draft of a bill for improving the mode of striking the fiars, to be introduced into Parliament by the Lord Advocate. 1834, ult.

——— *See* Annual Reports of Committee on Fiars.

Fife Synod. The register of the synod ordered to be transcribed. 1698. 14.

——— The old registers of the synod being found by Mr Bell

at Gladsmuir, were delivered up to the clerk of synod in presence of the Assembly. 1708. 9.

Fife Synod. The day of meeting changed from the first to the second Wednesday of October. 1776. x.

——— The day of meeting changed from second Wednesday to second Tuesday of October. 1777. viii.

Fines. Kirk-sessions discharged from receiving or exacting pecuniary fines from delinquents in cases of discipline, or from even adverting to such a subject in their presence, leaving it to the curators of the poor's funds in each parish to adopt such measures as they may deem proper. 1837, ult.

Finance. Acts anent the right application of the money granted by Her Majesty for defraying the public charges of the Church. 1712. vii.; 1719. viii.; 1723. viii.; 1761. v.

——— All applications for a share of the public money to be transmitted to the agent for the Church on or before the 1st of May yearly. 1763. vi.

——— A general contribution recommended in aid of the public funds of the Church. 1810. x.

——— An annual contribution of 5s. from each minister recommended. 1816. xi.; 1812, ult.

——— The Committee reported the various steps taken for the augmentation of the funds, and that money had been granted by the Treasury for payment of the debts of the Church. 1809. 8.

——— A collector to be appointed in each presbytery for collecting subscriptions. 1813, ult.; 1814. 9.

——— An abstract of the receipts and expenditure ordered to be published annually along with the Acts of Assembly; and a state of the processes, carried on at the expense of the Church, to be laid on the table on the first Monday of the Assembly. 1825. 9.

——— Ministers earnestly recommended to be zealous in raising the minimum contribution of 10s. in their respective parishes. 1835, ult.; 1847. 8; 1853. 4.

——— A full report given in, and ordered to be printed and transmitted to all the presbyteries of the Church 1856, ult.

——— A collection recommended in all churches and chapels

in aid of the funds for liquidating the debt which has been accumulated chiefly in connection with public measures recently before Parliament. 1854. 13.

Finance. Resolved that all accounts with which the Church is connected shall every year be brought to a balance on the 15th April—audited and reported to the Assembly; and that a general abstract of the whole shall be printed along with the Acts. 1840. 9.

——— A full report given as to the state of all the funds. 1841. *Appendix.*

——— The following may be quoted as examples of a few out of many instances in which aid was formerly given out of the public funds of the Church—viz.:

In a process against heritors to compel them to make a parish church a commodious place of public worship. 1801. 9.

In a process of augmentation. 1801. 9.

In a process for repairs on a manse, and rebuilding offices. 1802. 9.

In a process respecting the valuation of a parish. 1801. 9.

For obtaining, at the public expense, a decision in the civil courts on a preliminary point relative to the improvement of glebes. 1803. 4.

For carrying on, at the public expense, a case appearing to involve a general question not yet fully settled respecting the mode of declaring a manse free. 1815, ult.

Fire. A diet for prayer appointed on account of the sad and astonishing conflagration that fell out on Saturday, the 3d February 1700, in the Parliament Close. 1700. 5.

——— Several registers and papers belonging to the Church lost by the dreadful fire which happened in the Lawnmarket of Edinburgh on the 28th October 1701. 1703. xi.

Forbes. Remitted to a committee to consider a petition relative to the Forbes Mortification Fund. 1856. 4; 1858. 4.

Foreign Missions. A committee appointed to devise a specific plan for propagating the Gospel among the heathen abroad. 1824. 7.

——— Report of committee highly approved of. 1825, ult.

——— Dr Inglis submitted a scheme for the establishment of a missionary institution at Calcutta, which the Assembly

together until they have concerted and agreed upon a form of process for regulating the procedure of church judicatories for the future. 1704. xxv.

Form of Process. The form of process in the judicatories of the Church of Scotland with relation to scandals and censures, ratified and approved by the General Assembly. 1707. xi.

——— Committee appointed to revise the form of process. 1785. 8.

——— Sketch of a new form of process approved of by the Assembly, and transmitted as an overture to all the ministers of the Church. 1786. 6.

——— The overture of 1786 having been disapproved of by a majority of presbyteries, was dismissed. 1787. 8.

——— Committee appointed to consider certain proposed changes on the form of process, and their attention specially directed to the overture of 1786. 1814. 6.

——— Enacted that the Rules of the Form of Process, chap. vii., with respect to informations against ministers, be extended to probationers. 1745. ix.

Formula. Prescribed to be signed by such of the late conforming ministers as, having qualified themselves according to law, shall apply to be admitted into communion with the Church. 1694. xi.

——— To be signed by all such as shall pass trials in order to be licensed, or that shall be ordained ministers or admitted to parishes. 1711. x.

——— Presbyteries discharged from using any formula in licensing probationers, or admitting or ordaining ministers, but such as has been agreed upon by the General Assembly. 1717. x.

——— Ordained that all elders shall subscribe the Confession of Faith as the confession of their faith, and the Formula agreed upon in the Assembly held in the year 1694, Act xi. p. 6. 1700. xi.

——— An overture transmitted to presbyteries but not passed, proposing that all ruling elders and deacons should at their ordination subscribe the Formula prescribed by Act x. Assembly 1711. 1724. 14.

——— Declared to be competent for an elder who had not signed the Formula to purge the objection by signing it at the bar of the Assembly. 1769. 3; 1788. 3; 1754. 3; 1809. 3.

Formula. The conduct of a presbytery declared to be unjustifiable and deserving of censure, in proceeding to ordain a minister without requiring him to subscribe the Confession of Faith and Formula, as the law and practice of the Church require. 1790. 5.

——— A minister accused of unsound doctrine, declared his willingness to subscribe the Formula at the bar of the Assembly; and, having subscribed the same, the Assembly found that there was no call for further proceedings. 1807. 5.

Fort-William. The Commission instructed to take all proper measures for securing a settled salary for a minister in Fort-William, and meanwhile appoint the minister of Kilmallie to supply the garrison there as frequently as possible. 1726. 10.

France. The moderator authorised to answer a letter from certain Protestant ministers in Paris. 1836, ult.

——— The Assembly received a deputation from the Protestant Central Evangelical Society of France. 1849. 4; 1850. 9.

——— *See* REPORTS OF COMMITTEE FOR CORRESPONDING WITH FOREIGN CHURCHES.

Free Days. A presbytery having been cited to appear before the Commission, objection was taken to the competency on the ground that sufficient *induciæ* had not been given—only six free days intervening between the day of citation and the day of meeting. The Assembly repelled the objection. Com., Dec. 11, 1839.

——— *See* COMMISSIONS.

Freedom of Court. A minister allowed £5 out of the funds of the Church to enable him to carry on his defence in a process against him for an alleged freedom upon a person's character, when delivering his opinion as a judge in an ecclesiastical court. 1765. 9.

Freedom, Ministerial. Declared that due and regular ministerial freedom is left entire to all ministers, notwithstanding the decision of the Assembly in Act vii. Assembly 1733. 1735. ix.

Funds. The Commission instructed to do what they could for obtaining a certain fixed fund for defraying the public charges of the Church. 1707. 10.

Funds. Report concerning the debts of the Church. 1709. 10, 13.

——— A separate cash-book ordered to be kept. 1710. 14.

——— An Act anent the right application of the money granted by Her Majesty. 1712. vii.

——— An Act for sale of the Church's debenture notes in the fund of the equivalent. 1718. 15.

——— An Act for the right management of the Church's public money. 1719. viii.

——— Anent the powers of the agent in the management of the funds. 1741. 8.

——— The Assembly finds the Church's yearly income is £500 sterling. 1723. 8.

——— Committee appointed to devise means to relieve the Church from pecuniary embarrassments. 1792, ult.

——— Said committee instructed to apply to Government. 1793. 9.

——— *See* Finance.

G

Gaelic. 3000 Bibles, 1000 New Testaments, and 30,000 Catechisms in the Gaelic or Irish language, procured from London by contribution for distribution in the Highlands. The translation of the Psalms into Gaelic ordered to be expedited. 1690. xi.

——— All congregations and families who worship God in the Gaelic or Irish tongue recommended to use a paraphrase of the Psalms in Irish metre, with a translation of the Shorter Catechism appended, emitted by the Synod of Argyle. 1694. xx.

——— The Commission instructed to make application to the King and Parliament for some vacant stipends for the encouragement of students having the Irish language. 1700. 18.

——— Synods recommended to maintain bursars of theology having the Irish language. 1701. viii.

——— An Act for bestowing bursaries upon students having the Gaelic language. 1704. xiii.; 1724. 13.

——— Presbyteries discharged from settling in a lowland

parish any minister or probationer having the Gaelic language. All such settled in the lowlands to be transported on receiving a call from a Highland parish. 1708. xi.

Gaelic. Act anent probationers having the Gaelic language. 1709. v.

——— A Gaelic missionary appointed to minister to the Highlanders in and about Edinburgh who did not understand English, under the superintendence of the Presbytery of Edinburgh. 1710. 6; 1748, ult.

——— An Act concerning bursars and students having Irish. 1710. x.; 1711. 11; 1712. xii.; 1715. vii.

——— Presbyteries prohibited from planting in lowland congregations preachers having Gaelic, or transporting into the lowlands ministers planted in the Highlands, without the sanction of the Assembly. 1716. viii.

——— Reference to the Commission of an application from Mr David M'Colm, relating to his design of publishing an English and Irish Dictionary. 1735. 10.

——— A petition for Irish Bibles from the Presbytery of Kintyre. 1752, ult.

——— Referred to the Commission to consider the best method for having the inconveniences arising from the scarcity of students having the Irish language remedied. 1754, ult; 1756. 8; 1762, ult.

——— A presentee to the parish of Aberfoyle rejected as unqualified for that parish, from his ignorance of the Gaelic language. 1772. 9.

——— Collection ordered for translating the Bible into the Gaelic language. 1784. 9.

——— An overture anent students having the Gaelic language dismissed. 1787. 9.

——— Principals and professors of divinity to meet with the members of Assembly from presbyteries where the Gaelic language is spoken, to make up a list of Gaelic probationers, and send them to preach in Highland parishes. 1724. 13.

——— Ministers in Highland parishes to preach every Lord's day in English as well as Gaelic. 1756. vii.; 1829. 8; 1848. 5; 1831. 8.

——— Standing committee appointed to consider as to the means for procuring the best version of the Scriptures in

Gaelic. The use of every other version prohibited in churches, chapels, missions, and schools, except the editions published by the Society for Propagating Christian Knowledge. 1816. vi.

Gaelic. The quarto edition of the Bible published by the Society, and no other, authorised to be used in public worship. 1826. iv.

——— No Gaelic preacher to be settled in a lowland parish until he has been a year in the Highlands without getting a call. 1708. xi.; 1716. viii.

——— A presentee to the parish of Little Dunkeld rejected as unqualified from his want of Gaelic. 1825. 5.

——— Want of Gaelic held to be a relevant objection against the settlement of a presentee. 1831. 9; 1854. 2 and 10.

——— Reported to the Assembly that two hundred and twenty-eight ministers of the Church use the Gaelic language in conducting public worship. Report to Ass. 1842.

——— Anent preaching in Gaelic in the Old Church, Rothesay. Com., June 3, 1835.

——— An overture anent expediting the training of students and the licensing of probationers having the Gaelic language, referred to a committee. 1844. 3; 1845. 10 and 15.

——— The Ladies' Association for the support of Gaelic schools cordially welcomed by the Assembly. 1847. 7.

——— The committee authorised to bring before Government the importance of having the publication of editions of the Gaelic Scriptures placed under the same superintendence as editions of the English Bible. 1855. 14; 1859. 13; 1861. 14.

——— A committee appointed to take into consideration the alleged deficiencies of Gaelic preachers, and the practicability of devising a remedy for the same. 1858. 12.

——— Presbyteries enjoined to be careful, before inducting any presentee to a Gaelic charge, to satisfy themselves of his ability to afford religious instruction to the people in their vernacular tongue. 1860. 14.

——— The Assembly enjoin the continuance of a Gaelic service in the church of Tain. 1861. 14.

Gairloch. An Act erecting the Presbytery of Gairloch. 1724. v.

Galloway. The place of meeting of the Synod of Galloway

changed from Wigtown to Newton-Stewart—allowing the synod to adjourn occasionally to Kirkcudbright, Wigtown, Stranraer, or elsewhere. 1776. xi.

Garden. Dr George Garden, Aberdeen, deposed for being tainted with the dangerous and blasphemous opinions of M. Antonia Bourignion. 1701. xi.

General Assembly. *See* Assembly.

Geneva. An invitation from the company of pastors at Geneva to send a deputation to represent the Church of Scotland at the celebration of the third centenary of the Reformation, declined with sorrow, on account of the Neologian, Socinian, and infidel opinions prevalent among the Reformed Protestant Churches on the Continent. 1835. 3.

——— A letter from the Church at Geneva thereanent. Com., Aug. 12, 1835.

Gillespie. An Act deposing Mr Thomas Gillespie, minister at Carnock, for contumacy and disobedience. 1752. iv.

——— A petition from the parishioners of Carnock, praying the Assembly to remove the sentence of deposition from off Mr Thomas Gillespie, refused. 1753. 6 and 7; 1769, ult.; 1770. 9.

——— A petition from the congregation attached to the chapel occupied by the late Mr Gillespie, praying to be admitted into communion with the Church of Scotland, remitted to the presbytery. 1775. 9; 1776. 7; 1777. 5; 1778. 9.

——— The prayer of the petitioners granted. Regulations respecting the chapel of ease in Dunfermline. 1779. 8.

——— Recommendation anent buying Mr Patrick Gillespie's book on the Covenant. 1705. 12.

Gipps. An Act and declaration for vindication of the Church of Scotland from the calumny of Thomas Gipps, rector of Bury, in a sermon preached by him. 1698. v.

Glasgow. Regulations for a new Gaelic chapel in the city of Glasgow. 1798. 7.

——— The bicentenary of the General Assembly, which met in Glasgow in 1638, commemorated by special devotional exercises. Com., Nov. 21, 1838.

Glebes. Presbyteries enjoined to take an exact account of the extent of the stipend, glebe, grass, and other emoluments belonging to every minister within their bounds, and to record the same with accuracy in the presbytery books for the benefit of succeeding incumbents. 1762. viii.

Glebes. Synods enjoined to take care that presbyteries strictly obey the aforesaid Act. 1802. viii.

——— An overture anent the enclosing of glebes referred to the Commission to ripen the same. 1765. 5.

——— A special committee appointed to consider the overtures respecting the improvement of glebes. 1802. 9.

——— The procurator and agent instructed to select a proper case before the civil courts, that a decision might be obtained regarding the improvement of glebes. 1803. 4; 1805, ult.; 1809. 9.

——— A report anent the right of ministers to grass glebes, and a committee appointed to consider the subject. 1809. 7; 1813, ult.

——— Aid granted to enable a minister to prosecute his right to a grass glebe. 1810. 9.

——— Report concerning the right of sowing and reaping glebes in vacant parishes. The Assembly considering it a matter of civil right, declined to give any opinion. 1827, ult.

——— A petition from a minister, who had succeeded at law in establishing his right to work the coal on his glebe, craving a grant from the funds of the Church to assist in defraying the expense of the process, refused. 1809. 9.

——— A committee appointed to consider overtures anent feuing glebes. 1791. 7; 1847. 8.

——— The committee recommend the Assembly to endeavour to obtain a general legislative enactment on the subject of feuing glebes. 1791. 7; 1850. 8; 1854. 13.

——— The committee authorised to get such a measure carried through Parliament as soon as possible. 1862. 13.

——— Committee appointed to consider and report on the new Valuation Bill, as it affects manses and glebes. 1854. 8 and 13.

——— Found incompetent to appeal from a presbytery to a superior court against a sentence regarding a glebe, that being a matter of civil right. 1826. 7.

Glenelg. The Presbyteries of Gairloch, Abertarff, Skye, and Long Island, erected into the Synod of Glenelg. 1724. v.

Glenelg. Day of meeting of synod changed to the Wednesday preceding the opening of Assembly by one month. 1835. xiv.

——— Synod to meet at Broadford and Lochcarron alternately. 1811. vii.

——— Day of meeting changed to the third Wednesday of April. 1859. viii.

Glenorchy. The Assembly sanctioned an application to Parliament for an alteration of the rules or institutes of Lady Glenorchy's Church, Edinburgh, inconsistent with the formula of the Church of Scotland. 1837. 3.

Gorbals Church, Glasgow. Committee appointed to cooperate in recovering for the inhabitants of Gorbals the large and suitable building which was erected for their use, and the provision for the minister., 1858. 12.

Governors of Youth. Ministers to give in an account every half-year to the presbytery what schoolmasters, chaplains, governors, and pedagogues were in their respective parishes, that they might be called on to subscribe the Confession of Faith. 1700. x.

Graduates. An overture anent the admission of graduates of English universities to the divinity halls in the universities of Scotland transmitted to presbyteries. 1859. xi.

Grant, Parliamentary. A grant from the Treasury for payment of the debts of the Church. 1809. 8.

——— £20,000 granted by Parliament for the use of the Church of Scotland. 1822. 9.

——— A grant from Parliament for the augmentation of small livings reported to the Assembly, and the thanks of the House given to the Lord Advocate for his counsel and exertions thereanent. 1811. 9.

Greek. No student to be licensed as a preacher of the gospel until he has been examined by the presbytery, strictly and privately, on his knowledge of Greek. 1696. xxii.; 1782. viii.; 1849. xi.

——— An exercise and addition on some portion of the original text of the New Testament to be delivered by every student as part of his trials in the divinity hall. 1782. viii.; and also of his probationary trials. 1849. xi.

Greenock. Certain parishes disjoined from the Presbytery of

Paisley and Irvine, and erected into the Presbytery of Greenock. 1834. viii.

Greenock. New constitution granted for the Gaelic church, Greenock. 1855. 13.

Grievances. Act concerning the grievances of the Church from toleration, patronage, &c. 1715. ix.

——— Commissioners sent to London to petition for redress of the grievance of patronage, and for repeal of the Act of Queen Anne. 1736. vi.

——— The instructions annually given to the Commission to apply, if a favourable opportunity offered, for redress from the grievance of patronage, omitted for the first time. 1784. xii.

H

Hairdressers. A complaint against the barbers and hairdressers of Edinburgh for profanation of the Sabbath-day referred to a committee. 1795. 4 and 9.

Hanover. Ministers recommended in their public prayers expressly to mention the Princess Sophia, Electress and Duchess-Dowager of Hanover. 1711. iv.

Hebrew. No student to be licensed until he has satisfied the presbytery as to his proficiency in the Hebrew tongue. 1696. xxii.; 1782. viii.; 1849. xi.

——— Enacted that every student shall attend two sessions on the Hebrew class in one or other of the universities of Scotland. 1833. ix.; 1849. xi.

——— A critical exercise on some portion of the original text of the Old Testament to be delivered by every theological student in the course of his attendance on the divinity hall. 1836. x.

——— Proceedings connected with the appointment to the Hebrew Chair in the University of Edinburgh. Com., Nov. 17, 1847; 1850, ult.

——— An overture anent teaching Hebrew referred to the committee on the uniform examination of students. 1862. 13.

Hepburn. Sentence of deposition pronounced against Mr John Hepburn for divisive courses. 1705. vii.

Heresy. A minister deposed for holding and teaching doctrines, regarding the extent of the atonement and the necessity of assurance, inconsistent with the word of God and the Standards of the Church. 1831. 5; 1833. 6; 1841. 5.

——— A probationer deprived of his licence for heretical doctrines regarding the human nature of our Lord Jesus Christ. 1831. 6; 1833, ult.

——— A probationer deprived of his licence, he having voluntarily declared that he did not believe in the whole of the doctrines of the Confession of Faith. 1831. 8.

——— A minister deposed, he having, in a written paper, declared that he considered it sinful in him to have signed the Confession of Faith; and that, in preaching, he was resolved to be limited by no human authority. 1832. 6.

——— A minister ordered to lay before the synod a sermon preached by him as moderator, which it was alleged contained unsound doctrine. The Assembly, on a reference, found that the sermon was not chargeable with unsoundness of doctrine. 1841, ult.

Heritors. Enacted and ordained that in all time coming no minister shall make any composition with his heritors with respect to obtaining a decreet of modification and locality for his stipend, but at the sight, and with the advice and consent of, the presbytery of the bounds. 1759. vi.

——— Reference to the commission anent disaffected heritors forcing people to frequent meeting-houses. 1715. 12.

Highlands. Act anent erecting schools in every parish in the Highlands. 1694. xiv.

——— Petition to the King that vacant stipends should be applied for the support of ministers sent to supply vacant charges. 1695. xv.

——— Overtures for a more expedite planting the north approved. 1696. xii.; 1697. xvi.; 1696. xiv.; 1698. viii.; 1699. ix.; 1699. xi.; 1703. ix.; 1716. viii.

——— Overtures and regulations for promoting the knowledge of God in the Highlands. 1699. xvi.

——— Subscription ordered for erecting schools in the Highlands; and a return of parishes wanting schools. 1704. xiv.

——— An Act anent libraries in the Highlands. 1704. xvii.; 1705. xii.

Highlands. Students, natives of the Highlands, enjoined to apply themselves to the study of Gaelic, that they might qualify themselves for being sent to Highland parishes. 1709. v.

——— Application to the King for part of the rents of the forfeited estates to be applied towards the erection of new parishes in the Highlands. 1765. vi.

——— English schoolmasters to be appointed in all the Highland parishes. 1698. xvii.

——— A committee of ministers connected with the Highlands appointed to meet with a committee of the Society for Propagating Christian Knowledge, to consult about the most proper places for erecting charity schools in the Highlands. 1711. 11.

——— A minister sent by the Trustees of the Forfeited Estates to visit the Western Highlands and Islands to inquire concerning the natural productions, and the state of manufactures, agriculture, and commerce in those districts; instructed by the Assembly to inquire also into the state of religion, and the means of instruction there. 1764. 4; 1771, ult.; 1772. 8.

——— An Act anent the distribution of Bibles in the Highlands. 1690. xi.

——— Ministers and preachers sent to supply vacant churches to be punctually paid out of the funds of the Church. 1715. v.

Home Mission. The committees on church extension, aid to weak congregations, the employment of probationers, and the encouragement of young men to the office of the ministry, merged into a new committee, to be called the HOME MISSION COMMITTEE. 1842. xviii.

——— *See* ANNUAL REPORTS.

House-Tax. Intimated by the Moderator that the ministers of the Church of Scotland had been found liable to pay the house-tax. 1793, ult.

Hume. The writings of David Hume and Henry Home (Lord Kames), discussed in the Assembly, and an Act passed against infidelity and immorality. 1755. 4.

Hunter. A special minute entered on the record as a tribute to the memory of the Rev. Mr Hunter, missionary at Sealkote, who was murdered in the Indian mutiny. 1858. 13.

I

the alphabetical list was not carried into effect. 1699. vi.; 1700. xvi.

Index. Referred to the Commission anent printing, in a small volume, all the Acts of Assembly already printed, and an abridgment and alphabetical index thereof for the service of the Church. 1704. 15.

Indian Company. A petition from the African and Indian Company for ministers referred to the Commission. 1699. 16 and 17.

——— Ministers recommended to pray for those sent to remote places by said Company. 1699. 17.

——— A letter addressed to the ministers sent out as missionaries to the Company's territories. 1700. vi.

Indian Churches. Committee appointed to watch the progress of proceedings in Parliament for renewing the Charter of the East India Company, with a view to the appointment of chaplains in connection with the Church of Scotland. 1812. 4.

——— A constitution given to the Presbyterian Church in India, empowering them to send commissioners to the General Assembly. 1814.

——— The right of the commissioners to sit in the Assembly having been objected to, the Assembly, in respect of the constitution granted to the Church in India in 1814, of the subsequent practice, and all the circumstances of the case, repelled the objection and sustained the commission. 1821. 5.

——— Form of commission prepared for the Church in India. 1818. 3; 1845. 15.

——— The *first* and *second* ministers of the Church of Scotland in the several presidencies declared to be collegiate ministers, and co-ordinate in their stations and functions as members of their respective sessions. 1832. 7.

——— The new charter to the East India Company making it imperative that there should be a minister of the Church of Scotland settled at each of the presidencies, the Assembly appointed a committee to accommodate the constitution to the altered circumstances. 1834. 4.

——— The two clergymen at Calcutta, with the ordained missionaries and two elected elders, authorised to meet as the Presbytery of Calcutta, under the superintendence of the Presbytery of Edinburgh. 1834, ult.

Indian Churches. A similar authority given to the kirk-sessions of Madras and Bombay. 1837. 7; 1848. 6; 1854. 4 and 12.

——— Committee instructed to procure an increase of chaplains in connection with the Church of Scotland, corresponding to the proposed increase of Episcopalian chaplains. Com., Nov. 18, 1840; Com., March 3, 1841.

——— Petition to the Court of Directors anent the reduction in furloughs and retiring allowances. 1845. 15.

——— Petition to Parliament against the countenance given to idolatrous practices in India. 1838. 9.

——— Chaplains in India authorised to solemnise marriages in the ordinary exercise of ministerial duty. 1817. 9; 1818. 4; 1819, ult.

——— Committee appointed to consider the circumstances connected with the approaching expiry and probable renewal of the East India Company's Charter. 1851. 14; 1852. 10.

——— The Assembly authorise the Presbytery of Edinburgh to grant induction to Mr Walker as one of the chaplains of Madras, declaring, at the same time, that, under ordinary circumstances, they would strongly disapprove of opening up the Indian chaplaincies to preachers not regular licentiates of this Church, and yet more strongly of the appointment to the office of chaplain of those who have gone out to India as missionaries. Com., March 4, 1859; 1859, ult.

——— A collection ordered on the day of public fasting and humiliation appointed by the Queen, in connection with the unhappy mutiny in India, for the many families and individuals reduced by the mutiny to circumstances of indigence. 1858, ult.

——— *See* ANNUAL REPORTS.

India. Intimation given that the residue of the estate of Peter Bruce, Esq., was to be at the disposal of the Assembly for benevolent purposes. 1822. 9. The opinion of eminent English counsel being unfavourable to the claim of the Church, said claim was finally abandoned. 1823. 9; 1838. 4.

Indian Education. Resolutions relative to a despatch from the Directors of the East India Company to the Governor-

General of India on the subject of general education in India. 1855. 13; 1856. 6; 1857. 11.

India Mission. Committee appointed to devise and report a specific plan for the propagation of the Gospel in India. 1824. 7.

——— Standing committee for the Propagation of the Gospel in Foreign Parts appointed to meet on the first Tuesday of every month. 1835. viii.

——— *See* Annual Reports.

Induction. In Her Majesty's letter to the Assembly, it having been declared that the Church was justly entitled to expect the aid of Parliament in removing any doubts with respect to the right construction of statutes relating to the admission of ministers, the Assembly found it was most desirable that all such doubts should be removed with as little delay as possible. 1843. 7 and 9.

——— A bill to remove doubts respecting the admission of ministers to benefices in that part of the United Kingdom called Scotland, commonly called Lord Aberdeen's Bill, cordially approved of by the Commission, in the hope that it would fulfil the patriotic intention of the Government, by securing the peace and prosperity of the Church. Com., August 9, 1843.

——— An overture and interim Act on the regulations to be observed in the induction of ministers transmitted to presbyteries. 1843. xviii.; and after numerous alterations and amendments passed into a standing law of the Church. 1856. xii.

——— Resolved that if no specific objection is made, and no intention to object intimated on the day of moderating in the call, it shall not be competent to receive any objections at a subsequent meeting, but such as affect the life or doctrine of the presentee. 1844, ult.; 1846. 10. Com., May 28, 1844.

——— *See* Settlements.

Infants. An Act concerning the admission of infants to baptism, declaring that children of parents, one or both of whom profess the Christian religion, have a right to baptism. No other sponsors to be taken than the parents, unless they be absent, or dead, or unqualified. In the case of exposed infants or foundlings, the kirk-session to be sponsors. 1712. iv.

Infants. Recommendation to the Commission to consider what method should be taken in the case of exposed infants. 1746. 9.

Inferior Courts. An overture proposing to allow the members of inferior judicatories of the Church to sit, judge, and vote in the superior courts in cases of appeals, as in cases of reference again and again transmitted to presbyteries but never passed into a law. 1754. 9 ; 1773. 9.

——— Anent extracts from the records of inferior courts. *See* STANDING ORDERS. 1859. xii. 18, 19, &c.

Infidelity. An Act against infidelity. 1755. iv.

Informer. In the case of a process being raised at the instance of a party complaining, if the party cited be found innocent, the informer is to be censured either for his calumny or imprudence, as the judicatory shall find cause. 1707. xi. ; chap. ii. 8.

Infirmary. Recommendation for a voluntary contribution to be applied towards the erecting of an infirmary or hospital, for diseased poor at Edinburgh. 1728. vi. ; 1731. vii.

——— A general collection ordered throughout the Church in aid of the Edinburgh Infirmary. 1804. 7.

Innovations. An Act against innovations in the worship of God. 1707. xv.

——— An Act anent the method of passing Acts of Assembly of general concern to the Church, and for preventing innovations, commonly called the BARRIER Act. 1697. ix.

——— Members of the Church solemnly warned against the rash adoption of changes in the order and form of public worship ; and presbyteries enjoined, when such innovations are reported to them, to inquire into the extent of and reasons assigned for such innovations. 1858, ult.

——— Declared to be an innovation upon and contrary to the laws and usage of the Church in the celebration of public worship, for the minister to read the prayers from a book, either in manuscript or printed, and the minister enjoined to conform in offering up prayer to the ordinary practice of the Church. 1859. 6 and 7.

Insanity. A committee appointed to advise with a presbytery for having the spiritual interests of a parish provided for during the insanity of the minister. Com., June 1, 1858.

Insufficiency. A minister deposed for insufficiency. 1704. 12; 1707, ult.

Intemperance. A committee appointed to make inquiries, and use the most effectual means for correcting the evil of intemperance. 1848. 12; which committee gave in a very full report. 1849. 9.

Intemperate Language. A minister who had used intemperate language in a presbytery, having, at the bar of the Assembly, expressed his sincere sorrow and deep contrition, was solemnly admonished by the moderator to guard against any such impropriety in future. 1823, ult.

—— A minister having brought an offensive charge against a co-presbyter, the Assembly found the charge utterly unwarrantable, most uncharitable in spirit, and offensive in language. 1854. 9.

Intemperate. In the case of a minister charged with using intemperate language, the Assembly found that the language used by him was most discreditable and highly censurable, and appointed him to be rebuked by the moderator of the presbytery, admonished of the sinfulness of his conduct, and suspended from his judicial functions till the meeting of next General Assembly. 1849. 12.

Interim Acts. Enacted and ordained that no overture shall be converted into an interim act, which involves an essential alteration of the existing law or practice of the Church, it being of great importance to maintain the Barrier Act in its letter and spirit. 1848. xiv.

Intrusion. An Act anent intrusion upon kirks in an illegal and unwarrantable manner. 1694. xvi.

—— Presbyteries enjoined to send in an account of such ministers or preachers as intrude into parishes, that they may be removed according to law. 1701. xviii.

—— Declared that it is and has been, since the Reformation, the principle of this Church, that no minister shall be intruded into any parish contrary to the will of the congregation. Presbyteries enjoined to be at pains to avoid encouraging unreasonable exceptions in people against a worthy person that may be proposed to be their minister. 1736. xiv.

Intrusion. Declaration of 1736. xiv. renewed, and presbyteries instructed to reject a presentee, if the major part of the male heads of families in full communion with the Church disapproved of his settlement. 1834. xii.

——— Act xii., Ass. 1834, commonly called the Veto Act, repealed, as infringing on civil and patrimonial rights, and presbyteries instructed to proceed in the settlement of ministers according to the practice which prevailed previous to the passing of that act. 1843. ix.

Inverness. Recommendation in favour of Inverness, with a reference to the Commission anent settling a third minister in that town. 1704. 12.

——— A committee named to arrange regarding a stipend for a third minister at Inverness. 1705. 6.

——— The Presbytery of Inverness summoned to the bar of the Assembly to account for their proceedings in matters complained of relative to the settlement of a parish. 1823, ult. The presbytery, having appeared, were severely censured for disobeying a previous order of the Assembly, and for acting in an unwarrantable and unconstitutional manner. 1824. 6.

——— Found to be *ultra vires* of the church courts to divide the parish of Inverness in the manner proposed, and declared that the United Parish of Inverness is still but one parish *quoad omnia*, and the ministers and elders of the English, Gaelic, and West Churches but one undivided session; and, as such, entitled to send only one elder to the presbytery and synod of the bounds. 1844. 16.

Ireland. Petition to Parliament, that under the system of national education introduced into Ireland, the fullest liberty might be secured to every one of reading regularly in a daily Bible class the sacred Scriptures in the authorised version, without note or comment. 1832. 8.

——— Petition to Parliament against any further countenance being given to said system. 1833. 6.

——— Petition to Parliament against the bill for endowing the College of Maynooth. 1845. 5.

Irish Language. *See* GAELIC.

Irregularities. Presbyteries and synods enjoined to advert to irregularities committed by vagrant unfixed ministers. 1696. xxiii.

Irregularities. Any person receiving licence or ordination from any of the late prelates, declared to be incapable of ministerial communion for the space of three years *simpliciter*, and after that until the presbytery are satisfied of his repentance. 1701. xiv.

Irvine. Certain parishes disjoined from the Presbytery of Irvine, and united with others from the Presbytery of Paisley to form the Presbytery of Greenock. 1834. viii.

Islands. Report of a committee appointed to inquire into the spiritual interests of those islands in which Gaelic is not the vernacular tongue. 1846. 14 ; 1847. 9.

Islay. Certain parishes disjoined from the Presbytery of Kintyre, and formed into the Presbytery of Islay. 1836. vi.

J

Jacobites. A representation of grievances from the late insults of Jacobites' intrusion of kirks and parishes in Angus and Mearns, and from disaffected schoolmasters and chaplains. 1716. 4.

Jamison. Ministers recommended to buy a book entitled 'Cyprianus Isotimus,' by Mr William Jamison, Professor of History in the College of Glasgow. 1705, ult.

Jews. Committee appointed to collect information respecting the Jews, their number, condition, and character—whether there are any openings for a mission to their nation, and where these are most promising, &c. 1838. viii.

——— Prayer and thanksgiving offered up for the safe return of a deputation which had been sent to Palestine to visit and inquire after the scattered Jews. Com., Nov. 20, 1839.

——— Memorial to Government petitioning them to use their influence to prevent the persecution of the Jews at Damascus. 1840. 2.

——— Committee instructed to take steps for preparing and sending out missionaries to the most promising stations. The Jewish mission instituted as the fifth scheme of the Church, and a general collection ordered on its behalf. 1840. ix.

——— Committee found entitled to dispense with the services of an agent if they deemed it expedient. Com., May 29, 1844.

Jews. Authority granted to examine, and, if found qualified, to ordain as missionaries to the Jews, agents who had not passed through the curriculum prescribed by the laws of the Church. 1846. 2.

——— Petition to Parliament against the bill for admitting to seats in the legislature persons of the Jewish persuasion. 1848. 4.

——— Report anent missions to Cochin-China, Paris, Egypt, and Jerusalem. 1855. 4.

——— *See* ANNUAL REPORTS.

Jottings. Extracts from the jottings from which the minutes were made up allowed to a party to enable him to substantiate his case. 1812. 9.

——— Extracts from the jottings refused to a party. 1823. 4.

——— Jottings held not to be the record of presbytery, but the extended minute, after being engrossed, revised, and signed by the moderator and clerk. 1834. 4; 1839. 3.

Judges. Anent the right of members of the Commission to sit as judges in cases brought up by complaint from the Commission to the Assembly. 1724. 7; 1737. 8.

——— An overture proposing to allow members of inferior courts to sit, judge, and vote in the superior courts in cases of appeals, as in cases of reference, transmitted to presbyteries, but never passed. 1741. 8; 1754. 9; 1771. 6.

Judicatories. Provincial synods and presbyteries enjoined to be careful in revising of the registers of the judicatories under their immediate inspection, and when they find nothing to challenge, to attest them according to a prescribed form. 1700. ix.

——— An Act for preserving the subordination of the judicatories of the Church and good order therein. 1733. v.

——— Inferior judicatories discharged from exercising authority beyond their respective bounds. 1707. xi., chap. i. 6.

——— Overtures (the larger) anent the discipline and method of procedure in ecclesiastical judicatories transmitted to presbyteries. 1697. v.; 1707. xvii., &c., &c.

——— Presbyteries enjoined to send up their remarks on the larger overtures transmitted in 1710 (1718. x.) Said overtures referred to Commission (1719. 10); but not having received the approval of a majority of presbyteries, allowed to drop. 1721. v.

Judicatories. Standing orders for regulating the form of procedure in the General Assembly shall, in so far as they apply, be binding on and observed by all inferior judicatories. 1850. xiv. 43.

Judicial. A minister having manifested an *animus* against a student on trials before his presbytery for licence, declared by the Assembly unqualified to sit as a judge in any question relative to said trials, and no appeal taken by him to be received unless supported by two other members of presbytery. 1805. 8.

——— The right of a minister to exercise judicial functions in a particular case having been objected to, on the ground that he had taken an active part to the prejudice of the defender, the Assembly, considering that the circumstances did not clearly appear from the record, waived consideration of the objection. 1829. 6; 1830. 6.

——— Ministers suspended from their judicial functions for holding ministerial communion with the deposed ministers of Strathbogie. 1842. 17.

——— A minister accused of having used intemperate language, and of having brought groundless charges against certain of his co-presbyters, suspended from his judicial functions until the meeting of next Assembly. 1849. 12.

Jurisdiction. Declared that the spiritual jurisdiction of this Church as a Church of Christ extends over all her members in whatever part of the world they may reside, and that it is competent for the Church to call to an account of their conduct every individual who has received licence or ordination from her, and to insist on the fulfilment of the obligations to which they then became bound. 1832, ult; 1833, ult.

——— Declared that, while the Assembly does not review the sentences of colonial church courts recognised by the Church of Scotland, with reference to ministers who have been licensed or ordained by this Church, while they hold charges in branches thereof in the colonies, and are consequently under the jurisdiction of the colonial church courts, yet when the connection of such ministers with such colonial courts has been regularly brought to an end, said ministers revert under the cognisance and jurisdiction of the courts of this Church. 1841. 3; Com., May 30, 1843: Com., June 4, 1840.

Jurisdiction. Resolution and declaration anent the independent jurisdiction of the Church of Scotland. 1838. xiv.

Jus Devolutum. Regulations anent the planting of vacant churches, especially *tanquam jure devoluto*, transmitted to presbyteries as an overture, but not passed. 1711. 10; 1721. v.

——— Another overture on the same subject transmitted to presbyteries and passed (1732. viii.); but repealed two years afterwards, as having been passed in violation of the Barrier Act. 1734. v.

——— Another overture on the same subject transmitted, but not passed. 1766, ult; 1769, ult.

——— A presbytery ordered to proceed towards the settlement of a crown presentee by a certain day, unless they had before then raised a summons of declarator of their right to present *tanquam jure devoluto*. 1800, ult.

——— The judgment of a presbytery nominating a probationer to a vacant charge, *tanquam jure devoluto*, reversed —an interesting and important debate. 1837. 3; 1847. 8.

——— The right of presenting to a parish having fallen to a presbytery, they resolved to leave the choice to the male inhabitants in full communion with the Church, the Assembly, on a complaint, remitted the matter to the presbytery, with instructions to issue a presentation, and proceed according to the rules of the Church. 1843. 9.

K

Kailzie. Referred to the Commission to consider a petition praying for re-erecting the church of Kailzie. 1695. 16.

Kaimes. An overture regarding the writings of Henry Home, Lord Kaimes, and David Hume, led to the passing of the Act against Infidelity and Immorality. 1755. iv.

Keys. Unanimously declared that it is the ecclesiastical right of the ministers of parishes to have free entrance to their churches, for the purpose of Divine worship and religious instruction, and that, during vacancies or suspensions, this right is vested in the presbytery of the bounds. 1828. 8.

Kilda, St. Pious persons to be sent to St Kilda to instruct the natives in the grounds of the Christian religion and the Shorter Catechism. 1704. 12.

——— The catechist in St Kilda allowed 400 merks out of the Church's funds. 1706. 12.

——— A minister ordained to St Kilda, and a committee appointed to go and endeavour to suppress the pagan and superstitious customs observed there. 1708. 11.

——— A deputation sent to St Kilda to assist the minister in dispensing the sacrament of the Lord's Supper. 1718. 7.

Kintyre. Disjunction of certain parishes from the Presbytery of Kintyre, and their erection into the Presbytery of Islay and Jura. 1836. vi.

Kirkcudbright. The parishes of Dalry and Carsphairn re-united to the Presbytery of Kirkcudbright. 1703. xiii.

Kirks. A committee appointed for considering what concerns the building and repairing of kirks and manses. 1762. 4.

——— Declared to be competent for synods to enjoin presbyteries to do their duty with respect to visitation of kirks according to law. 1762. 9.

Kirk-Sessions recommended to supply themselves with copies of all Acts of Parliament that concern the Church. 1695. 6.

——— Enacted and appointed that every minister and kirk-session have a copy of all the printed Acts of the General Assembly, and that inquiry be made into this at presbyterial and synodical censures. 1700. xvi.; 1772. vii.

——— Concerning processes which begin in kirk-sessions, but are not to be brought to a final determination therein—such as scandals of adultery, trilapse, &c. 1707. xi. chap. vi. 1.

——— The erecting of a new or separate session for the High Church of Paisley prohibited till that part of the town should be disjoined and formed into a separate parish. 1758. 6.

——— The decreet of erection vesting the right of choosing the session-clerk of the town and parish of Paisley in the magistrates, the session were enjoined to admit the nominee of the magistrates accordingly. 1761. 6.

Kirk-Sessions. The Presbytery of Glasgow authorised to appoint a committee for nominating proper persons to be members of session for the new erected church of Glasgow called the Wynd Church. 1766. 9.

——— Overtures concerning kirk-sessions and presbyteries transmitted to presbyteries for their consideration, but not passed. 1720. 11; 1721. v.

——— The assistance of a law-agent unanimously refused to a party before a kirk-session in a case in which she was pursuer. 1827. 9.

——— A presbytery having, from an examination of a session record, found that there had evidently been a culpable neglect of duty on the part of the clerk to said session, without calling him to account for his neglect, the Assembly remitted the case to the presbytery, with instructions to them to give the session-clerk a full opportunity of being heard in his own defence. 1847. 10.

——— The clerk of a kirk-session having been dismissed by the session, appealed to the presbytery, who declined to interfere, on the ground that he had not been elected *ad vitam aut culpam*. The Assembly, on appeal, found that the matter resolved itself into a question of civil right, which could only be competently tried before the civil courts, and that, therefore, it was not competent for the presbytery to pronounce any sentence on the merits of the case. 1819. 9.

——— Persons filling certain offices declared amenable to the kirk-session in the discharge of their duties. 1823. 5.

Konigsberg. A collection ordered in aid of the funds for building a church for those of the reformed religion at Konigsberg. 1698. 12.

L

Langholm. Certain parishes disjoined from the presbyteries of Middlebie, Lochmaben, and Jedburgh, and formed into the new presbyteries of Annan and Langholm. 1743. v.

Language. A minister rebuked for unsuitable expressions uttered by him in the Assembly. 1711. 8.

——— A probationer deprived of his licence, and said licence declared void and null because of his insolent behaviour before the General Assembly. 1713. 8.

——— In the case of a minister who had been found guilty by his presbytery of great imprudence in throwing out a story affecting the character of a brother, the Assembly dismissed the appeal, and recommended the brethren of the said presbytery to bury their differences in oblivion, and to live in brotherly love and friendship. 1745. 6.

——— A minister rebuked and admonished from the chair for emitting unfounded and intemperate expressions in the Assembly affecting the character of a brother. 1748. 9.

——— A presbytery rebuked at the bar of the Assembly for censurable expressions in conducting a case, and the offensive passages expunged from the record by the clerk of Assembly. 1794. 7.

——— *See* INTEMPERATE.

Larbert. A sentence of the Synod of Perth and Stirling affirmed relative to the minister of Larbert and Dunipace officiating in the churches of said parishes. 1802. 5.

Larger Overtures concerning the discipline and method of proceeding in the ecclesiastical judicatories of the Church of Scotland transmitted to presbyteries for their consideration (1698. ix.), printed with the Acts in 1705, and frequently retransmitted down to 1718, when they seem to have been allowed to drop. 1718. x.

Latin. Enacted that no student shall be admitted into any of the divinity halls unless he shall produce to the professor of divinity, and to the presbytery within whose bounds he resides, a certificate of having attended the Latin class in some university for at least one session, and made satisfactory proficiency as a Latin scholar. 1843. xiv.; 1849. xi.

——— Ordained that, before agreeing to the proposal to take a student on trials for licence, the presbytery shall examine him strictly and privately on his knowledge of the Latin language. 1813. viii.; 1849. xi.

Law-Agent. The assistance of a law-agent refused to a party in a case before a kirk-session. 1827. 9.

Lawyers. The thanks of the Assembly given to several lawyers, members of the House, who, in order to save the expenses of the Church, had signified their readiness to appear, gratis, in causes wherein the Church was concerned. 1752. 9; 1764. 9.

——— Lawyers, members of Assembly, prohibited from acting as procurators, counsel, or agents in any causes before the House—the Assembly considering that they have a title to the advice and assistance of all the members as judges in every cause brought before them. 1751. iv.; 1783. viii.

Lay Association. The association of laymen for supporting the several schemes of the Church, and promoting education and religion at home and abroad, recommended to the members and friends of the Church. Com., Aug. 9, 1843.

——— The thanks of the Assembly given to the convener and committee of the Lay Association for the valuable services rendered by them to the Church. 1844. 16.

Lay Preaching. The practice of lay preaching highly disapproved of, and presbyteries enjoined to exercise all due care and vigilance to prevent its occurrence. 1848, ult.

——— All ministers of the Church discharged and prohibited from giving countenance or permission to any persons to engage in the public ministry of the Word, except to those who have been regularly ordained or licensed to preach the Gospel. 1854. xii.

Leadhills. The Earl of Hopetoun's pious design of maintaining a catechist or preacher at Leadhills cordially approved of. 1738. 9.

Learning. The Commission recommended to think upon means to promote and encourage learning, and how young men may be enabled to follow such studies as may be useful for defence of the doctrine, worship, discipline, and government of this Church. 1706. 12; 1707. vi.

Lecturing. Ministers recommended, in their exercise of lecturing, to read and open up to the people some large and considerable portion of the Word of God. 1694. ix.

——— Presbyteries and synods enjoined to see that Act ix. Ass. 1694 was observed within their respective bounds. 1704. v.; 1706. x.

Leechman. An Act concerning Mr William Leechman, professor of divinity in the College of Glasgow, relative to certain charges brought against him for a sermon preached and published by him. 1744. ix.

Lerwick. The presbyteries of Lerwick and Burravoe erected and appointed to form a synod to be called the Synod of Shetland. 1830. viii.

Leslie. A reference respecting the election of Mr John Leslie to be professor of mathematics in the University of Edinburgh, "after long reasoning," dismissed. 1805. 7.

Lethendie. A reference concerning the proposed annexation of the parishes of Lethendie and Kinloch referred to the Commission. 1758, ult.

Letter. An original letter by King James VI. to the clerk of Assembly, ordering him to deliver up the Registers of the Church to the Earl of Arran, then chancellor, dated the 2d of November 1584, produced and recorded. 1737. 8.

——— A letter from the Assembly to four ministers sent to the African and Indian Company's colony in Caledonia in America, "or wherever they are." 1700. vi.

——— A letter to the King congratulatory on the suppression of the rebellion. 1716. vi.

——— A letter or address to His Majesty from the commissioners sent to London to endeavour the redress of the grievance of patronage, and repeal of the Act *anno decimo Annæ* reimposing the same. 1736. vi.

Leven. An address recorded in the minutes to the Right Hon. the Earl of Leven and Melville on his resignation of the office of Lord High Commissioner, the duties of which exalted station his Lordship had discharged during the long period of nineteen consecutive assemblies in a manner that had commanded the respect and veneration of the Assembly. 1802. 8.

Lewis. An Act disjoining the Presbytery of Longisland, and erecting the same into the two presbyteries of Uist and Lewis. 1742. 4.

Libel. A copy of the libel, with a list of witnesses, ordered to be served on the party accused, either personally or at his dwelling-house, at least ten free days before the day of compearance. 1707. xi., cap. vii. 5.

——— Referred to the Commission to cognosce and finally

determine, in an appeal from a sentence ordaining a minister to prosecute before the kirk-session of another parish an accusation by him against an elder, member of said session. 1747, ult.

Libel. A minister ordered to be served with a libel for holding in tack great and extensive possessions in his parish, and for sundry acts of alleged oppression of the tenants of the said possessions, as also for his prevarications and other miscarriages. 1748, ult.

——— A libel against a minister dismissed, in respect that it did not appear, from the precognition taken by the presbytery, there was any evidence of the facts charged against him, the same containing nothing but hearsays. 1755. 9.

——— In a charge against a minister, the Assembly found that there was no necessity for giving him a libel, in respect that there was no private party offering to insist in a prosecution against him, and also because his conduct had been imprudent and irregular rather than criminal. 1765. 6.

——— A libel against a minister dismissed as *ex facie* irrelevant and improper, and the whole proceedings declared to be null and void. 1766. 9.

——— A committee appointed to consider an overture anent the method of carrying on processes against ministers when private parties do not come forward to libel them. 1795. 8.

——— Declared that when any criminal act is charged in a libel, it is necessary to mention the time within which such criminal act is said to have been committed, and that such time shall in no case exceed the period of one year. 1799, ult.

——— A charge in a libel respecting an instance of intoxication said to have happened about ten years previously, found irrelevant. 1798, ult.

——— Enacted that in all cases originating with presbyteries as prosecutors, except in those which involve error in doctrine, presbyteries shall, before serving the libel, lay it before the procurator for revision, and after the relevancy has been found, shall proceed, notwithstanding all appeals, to prepare the case for final judgment. 1851. ix.

——— The party accused bound to lodge defences, along with a list of witnesses, within twenty days after the libel has been served upon him, or otherwise shall be held to have no defence excepting a simple denial of the libel. 1850. xii.

Libel. A presbytery ordered to admit a proof only of such facts and circumstances tending to support a libel as fall within five years from the date thereof. 1800. 9.

——— A libel dismissed as laid, leaving it to the libellers to serve the accused with a new libel if they saw cause. 1805. 8.

——— Found that a presbytery did wrong in allowing libellers to withdraw an original libel and present a new one, and remitted to the presbytery to take probation on the original libel as formerly found relevant. 1805, ult.

——— A presbytery allowed to withdraw a libel served by them against a minister, that the parishioners might libel him in their own name. 1812. 8.

——— A presbytery having permitted the libellers to withdraw a libel and to serve the party accused with a new one, the Assembly found that the presbytery must discharge the former libel before taking any further proceedings in the case. Com., June 1, 1836.

——— A charge in a libel found to be too vague as laid, but the libellers allowed to amend their libel by giving in a particular condescendence of the special offences charged. 1806. 5.

——— In a similar case the libellers were permitted either to amend the libel, or to serve the party accused with a new one as they might be advised. Com., Aug. 12, 1835.

——— The defender in a cause being prevented, as was alleged, by sickness from appearing personally before the presbytery, the presbytery referred to the Assembly for advice as to whether they might proceed with the proof in the absence of the defender. The Commission found that the absence of the defender personally was no obstacle to the presbytery going on with the cause, and instructed them to proceed accordingly. Com., June 2, 1842.

——— In a case of libel the defender did not appear personally on the day fixed for considering the relevancy, but his agent sent in a letter craving a month's delay. The presbytery refused the petition and found the libel relevant, whereupon the defender brought the matter before the Assembly by petition, on the ground that the conduct of the presbytery in pronouncing judgment on the relevancy in his absence was precipitate and unwarrantable. The Assembly unanimously dismissed the petition, and affirmed the judgment of the presbytery. 1845. 13.

Libel. A minister under libel having repeatedly failed to obtemper peremptory citations, the presbytery found him guilty of contumacy, and resolved that he should be deposed. The Assembly, on appeal, recalled the resolution to depose, and instructed the presbytery to proceed with probation of the libel. 1850. 8.

——— A presbytery having proceeded against a party by libel, the Assembly dismissed the libel as irrelevant, and ordered the libel and all the proceedings in the case to be expunged from the record. 1806. 9.

——— A libel not having been duly signed, the Assembly found it relevant, but ordered it to be signed by the moderator and clerk before any proof was led. 1812. 5.

——— It having been objected that there was no attestation of the date and place of signing a libel, and that there was no warrant by the presbytery to cite the defender, the Assembly repelled the objection. Com., May 29, 1844.

——— A committee appointed to consider anent the performance of duty by ministers under libel, having laid on the table the draft of a bill introduced into the House of Lords by Lord Belhaven to give legal effect to the recommendations of the committee, the thanks of the Assembly were given to Lord Belhaven, and the committee was instructed to give him every assistance. 1862. 14.

——— *See* STANDING ORDERS and FORM OF PROCESS.

——— A presbytery enjoined not to allow one of their members to sit with them as a judge in any question relative to a particular case, nor to permit any charge or appeal at the instance of said member to stop their procedure. 1805. 8.

——— It was objected that the copies of the libel and lists of witnesses served on the defender did not bear that the originals had been dated and subscribed by the moderator, but only by the clerk and officers ; and that, if the originals had been so dated and subscribed, the service copies were, in that important particular, disconform to the originals ; and that, in either view, the service was bad. The Assembly repelled the objection and dismissed the appeal. Com., June 3, 1840.

Libel. Objected that the warrant of citation, and citation following thereon, did not allow ten free days to lodge answers before the day of compearance, and a second ten free days between the lodging of the answers and the day of compearance. The Commission repelled the objection, and instructed the presbytery to proceed with the case until it was ripe for final judgment. Com., June 3, 1840.

——— The Assembly dismissed a libel, in respect it did not appear that list of witnesses had been regularly served on the defender, and remitted to the presbytery to proceed *de novo* if they should see cause. 1816. 8.

——— Found that a presbytery may refuse to receive a libel by the parishioners against a minister, if, after inquiry, they are satisfied that there are no adequate grounds for it. 1832. 5.

——— Declared that a libel against a schoolmaster may be insisted in at the instance either of the heritors, of the minister and elders, or of the presbytery of the bounds. 1812. 9.

——— A presbytery found to have acted prematurely, unconstitutionally, and unjustly, in suspending a probationer, citing parties, and taking evidence, without having previously served him with a libel, and the evidence ordered to be expunged from the minutes. 1814. 9.

——— A minister under libel found to have the same right to dispense the ordinances of religion in his parish during the dependance of the process against him as before. 1812. 8.

——— In the case of a minister under libel, the Assembly instructed the presbytery to proceed, and authorised them, if they saw cause, to make provision for the dispensation of religious ordinances in the parish for those members of the Church who were unwilling to attend the ministry of the defender. 1842, ult.

——— A presbytery having craved power to suspend a minister, pending a process of libel against him, the Assembly found the libel relevant, and remitted the case to the presbytery to proceed with the same until the case was ripe for judgment, disregarding all appeals. 1847. 9.

Libel. An overture, to the effect that in all cases of libel against a clergyman on charges of heresy or immorality, inferring deposition or suspension, it shall not be competent for the party libelled to exercise the functions of his office from the date of the service of the libel till the decision of the case upon the merits. 1842. xxv.

——— This overture was not re-transmitted; but a similar overture was remitted to the committee on the Form of Process. 1846. 14.

——— In a process by libel, the presbytery, before considering the relevancy, agreed to take evidence, to be sealed up, and kept *in retentis*, the witnesses being about to sail for India. The Assembly dismissed the appeal, and affirmed the sentence of the presbytery. 1848. 5.

——— A presbytery having been petitioned to inquire into certain circumstances affecting the character of a minister, and as two individuals cognisant of these circumstances were about to leave the country, they were further petitioned to proceed immediately to take the evidence of these parties, to seal it up and keep it *in retentis*, to be made available, if necessary, in the future proceedings of the case. The Assembly found that the presbytery had acted irregularly in taking extrajudicial evidence in absence of any charge having been made, and before any libel had been served. 1834. 5.

——— A presbytery having resolved to libel a minister, he appealed to the synod, who sustained the appeal, and remitted the case to the presbytery, with instructions to state explicitly to the defender the charges they had to prefer against him, and to exhibit the documents on which these charges were founded. The Assembly reversed the sentence of the synod, and remitted to the presbytery, with instructions to proceed to consider the relevancy. 1845. 13.

——— In a process of libel for heresy, the defender requested the presbytery to deal with him in writing. The presbytery declined, and resolved to deal with him orally. Against this decision he appealed, on the ground that it was impossible that loose conversational interviews could enable him to explain and reconcile detached passages in a number of different published works. The Assembly repelled the objection, and dismissed the appeal. 1841. 3.

Libel. It having been reported that the military had been withdrawn from the preaching of a minister, and further, that he had preached in a Chartist place of worship, the Commission suspended him from the exercise of his ministerial and pastoral functions until the next General Assembly, and instructed the presbytery to serve him with a libel. Com., June 1, 1842.

——— A libel having been instituted against a minister by the patron, who was also a resident heritor, objection was taken to the competency, on the grounds that the heritor was not in communion with the Church of Scotland, and that, as patron, he had a pecuniary interest in ejecting the minister. The Assembly repelled both objections, and found that it was competent for the patron to institute the libel. 1845. 8.

——— A presbytery having allowed reprobatory proof to be taken on the part of the prosecution after the exculpatory proof, but, *quoad ultra*, holding the proof on either side to be closed, this sentence was appealed against, on the ground that it was contrary to justice to allow a prosecutor in a criminal case to lead proof after the accused party had brought evidence against that on which the prosecution proceeded. The Assembly sustained the appeal, to the effect of expunging all the evidence led after the defender's witnesses had been examined. 1853. 5.

——— An appeal was taken, on the ground that the place of the presbytery meeting was not set forth in either the warrant or the citation; and that it was not stated with whom the defences were to be lodged—the warrant and citation being in these words, "to cite him to appear personally before the said presbytery at their next meeting, which is appointed to take place at St Andrews, on Friday the third day of September next, in the hour of cause, at 11 o'clock forenoon." The Assembly dismissed the appeal. 1853. 5.

——— A presbytery having rejected a proposal to examine a minister and his wife in a case affecting their characters, an appeal was taken to the Assembly, who dismissed the appeal, and remitted to the presbytery, with instructions to sist all further procedure and dismiss the cause, unless a libel was laid before them before a specified time. Com., May 30, 1837.

Libel. It having been stated by a member of Assembly that a minister had attempted to force his way into the House in a state of intoxication, the Assembly appointed a committee to inquire into the circumstances, and the minister, being present, was called to the bar, and cited, *apud acta*, to appear at a subsequent diet: at which diet, the committee having reported that, having taken a precognition, they were unanimously of opinion that there was ground for proceeding against the said minister, the Assembly transmitted the precognition to the presbytery to which the minister belonged, with instructions to serve him with a libel, and to apply to the Presbytery of Edinburgh to examine such witnesses as were resident within their bounds, and to go on according to the laws of the Church. 1838, ult.

——— The Commission, on appeal, found the libel proven, and deposed the said minister from the office of the Holy Ministry, which sentence was affirmed by the General Assembly. 1839, ult.

——— A verdict of "NOT PROVEN," by the forms of the Church courts, said to be equivalent to a verdict of "NOT GUILTY" in the civil court. 1839. 4.

——— "Habitual drunkenness for and during the space of fifteen years or a portion thereof," held to be not a relevant charge in a libel. 1835. 5.

——— "Secular employments, managing and superintending a farm and fruit-garden, so as to occupy an undue portion of time, to the neglect of the duties of the Holy Ministry, and persisting in a neglect of duty, with a view to disperse the congregation," held to be relevant charges in a libel; and being found proven, the minister was deposed. Com., June 1, 1836. 1837. 9.

——— Frequent neglect of pulpit and parochial duties, and the discharge of them in an unsuitable and irreverent manner, found relevant charges in a libel. 1847. 9.

——— "To exhibit a purpose" of doing an improper action held not to be sufficiently specific as a charge in a libel. Com., May 30, 1837.

Libel. Poaching, Sabbath profanation, and falsehood, found relevant charges in a libel. 1851. 5.

——— Declared to be essential to the wellbeing and purity of the Church that a fund should be raised for defraying the expenses incurred in the prosecution of libels. Kirk-sessions earnestly recommended to contribute for that purpose. 1849. 12.

——— An overture on the expenses of prosecution in cases of libel referred to a committee, with instructions to prepare a remedial scheme for removing or mitigating the evils complained of, and to consider how funds may be raised to meet the expenses that now fall upon presbyteries when necessitated to carry on prosecutions. 1854. 4 and 12.

——— An overture transmitted to presbyteries for several years, but not adopted, proposing that all prosecutions of ministers (except for heresy) should run in the name of the procurator, and be conducted by him before the presbyteries, &c. 1845. viii., &c. &c.

Library. A committee appointed to examine the library belonging to the Church, to cause to be made out a catalogue of the books and papers contained in said library, and take all necessary steps for the preservation of the same. 1811, ult.

——— An overture for the establishment of a library for the General Assembly referred to a committee (1835. 8). Which committee gave in a full report, and were instructed to collect funds and take all measures which appeared to them calculated for carrying into effect the establishment of said library. 1837. 6; 1838. 7.

——— Committee authorised to remove the books and MSS. belonging to the Church into the room provided for them in the new Assembly Hall. 1843. 10.

Libraries in Highlands. The Assembly approve of a project for erecting libraries in the Highlands and Islands, name the places where such libraries should be fixed, and instruct the Commission to give their best advice and assistance for making the project effectual. 1704. xvii.

——— Committee appointed to take charge of the distribution of said libraries. 1705. xii.

Libraries in Highlands. The Commission instructed to require a full and clear account from said committee. 1706. xviii.

——— Letter of thanks to Mr Strachan, a minister in England, and others there, for their care and liberality in procuring libraries for the use of this Church. 1706. 14; 1709. 12.

Libraries, Presbyterial. Public libraries for the advancement of learning recommended to be established at every presbytery seat, and parochial collections ordered for that purpose. 1709. xi.

——— Procurator instructed to concur in a process of spulzie of presbyterial and parochial libraries taken in the late rebellion. 1720. 4.

——— Commission instructed to prepare a special report as to the state of the libraries, &c. 1729, ult.

——— Commission instructed to make further inquiries into the state of parochial, presbyterial, and synodical libraries. 1730, ult.; 1738, ult.; 1740. 10.

——— The Presbytery of Dunblane desired to send an account to the Commission anent the library of Dunblane. 1705. 13.

Licence. Enacted that any person who shall receive licence or ordination from any of the late prelates, shall be incapable of ministerial communion for the space of three years *simpliciter*, and even after that time, until the presbytery shall be satisfied of his repentance. 1701. xiv.

——— Students of divinity inhibited from going to foreign places to offer themselves for trial for licence or ordination, unless they carry along with them sufficient testimonials. 1711. xii.

——— The foregoing Act renewed, and enacted that licences received in the manner therein described shall have no effect in this Church; and that preachers who go abroad for ordination shall forfeit the licences formerly given them. 1777. ix.

——— An overture anent a uniform form of licence transmitted to presbyteries, but not passed. 1724. 4; 1740. 10.

——— Presbyteries warned to take notice of one alleged to have a counterfeit licence. 1706. ult.

——— A probationer's licence declared null because of his errors. 1714, ult.

Licence. A licence granted by a classical meeting of Presbyterian ministers at Newcastle sustained. 1773. 4.

——— An appeal against a sentence of presbytery refusing to grant licence to a student ultimately dismissed, and the sentence of presbytery affirmed. 1777. 7; 1778, ult.; 1781. 9.

——— A licence granted by the Scots Presbytery in London not sustained, as inconsistent with Act ix., Assembly 1779. 1790. 5.

——— A similar case. 1798. 5.

——— Presbyteries strictly prohibited from receiving on trials for licence young men who have never studied at a university. 1781. vii.

——— Licentiates coming with a licence from abroad not to be allowed to preach in Scotland until they have been re-examined, and have signed the Formula. 1736. xvi.

——— No student to be licensed under twenty-five years of age (1704. x.) This law changed, and enacted that students, at the time of their being admitted to trials, must be twenty-one years of age complete. 1782. viii.

——— Acts anent the trials and licensing of students. 1727. xii.; 1742. vi.; 1782. viii.; 1813. viii.; 1849. x.; 1863. x.

——— An abstract of all the Acts in force relative to the trials and licensing of students transmitted to presbyteries as an overture. 1856. x.

Licentiate. *See* PROBATIONER.

Lining. Mr Thomas Lining and others admitted into communion with the Church, on their promising subjection and obedience. 1690. v.

Lithuania. Letters from the Protestant Synod at Lithuania, thanking the Assembly for undertaking to educate two young men, students of divinity, at the University of Edinburgh. 1724. 3.

——— Acts in favour of students from Lithuania. 1722. v.; 1740. viii.

Liverpool. Found to be imprudent to receive the Presbyterian congregation in Liverpool, or any congregation however respectable, into connection with the Church of Scotland. 1823. 7.

Livingston. A committee appointed for receiving from the representatives of the late Mr John Livingston, minister at Ancrum, his Notes on the Holy Bible. 1704. 11; 1707, ult.

M

M'Millan. Act anent the schismatical and disorderly proceedings of Mr John M'Millan. 1704. xviii.

Maitland. Ministers recommended to give every assistance to Mr Thomas Maitland in his intended design of writing a history of Scotland. 1741. 3.

Male Appellatum. An appeal, containing a complaint against the Synod of Argyle for certain acts passed by them respecting the number of sermons to be preached before and after the celebration of the Lord's Supper, dismissed as not properly brought before the Assembly. 1756. 7.

Male Appellatum. An appeal dismissed, and sentence declared final, no regular appeal having been taken and followed forth against it. 1772. 9.

Man. Mr James Man allowed access to the records, &c., to enable him to prosecute his design of publishing an historical account of affairs transacted in Scotland, from the beginning of the civil wars to the conquest of Scotland by Oliver Cromwell. 1746, ult.

Mandate. A manifest clerical error in a mandate held not to invalidate the document, the contents expressly specifying the purpose for which the mandatory was appointed. 1836. 9.

Manses. Presbyteries instructed to inquire and report to the procurator what ministers want manses, glebes, grass, or other accommodation, that diligence may be taken out thereon. 1719. iv.

——— Members of a presbytery ordered to be rebuked for ordering a process of ejection to be carried on against the widow of a deceased minister for not removing from the manse and offices. 1741, ult.

——— Committee appointed to prepare an overture anent the proper reparation and rendering more commodious manses, churches, and schoolhouses. 1764. 9.

——— On a petition relative to repairs on a manse and offices, the Assembly directed the petitioner to apply to his presbytery, on the ground that presbyteries are the only Church courts competent to discuss questions regarding manses, &c. 1823. 8.

——— An overture anent the jurisdiction of the Church respecting the building or repairing of manses, churches, &c., referred to a committee. 1815, ult.

Manses. Unanimously found that neither the synod nor General Assemblies of this Church have any jurisdiction in regard to repairs on manses, &c.; and the party instructed, in the event of the presbytery refusing to do him justice, to resort to the civil court for redress. 1826. 7.

Manuscripts. Committee appointed to advise anent printing certain MSS. of Messrs Samuel Rutherford, John Baird, and Matthew Crawford. 1698. 12.

——— Committee appointed to examine the several MSS. belonging to the Church, to prepare a catalogue of the same, and to take what steps they thought necessary for preservation of the books and papers of the Church, and for procuring additional documents and MSS. 1819. 5.

——— An elaborate report given in by Dr Lee, along with a list of the MSS. belonging to the Church. 1820. 9; 1821. 9.

——— Committee instructed to correspond with Zion College respecting access to certain MSS. in said college which formerly belonged to the Church of Scotland. 1822, ult.

——— Petition to Parliament for restitution of said MSS. 1828, ult.

——— Committee instructed to take all necessary steps for the recovery of "that interesting record, the Buk of the Universal Kirk." 1829. 8.

——— Dr Lee reported the near prospect of said record being recovered. 1834, ult.

——— Reported that said records were supposed to have been burned with the Houses of Parliament. The records, &c., of the Church ordered to be deposited in the Register Office, until a proper place should be provided for them. 1837. 3.

——— The Assembly expressed their gratification at hearing that the Bannatyne Club intended to print the Buk of the Universal Kirk and Baillie's Letters, and willingly allowed the Club the use of the Church's copy of Baillie's Letters for that purpose. 1838, ult.

——— Ordered that no MS., or part of a MS., should be given out without the authority of the Convener, and a written receipt for the same. 1826. 8.

Manuscripts. *See* Annual Report of Committee on MSS.

Markets. Resolved that application be made to Parliament for altering all markets that are held on Saturdays and Mondays. 1690. vii. 7; 1705. 12; 1708. 13; 1720, ult.

Marriage. The celebration of marriage without due proclamation of banns on three separate Sabbaths discharged. Contraveners to be censured. 1690. vii. 3.

——— A marriage declared unlawful, being within the forbidden degrees, and the parties discharged from cohabiting. 1696, ult.

——— Ministers recommended to dehort their people from marrying with Papists, and to show them the dangerous effects thereof. Application to be made to Parliament for discharging such unequal marriages. 1704. xxii.

——— A man's marriage declared incestuous because the woman had formerly borne a child to his granduncle. 1710. 4.

——— Ordained that the Act concerning proclamation of banns be duly observed, and that inquiry be made that the persons desiring marriage be not within the forbidden degrees, and be single and free, and that all concerned do consent. 1711. v.

——— The minister of Aberlady's irregular marriage while a probationer, referred to the Commission. 1717. 10.

——— Referred to the Commission to give advice anent the proposed marriage of a man with the daughter-in-law of his deceased wife. 1746. 6.

——— Do. between a man and his former wife's brother's daughter. 1748, ult.; 1749, ult.; 1756. 9; 1758. 7.

——— Referred to the Commission to give advice anent a man and woman who had been irregularly married by a probationer. 1720. 11.

——— Representation from the Synod of Merse and Teviotdale with respect to the frequency and bad effects of irregular marriages in their bounds. 1755. 4.

——— Referred to the Commission anent a clandestine marriage. 1760, ult.

——— An overture anent irregular marriages remitted to the Synod of Lothian and Tweeddale that they may suggest effectual means for remedying the evils complained of. 1775. 4.

Marriage. Regulations adopted by the Presbytery of Edinburgh for correcting abuses in the solemnisation of marriages sanctioned by the Assembly, and a strict observance of said regulations enjoined. 1782, ult.

——— Enacted that no session-clerk shall proclaim any persons in order to marriage until he has given the minister written intimation of their names, designations, and places of residence. In case of a vacancy, said intimation to be given to two elders. 1784. viii.

——— A man and woman who had married while the woman had a husband living, wished, upon the death of said husband, to be married regularly. The Assembly found that they might be admitted to the privilege of marriage if they purged the scandal under which they lay by giving evidence of penitence and submitting to the discipline of the Church. 1810, ult.

——— The Presbytery of Edinburgh having prohibited the Scottish chaplain at Calcutta from solemnising marriage, he brought the case by petition before the Assembly, who saw no reason why the chaplain should not be permitted to solemnise marriage when called upon to do so in the ordinary exercise of his ministerial duty (1817. 9). It was reported to the following Assembly that a bill had been introduced into Parliament to remove doubts on the subject, and to legalise marriages performed by ministers of the Church of Scotland in India (1818. 4), which bill having been passed, a copy thereof was laid on the table of Assembly. 1819, ult.

——— Resolved to petition Parliament to adopt immediate measures for declaring valid marriages between Presbyterians and members of the Church of Ireland, and for securing to Presbyterian ministers the right to perform marriages. Com., March 2, 1842.

——— Referred to the Colonial Committee anent marriages by ministers ordained by this Church in New Zealand. 1854. 12.

——— The procurator instructed to apply to the Crown Counsel to take a precognition in any case that occurred of irregular, clandestine marriage, celebrated without proclamation of banns, or in which a false certificate of proclamation was produced. 1812. 6.

Marriage. Committee appointed to consider what means were best calculated to prevent the evil of clandestine and irregular marriages, and to write letters to all the presbyteries of the Church, requesting full information on the subject. 1826. 8.

——— Report of said committee. 1827. 9.

——— A summary of notes on irregular marriages read to the Assembly and ordered to be printed. 1853. 14.

——— Petition to Parliament against a bill to amend the law of Scotland affecting the constitution of marriage. 1847. 5; 1848. 13; 1849, ult.

——— Marriage between a man and the sister of his deceased wife declared to be within the degrees of affinity prohibited by the Word of God, and contrary to the Confession of Faith. Com., May 28, 1839.

——— Petition to Parliament against a bill to amend the law of marriage in so far as relates to marriage within the prohibited degrees of affinity. 1849. 8; 1850. 15; Com., March 7, 1849; Com., March 6, 1850; 1855, ult.; Com., March 2, 1859.

——— Principal Lee requested to confer on the Church and people of Scotland the very great benefit which must arise from the results of his extensive knowledge and careful inquiries in regard to the law of marriage being given to the public in a permanent form. 1850. 15.

'**Marrow of Modern Divinity**.' Edict concerning a book called 'The Marrow of Modern Divinity.' 1720. v.

——— An Act confirming and explaining Act v. 1720. 1722. vii.

——— An Act concerning a sermon preached by Mr Gabriel Wilson, minister at Maxton. 1723. xi.

Masquerades. A reference to the Commission anent. 1669. 18.

Mathematics. Enacted that mathematics shall be studied by students of divinity for at least one session in a university before they enter the class of natural philosophy. 1845. xviii.; 1849. xi.

Maynooth. Petition to Parliament and address to her Majesty against the bill for endowing the College of Maynooth. 1845. 5 and 13.

Meeting-Houses. The performance of divine service or any part of public worship by ministers of this Church in meeting-houses of Dissenters declared to be irregular and unconstitutional. 1818. 9.

Member. An elder duly elected to represent a kirk-session in presbytery having been excluded from the roll of presbytery, the commission from said presbytery to the General Assembly was in consequence declared null and void. 1766. 4.

Members. *See* ASSEMBLY and COMMISSIONS.

Middlebie. Certain parishes disjoined from the Presbytery of Middlebie and joined to the new presbyteries of Annan and Langholm. 1743. v.

Ministers. An Act anent ministers who observe not the public orders of the Church. 1690. vi.

——— Ministers prohibited from leaving their charges without consent of the Church judicatories. 1690. ix.

——— An Act declaring all Acts passed against ministers from the year 1650 to the Revolution null and void. 1690. xiii.

——— Ministers enjoined to be punctual in obeying all the appointments of their presbytery. 1697. viii.

——— An Act anent the transportation of ministers. 1694. vi.

——— Recommended to preach Catechetical doctrine. 1696. xviii.; 1720. vii.

——— Do. on the principles of the Reformation and Revolution. 1749. 4.

——— Presbyteries enjoined to take special notice of any books published by ministers. 1707. vii.

——— Ministers declared to be not liable to the censure of kirk-sessions, but of the superior judicatories. 1707. xi. chap. i. 7.

——— All processes against ministers must begin before the presbytery of the bounds, and not before the kirk-session of his own parish. 1707. xi. chap. vii. 1.

——— Questions appointed to be put to ministers at their ordination, and a Formula to be subscribed by them. 1711. x.

Ministers. Presbyteries prohibited from putting any other questions than those which are implied in the Formula. 1799. 8.

——— An Act concerning the character and behaviour of ministers. 1745. ix.

——— Missionary ministers or preachers not eligible as commissioners to the Assembly. 1753. iv.; 1789. 7.

——— Ministers admitted to parishes are, *ipso facto*, members of the synod and presbytery of the bounds. 1754. v.

——— Presbyteries and synods enjoined to send to the clerk of Assembly a report of all ministers deposed or suspended. 1709. xv.

——— Students of divinity prohibited from going abroad for licence, or for ordination to the holy ministry. 1711. xii.; 1779. ix.; 1799. v.

——— If a minister be convicted or plead guilty of a scandalous offence, he shall, *instanter*, be deposed, whatever be the nature of his penitence, though manifest to all. 1707. xi. chap. vii. 5.

——— Ministers prohibited from attending the theatre. 1757. v.

——— Ministers prohibited from preaching in vacant churches not within the bounds of their own presbytery, without an invitation either from the presbytery of the bounds or a member thereof. 1711. xv.

——— Ministers and probationers of this Church called home from abroad. 1695. 18; 1698. 15.

——— Petition from the widows and children of ministers ejected from their parishes in 1660, referred to the Commission. 1713. 10; 1717. 12.

——— A minister rebuked for not being present at an ordination. 1774. 7.

——— An overture anent processes against ministers dismissed as unnecessary. 1797, ult.

——— Declared to be not agreeable to the Acts of Assembly and practice of this Church for burghs to send ministers to represent them in the General Assembly. 1732. 3.

——— Declared that any minister of this Church who exercises his pastoral functions in a vagrant manner, preaching during his journeys from place to place, without the special invitation or consent of the minister of the parish, is guilty of conduct disorderly and unbecoming the character of a minister of this Church, and calculated to weaken the hands of the minister of the parish. 1818. 9.

Ministers. The practice of ministers intruding themselves into the parishes of other ministers declared to be inconsistent with the principles of an Established Church, and with the laws and constitution of the Church of Scotland. 1843. 10.

——— Declared to be not competent for a minister to appoint another minister to act as his substitute during a lengthened absence from his parish, without consulting the presbytery of the bounds. 1835. 3.

——— A minister in the stated and regular exercise of the ministerial office, not eligible to sit as a ruling elder in the General Assembly. 1829. 3.

——— A retired minister, when returned as a commissioner to the Assembly, must come under the same regulations in regard to the certificate of *bonâ fide* eldership as other ruling elders. 1840. 3.

——— The resignation of a minister, and the appointment of an assistant and successor, sanctioned by the Assembly. 1838. 4 and 7.

——— An overture regarding the formation of a system of mutual assurance, or of a general fund for the *superannuation* of aged and infirm ministers, referred to a committee, with instructions to digest into proper form such information as they might receive on the subject. 1852, ult.; 1853. 14; 1854. 13; 1859, ult.; &c.

Ministerial Communion. Ministers prohibited from employing to preach or to dispense any of the ordinances of religion within any congregation under the jurisdiction of this Church, any person not qualified to receive a presentation. 1799. v.

——— The foregoing Act rescinded. 1842. ix.

——— The Rescissory Act of 1842 rescinded. 1843. xv.

——— Overture and Interim Act anent ministerial communion. 1844. vi.; 1845. xvi.

——— Foresaid overture remitted to a committee, on whose report the Assembly found that there was no ground or occasion for introducing any change into the laws of the

Church as they now exist in regard to the matter of ministerial communion. 1847. 11.

Ministerial Communion. A committee appointed to consider whether any Act can be passed in consistency with the laws and practice of this Church whereby the Church of Scotland may hold ministerial communion with other evangelical Churches, and nnder what provisions the same may be safely guarded. 1860. 8; 1861. 15; 1862. 14.

Ministerial Freedom. An Act concerning ministerial freedom in this Church. 1734. ix.

Ministerial Visitations. Recommendation and direction concerning ministerial visitation of families. 1708. x.

Ministerium Vagum. Presbyteries prohibited from ordaining any one to the ministry without appointing him to some particular office or charge. 1771, ult.

——— Presbyteries recommended to be very cautious in granting ordination to any one who has not a fixed charge, nor a reasonable prospect of such provision as may enable him to support the ministerial character. 1784. ix.; 1827, ult.

——— Presbyteries enjoined to be vigilant in guarding against the evils necessarily connected with a *ministerium vagum*, and to observe the standing laws of the Church thereanent. 1808. 7.

——— Presbyteries enjoined not to grant ordination to any person who has a near prospect of removing from their bounds into the bounds of another presbytery. 1811. 6; 1826. 7; 1827. 5, ult.

Ministry. Committee appointed for the purpose of aiding promising young men having views to the ministry. 1839. 10.

——— Said committee merged in Home Mission. 1842. 17.

Minutes. The judicatories of the Church enjoined to take special care that their minutes are correctly written, and that they allow no blottings or interlinings therein; and that, if anything happen to be blotted out as superfluous, it be marked on the margin how many words or lines are blotted out, that it be done by the authority of the court, and subscribed by the moderator and clerk; and if anything be omitted, that it be written on the margin, and subscribed by the clerk. 1706. ix.

Minutes. A synod enjoined to be more accurate in engrossing their minutes, and particularly to avoid interlineation and erasements. 1779. 9.

——— All the minutes relating to a case before a presbytery ordered to be erased, and all papers lying *in retentis* to be destroyed. 1738. 10.

——— Minutes, when extended and approved by a subsequent meeting, declared to be the only authentic record of the court, and not the jottings or scroll, though subscribed by the clerk. 1823. 4; 1834. 4; 1839. 3.

——— In one case dissenting members of a synod were found entitled to the original jottings of a minute of presbytery as the only means of substantiating their complaint before the Assembly. 1812. 9.

——— Found that, in all causes where there are private parties, they are entitled to have extracts of the minutes immediately if they require them. 1813. 4.

——— Presbyteries recommended to order the minutes of every sederunt to be read in their hearing before the court rises, and authenticated by the signature of the moderator. 1813. 4.

——— A synod found to have acted in a manner incompetent and highly irregular in ordering the minute of a preceding meeting to be expunged. 1817. 7.

——— The Assembly having ordered the minutes in a certain process to be expunged, the party complained to the following Assembly that it had not been done sufficiently. The Assembly declared him entitled to have all the proceedings in his case *expunged so as to be illegible,* and to have all the relative papers destroyed. 1818. 9.

——— The Assembly, finding that in the minute-book of a synod several printed papers and other documents had been pasted on the pages thereof, disapproved of the practice, as tending to suggest doubts of the authenticity of the record, and ordered said practice to be discontinued. 1845. 10.

——— *See* REGISTERS.

Missions. An overture, relative to the diffusion of the gospel, praying the Assembly to appoint a committee to consider the subject, dismissed as inexpedient, and not suitable to the circumstances of the times. 1796. 8.

Missions. Four ministers sent out to the African and Indian Company's Colony in America. 1700. vi.

Mission, Foreign. A standing committee appointed to meet statedly on the first Tuesday of every month for the propagation of the gospel in foreign parts. 1824. 7.

——— The committee authorised to look out for a proper person who, as an ordained minister of our national Church, might be sent to India for the purpose of laying the foundation of such a seminary of general education and religious instruction as the Assembly had from the beginning projected. 1828. 7.

——— The appointment of Dr Duff as first missionary formally ratified. 1829.

——— An Act in favour of the India Mission. 1835. 8.

——— *See* ANNUAL REPORTS.

Mission, Home. The Home Mission Committee constituted by the amalgamation of the Committees on Church extension; on aiding congregations already established; on the employment of probationers; and on the encouragement of young men to the ministry. 1842. xviii.

Mission, Colonial. Declaratory enactment and recommendation relative to colonial churches. 1833. v.

——— A standing committee appointed, to be called "The General Assembly's Committee for promoting the Religious Interest of Scottish Presbyterians in the British Colonies." 1836. ix.

——— *See* ANNUAL REPORTS.

Mission, Jewish. Committee appointed to collect information respecting the Jews, their number, condition, and character; what means have been employed for their spiritual good, and with what success; whether there are any openings for a mission to their nation, and where these are most promising, and to use all prudent measures at home and abroad for the advancement of their cause. 1838. viii.

——— The Conversion of the Jews adopted as a fifth Scheme of the Church. 1840. ix.

——— *See* ANNUAL REPORTS.

Moderation. The moderation of a call in the settlement of ministers declared to be agreeable to the immemorial and constitutional practice of the Church. 1782. vii.

Moderator. An overture anent the mode of electing the moderator of the General Assembly withdrawn after discussion, the Assembly finding it unnecessary to discuss the question. 1833. 10; 1836. 7; 1860. 4.

Montreal. The Presbyterian Church at Montreal declared to be in communion with the Church of Scotland so long as they elect pastors who have been licensed or ordained by this Church. 1817. 8.

——— A petition for a collection for the relief of the sufferers by a great fire at Montreal refused. 1766. 8.

Monument. Ministers recommended to promote subscriptions and collections for the erection of the National Monument on the Calton Hill, Edinburgh. 1819, ult.

Moray. The Presbytery of Strathbogie disjoined from the Synod of Aberdeen, and annexed to the Synod of Moray. 1700. iv.

'**Morning and Evening Sacrifice**,' and other books, remitted to the Presbytery of Dalkeith to inquire into the *fama* regarding them, and proceed according to the laws of the Church. 1839. 3.

Mortifications. Presbyteries enjoined to be particular in inquiring into the management of all mortifications. 1700. xxii.

——— Presbyteries enjoined to give information to the Commission anent mortifications and stipends that have been dilapidated or suppressed. 1706. xii.

——— An humble address to Her Majesty concerning a mortification of the deceased Viscountess of Kenmuir in favour of suffering ministers. 1709. 11; 1714. 3.

——— The Commission instructed to give advice for rendering effectual a mortification made by the deceased George Earl of Cromarty for maintaining catechists in Ross. 1718, ult.

Motions. Resolved that in future all motions and amendments be given in to the Assembly in writing. 1782. 7; 1850. xiv. 37.

——— A motion in possession of the House not to be altered without the consent of the mover and seconder of the countermotion or amendment. 1850. xiv. 39; 1859. xii. 38.

——— All motions after the first shall be dealt with as amendments. Where there is more than one amendment, the vote shall be first taken upon the question which of the amendments shall be put against the motion. 1859. xii.

Motions. *See* STANDING ORDERS.

Mull. An Act dividing the Presbytery of Lorn, and erecting the new Presbytery of Mull. 1729. v.

Murdering of Children. An Act of Parliament against murdering of children ordered to be read from all the pulpits of the Church twice every year. 1762. iv.

Music. Presbyteries recommended to employ all prudent means for promoting the cultivation of church music in schools, according to the practice of former times. 1839. 11.

——— *See* PSALMODY.

N

Nassau. The minister of Nassau, New Providence, admitted into communion with the Church. 1814. 5.

Netherlands. A letter of brotherly sympathy and encouragement sent to the General Synod of the Reformed Church of the Netherlands. 1853, ult.

New South Wales. A pastoral letter transmitted to the ministers, elders, and people of the Presbyterian Church in New South Wales, with reference to the evils which had arisen in that Church. Com., Aug. 8, 1838.

New York. A committee appointed to apply for a royal mandate, authorising the governor of New York to grant to the Presbyterian Church there a charter of incorporation. 1766. 8, 9.

——— A standing committee appointed to correspond with the Synod of New York. 1770, ult.

——— Collection recommended in aid of the congregation at New York in their distressed circumstances. 1724. 3.

——— A representation anent the financial difficulties of the congregation at New York. 1738. 11.

New Churches. An overture anent constitutions to new churches transmitted to presbyteries. 1835. xx.

——— An order as to the titles of new churches. 1842. xv.

Nobile Officium. It having been reported that a presbytery had compromised a case by dropping a libel, the Assembly, in the exercise of its *nobile officium*, ordered a special meeting of the synod of the bounds for the purpose of revising the records of the presbytery, from which judgment many members dissented, as being in violation and subversion of the laws and constitution of the Church. 1837, ult.

Nobile Officium. In a similar case the Assembly reversed the sentence of a synod, in so far as it opened up a case which had been finally settled by a judgment of the presbytery, from which there had been no complaint or appeal. 1839. 5; 1811. 4.

Non-intrusion. Declared to be a fundamental law of the Church, that no pastor shall be intruded on a congregation contrary to the will of the people. 1834. xii.

——— Said Act repealed, as infringing upon civil and patrimonial rights, with which it was not competent for the Church courts to intermeddle. 1843. ix.

Non-residence. The Commission empowered to judge finally any question that might be brought before them, relative to a complaint against a minister for non-residence. 1752, ult.

——— Mr David Malcolm of Duddingston, an enthusiastic Celtic scholar, deposed for leaving his charge. Com., March 24, 1742.

——— A minister deposed for non-residence. 1801. 6; 1841, ult.

Normal Seminary. The proposal to erect a normal seminary in Glasgow for the training of schoolmasters approved of, and the committee recommended to encourage the establishment of similar institutions in Edinburgh and other suitable places. 1835. 6.

Norrieston. A collection ordered for aiding in the erection of a new parish at Norrieston, and encouraging a young man to preach there in the mean time. 1720. 11.

——— 13,000 merks collected and laid out at annual rent. 1738, ult.

——— Committee appointed to consider a petition for a new church. 1766. 7.

——— Committee appointed to consider a petition for a new manse. 1770. 9.

——— The minister of Kincardine found not entitled to present a minister to Norrieston Church. The presbytery ordered to proceed towards the settling of one who shall be agreeable to those usually attending divine ordinances there. 1771. 5.

Norrieston. Resolution regarding the salary and manse. 1772. 9; 1776. 8.

——— The elders in the Presbytery of Dunblane found entitled to vote in the management of Norrieston fund. 1797. 8.

Northumberland. A petition and memorial from the Northumberland class of dissenting ministers favourably received. 1786. 4.

Notarial Protest. A presentee cited to appear at the bar of the Assembly to be heard in regard to his having taken a notarial protest that the members of presbytery should be held liable for the consequences of refusing to take him on trials, and after explanation discharged. 1838. 7, and ult.

——— A similar case. Com., December 11 and 12, 1839.

Novations. An overture anent novations, commonly called the Barrier Act, transmitted to presbyteries, 1695. xi.; and passed into a standing law of the Church, 1697. ix.

O

Oath, Accession. The oath taken by His Majesty at his accession to maintain and preserve the Protestant religion, with the government, worship, discipline, rights, and privileges of the Church of Scotland, as established by law, openly read in the Assembly, and ordered to be recorded. 1715. iv.; Com., Aug. 11, 1830.

Oath, Abjuration. An Act concerning the oath of abjuration. 1712. xvi.

——— An address to the Queen concerning the oath of abjuration. 1712. xvii., xviii.

——— An Act for maintaining the unity and peace of the Church with reference to the abjuration oath. 1713. vi.; 1714. viii.

Oath, Purgation. Found that a party could not be obliged, upon alleged presumptions of guilt, to take an oath of purgation, and that he was not liable to Church censure for refusing the same. 1706. 11.

Oath, Purgation. The oath of purgation not to be pressed upon any one; and, if offered, to be accepted or not as the judicatory shall see cause, and never but by the advice of the presbytery. 1707. xi. chap. iv. 8.

——— Refused to admit a party to purge himself of a scandal by the oath of purgation, in regard it was judged his so doing would not remove the scandal, the presumption of guilt being so pregnant. 1711. 4.

——— Committee appointed to take into consideration the oaths administered to preachers and others admitted to offices under Government, and to correspond with the law officers of the Crown. 1826. 7.*

Objections. Edictal notice to be given that on the day for moderating in the call the presbytery will be ready to receive any objections to the presentee, or any reasons against his settlement. 1856. xii.; 1862. vii.

——— Objections can only be received from those who are both parishioners and members of the congregation, and who appear personally before the presbytery to give in their objections. 1862. vii. sect. vii.; 1846. 4; 1848. 8.

Officers, Church. Parish officers amenable to the kirk-session in the discharge of their duties, though appointed by heritors or magistrates. 1823. 5.

——— Kirk-sessions, presbyteries, and synods enjoined to observe all the Acts of Assembly relative to the office-bearers of the Church. 1722. ix.

Officers, Assembly. A petition from the officers of the Assembly in regard to their salaries remitted to the Finance Committee. 1854. 12.

——— The clerks of Assembly empowered to name the beadles in time coming, upon any vacancy, and to dismiss them when they see cause. 1774. 5.

——— Petition from officers for augmentation of salary. 1775, ult.; 1776, ult.

* In regard to the necessity of a patron qualifying by taking the oath of allegiance every time before issuing a presentation, see the debate on the Dreghorn case. 1834. 10.

The oath of allegiance may be taken by a presentee at any time before ordination; doubtful if necessary to be taken again by a minister already ordained. Court of Session, North Leith Case, 1859.

Ordained Assistants. An overture and interim Act transmitted to presbyteries for four successive years, but not passed, whereby it was proposed that an ordained assistant and successor should be a constituent member of session as well as the minister, and eligible as a commissioner to the General Assembly. 1784. vii.

Ordinances, Sealing. Sealing ordinances to be dispensed to strangers, with all tenderness, when they desire the benefit thereof. 1711. xiii.

Ordinances. On the report of the Committee on the Administration of Divine Ordinances, the Assembly earnestly called the attention of the members of the Church to the importance and necessity of the regular and stated observance of the Lord's Supper, and expressed their desire to see the ordinance administered not once only, but twice every year in all the churches. 1846, ult.

Ordination. Questions appointed to be put to ministers at their ordination. 1711. x.

——— Presbyteries prohibited from imposing any other upon those about to be ordained than those implied in the questions appointed by Act x., Assembly 1711. 1809. 5.

——— A presbytery having ordained a probationer, who for many years had resided in England, without any certificate of character or evidence of provision for his support in the ministerial character, the Assembly declared the ordination altogether irregular, and ordered all the proceedings to be expunged from the records of the presbytery. 1827. 5.

——— Presbyteries recommended to use great caution in ordaining ministers going to foreign parts, or who have no relation to a particular charge. 1827, ult.

——— On the day of ordination presbyteries entitled to disregard all charges against a presentee, unless they are substantiated *instanter*, and to proceed with the ordination in the face of a protest from the people. 1832. 5.

——— *See* MINISTERS and ELDERS.

Order in Council. A motion to the effect that no civil authority can constitutionally prescribe either forms or heads of prayer to the ministers and preachers of this Church; and that the Orders in Council which have been issued from time to time respecting prayers for the Royal family, are inconsistent with the rights and privileges secured by law to our ecclesiastical establishment. 1820. 6.

Orkney. Representation relative to vacant charges, ruinous kirks and manses, and the want of schools. 1699. 10; 1701. 21.

——— Act anent the state of the Church in Orkney, Zetland, and Caithness. 1700. vii.

——— A commission appointed to visit Orkney, &c. 1700. xiii.

——— Application to Government for the repair of churches and manses there. 1700. 14.

——— An Act concerning the Synod of Orkney and Caithness. 1842. xxii.; 1704. iv.; 1706. 9; 1725. v.

——— Presbytery of Orkney divided into the two Presbyteries of Kirkwall and Northisles. 1707. x.

——— The Presbytery of Zetland disjoined from the Synod of Orkney, and declared to be subordinate only to the General Assembly. 1715. 9.

——— The Commission to use every endeavour to obtain gifts of the bishops' rents, for maintaining more ministers and catechists in Orkney. 1717. 11.

——— A committee appointed to correspond with heritors and ministers in Orkney regarding the state of churches and schools. 1797, ult.; 1800. 10, ult.

——— Report of committee on the state of religion in Orkney. 1847. 9.

Original Burghers. The proposal of the Original Burgher Synod to enter into a conference with the General Assembly, with a view of their entering into reunion with the Church, cordially approved of, and a committee appointed for that purpose. 1835. 4 and 11; 1836. 5; 1837. 8.

——— An overture for reunion transmitted to presbyteries, 1838. 9; and passed into a law, 1839. 10.

Orphans. Recommendation of a fund for maintaining the indigent widows and orphans of ministers. 1718. iv.; 1735. iv.; 1723. x.

——— Presbyteries and ministers enjoined strictly to observe the regulations prescribed relative to the "Act for raising and establishing a fund for a provision for the widows and children of the ministers of Scotland." 1744. iv.; 1745. iv.

——— Proposals for more effectually executing a scheme for

maintaining and educating the infants and orphans of soldiers. 1767. iv.

Orphans. Collection appointed in aid of the widows and children of soldiers and sailors engaged in the war. Com., Mar. 22, 1854.

Overtures. Enacted that when anything of public concern and great weight is proposed to the General Assembly to be passed as an overture or Act for a standing rule of the Church, it shall, after the first reading, be delayed till the next day, and lie on the table to be seen and considered by all the members; and ordained that presbyteries shall publicly read all overtures transmitted to them from the Assembly before the first meeting of the synod after the rising of the Assembly. 1700. xvi.

——— Enacted that when an overture has been twice transmitted, the Assembly shall, without further transmission, take such overture into consideration, and pass it into an Act, or reject the same, as they shall see cause, although presbyteries have not sent up their opinions. 1752. vii.

——— Remonstrances having been made against the passing of foresaid Act, as a violation of the Barrier Act, it was in 1753 transmitted as an overture to presbyteries, and finally passed into an Act. 1758. v.

——— Overtures retransmitted only to such presbyteries as had neglected to send up their opinions thereon. 1758, ult.; 1769. 5, &c.; 1797. 8; 1812, ult.

——— Expressly enjoined that returns be made by presbyteries *every year* to the overtures transmitted by the authority of the Assembly; said returns to be each written on a separate sheet. 1848, ult.; 1855. viii.

——— A note appended to every overture transmitted reminding presbyteries that even in cases of overtures retransmitted without alteration, it is necessary that their approbation of them be annually renewed. 1853. 14.

——— Found that the necessary consent of the Church had not been obtained in favour of an overture, in respect that there were not *that year* returns from a majority of the presbyteries of the Church approving of it, although, including the returns of former years, it had obtained the consent of a majority of presbyteries. 1849. 9.

Overtures. Found that no individual, not being a member of the House, is entitled to introduce an overture to the Assembly, or to be heard in support of it. 1780. 6; 1837. 4.

——— The Committee of Overtures, highly disapproving of the language, tenor, and spirit of an overture, refused to transmit the same; and the Assembly warmly approved of their resolution. 1837. 3.

——— An overture anent the transmission of overtures after discussion withdrawn as unnecessary. 1816. 7.

——— Presbyteries recommended, at a previous ordinary meeting, to fix a day for considering the overtures transmitted from the General Assembly. 1797. 8.

——— Presbyteries enjoined, at their first meeting after receiving the printed Acts of Assembly, to fix a day for the consideration of overtures transmitted. 1798, ult.

——— Resolved that, as far as possible, separate days shall be set apart for hearing of causes, and consideration of overtures. 1832. vi.

——— No overture to be entertained or transmitted by the Committee of Overtures, unless there be some person present to explain and support it. 1850. xiv. 14; 1859. xii. 15.

——— All overtures to the Assembly to be printed in such numbers as to allow a copy to each member, 450 at least, and laid on the table on or before the first Monday of the Assembly. 1850. xiv. 27; 1859. xii. 29.

Owen. The conduct of the Presbytery of Lanark highly approved of in the business of Mr Owen's school at New Lanark. 1823, ult.

P

Pagan. Referred to the Commission to use all the means in their power for extirpating the remaining idolatrous Pagan and Popish superstitions in the Highlands and Islands. 1707. xiii.

Paisley. Act disjoining certain parishes from the Presbyteries of Paisley and Irvine, and forming them into the Presbytery of Greenock. 1834. viii.

Papers, Printed. Parties concerned in causes before the

Assembly ordered to distribute their printed cases at least twenty-four hours before the causes are to be heard. 1772. 6.

Paraphrases. Referred to the Commission to consider an overture about turning some passages of the Old and New Testaments into metre, in order to be used in churches as well as in families, and to take the assistance of learned divines who have employed their time and pains on subjects of that sort. 1741, ult.

——— A committee appointed to make a collection of translations into English verse or metre of passages of the Holy Scriptures, or to receive in performances of that kind from any who may transmit them. 1742. 7; 1744. 10.

——— Some pieces of poetry, under the title of "Translations and Paraphrases of several Passages of Sacred Scripture," transmitted to presbyteries as an overture. 1745. vi.; 1747. 8.

——— Said Paraphrases recommended to be used in private families. Presbyteries to have a sufficient number of copies within their bounds. 1751, ult.

——— The committee having reported that they had at length prepared such a collection of sacred poems as they thought might be submitted to the judgment of the Church, the Assembly ordered the same to be transmitted to presbyteries for their perusal—the printer for the Church to have the sole privilege of printing said Paraphrases for five years. 1781. 3, 8.; 1786. 8.; 1795. 8.

——— The sole right of printing the Paraphrases granted to the printer of the Church for fourteen years. 1803, ult.

——— The Assembly allow the committee to print 250 copies of a new version of 17 Psalms and 21 Paraphrases. 1811, ult.

——— Presbyteries enjoined to take the collection into their consideration. 1821. 7.

Parishes. Overture respecting the annexation and suppression of parishes. 1793. ix.

——— Presbyteries prohibited from consenting to the supression of parish churches. 1740. v.

——— Synods prohibited from disjoining or annexing parishes from one presbytery to another, without the authority of the General Assembly. 1745. v.

——— Presbyteries enjoined to inform synods of any proposed

annexations or suppressions, and not to concur therein without consent of the synod. 1794. viii.

Parishes. Practice of attending other than the parish church disapproved of, and the conduct of ministers who encourage or give countenance to any such practice declared to be unbecoming and schismatical. 1810. 5 ; 1747. 4.

——— Committee appointed to consider overtures on the subdivision of parishes, and report. 1834. 7.

——— A committee appointed to communicate with the Lord Advocate, with a view to obtain a legislative enactment in regard to parochial registers. 1816. xii. ; 1817, ult.

——— Presbyteries recommended to be careful and diligent in visiting the parishes within their bounds. 1700. xxii.

——— Ministers to visit all the families in their respective parishes once a-year at a convenient season. 1708. 10.

Parliament. Commission to name ministers to preach before Parliament. 1701. 13.

Parliament House. The bar-keeper or crier allowed one guinea per annum in addition to the allowance which, for a number of years past, he has received out of the funds of the Church. 1812, ult.

Parliamentary. *See* CHURCHES.

Parliamentary Burghs. A committee appointed to consider the claims of the parliamentary burghs to be represented in the General Assembly. 1834. 9.

——— A motion having been made to allow the parliamentary burghs to send representative elders, the Assembly considered the proposal premature, and did not feel prepared to adopt so material a change in the constitution of the House. 1836. 7.

Pastoral. Admonition from the General Assembly to all the people under their charge in regard to false teachers, infidel publications, and seditious principles. 1799. xi.

——— Admonition on the subject of Sabbath profanation. 1834, ult.

——— On the prevailing sins of the land. 1835. xxi.

——— On family worship. 1836. xix.

——— On privileges and responsibilities. Com., June 1, 1838.

——— On the trying circumstances of the Church. 1839, ult.

Pastoral Letter to the Churches in the colonies. Com., Aug. 13, 1840.

——— On the present circumstances of the Church. 1841, ult.; 1842. 18.

——— To the people of Scotland on the present afflicted state of the Church. 1843. 7.

——— In regard to the missionary schemes of the Church. 1845. 12.

——— On the subject of Sabbath observance. 1847. 9.

——— On the distresses prevailing in the United Kingdom and among other nations. 1848. viii.

Pastoral Address. On the prevalence of intemperance. 1850, ult.

——— On the condition of the non-churchgoing population. 1851. 12.

——— On the subject of Sabbath schools. 1852. 8.

——— On the increase of immorality in the rural districts. 1861, ult.

——— A committee appointed to superintend the publication of the admirable pastoral addresses drawn up by the late Principal Lee, as a fitting memorial of the relation in which their distinguished author stood to the Church. 1859. 12.

Patronage. An address to the Queen anent the "Bill for restoring of Patronages," representing that, "from the first reformation from Popery, patronages have always been considered a yoke and a burden upon the Church," and deprecating the Bill as "an encroachment evidently prejudicial to the work of the gospel and the peace of the Church." 1712. x.

——— Memorial concerning the grievance of patronage. 1715. ix.

——— Report of the Commissioners sent to London to solicit the redress of the grievance of patronage, and the repeal of the Act Anno decimo Annæ, restoring the same. 1735. 4; 1736. vi.; 1736. 9; 1737, ult.

——— Presbyteries enjoined to take care that both patron and presentee were qualified in terms of law, and to use their best endeavours to remove groundless objections. 1754. iv.

——— The instruction annually given to the Commission to "make due application to the King and Parliament for redress of the grievance of patronage," omitted for the first time. 1784. vi. ; 1784. 5 ; 1785. 7.

Patronage. Act anent the planting of vacant kirks, *tanquam jure devoluto.* 1732. viii.

——— Said Act repealed. 1734. v.

——— Presbyteries enjoined to give in returns of the churches within their bounds that were of the Queen's presentation. 1711. 13.

——— Referred to Commission anent preventing unqualified patrons from substituting others to present *pro hac vice.* 1750, ult. ; 1751. 7.

——— Committee appointed to consider an overture respecting the law of patronage. 1768. 6.

——— Committee discharged as inexpedient. 1769. 6.

——— An overture on the mode of supplying vacant parishes dismissed as incompetent and of a dangerous tendency. 1781. 7 ; 1784. 5.

——— Commission to consider what should be done with ministers and probationers who show a willingness to accept presentations. 1724. 13.

——— A preacher prohibited by a presbytery from accepting a presentation. 1729. 6 ; and suspended for having done so. 1731, ult.

——— Anent a finding by a presbytery, that a presentation by a patron was no hindrance to a free and unlimited moderation of a call. 1740. 6.

——— An overture to consult with patrons as to whether they would consent to an alteration in the Act of 1712, restoring patronages, after discussion dismissed. 1785. 7 ; 1786. 9.

——— An overture anent the sale of the right of patronage during a vacancy referred to a committee. 1787. 7 ; 1788. 6.

——— Objection taken to the constitution of St Thomas' Church, Leith, in regard to the right of patronage. 1839, ult.

——— A patronage having been sold during a vacancy, the presbytery refused to sustain the presentation, and referred the matter to the Assembly. The Assembly, in respect there did not appear to be any law prohibiting an absolute sale of a patronage during a vacancy, remitted the case to the presbytery, with instructions to sustain the presentation, and proceed according to the rules of the Church. 1818. 4.

stances, but the presbytery instructed to pay all due attention if an application should be made to them by the magistrates or kirk-session for an additional place of worship. 1794. 6.

Perth. A memorial from the presbytery respecting the Hospital of Perth referred to a committee. 1782. 4, 9.

Perth and Stirling. The synod appointed to meet in Crieff in April 1743, and there resolve on their future places of meeting; that if they agree the same may be authorised by the Assembly; 1742. 10. The synod met accordingly, and resolved to meet at Perth in October, and at Stirling in April, *per vices*, in all time coming; to which resolution the Assembly did interpone their authority. 1743. viii.

Petition. A petition rejected because it contained expressions indecent and unbecoming. 1765. 5.

——— Found that parties who had made no appearance before the inferior court were not entitled to be heard by the Assembly on petition. Com., June 2, 1835.

——— A minister under libel for non-residence sought to bring his case before the Assembly by petition, on the ground that he had been prevented by indisposition from being present when the sentence complained of was pronounced. The Assembly refused to sustain his petition. 1801. 6.

——— Declared that no petition for charity shall be transmitted to, nor regarded by, the Assembly, unless the petitioners produce therewith ample testimonials as to their life and conversation. 1710. viii.

Pluralities. Overture from the Synod of Perth and Stirling concerning plurality of benefices dismissed by a large majority. 1763. 8; 1780. 6; 1796. 7.

——— The Assembly of 1814 having passed an enactment anent the residence of ministers, and the union of offices in the persons of ministers, the Assembly of 1816 declared the same not binding, as having been passed in violation of the Barrier Act. An overture on the subject was transmitted to presbyteries, 1816. v., and passed into a standing law of the Church, whereby it is enacted and declared that the same person shall not hold at the same time a professorship in a university and a parochial charge which is not situated in the city which is the seat of the university, or in the suburbs thereof. 1817. vi.

Pluralities. An overture proposing that the holding of a principality or professorship in a university should be incompatible with the holding of a parochial charge in the city that is the seat of the university, dismissed as inexpedient. 1825. 6; 1826. 6; 1827. 6; 1828. 4.

——— A similar overture transmitted. 1842. xxix.

——— A similar overture approved of by the Assembly, and a committee appointed to memorialise Government for adequate endowments to the theological chairs. 1847. 6; 1852, ult.

——— The union of the Professorship of Church History in the University of St Andrews with a country charge sanctioned by a majority of 5. 1813. 6.

Poaching. Found relevant as a charge in a libel against a minister. 1851. 5.

Poole. Ministers instructed to recommend Poole's 'Annotations' from their pulpits. 1700. 16.

Poor. Address to the Privy Council anent the poor. 1699. 13.

——— Presbyteries to be careful in seeing after all mortifications for behoof of the poor. 1700. xxii.

——— Memorial anent interference of justices of the peace with the poor's funds. 1709. 11.

——— Committee appointed to consider laws regarding the poor. 1747. 5; 1751, ult.

——— Presbyteries recommended to apply to justices of the peace to put in execution the laws concerning the poor and vagrant beggars, and to provide work and maintenance for them. 1711. xi.

——— Every parish to maintain its own poor. 1724. vii.

——— A return to Parliament regarding the poor. 1817. 10.

——— Report of committee concerning. 1818. 9; 1819. 10.

——— Petition to Parliament against new Poor Law Bill. 1824. 6.

——— Return ordered of all funds mortified for behoof of the poor, or for educational purposes. 1825, ult.; 1826. 10.

——— Committee appointed to prepare a digest of the laws regarding the management of the poor. 1827. 10.

——— Report on the state of the poor requested by Government; 1838. 3. Given in and approved; 1839. 4. Resolution regarding. 1841. 15.

Poor. General collection ordered for the poor and destitute. 1842. 3. Com., Nov. 17, 1842.

Popery. Presbyteries enjoined to take special notice what Papists are in their bounds, and take pains to reclaim them; to see how their children are educated, and, if need be, apply to the civil authority concerning them. 1690. vii.

——— An Act anent trafficking priests and the education of young noblemen and others, children of Popish parents. 1695. ix.; 1705. 9.

——— Ministers enjoined to study Popish controversies more, and deal wisely and convincingly with the consciences of those who have fallen to Popery. 1699. viii.

——— An Act regulating the reception of such as come off from Popery. 1700. xviii.; 1703. x.

——— Scandalous persons becoming Papists to be excommunicated. 1704. viii.

——— Presbyteries enjoined to send in lists of all Papists to the Privy Council. 1704. xxi.

——— Ministers enjoined to dehort their people from marrying with Papists, and to hold forth the dangerous effects thereof. 1704. xxii.

——— An Act for suppressing of Popery, and preventing the growth thereof. 1707. viii.; 1714. xi.; 1717. viii.; 1720. vii.; 1747. v.; 1779. vii.

——— Ministers enjoined to warn their people against the abominable errors of the Church of Rome, and instruct them in the truth of the Reformed religion. 1708. iv.; 1724. 6, 14.

——— Petitions to both Houses of Parliament respecting the political privileges of the Roman Catholics. 1813. v.

——— A letter to the Earl of Aboyne congratulating him on renouncing the Popish and professing the Protestant religion. 1699. 10 and 13.

——— Converts from Popery required to sign the Confession of Faith before a Church judicatory. 1700. xviii.; 1703. x.

——— Many Papists reported to be in the country of Glenlivet. 1760. 6.

——— A discussion in regard to Catholic Emancipation. 1778. 7.

Popery. Presbytery of Edinburgh instructed to get the mass meetings held in some places about the town of Edinburgh, suppressed. 1719. 8.

——— A Popish priest publicly renounces the errors of Popery, and is admitted into communion with the Church. 1735. 6.

——— Reports from the several presbyteries in regard to the state of Popery in Scotland. 1737. 8.

——— Committee appointed to collect information as to the present state of Popery in Scotland. Ministers recommended to preach on the errors of Popery and the principles of the Reformation. 1834, ult.

——— Report of committee. 1837. 9.

——— A note in New Statistical Account ordered to be cancelled. 1837. 9.

——— Committee instructed to correspond with other Reformed Churches in regard to the most prudent means for counteracting the evils of Popery, and to petition against the endowment of Popery. 1839. 10.

——— Petition to Parliament against the Papal-Aggression Bill. 1851, ult.

——— Resolutions in regard to Popery, and a memorial from the Scottish Reformation Society. 1852. 13; 1853. 13; 1856, ult.; 1859. 13.

Prayer. Enjoined that all ministers, after praying for the Queen, shall expressly mention the Princess Sophia and the Protestant line in that family. 1711. iv.

——— Acts about praying for the Royal Family. 1736. v.; 1795. vi.; 1830, ult.

——— Two ministers deposed for not praying for King George *nominatim*. 1715. 5.

——— Found to be unnecessary and inexpedient to adopt any declaration with regard to the late or any former orders in Council relative to prayers for His Majesty and the Royal Family. 1820. 6.

——— Congregational prayer meetings recommended. 1840. 10.

——— Forms of worship for the use of soldiers, sailors, colonists, sojourners in India and in foreign countries, and other parties destitute of a settled minister, laid on the table. 1858, ult.; 1859. 13; 1862. 5.

Prayer. Reading prayers from a book, either in manuscript or printed, declared to be an innovation upon, and contrary to, the laws and usage of the Church in the celebration of public worship. 1859. 7.

Preachers. *See* PROBATIONERS.

Preaching. Ministers enjoined to preach catechetical doctrine, insist upon the fundamental truths of religion, and suit themselves to the capacities of their hearers. 1720. viii.

——— Ministers enjoined to observe the Directory of 1645 anent the preaching of the Word. 1736. vii.

——— Overtures anent the method of preaching. 1726. 12; 1734, ult.; 1735, ult.

——— Ministers prohibited from employing students of divinity to preach or conduct public worship. 1854. xii.

Precentor. Assistance granted from the funds of the Church to the kirk-session of Elgin, in defending their rights in choosing their own clerk, precentor, and beadles. 1738, ult.; 1739, ult.; 1741. 8.

Prelatical. Grievances complained of from the illegal attempts of prelatical parties. 1703. 9.

——— Preachers receiving licence or ordination from any of the late prelates, declared incapable of ministerial communion for three years. 1701. xiv.

——— Prelatical preachers and separatists discharged from exercising Church discipline. 1715. xiv.

Presbyteries to take notice of ministers who fail to observe the public orders of the Church. 1690. vi.

——— Ministers of different presbyteries allowed to associate themselves into one presbytery until the vacancies in consequence of the Revolution settlement were filled up. 1690. viii.

——— An Act regulating the representation of presbyteries in the General Assembly. 1694. v.; 1704. vi.; 1712. vi.; 1717. ix.; 1835. xix.; 1839. vii.

——— Presbyteries enjoined to set up the use of the exercise and addition, and of privy censures. 1694. xvii.

——— Recommended to institute parochial and presbyterial libraries. 1705. xii.

——— Declared that ministers admitted to parishes are *ipso facto* members of presbytery and synod. 1754. v.

Presbyteries. Presbyteries of Lerwick and Burravoe erected out of the Presbytery of Shetland. 1830. viii.

——— Act erecting the Presbytery of Olnafirth. 1848. xviii.

——— Act erecting the Presbytery of Greenock. 1834. viii.

——— Act erecting Presbyteries of Jura and Islay. 1836. vi.

——— Act erecting the Presbytery of Weem. 1836. vii.

——— Parish of Fullarton added to Presbytery of Irvine. 1837. xv.

——— Presbytery of Kinross erected out of certain parishes disjoined from Presbyteries of Perth, Kirkcaldy, Auchterarder, and Dunfermline. 1856. viii.

——— Presbytery of Nairn erected. 1773. 9.

——— Presbytery of Dunfermline censured for disobedience. 1733. 8.

——— Presbytery of Linlithgow censured for disobedience. 1751. 5, ult.

——— Presbytery of Kintyre censured for irregularities. 1758. 6.

——— Presbytery of Gairloch changed into the Presbytery of Lochcarron. 1775, ult.

——— Parish of Monedie disjoined from Presbytery of Dunkeld and annexed to Presbytery of Perth. 1758. 9.

——— Proposed disjunction of the Presbytery of Aberdeen declared to be inexpedient. 1836, ult.

——— Not competent for the Commission to disjoin or annex parishes from one presbytery to another. Com., Aug. 13, 1835.

——— A presbytery severely censured for presuming to institute an inquiry into the grounds of charges which had been already under the view of the General Assembly. 1803. 5.

——— Not competent for a presbytery to meet beyond its own bounds without the authority of a superior court. 1811. 5.

——— All the members of a presbytery ordered to attend at the settlement of a minister which was opposed by the people. 1812. 6.

——— Declared to be incompetent and unconstitutional for a synod to appoint corresponding members to act with a presbytery within their bounds. 1812. 7.

——— An absent member exonerated from sharing in any

blame attaching to those who concurred in a sentence passed at a meeting at which he was not present. 1813, ult.

Presbyteries. Declared irregular and incompetent for a presbytery to pass judgment in a cause before the appeals taken against certain interlocutory judgments had been decided by the Assembly. 1814. 8.

——— Certain members of a presbytery exempted from sitting as judges in a particular case. 1814, ult.

——— Found that there is no appeal from sentences of presbyteries regarding manses and glebes to a superior ecclesiastical court. Parties aggrieved must apply to the civil court. 1826. 7.

——— The ordinary place of meeting for a presbytery fixed by the General Assembly. 1828. 7.

——— Leave to a presbytery to meet during the sitting of the Assembly to attest a commission, granted by a majority of 61 to 38. 1835. 2.

——— An Act concerning presbyteries neglecting to send up their opinion on overtures transmitted to them. 1758. v.

——— Ministers of a different presbytery appointed to act as assessors along with a presbytery, in conducting a process of libel. Com., June 1, 1842.

——— Objection to the competency of a presbytery proceeding with a case on the day after the meeting of synod, before new commissions could be issued in favour of ruling elders—repelled. 1845. 8.

——— Presbyteries that had become defunct resuscitated by the General Assembly. 1775. 4; 1841, ult.; 1843. 3; 1843.; 9; 1849. 14; 1847. 17.

——— A presbytery having been prevented from meeting by the stormy state of the weather, became defunct, and applied to the Commission to appoint them to meet on an early day, for important business, which the Commission did accordingly. Com., Nov. 17, 1847. 1849, ult.

——— Presbyteries that had become defunct resuscitated by calling a *pro re nata* meeting for the purpose of fixing a day for the transaction of ordinary business. 1843. 3.

——— Committee appointed to consider in what manner, when presbyteries become defunct, they shall be revived. 1843. 3.

Presbyteries. Interim Act anent appointing a day of meeting of a presbytery for ordinary business, when from any cause such has not been previously fixed. 1862. viii.

——— Clerk held to be not entitled to withhold the commission of a burgh elder because of the non-payment of the fee for attestation. 1825. 3.

——— Peremptorily enjoined to send up the reports of the examination of schools. 1829. 9.

——— The visitation of parishes by presbyteries declared to be a practice recognised by the laws and constitution of the Church. 1837. 5.

——— A committee appointed to draw up regulations for trials of presbyteries and privy censures. 1840, ult.

——— Anent the proposed subdivision of the Presbyteries of Edinburgh and Glasgow into presbyteries of an extent fitted for the most efficient performance of the duties of these courts. 1839. 10.

Prescription. A party who had judicially confessed his guilt and been sentenced to be rebuked failed to appear. On being refused Church privileges some years afterwards, he pled that the cause was prescribed, and could not be revived in order to censure. The Assembly, on appeal, did not decide the general question of prescription, but found that, "in the special circumstances of the case, it was inexpedient to revive the scandal." 1804. 6.

Presentee. Found that a fama affecting the character of a presentee can only be prosecuted by libel, and does not warrant a presbytery from sisting procedure in regard to the moderating in of a call. 1771. 7.

——— A presentee having, after it had been sustained by the presbytery, resigned his presentation, the Assembly held that, as he was in the hands of the Church courts, the proper course for him was to ask leave to withdraw his letter of acceptance. 1838. 4.

——— A presbytery having refused to sustain the trials of a presentee, the Assembly, on appeal, appointed a committee to examine him, and sustained his trials. Com., June 1, 1847.

——— Before taking any steps towards a settlement, in consequence of a presentation, presbyteries to take care that

Printing. An overture to report on any alterations which it was advisable to make on the printing of the Acts, and republishing such as were out of print. 1832. 9.

Printer to the Church. Margaret Gib, relict of the deceased George Mossman, continued in her deceased husband's office of printer to the Church during the Assembly's pleasure, provided she kept a printing-house of her own, and sold the Acts of Assembly at one penny sterling each sheet. 1708. 13; 1709. 10.

——— Agnes Campbell, relict of Andrew Anderson, printer to Her Majesty, appointed printer to the Church. 1712, ult.

——— The executors of the deceased Agnes Campbell appointed printers to the Church in her room. 1717. 3.

——— Referred to the Commission to settle with proper persons for printing the Acts of Assembly and other public papers of the Church, who appointed James Davidson and Robert Fleming joint printers. 1723. 8.

——— Robert Fleming, junior, conjoined with his father. 1769. 9.

——— Mr James Dickson conjoined with R. Fleming. 1777. 8.

——— Mr Charles Dickson printer in 1801.

——— Mr Peter Hill in 1803.

——— Mr John Waugh appointed printer and stationer. 1824, ult.

——— Neill & Co. appointed. 1837. 8.

——— Report of a committee on the duties and emoluments of the printer to the Church. 1837. 8.

Printers. A petition from the printers for the Church complaining that, of five hundred copies of the Acts of Assembly printed yearly for twenty years past, scarcely one half were disposed of, referred to the Commission. 1744, ult.

Prisons. A committee appointed to consider the most effectual measures for providing the means of religious instruction and public worship in prisons and bridewells. 1819. 3; 1825, ult.

——— A committee appointed to correspond with the Home Secretary anent the appointment of prison chaplains. 1860. 14.

——— The committee reported that they had succeeded in preventing the insertion of a clause into the new Prison

Act, to the effect that chaplains of prisons might be appointed who were not licentiates of the Church of Scotland. 1861, ult.

Printer. Committee appointed to attend to any proceedings connected with the renewal of any privileges or patent to His Majesty's printers. 1838. 4; 1839. 11, 12; Com., May 30, 1837; Com., June 1, 1841.

Privy Censures. Presbyteries enjoined to set up the practice of privy censures, conform to the ancient practice of this Church. 1694. xvii.

——— Presbyteries enjoined annually to obtain answers from the different ministers within their bounds to a prescribed list of queries, and to record them in their minutes, and to transmit a copy to the synod. 1848. xvi.

Probationers. Not to be taken on trials without sufficient testimonials—to preach only within the bounds of the presbytery that licensed them. On removing into the bounds of another presbytery, to carry with them an extract of their licence and presbyterial certificate. All sentences pronounced against them to be intimated to the neighbouring judicatories. 1694. x.; 1736. ix.

——— Presbyteries enjoined to send up to the Assembly annual lists of all probationers within their bounds, to be recorded in the Assembly registers. 1697. iii.; 1736. ix.; 1704. 15; 1735, ult.; 1737, ult.; 1769, ult.; 1781, ult.; 1801, ult.

——— Enacted that the rules of the form of process, with respect to informations against ministers, be extended to probationers. 1697. iii.; 1745. ix.

——— Presbyteries prohibited from putting a call into the hands of any probationer until after his trials. 1711. x.

——— Questions to be put to all probationers when licensed, and Formula to be subscribed. 1711. x.

——— Acts concerning the trials and licensing of probationers. 1695. xiii.; 1699. xi.; 1708. xiii.; 1709. xv.; 1710. iv.; 1711. x.; 1714. vi.; 1727. xii.; 1742. vi.; 1782. viii.; 1813. viii.

——— Act anent the study of divinity, and the trials and licensing of probationers, re-enacting and consolidating former Acts. 1849. xi.; 1856. x.

Probationers. Declared ineligible as commissioners to the General Assembly. 1753. iv.

——— Proceedings against a probationer for counterfeiting a testimonial. 1695. 12; 1716. 8.

——— Having the Irish language not to be settled in lowland parishes till the Highlands were sufficiently provided 1694. xxi.

——— Synod to restore his licence to a probationer who had been silenced, should they see cause. 1744. 9.

——— Committee appointed to consolidate the Acts concerning probationers. 1739. 10.

——— Directions how to proceed against a probationer who was also a schoolmaster. 1814. 9.

——— Inconsistent with the consuetudinary practice of the Church to allow probationers to supply the pulpit of a vacant parish, as it might affect the usefulness of the presentee to be nominated by the patron. 1829. 7.

——— Committee appointed to enforce the superintendence of probationers, and report anent their useful employment. 1838, ult.

——— Said committee reported the number of probationers as 700—of whom 276 were employed as missionaries or assistants, 148 as teachers, 131 were unemployed, 37 were engaged in secular pursuits, and 65 could preach in Gaelic. 1839, ult.

——— In a case of *fama* against a probationer, reference was made for advice as to whether it should be prosecuted by the presbytery by which he was licensed or the presbytery in which he resided. Found to be the latter. Com., June 4, 1840; Com., March 17, 1841.

——— The Assembly recorded the value they attached to the services rendered to the Church by the probationers in her season of peculiar difficulty. 1844. 10.

——— A student, who had finished the curriculum of theological study prescribed by the Church, went to Ireland, and was licensed by the Presbytery of Dublin. On his return to Scotland, the Assembly directed the presbytery to whom he applied to take him on trials *de novo*, and, if found qualified, to license him in the usual manner. 1848. 9.

——— Schedule sent down to presbyteries for a return of the

probationers residing within their respective bounds. 1848, ult.

Probationers. Report of said committee. 1850. 10.

——— Probationers resident in England, within the bounds of a presbytery in connection with this Church, required to report themselves within two months to the moderator of said presbytery, and to make such acquaintance with the members thereof as will enable them, when they return to Scotland, to bring along with them a favourable certificate. 1850. 15.

——— Unemployed probationers earnestly entreated to consider the destitute condition of our expatriated countrymen, and to put themselves into communication with the colonial committee. 1852. 4.

——— Remitted to a presbytery to take further trial of a probationer, to take down in writing their questions and his answers, and to receive written copies of his sermons. 1738. 4.

Procedure. Larger overtures concerning the discipline and method of procedure in the ecclesiastical judicatories of the Church of Scotland, transmitted to the several presbyteries to be further considered. 1705. 15.

——— Act anent overtures concerning the method of procedure in ecclesiastical judicatories. 1697. v.; 1698. ix.; 1707. xvii.; 1710. xvi.; 1718. x.

Process. Committee appointed to receive overtures anent the form of process in church judicatories, in order to make a frame thereof. 1694. 14.

——— Committee appointed to revise and remodel said overtures. 1703. xii.; 1704. xxv.; 1706. v.

——— Form of process in the judicatories of the Church of Scotland with relation to scandals and censures. 1707. xi.

——— Committee appointed to take under their consideration the form of process, and what additions or alterations may be made thereupon. 1765. 9; 1819. 5.

——— An Act on the form of process ordaining that when a presbytery have resolved to libel a minister or probationer, no complaint or appeal shall prevent the cause from going on till the relevancy shall be determined. 1835. xi.

Process. In all cases, except those which involve error in doctrine, presbyteries shall, after a libel has been found relevant by them, proceed, notwithstanding all appeals, to prepare the case for final lodgment. 1850. xiii.

——— All papers in processes to be given in to the clerk of Assembly between diets, and not while the house is sitting. 1694. vii.

——— No person to print papers in a process without consent of court. 1700. xvii.

——— All papers forming part of the record, or produced in evidence before any of the inferior courts, to be dated, numbered, and initialed by the clerks of said courts. 1850. xiv. 15.

——— *See* FORM OF PROCESS. 1707. xi.

——— *See* STANDING ORDERS. 1850. xiv.; 1859. xii.

Procurator. Mr John Dundas, of Philipstoun, Advocate, appointed advocate in ordinary and procurator for the Church. 1706. 13.

——— Mr William Grant, afterwards Lord Prestongrange, appointed in room of Mr John Dundas, deceased. 1731. 7.

——— Mr David Dalrymple appointed in room of Mr Grant, promoted to be Lord Advocate. 1746. 7.

——— Mr William Robertson appointed in room of Mr Dalrymple, promoted to the bench as Lord Westhall. 1778. 5.

——— Mr John Connell appointed in room of Mr Robertson, promoted to the bench as Lord Robertson. 1806. 1.

——— Mr Robert Bell appointed in room of Sir John Connell, deceased. 1831. 1.

——— Mr Alexander Shank Cook appointed joint procurator with Mr Bell. 1856. 10.

——— The offices of procurator and principal clerk disjoined. 1746. 7.

——— Report of committee on the duties and emoluments of the office of procurator. 1746. 9; 1856. 10.

——— Fee allowed to procurator's clerk. 1750. 3.

——— Procurator to be appointed *ad vitam aut culpam.* 1780. 7.

Profaneness. Kirk-sessions to apply to magistrates to put in execution the Acts of Parliament against profaneness. 1694. xiii.; 1706. xv.

Profaneness. An Act against profaneness to be read yearly. 1697. xi.; 1699. vii.; 1704. xi.

——— The Acts against profaneness, with a royal proclamation, to be printed in a small volume, sent to every parish, and read from every pulpit. 1714. v.; 1715. xiii.; 1722. ix.

——— Anent reprinting an abbreviate of the laws against profaneness. 1746. ix. xiii.

Professors enjoined to take very particular notice of the piety and Christian carriage of their students, and to certify accordingly in their testimonials. 1705. v.

——— To use their best endeavours to have their students well acquainted with the best method of preaching the Gospel. 1736. vii.

——— Preachers nominated to be professors of Divinity, Church History, Biblical Criticism, or Hebrew, to be taken on trials by the presbytery of the bounds, and, if qualified, ordained previously to their induction as professors. 1838. xii.

——— Anent the right of professors to sit in presbytery. The Presbytery of St Andrews appointed to receive and enrol the Professor of Divinity and Church History as a member of their presbytery at their first meeting. 1758. 5.

Property-Tax. Claim for exemption on behalf of ministers, to be submitted to Government. 1806. 6.

——— Opinion of Lord Advocate unfavourable to exemption of ministers from direct taxation—claim reserved, but proceedings dropped. 1808. 7.

——— A minister having refused payment and applied to the Assembly for assistance, the Assembly disclaimed concurrence or implication in his action, as inconsistent with the resolution of 1808. 1812. 5.

Protestation. Committee appointed to prepare an overture to prevent protestations of parties or their procurators against sentences of the Assembly. 1717. 7.

——— A minister who had been deposed appeared at the bar and offered what he called a protest, which the Assembly prohibited their clerk to receive. 1768, ult.

——— Entering a protestation by parties against a judgment of the Supreme Court, declared irregular and unconstitutional. 1770. 9.

Q

Quoad Sacra. The Act aforesaid declared to be founded on a fundamental principle of this Church, to which she is determined at all hazards to adhere. 1842. xxi.

——— The foregoing Acts rescinded as having been incompetently passed. 1843. 10.

Quorum. 15 declared to be a quorum of the Commission of the Assembly, of whom 10 to be ministers. 1694. xviii.

——— 15 to be quorum, of whom 9 to be ministers. 1696. xx.

——— 21	do.	14	do.	1703. iv.
——— 21	do.	15	do.	1705. xiii.
——— 31	do.	21	do.	1717. v.

R

Rabblers. The procurator instructed to prosecute certain rabblers at Aberdeen. 1714. 10.

——— A minister's widow allowed £320 Scots, out of the public money, on account of the charges her husband had been at in prosecuting rabblers. 1715. 7.

Rae. The thanks of the Assembly given to Sir William Rae, Lord Advocate, for his active and unwearied exertions at all times to promote the interests of the Church. 1819. 1.

——— Anent a proposed new metrical translation of the Psalms by Mr William Rae. 1850. 15.

Raining. Anent Mr John Raining's mortification for the support of schools in Scotland. 1724. 12; 1725. 9; 1726. 6; 1746. 9; 1747. 5.

Reading. Ministers recommended to read at one of the meetings for public worship such portion of the Old and New Testament as they may judge expedient. 1812. ix.

——— Ministers enjoined to observe the recommendation respecting the reading of the Holy Scriptures of the Old and New Testament at each diet of public worship. 1856. xi.

Reasons. Enacted that reasons of dissent against the determination of Church judicatories shall not be entered in the registers, but kept *in retentis*, to be laid before the superior judicatories. 1730. vii.; 1813, ult.

Reay. A letter of thanks to Lord Reay for his zeal in promoting religion in his country. 1724. 3.

Rebellion. Congratulatory address to the King on the suppression of the rebellion. 1716. vi.

——— A minister deposed for taking part in said rebellion. 1716. 12; 1717. 10.

——— A warning and exhortation against the wicked and desperate rebellion. Com., Nov. 15, 1745.

——— A minister suspended for taking part in the rebellion. Com., May 20, 1747.

——— Congratulatory address to the King upon the victory obtained by his army over the rebels in this country. 1746. v.

——— Committee appointed to assist ministers in obtaining redress for the damages they sustained by the rebels plundering them, and in recovering public libraries carried away by the rebels. 1716. 10; 1717. 11.

——— A petition from Mr Thomas Montford, minister at Kilmalie, craving relief in his present distressed circumstances, occasioned by the want of his stipend, resting by those in the rebellion, remitted to the committee on public accounts. 1746. 7.

——— The moderator represented that he, with several other members, had paid the compliments of this Church to his Serene Highness Prince Frederick of Hesse Cassel, then present in the Assembly. 1746. 10.

——— Proclamation issued by the Duke of Cumberland for discovering such of the rebels as have carried arms, and such as harbour or entertain them, appointed to be read in all the churches within Scotland. 1746. 10.

——— Presbyteries enjoined to inquire into the conduct of ministers and elders during the late unnatural rebellion, and to commence processes against offenders. 1746. x.

Rebuke. A minister sentenced to be sharply rebuked by the moderator from the chair, for having in the heat of passion uttered expressions irreverent towards Almighty God. 1788. 7.

——— A minister rebuked at the bar for throwing out unsubstantiated charges against his brethren. 1788. 8.

Records. Synods recommended to have their record completely filled up annually before the meeting of Assembly, signed by the moderator and clerk, and timeously produced to the General Assembly yearly. 1698. xi.

Records. Records of the several judicatories to be regularly revised by the next superior court, and attested according to the form prescribed. 1700. ix.

——— An Act for supplying and preserving the records and papers belonging to the Assembly. 1703. xi.; 1704. xxvii.; 1706. ix.; 1712. xiv.; 1816. xii.; 1839. xiv.

——— A copy of the proceedings of every Assembly to be sent to each of the University libraries. 1712. xiv.

——— Referred to a committee anent the records of Assembly, and other papers lost in the fire of 28th October 1701. 1703. 6, 9.

——— Committee appointed to speak to the Earl of Cromarty to receive some records of the Assembly, from 1560 to 1610, said to be in his lordship's hands. 1707. 8; 1708. 7; 1709. 13.

——— Committee appointed to revise the old records, and endeavour to supply what was wanting. 1708. 13.

——— Reported that the records of the Assembly for the years 1690 and 1692, with copies of their proceedings from 1702 to 1736 inclusive, are lodged in the four universities; the records from 1694 to 1700 having been lost by the fire of 28th October 1701, and the principal registers of Assembly and Commissions, down to the year 1736, except for the said years above lost, are in the clerk's hands, together with an old register of Assembly from 1560 to 1608. 1737, ult.

——— Commission appointed to inquire anent presbytery records and old MSS. 1741. 8.

——— The Commission instructed to use all possible endeavours to recover the old registers of the Church, which were lodged by Mr Secretary Johnstone in the hands of the deceased Mr George Redpath at London. 1726, ult.

——— A committee appointed to negotiate for their recovery. 1733. 9; 1738. 9; 1739, ult.

——— The moderator appointed to sign the records of several former Assemblies, the moderators of which had been removed by death. 1733. 9.

——— A recovered transcript of the proceedings of Assembly from 1560 to 1608 attested as a true copy. 1734, ult.

Records. Certain volumes of MSS. purchased from the executors of Professor Crawford, and lodged in the clerk's hands. 1737. 8.

——— A room obtained in the Register Office for the preservation of the Assembly records. 1790. 9.

——— *See* Annual Reports.

——— Committee on the Schemes instructed to make provision for increasing the interest and widening the circulation of the 'Missionary Record,' as the organ of the Church in reference to its missionary operations. 1849, ult.

Registers. An Act and recommendation for keeping parochial registers of the dead. 1746. xii.

——— Every parish recommended to keep three separate registers—viz., for births, marriages, and deaths, and to submit them annually to the presbytery of the bounds. 1816. xii.; 1817, ult.

——— Registers of baptisms and proclamations of banns appointed to be kept in every parish. 1856. vii.

——— Presbyteries ordered to keep a separate register for particulars relating to the Ministers' Widows' Fund. 1744. iv.

Registration. Committee appointed to confer with the Lord Advocate anent registration of births, &c. 1817. 10; 1819. 8; 1821. 7; 1828. 10.

——— Petition to Parliament against Registration Bill. 1837. 3; Com., March 7, 1849; 1852. 15; 1853. 14; 1854, ult.

Regiments. Committee appointed to consider in regard to the administration of ordinances in Scotch regiments. 1806. 10; 1807. 10; 1812. 4.

——— Petitions to Parliament for the appointment of Presbyterian chaplains for Scotch regiments. 1839, ult.

Regulations. Anent the calling of ministers. 1836. xi.; 1840. xiii.; 1856. xii.

References. Recommendation concerning the method of giving in references to the General Assembly. 1706. vi.

——— A reference must be made to the next superior judicatory. The Assembly refused to consider a reference from a presbytery, on the ground that it had been made direct to the Assembly, and not to an intervening meeting of synod. 1821. 6.

References. Found that the party concerning whom a reference is made must be formally cited to appear at the bar of the superior court, and that where there was no citation there was no case. 1832. 6.

——— *See* STANDING ORDERS.

Reformation. Proceedings in regard to the Tricentenary of the Reformation. 1858, ult.; 1860. 6.

Relief. Act deposing Mr Thomas Gillespie, the Father of the Relief Church. 1752. 4.

Religious. The Religious Instruction Commission declared to be not entitled to the confidence of the Church. Com., Aug. 13, 1835.

——— Petition for placing nunneries and other religious houses under the supervision of the civil authorities. 1853. 13.

Reponed. Enjoined that when a minister has been deposed, the filling up of the vacancy should never be delayed in the expectation of his being reponed, "it being almost impossible that ever he can prove useful in that parish again." 1707. xi. cap. vii. 14.

——— In a particular case, "in its so peculiarly favourable circumstances," the Assembly authorised a presbytery to repone a minister in his former parish; but at the same time declared that no minister deposed for immorality shall be capable of being restored to his former charge in any circumstances whatsoever, without the special authority of the General Assembly appointing it. 1748. 6.

Representation. The representation of presbyteries in the General Assembly to hold proportion to the number of parishes in each, *i. e.*:—

	Ministers.		Elders.
Presbyteries consisting of less than 12 parishes shall send	2	and	1
Presbyteries consisting of 13 to 18 shall send	3	,,	1
Do. do. 19 to 24 do.	4	,,	2
Do. do. 25 to 30 do.	5	,,	2
Do. do. 31 to 36 do.	6	,,	3
Do. do. 37 to 42 do.	7	,,	3
Do. do. 43 to 48 do.	8	,,	4
Do. do. 49 to 54 do.	9	,,	4
Do. do. 55 and upwards do.	10	,,	5

1694. v.; 1712. vi.; 1835. xix.; 1839. vii.

Representation. Presbyteries strictly enjoined to send their full number of representatives to the General Assembly. 1709. vii.

——— Act declaring who have a right to vote in the election of a commissioner from the University of Edinburgh. 1723. vi.

——— Representative elders prohibited from acting as procurators or agents in any causes before the Assembly or Commission. 1751. iv.

——— Representative elders to be *bona fide* acting elders, which must be certified by the kirk-session of which they are a member. 1839. xii.

——— An overture on the status and qualifications of representatives to the General Assembly referred to a committee. 1857, ult.

Rescissory. Enacted that no Act rescissory of any standing Acts of Assembly shall be passed without being first transmitted as an overture to presbyteries in terms of the Barrier Act. 1736. s.

——— An Act rescinding Act 1799. v. anent ministerial communion (1842. ix.) itself rescinded. 1843. xv.

——— Act rescinding the Act 1835. ix., on the calling of ministers, commonly called the Veto Act. 1843. ix.

——— Act rescinding the Acts of 1833, 1834, and 1839, as to ministers of chapels-of-ease. 1843. x.

——— Act rescinding Act 1845. vii., on the mode of taking the vote. 1846. viii.

Residence of Ministers in their respective parishes required by the fundamental laws of the Church. 1817. vi.

——— Found that the existing laws of the Church and State make sufficient provision for ensuring the residence of the ministers of the Church of Scotland, and presbyteries recommended to continue their vigilant attention to the execution of those laws of which they are the constitutiona guardians. 1801. s.

——— Presbyteries not to examine students for enrolment in the Divinity Hall, unless their chief residence during the preceding six months has been within their bounds. 1714. vi.; 1851. s.

——— Presbyteries not to take students on trials for licence

unless their residence during the year has been chiefly within their bounds. 1813. viii.; 1849. xi.

Residence. Students not resident within the bounds of the Church to be examined by the presbytery within whose bounds the University at which they study is situated. 1835. xv.

——— *See* NON-RESIDENCE.

Resignation. A minister having resigned, and the presbytery having accepted his resignation, he was summoned to appear before the Assembly to answer for his conduct in giving up his ministerial charge. The Assembly reversed the sentence of the presbytery, disapproving thereof as highly reprehensible and irregular in accepting *simpliciter* under the circumstances of the case the said resignation, and ordained the minister to return to his charge. 1799. 3 and 6.

——— The resignation of a minister having been accepted by a presbytery, the Assembly declared him no longer a minister of the Church of Scotland, and incapable of receiving a presentation or call. 1799. 6.

——— A minister having given in the resignation of his parish to the presbytery, he being appointed to a professorship, the presbytery allowed it to lie on the table till next ordinary meeting. A question arose as to whether the parish became vacant on the day when the resignation was given in, or on the day when it was accepted, the Assembly found that the vacancy took place only on the acceptance of the resignation by the presbytery. 1859. 14.

——— A minister having sent in a resignation of his parish to the parish on the plea of bad health, the presbytery at once accepted the resignation, and declared the parish vacant. At a subsequent meeting the minister solicited the presbytery to reconsider their judgment, on the ground that he had been concussed into signing the letter of resignation. The presbytery found that it was incompetent for them to comply with the request, the matter being *res judicata.* The Assembly reversed the procedure of the presbytery in accepting the resignation, and remitted the case to them, with instructions to prosecute the matter on the original letter of resignation according to the rules of the Church. 1848. 7.

——— A presbytery having accepted the resignation of a minister in very peculiar circumstances, the Assembly, on the ground that these circumstances were not explained in the extract minutes produced, cited the presbytery to appear before the Commission, and to bring the records of presbytery, with all the minutes relating to the matter engrossed. At which meeting the Commission found that the presbytery had acted irregularly in not summoning the parishioners as parties; and in accepting the resignation without specifying distinctly in their minutes the ground on which they came to that judgment. Com., May 31, 1853; August 10, 1853.

Resignation. A presbytery having accepted the resignation of a minister while he was under a *fama*, without duly intimating such resignation to the parishioners, and citing them to appear for their interests, the Assembly expressed their decided disapproval of their conduct in acting so precipitately. 1858. 3.

Resolution. Declaring patronage a grievance, and that it ought to be abolished. 1842. xii.

Restored. Enacted that before a minister deposed for scandalous carriage can be restored to the exercise of the ministerial functions, there must be not only convincing evidences of a deep sorrow for sin, but an eminent and exemplary humble walk and edifying conversation. 1707. xi. cap. vii. 14.

——— Messrs Thomas Lining, Alexander Shields, and William Boyd restored to the fellowship of the Church. 1690. v.

——— Mr Robert Dalrymple restored. 1776. ix.

——— A minister who had been deposed restored to the status of a licentiate. 1858. vii.

——— See also 1860. 13; 1862. 10.

Reunion. An Act anent reunion with Seceders. 1839. viii.

Revised. Certain proceedings of a presbytery having been brought under the notice of the synod, were referred by the synod to the Assembly. The Assembly cited the presbytery to appear at their bar and explain. The presbytery having compeared, the Assembly found that their decision required to be reconsidered, and instructed them accordingly. 1851. 4 and ult.

Revivals. On an overture on revivals, the Assembly, while by no means committing itself to an approval of all that had accompanied recent religious movements, recommended to all ministers and elders special watchfulness and prayer in regard to the progress of vital religion in their parishes. 1860. 13; 1861. 15.

Revolution. A national thanksgiving appointed to be kept as the centenary or secular anniversary of the Happy and Glorious Revolution. 1788. x.

——— Address to the King anent commemoration of the Revolution. 1788. iv.

Rioting. Referred to the procurator to bring a process, if necessary, against Mr Rattray of Dulrulzian, for rioting in the kirk of Kirkmichael. 1786, ult.

Roll. A roll of communicants to be made up annually in every parish. 1835. x.

——— Every kirk-session required to make up annually a duly purged roll of communicants, and presbyteries to see that this is regularly done. 1862. vii.

——— Of causes before the Assembly to be put up daily in a conspicuous place. 1768. 3.

——— Ordained that before the roll begin to be called for taking a vote, the doors of the Assembly House shall be shut, and not opened until the judgment has been declared. 1789. vi.

Ross. An Act anent the supply of Ross, Sutherland, and Caithness. 1696. xiv.

——— The Synod of Ross appointed to meet once in the year only, instead of twice. 1759. iv.; 1761. ix.

Rotterdam. Referred to the Commission to settle any question that might come before them about planting the Scots congregation at Rotterdam. 1736. 10.

Royal Bounty. The Commission instructed to address the government for a suitable fund yearly, during His Majesty's pleasure, for maintaining more preachers and catechists for travelling in countries where popery abounds. 1723. 8.

——— A warrant under His Majesty's hand, delivered to the Assembly, signifying his gracious inclination to contribute yearly £1000 sterling for the encouragement of itinerant preachers and catechists, to assist the ministers of large parishes in the Highlands and Islands where popery and ignorance do prevail, and giving thus to the Assembly £1000 to be disposed of by them for the foresaid purposes as they thought fit. 1725. 2.

S

sailing; application to Parliament to alter all markets in royal burghs kept on Saturdays and Mondays. 1690. vii.

Sabbath. Acts for the better observance of the Sabbath. 1705. ix; 1708. xii; 1722. ix.

——— Opinion of Lord President Blair on the statutes in force with respect to the observance of the Sabbath-day—said statutes printed with the Acts and transmitted to presbyteries, along with an admonition and information respecting the profanation of the Lord's Day. 1794, ult.; 1823. x.

——— Pastoral admonition on the sanctification of the Sabbath. 1834. 7. and ult.

——— Petition to Parliament on the Bill for explaining the Scots Acts on Sabbath observance. 1834, ult.

——— Committee instructed to endeavour to get a legislative enactment to prevent fishing on the Sabbath in the Solway. 1804. 5; 1805. 5 and 10.

——— Procurator to endeavour to prevent the running of stage-coaches on the Lord's Day. 1807. 8.

——— Anent salmon-fishing with stake-nets. 1804. 5; 1826. 4.

——— Anent state processions during the sitting of Assembly. 1834. 1-4.

——— Petition to Parliament against railway travelling. Com., Nov. 18, 1846; 1847. 9; 1836. 2; 1837. 4; 1841. 15.

——— Petition to Parliament against sale of spirits on Lord's Day. 1838. 9; 1840. 9.

——— Anent blast-furnaces going on Lord's Day. 1850. 13.

——— Anent unnecessary labour in the Post-office on the Lord's Day. 1850. 8; 1851. 15. Com., March 6, 1850.

——— Reference to the commission to use all proper endeavours to put a stop to the going of the salt-pans of Dysart on the Lord's Day. 1737, ult.

——— *See* ANNUAL REPORTS OF COMMITTEE ON SABBATH OBSERVANCE.

Sabbath Schools. A report concerning vagrant teachers and sabbath schools by the Committee appointed to inquire into the existing laws which place teachers and schoolmasters under the control of the Established Church, ordered to be printed, and a copy sent to every minister. 1799. xii. and ult.

——— Sabbath schools during the hours of divine service

declared to be a violation of the Sabbath, which the civil magistrate should be called on to prevent. 1811. 9.

Sabbath Schools. Declared that the safest course to be pursued in regard to text-books in Sabbath schools is to use the books of Scripture, the metrical versions of the Psalms and Paraphrases, with the Catechisms already authorised by the Church. Com., June 1, 1837.

——— Committee instructed to procure from ministers returns in regard to the state of Sabbath schools in every parish, and to publish these with the reports from presbyteries on education. 1841. 11 ; 1850. 4.

——— *See* Annual Reports of Committee.

Sacraments. An Act anent the administration of the sacraments, prohibiting the administration of the Lord's Supper to sick persons in their houses, and of baptism in private, or at any time when the congregation is not orderly called together to wait on the dispensing of the Word. 1690. vi. ; 1690. x.

——— Ordained that no grossly ignorant nor scandalous person be admitted to the Lord's Table. 1694. xiii.

——— Recommended that the Lord's Supper be more frequently administered, and the number of ministers assisting thereat restricted, that neighbouring churches be not thrown desolate. 1701. xix.

——— Ministers enjoined diligently to examine and instruct young communicants. 1706. xi. ; 1727. viii.

——— Presbyteries enjoined to do what they can to get it so ordered that the Lord's Supper may be administered in the several parishes within their bounds, at different times through the several months of the year. 1711. vi. ; 1724. vi.

——— Ministers neglecting to celebrate the Supper for a whole year to be called to account by their presbyteries and synods. 1712. xi. ; 1724. 6. ; 1751. vii.

——— Ministers recommended to show all tenderness to persons educated in other Protestant Churches when they desire sealing ordinances, and cheerfully to comply with their desire. 1711. xiii.

——— Children, one or both of whose parents are members of the Church, have a right to baptism ; no other sponsor to be taken than a parent unless they be dead or absent, under scandal, or grossly ignorant, in which circumstances one related to the parents to be sponsor. The parent or sponsor to speak to the minister before baptism. In the case of children exposed, the kirk-session to order the presenting of the child for baptism. 1712. iv.

Sacraments. Recommendation anent buying Mr John Spalding's book on the Sacrament of the Lord's Supper. 1705. xv.

——— Anent the administration of sacraments by deposed and excommunicated ministers or others not qualified. 1719. 8.

——— Thursday ordered to be continued as a fast-day before the Sacrament of the Supper as formerly. Declared to be inexpedient for synods or presbyteries to appoint any general alteration of the diets of public worship at such solemn occasions till the matter be considered by the General Assembly. 1751. 9.

——— The Synod of Argyle having appointed the sermons on the Saturday before and Monday after the Sacrament to be discontinued, the Assembly, on appeal, allowed the appellants to have sermon on the Saturday, as they saw it to be for edification. 1762. 6.

——— Declared, that the Sacrament of the Lord's Supper ought to be dispensed within the bounds of the Church at least once every year; that the time of dispensing it is left in every parish to the discretion of the minister and elders, yet that is not a wise exercise of this discretion to select such times as must be known materially to interfere with the temporal interests of the parish, and particularly that it should not interfere with seed-time or harvest. 1826. 4.

——— It having been reported to the Assembly that many children in the parish of Bracadale were unbaptised, the Assembly instructed the Presbytery of Skye to see that the ordinance of baptism was regularly administered in said parish. 1826. 5.

——— A presentee having been required by the parishioners to declare in writing his consent to their receiving sealing ordinances from any other minister of the Church, as they had not freedom to receive them from him, the Assembly declared their high disapprobation of any such arrangement, as inconsistent with the constitution of the Church of Scotland and subversive of good order. 1809. 5.

Sacraments. A kirk-session and presbytery having refused the privilege of baptism to a child because the father of said child did not attend the ordinances of religion in his own parish church, the Assembly reversed said judgments, and ordered the child to be baptised, on the ground that the father had a business concern in another parish, which obliged him to be frequently in that parish in the end of the week; and that he regularly attended divine worship in said parish. 1809, ult.

——— Declared to be contrary to the laws and constitution of this Church for any minister to administer sealing ordinances to those who desert the ministry of their established pastors, and unbecoming and schismatical in neighbouring ministers to give countenance or encouragement to those who statedly withdraw themselves from their own congregations. 1810. 5.

——— Declared that it is the law, and has been the immemorial practice of the Church of Scotland to dispense the sacrament of the Lord's Supper to the people seated at or around a communion table or tables, and presbyteries enjoined to use their best endeavours, when churches are rebuilt or reseated, to have a suitable table or tables provided for the solemn service of the Lord's Supper. 1825. 4; 1827. 5.

——— On a reference for advice anent certain alleged irregularities in the dispensation of the Lord's Supper, the Assembly remitted to the presbytery to give such admonition as the circumstances of the case required. 1826. 9.

——— It having been reported to the Assembly that the Lord's Supper had not been administered in certain parishes for more than a year, the Assembly enjoined the presbytery of the bounds to see that said ordinance was dispensed during the current year in all their parishes, and to report to next Assembly. 1837, ult.

——— A minister and kirk-session found to have acted judiciously in refusing to baptise the child of a person who pled guilty to several charges, but refused to express his penitence until his child should be baptised. Com., May 28, 1833.

Sacraments. The kirk-session of a city parish having resolved to dispense the Sacrament of the Lord's Supper four times in the year, the presbytery prohibited the minister from administering it more frequently than it was administered to other congregations in the city, on the ground that the dispensation of the communion was one of the points in which the city must be held to be one parish. The synod reversed the sentence complained of, and left it to the kirk-session to proceed with the administration of the Lord's Supper as to them might seem expedient. The Assembly found that, while legally constituted, kirk-sessions have a right under the control of their respective presbyteries to determine as to the frequency of dispensing the Sacrament of the Supper, such a degree of uniformity as to the dispensation of ordinances in the city churches ought to be observed as may insure a similarity of practice in regard to the frequency of dispensing the Sacrament of the Supper. 1833, ult.

——— A committee appointed to take the matter of the more frequent celebration of the Lord's Supper into their serious consideration, to inquire carefully into the practice of the Church in former times, and report to next Assembly. 1842. 4.

——— Attention earnestly called to the importance and necessity of the regular and stated observance of the Lord's Supper, and recommended that that ordinance should be administered, not once only, but twice every year in all the churches. 1846, ult.

——— An overture anent dispensing the Lord's Supper to congregations in private, after discussion withdrawn. 1852. 13; 1853, ult.; 1856. 10.

——— An overture on the mode of administering the Lord's Supper, praying the Assembly to enjoin that all participating should communicate simultaneously and not in detached parties, after discussion withdrawn. 1853. 13.

——— A deputation appointed to proceed to Skye to confer with the presbytery, and arrange for the regular dispensation of divine ordinances in a parish there. 1853, ult.; Com., Nov. 16, 1853.

——— Ministers administering the Sacraments in private, to be noticed and censured accordingly. 1690. vi.

Sacraments. An Act anent the administration of the Sacraments. 1690. x.

Sacred Poesy. *See* PARAPHRASES.

Sackloth. A kirk-session ordained to admit a man to make satisfaction without sackloth. 1737, ult.

Sailing. Presbyteries enjoined to put in execution the Acts of Assembly against unnecessary sailing and travelling on the Lord's Day. 1690. vii.

Salmon-fishing. A committee appointed to watch over a Bill before Parliament anent salmon-fishing, and to take measures for preventing the profanation of the Lord's Day. 1801. 5; 1805, ult.

Scandals. Reference to the Commission anent old scandals, and scandals committed out of the kingdom by persons now residing therein. 1699. 18.

——— A minister deposed for scandal and other miscarriages. 1704, ult.

——— Refused to admit a party to purge himself by oath of a scandal he was alleged to be guilty of, in regard it was judged the same could not remove the scandal, the presumptions of guilt being so pregnant. 1711. 4.

——— The Commission instructed to give advice to the Synod of Moray, relating to the fourth section of the first chapter of the form of process concerning the five years' prescription of scandals. 1744, ult.

——— Enacted that if a scandal shall not happen to be noticed in order to censure for the space of five years, it should not be again revived, unless it be of a heinous nature, or become again flagrant. 1707. xi. chap. i. 4.

——— Presbyteries allowed, if they saw cause, to send in to the General Assembly the names of scandalous persons of whatever quality, that the Assembly might proceed against them as they thought meet. 1700. xv.

——— An Act concerning the method and form of procedure of judicatories of the Church against scandalous persons. 1705. iv.

——— Ordained that if parties under scandal live in different parishes, the process against them shall be before the session of the parish where the woman liveth, or where the scandal is most notour. 1707. xi. chap. iv. 15.

Scandals. Presbytery enjoined to apply to magistrates and commanding officers to compel soldiers under scandal to submit to the discipline of the Church. 1710. v.

——— Enacted that if a minister be convicted or plead guilty of a scandalous offence, he shall *instanter* be deposed, whatever be the nature of his penitence, though manifest to all. 1707. xi. chap. vii. 5.

——— Scandalous and contumacious persons to be excommunicated. 1704. viii.

Scarcity. A day set apart for fasting and prayer on account of a visitation of Providence in afflicting the land with an uncommon scarcity of provisions. 1783. vii.

Schedules. Printed schedules first issued to presbyteries for their annual reports on the examination of schools. 1819. viii.

Schemes of the Church. Committee appointed to inquire into the expenses connected with their management, and whether any means could be devised by which these expenses might be reduced without impairing the efficiency of the schemes. 1848. 4 and 11; 1852. 6.

——— A committee appointed, consisting of the several conveners, and two other members from each committee, to confer and arrange in regard to matters of common interest to the committees. 1849, ult.

——— The India Mission Scheme, instituted 1824. 7.

——— The Education Scheme, instituted 1824. 7.

——— The Home Mission Scheme, instituted 1842. xviii.

——— The Colonial Mission, instituted 1836. ix.

——— The Jewish Mission, instituted 1840. ix.

——— The Endowment Scheme, instituted 1849. vi.

Schemes. Committee authorised to carry into effect certain suggestions in regard to more suitable accommodation for the Committees of the Church. 1851. 14; 1854. 11.

Schism. Acts for suppressing schism and disorders in the Church. 1704. xviii.; 1708. vi.

——— The Commission instructed to use all suitable means for remedying of schism, and for recovering those who on either hand do withdraw from the communion of the Church. 1706. 12.

——— Committee appointed to inquire anent the number of

meeting-houses erected by those who had seceded from the Church, and the state of the congregations thereto belonging. 1765. 8.

Schism. An overture anent the causes and growth of schism, with the foresaid Committee's report thereon, considered, and after a long debate rejected. 1766. 8.

Schools. Synods and presbyteries enjoined to see that schools are erected in every parish conform to Acts of Parliament and former Assemblies. 1690. xi.; 1699. x.

——— A report in regard to the state of education in the Highlands; schools to be erected there; a general subscription ordered. 1704. xiv.; 1707. v.

——— Ministers enjoined to see that a school is erected in every parish. Children to be instructed in the principles of the Christian religion. Poor scholars to be taught on charity. 1705. v.; 1719. iv.

——— Grammar schools to be visited by presbyteries at least twice every year. 1706. xiii.; 1707. v.

——— Presbyteries earnestly enjoined to take a watchful inspection of all schools within their bounds, and of the character and behaviour of schoolmasters. 1749. iv.

——— Presbyteries enjoined to hold visitations in all parishes where schools are awanting, and to take all proper and legal steps for erecting schools therein, with competent salaries and schoolhouses as the law directs. 1749. vi.

——— The Society for Propagating Christian Knowledge having reported that there were not less than 475 parishes in which no parochial schools had been erected, the Assembly renewed the injunction on presbyteries to take the necessary steps for remedying the evil. 1758. vi.; 1762. 4.

——— A statement of the laws which place schools and schoolmasters under the inspection and control of the Church. 1799. xiii.

——— Presbyteries enjoined to continued diligence in attending to the different schools within their bounds. The Presbytery of Brechin commended for the firmness and propriety with which they had asserted their unquestionable right to examine all schools of every description. 1817. v.

——— A similar case. 1836. 8; 1837. 4; 1838. 4. 8.

Schools. Presbyteries enjoined to be regular in examining schools, and to report annually to the Assembly. 1810. ix.; 1813. x.; 1820. vii.; 1819. viii.; 1830. 4.

——— *See* ANNUAL REPORTS.

——— Presbyteries recommended to use all prudent means for promoting the cultivation of church music in all schools under the superintendence of the Church, according to the practice in former times. 1839. 11.

——— Presbyteries peremptorily required to send up with their commissioners annual returns of the examination of schools, specifying the names, not only of the schools examined, but also of every school which has not been examined, and the cause of the omission. 1829. 9.

——— The erection of schools in connection with *quoad sacra* churches recommended. 1839. 11.

——— The Presbytery of Elgin having vindicated the right of the Church to examine burgh schools, the Assembly strongly recommended their claim to relief, by pecuniary contributions, from a burden incurred by them by the advice and for the interest of the Church. 1861. 11.

——— A full report in regard to the existing provision for education, and the existing deficiences. 1854. 7.

School Books. Overtures in regard to a new series of books for the use of schools, referred to the immediate attention of the Education Committee. 1838. 8.

Schoolmasters to be appointed to teach English in every Highland parish. 1699. ix.

——— Presbyteries enjoined to require all schoolmasters to sign the Confession of Faith. 1699. xiii.; 1700. x.; 1706. xiii.

——— Those who had the power of settling schoolmasters, recommended to prefer men who had passed their course at college and taken their degrees. 1706. xiii.

——— Schoolmasters required to teach the common church tunes, and not only to pray with their scholars, but to sing part of a psalm with them every day. 1713. vii.

——— Presbyteries enjoined to call before them all teachers of youth, whether in parochial or other schools, and to take trial of their sufficiency and qualifications. 1799. xii.; 1800. xi.; 1801. viii.; 1802. vi.; 1808. ix.

——— The exclusive jurisdiction of the Church, with regard

to the qualifications of parochial schoolmasters, having been decided by the House of Lords in the case of Bothwell, the Assembly recommended a general subscription throughout the Church to assist in defraying the expenses of the appeal. 1800. xii.

Schoolmasters. Declared that the parochial schoolmasters are a body of men who have been highly useful in diffusing knowledge and learning among the people of Scotland; that in the opinion of the Assembly their provision for maintenance was generally too small, and therefore that they deserved further encouragement from the public. 1784, ult.; 1802. vii.

——— Anent the right of a minister to vote in the election of a schoolmaster. 1756. 8.

——— Recommendation relative to the proposed establishment of a fund for making a provision for the widows of parochial schoolmasters. 1761. 5; 1762. 4.

——— Anent the power of the superior ecclesiastical courts to review the sentence of a presbytery relative to the qualifications of a schoolmaster. 1791, ult.

——— Reports from presbyteries relative to vagrant teachers. 1801. 9.

——— The new Act of Parliament in favour of parochial schoolmasters to be printed by the Clerk of Assembly, and transmitted to presbyteries. 1803, ult.

——— The Assembly dismissed as incompetent an appeal from the sentence of a presbytery regarding the character and qualifications of a schoolmaster. 1809. 9.

——— Found that a libel against a schoolmaster may be insisted in, either at the instance of the heritors, minister, or elders, or at the instance of the presbytery of the bounds. 1812. 9.

——— Anent an action of reduction of a sentence of a presbytery deposing a schoolmaster. 1824, ult.

——— With reference to a Bill before Parliament, the Assembly declared their decided opinion that no person ought to be admitted to the office of a parish schoolmaster who shall not be found by the presbytery of the bounds qualified to teach the Latin language, with power to the presbytery, in every case, to determine what other qualifications may be necessary; and further, that the right of appeal from the sentence of presbyteries in the case of schoolmasters to the supreme ecclesiastical courts, according to the ancient laws of the Church, ought to be restored. 1825, ult.

Schoolmasters. A memorial and petition from the parochial schoolmasters of Scotland, laid before the Assembly by Thomas Maitland, Esq., advocate, proposing amendments on Act 1803, was cordially approved of, and recommended to Her Majesty's government. 1834, ult.; 1844. 17; 1845. 14.

—— A schoolmaster having refused to compear before the presbytery for examination, the Sheriff interdicted him from teaching till he had satisfied the presbytery, and found him liable in expenses. 1804. 7.

—— A Bill before Parliament for the regulation of schools and the appointment of schoolmasters in those newly erected parishes in the Highlands, for which an endowment had been secured, approved of. 1838. 8 and ult.

—— Resolved to maintain, and endeavour to extend in its connection with the Church, the admirable system of National Schools, which has, by the blessing of God, been productive of inestimable benefit to the people of this country. 1854. 7.

—— Bill for regulating Reformatory and Industrial Schools, remitted to Education Committee, with authority to take such steps thereanent as to them might seem meet. 1854, ult.

—— The magistrates of a burgh having refused to allow the presbytery to examine the burgh school, the Assembly instructed the presbytery to apply to the Lord Ordinary, and authorised the procurator to give all needful advice and assistance. 1836. 8; 1846. 14; Com., June 1, 1851.

—— Committee appointed to consider and advise presbyteries in regard to certain schoolmasters who refused to comply with the statutory duty to acknowledge and subscribe the Confession of Faith, and conform to the government and discipline of the Church. 1845. 11.

—— The Education Committee instructed to bring under the attention of the Privy Council the claims of the teachers of the Parochial and Assembly Schools to a due share of the grant for the advancement of education in Scotland. 1848. 10.

Schoolmasters. Petitions to Parliament against School Bills. 1850. 10; 1851. 7; Com., Mar. 6, 1850.

——— Committee appointed to consider the best means to be adopted for raising the emoluments and improving the condition of the parochial schoolmasters, a body of men whose services have been of incalculable benefit to the country. 1850. 12.

——— The Assembly approved of the steps taken for introducing the elements of industrial education into the Highlands and Islands. 1852. 8.

——— Petition to Parliament for prevention of the diminution of the salaries of schoolmasters about to take place under the Act of 1803. 1853. 3.

——— Debate on the inspection of schools and government grants. 1853. 3.

——— A schoolmaster having for years absented himself from public worship, the presbytery referred the matter to the Assembly, who found that the case came under the description of divisive courses, and recommended the presbytery to exercise their statutory powers and proceed against him to deposition, or take such steps as they in their own judgment might consider proper. 1853. 13.

——— Resolved to use every constitutional means for preserving the parochial schools in strict connection with the Church, as the best security, under the Divine blessing, for continuing and perpetuating the religious element in the education of the youth of the land. Com., Nov. 16, 1853.

Scriptures. Ministers enjoined in their exercise of lecturing to read and open up to their people a large and considerable portion of the Word of God, that the old custom established by the Directory might by degrees be recovered. 1694. ix.; 1704. v.

——— Ministers enjoined to read at one of the diets for public worship such portion of the Old or New Testament, or both, as they may judge expedient. 1812. ix.

——— Ordained that every congregation, at each diet of public worship, should have the advantage of hearing a portion of the Old or New Testament read, and that there should be always included in the service of every Lord's

Day, not only a sermon, but a lecture on a passage of the Holy Scriptures. 1856. xi.

Scriptures. Committee appointed to watch over the correction of the impressions of the Scriptures, Confession of Faith, and other books authorised by the Church. Com., May 31, 1836; Com., May 30, 1837.

Scripture Songs. Commission instructed to revise a collection of Scripture songs. 1695. 17; 1705. 12.

——— Presbyteries recommended to promote the use of said songs in private families, for facilitating the Assembly's work in preparing said songs for public use. 1706. iv.

——— Said songs re-transmitted to presbyteries for further consideration. 1707. xvi.

——— The Commission empowered to publish and emit said songs for the public use of the Church, as was formerly done on the like occasion when our version of the Psalms was published in the year 1649. 1708. xv.

Seat-Rents. Committee appointed to inquire into the origin, extent, and legality of the practice of exacting seat-rents in endowed parish churches, and the course which the Church should adopt in regard to it. 1839. 10.

——— A circular address on the subject of seat-rents to be read from all the pulpits of the Church. 1842, ult.

Seceders. An Act concerning some of the ministers of the Presbytery of Dunfermline for preserving the subordination of the judicatories of the Church and good order therein. 1733. v.

——— Act and sentences concerning Mr Ebenezer Erskine for contempt. 1733. vii.; 1734. viii.; 1738. iv.; 1739. iv.

——— Act and sentence of deposition against eight ministers who had seceded from the Church. 1740. iv.

——— Magistrates exhorted to debar deposed ministers from access to officiate in parish churches. 1742. 8.

——— Mr Thomas Boston having seceded and demitted his charge, declared incapable of receiving a call or presentation to any parish in this Church. 1758. iv.

——— A similar Act concerning Mr James Bain. 1766. vi.

——— Enacted that all the ministers of the Associated Synod of Original Seceders, and their congregations, desirous of being re-admitted into connection and communion with the Church, be received accordingly. 1839. viii.

Seceders. Act of separation and deed of demission given in by certain ministers and elders who left the Assembly on the 18th of May 1843. All the ministers and elders who had signed said deed declared to have ceased, by their own voluntary act, to be ministers or elders of the Church of Scotland. 1843. xi.

Secession. Committee appointed to prepare instructions to presbyteries anent the proceedings necessary in consequence of the recent secession. 1843. 7.

Secular Pursuits. A minister who had accepted the office of sheriff-depute, having been censured for so doing, gave up the appointment. 1735, ult.

——— A minister deposed (*inter alia*) for unministerial conduct, and engaging in secular pursuits. 1837. 9.

——— The Assembly declared their high disapproval of ministers engaging in such secular employments as are inconsistent with the full and faithful discharge of their professional duties. 1819. 7.

Semple. A committee appointed to inquire at the representatives of the late Mr Jones Semple, minister at Liberton, what progress he had made in the history he was encouraged to write of this Church, and what registers or MSS. he had left behind him. 1742. 9.

Separate. *See* REGISTERS.

Sermon. An Act concerning a sermon preached by Mr Gabriel Wilson, minister at Maxton, before the Synod of Merse and Teviotdale. 1723. xi.

Servants. Ministers enjoined to take care that servants removing from one parish to another take with them testimonials of their honest and Christian behaviour. 1694. xiii.

Session. *See* KIRK.

Session, Court of. The Commission instructed to consider certain interlocutors of the Court of Session, whereby it was apprehended the rights and privileges of the judicatories and ministers of the Church were encroached upon. 1735. 11.

——— Claim, declaration, and protest against the encroachments of the Court of Session. 1842. xix.

Sessions, General. Presbyteries within whose bounds there are burghs including several congregations, to inquire into the constitution and practice of general sessions, and report. 1720, ult.

Settlement. Instructions to the Commission anent the settlement of parishes. 1743. vii.

——— Presbyteries recommended to use their best endeavours for obtaining the consent of the inhabitants in planting of parishes with ministers. 1715. 12.

——— Act anent the calling of ministers, commonly denominated the Veto Act, with regulations for carrying the same into effect in the settlement of parishes. 1835. ix. and x.

——— Said Act repealed, as infringing on civil and patrimonial rights, and presbyteries ordered to proceed in the settlement of parishes according to the practice which prevailed previously to the passing of that Act. 1843. 10.

——— Overture on the regulations to be observed in the case of the settlement of ministers. 1843. xviii.

——— Overture and Interim Act respecting the induction of ministers transmitted to Presbyteries—1844. ix., and retransmitted with various alterations and amendments every year thereafter till 1856, when, having obtained the consent of a majority of presbyteries, it was passed into a standing law of the Church. 1856. xii.

——— Overture anent certain proposed alterations on the regulations to be observed in the induction of ministers. 1860. vii.; 1861. vii.; 1862. vii.

Settlements, Disputed—and in regard to which references, complaints, or appeals came before the General Assembly :—

Abbotshall, 1741. 3; 1810. 7.
Abdie, 1720. 5; 1752. 8.
Aberdalgie, 1718. 14.
Aberdeen, 1695. 9; 1699. 3; 1700. 4, 5; 1701. 12; 1704. 6; 1714. 6; 1725. 4; 1831. May 31.
Aberdour, 1733. 12.
Aberfoyle, 1772. 9.
Aberlour, 1719. 9.
Airth, 1700. 10; 1697. 6; 1743, ult.; 1844, ult.
Aiton, 1752, ult.
Alloa, 1703. 4; 1750, ult.
Alness, 1726. 4.
Alyth, 1736. 6.
Alves, 1697. 6.
Ancrum, 1791. 7.
Ardnamurchan, 1761, ult.
Arbroath, 1697. 9; 1699. 10, 12; 1735. 7; 1789. 8.
Arbuthnot, 1714. 8.
Arderseir, 1709. 12.
Arrochar, 1725. 11; 1782. 5.
Auchterarder, 1835. 10; 1836. 9; 1838. 7, 9, ult.; 1839. 6; May 28 and Aug. 14; 1840. June 3; 1841. 12; 1842. Nov. 16.

Settlements, Disputed—*continued.*

Settlements, Disputed—*continued.*

Settlements, Disputed—*continued.*

Settlements, Disputed—*continued.*

Settlements, Disputed—*continued.*

Tain, 1750. 10.
Tannadice, 1743. 4.
Tarbart, 1750, ult.
Tarbolton, 1694. 10.
Tealing, 1718. 14; 1731. 5.
Temple, 1738. 5.
Terregles, 1751. 7; 1752. 5; 1781. 5.
Tongland, 1748. 4.
Tongue, 1726. 6, 7;
Torphichen, 1749. 9; 1750. 9; 1751. 6.
Torryburn, 1724. 13.
Towie, 1709. 6; 1729. 3; 1823. 9.
Tranent, 1740. 5; 1744. 5.
Trinity Gask, 1835. 7; 1836. 6.
Troqueer, 1733. 9; 1734, ult.; 1735. 9; 1736. 10; 1743, ult.
Tulliallan, 1713. 7; 1718. 15.
Tulloch, 1791. 5.
Twynholm, 1776. 7.
Tyree, 1861. 12, 13.

Udny, 1850. 6, 7.
Uist, South, 1736. 6; 1745. 9; 1746. 9.
Ullapool, 1834. 4.
Urquhart, 1733, ult.
Urr, 1836, ult.; 1837. 4.
Urray, 1749. 3; 1812. 6.

Watten, 1732. 6.
Westkirk, 1732. 7.
Whitsome, 1724. 10.
Wick, 1697. 4.
Wigtown, 1700. 6.

Sheep. A petition from the Presbytery of Zetland respecting a distemper among the sheep in that country, to be transmitted to the Lord Advocate, with a request for his interposition on behalf of the petitioners. 1790. 9.

Simony. An Act against simoniacal practices appointed to be read by presbyteries to every person before he be licensed to preach the gospel. 1753. v.

——— The aforesaid Act explained and amended. 1759. viii.

——— An overture and interim Act for the more effectual preventing of simony. 1818. vii.

——— Committee appointed to consider a cause relating to certain alleged simoniacal pactions in the case of the settlement of the parish of St Vigeans. 1756. 8.

——— An overture transmitted to presbyteries anent ministers making agreements with their heritors concerning the extent of their stipends. 1756. 5.

——— A minister, before being appointed assistant and successor to his father, having granted to the patron an obligatory letter for £50, the procurator and agent were appointed to appear in defence of the minister in case the patron pursued him for payment. 1761. 4.

——— A committee appointed to revise the laws concerning simony. 1787. 7.

——— On a reference for advice respecting an alleged simoniacal paction, the Assembly highly approved of the conduct of the presbytery in delaying proceedings, and instructed them not to take any steps in the settlement of the presentee until the question was determined, without directions from the General Assembly. 1790. 5.

Simony. The Court of Session having decided that a simoniacal transaction had been entered into, but that the presentee had no knowledge of nor accession thereto, the Assembly authorised the presbytery to proceed with his settlement. 1791. 9.

——— In a process of simony the Assembly found that there was no foundation for the charge against the presentee, and assoilzied him from the same. 1793. 8.

——— Simoniacal practices in order to obtain a presentation found relevant as a charge in a libel against presentee. 1806. 5.

——— A presbytery having found a libel, charging a presentee with simoniacal practices, proved, and deprived him of his licence, the Assembly reversed their sentence *in hoc statu*, and remitted to them to take additional evidence. 1833. 7.

——— A probationer having written a letter to the patron of a vacant parish, soliciting the presentation, and offering to pay £100 per annum for five years, the Assembly affirmed a sentence of the presbytery, depriving him of his licence as a preacher of the gospel. 1826. 9.

Simson. An Act and Commission for preserving purity of doctrine, and concerning Mr John Simson. 1727. x.

Singing. Private families recommended, in singing the praises of God in their religious exercises, to go on without the intermission of reading the line, and schoolmasters enjoined to be careful to instruct the youth in singing the common tunes. 1746. 8.

——— Presbyteries recommended, for the more decent performance of the public praises of God, to use endeavours to have such schoolmasters chosen as are capable of teaching the common tunes, and to see that children be taught to sing the said common tunes, by singing part of a psalm in the school at least once every day. 1713. vii.

Skye. An Act erecting the Presbytery of Skye and three others into the Synod of Glenelg. 1724. v.

their fellow-soldiers in communion with the Church of Rome, dismissed as unnecessary. 1827. 5.

Songs, Scripture. Referred to the Commission to cause revise the Scripture songs. 1695, ult.; 1705. 12.

——— Presbyteries recommended to promote their use in private families to facilitate their introduction for public use. 1706. 4.

——— Commissions authorised to publish and emit said songs for public use, as was formerly done on like occasion when our version of the Psalms was published in the year 1649. 1708. xv.

Spalding. Recommendation in favour of buying Mr John Spalding's book on the Sacrament of the Lord's Supper. 1705, ult.; 1707, ult.

Special. *See* Commission.

Speeches. Unanimously agreed that not more than three speeches be heard from each side of the bar. 1824. 6.

——— Ordained that in no case shall more than two speeches be allowed to each party at the bar, besides the reply to which the appellant or complainer shall be entitled; and that when there are more than two parties on one side, there shall be only one speaker and one speech for each besides the reply. 1850. xiv. 31; 1859. xii. 31.

Spirit Licences. Petition presented to Parliament on the subject of licences for the sale of spirits. 1836. 14.

——— Resolved to use every possible means for diminishing the number of houses licensed for the sale of spirits. 1849. 9.

Spiritual Independence. A resolution anent the spiritual independence and exclusive jurisdiction of the Church. 1838. 6.

Spiritual Songs. *See* Scripture.

Sponsor. A man who had been several years married to a woman, by whom he had four children, who were all baptised without objection, was refused baptism for a fifth child, on the ground that the woman had been previously married to another man still living. The Assembly found, that, as the man at the birth of said child was in possession of his status as husband of the said woman, and legal father of his children by her, there was nothing in his conduct to

far as they apply, shall be binding on and observed by all the inferior judicatories of the Church. 1850. xiv. 43.

Standing Orders. In a case of petition and complaint, the Assembly unanimously found that the petition, not having been printed in terms of the standing orders, could not be received. 1846. 3.

——— In a case of appeal, the standing orders with respect to the printing of papers dispensed with. 1850. 5.

——— The standing orders with respect to printing papers not having been complied with, a party was held to have deserted his case, and the sentence appealed from declared to be final. 1843. 9; 1848. 3; Com., May 31, 1853.

——— Found that when a case is brought before the synod by appeal, and referred *simpliciter* to the Assembly, the appellant stands in the same character in the Assembly, and is bound to pay the expense of printing in terms of the 7th standing order of June 2, 1834. 1844. 8.

——— A new code of standing orders adopted for regulating the business of the House. 1859. xii

Statistical Account. Ministers recommended to furnish Sir John Sinclair with statistical accounts of their respective parishes, and to contribute with all the expedition in their power to complete a work of such apparent utility. 1793, ult.

——— Ministers recommended to consult their respective parishes as to the most effectual means for procuring a copy of the whole Statistical Account for every parish in the kingdom. 1798, ult.

——— A copy of the whole work presented to the General Assembly by Sir John Sinclair, which was gratefully received, and ordered to be deposited with the records and papers of this Church. 1799, ult.

——— The Right Hon. Sir John Sinclair laid on the table a copy of the 'Statistical Account of Scotland,' in 21 vols., of which he begged the Assembly's acceptance. The unanimous and hearty thanks of the Assembly were given to Sir John for his communication, and his friendly sentiments towards the Church on all occasions. 1820. 8.

——— An analysis of said Account presented by Sir John Sinclair. 1825. 8.

Statistical Account. The scheme of a New Statistical Account announced to this Assembly. Ministers recommended to give it all the aid in their power. 1832. 7.

——— Ministers earnestly recommended to prepare the reports of their several parishes with all possible despatch. 1836, ult.

——— The Assembly expressed their strong disapprobation of a passage in the New Statistical Account, and ordered it to be cancelled. 1837. 9.

——— Statistical Account reported as completed. 1845. 14.

Stipends. The Lord High Commissioner requested to apply to their Majesties, &c., that ministers serving vacant charges may have access for maintenance out of the vacant stipends. 1694. xv.

——— Presbyteries enjoined to give information to the Commission anent mortifications or stipends that have been dilapidated or suppressed. 1706. xii.

——— Presbyteries enjoined to report to the clerk or the agent for the Church any parishes within their bounds that want legal stipends, or decreets for their stipends and communion elements. 1702. v.

——— An Act and recommendation concerning an application to Parliament for an augmentation of ministers' stipends. 1750. iv.

——— Ministers prohibited from making any composition with their heritors with respect to obtaining a decreet of modification of stipend without the consent of the presbytery. 1759. vi.

——— Presbyteries enjoined to take an exact account of all the stipends within their bounds, and to record it in their minutes. 1762. viii.

——— Synods enjoined to see that presbyteries strictly observe the foregoing Act. 1802. viii.

——— A committee appointed to inquire into the just value of all the stipends in Scotland, the true extent and state of the tithes, and all funds that may be applied with or without the authority of Parliament for augmenting of stipends, and to correspond with persons in power for their assistance in promoting the relief of ministers not sufficiently provided. Presbyteries enjoined to give all needful assistance and information. 1749. 8.

Stipends. A full and particular report by said committee, with resolution thereanent. 1750. 4, 7, 10.

——— Report of the commissioners appointed to apply to the King and Parliament anent the scheme for augmenting ministers' stipends. 1752. 4.

——— The procurator instructed to advise presbyteries how to oblige patrons of churches to apply vacant stipends as directed by law. 1756. 8.

——— A minister having been settled under a presentation granted by a gentleman afterwards found not legally entitled to present, the legal patron detained the stipend from said minister. The Assembly appointed a committee to endeavour to get the matter amicably settled. 1761. 4.

——— A scheme for the augmentation of stipends approved of, and a committee appointed to digest it into the form of a bill to be laid before Parliament. 1792. 9; 1793. 9.

——— A memorial regarding the augmentation of small stipends, and a list of parishes in which the stipends were inadequate. 1809. 7.

——— An Act of Parliament for the augmentation of small stipends reported to the Assembly. 1811. 9.

——— A committee appointed to take every proper measure for having a Parliamentary grant of £20,000 for the use of the Church of Scotland made good. 1822. 9.

——— A presbytery authorised to proceed with the ordination of a chapel minister on obtaining a bond from the managers for the yearly payment of £70, together with a house and garden. 1811. 9.

——— The augmentation of small livings considered most desirable, and a committee appointed to watch over this important subject. 1825. 4; 1826. 9; 1829. 8.

——— Committee appointed to consider an overture for raising the stipends of the clergy, with power to apply to any quarter from which relief is likely to be obtained. 1851. 14.

——— Committee appointed to consider an overture on the subject of the reduction which had taken place in the stipends of those ministers who derived their living from teinds. 1852. 10, 14; 1853. 15.

Stipends. The thanks of the Assembly given to Dr Cook of Haddington for a very able report on the reduction which had taken place in the stipends of ministers. 1853, ult.

Stirling. The Presbytery of Stirling enjoined to take all proper care to preserve the erection of a third minister in that town, and the synod to give them their advice and assistance in the matter. 1745. 9.

——— The presbytery instructed to arrange the services of the three ministers of Stirling in such a manner as shall appear most to serve the purposes of edification. Com., May 31, 1831.

——— The kirk-session having selected additional elders entirely out of the East Church congregation, the Assembly expressed their high disapprobation of such a mode of selection, and appointed the kirk-session forthwith to make such a selection as should equalise the number of elders connected with each of the congregations in the town. 1819. 6.

——— Appeal of five elders of the kirk-session of Stirling with relation to several extraordinary steps taken by their ministers as to the admission and exclusion of members from the Lord's Table. 1737, ult.

Strangers educated in other Protestant Churches to be received with all tenderness when they come desiring to join in communion with this Church, and seeking the benefit of sealing ordinances. 1711. xiii.

Stranraer. Certain parishes annexed to the Presbytery of. 1699. iv.

Strathbogie. An Act disjoining the Presbytery of Strathbogie from the Synod of Aberdeen, and annexing the same to the Synod of Moray. 1700. iv.

Students. Anent the qualifications of students of divinity, the usual school degrees to be inquired after, but not made a necessary qualification. None to be licensed until they give proof of their knowledge of Greek and Hebrew. The study of other Oriental languages recommended, particularly Chaldaic and Syriac, and of the great controversies about religion and Church government, particularly the history of our own Church. 1696. xxii.

——— Presbyteries enjoined to send up to the Assembly the names of all students residing within their bounds. 1697. iii.

Students. Former Acts anent the trials and licensing of students ratified and revived—viz., Act of 1596; 1638. xiii. 7; 1647. 27; 1694. x.; 1696. xxii. None to be admitted to the ministry under twenty-five years of age, except such as have rare and singular qualities—their catechetical trials not to be perfunctoriously gone about—to be required to answer objections, and give trial of their gifts as to lecturing, &c. 1704. x.

——— An Act anent students and entrants to the holy ministry. 1705. xvi.

——— Students to attend the profession of divinity for six years, or at least to follow closely the study of divinity and the languages for that space, after they have passed their course of philosophy. None to be licensed by any presbytery, unless they have resided within the bounds for the space of six years, or produce sufficient testimonials. Students coming from abroad not to be entered on trials for the space of a whole year after they come to Scotland. Circular letters to be written by the presbytery before which the student has passed his preliminary private trials, to all the presbyteries within the bounds of the synod, intimating the intention of the presbytery to take him on public trials for licence. A list of questions appointed to be put to all such as pass trials in order to be licensed, and Formula to be subscribed. 1711. x.

——— Students prohibited from going abroad for licence without testimonials from the professors under whom they studied, the minister of the parish, and the presbytery of the bounds. 1711. xii.

——— Students required to finish their private trials before the presbytery of the bounds before they can obtain a transference to another presbytery. 1713. x.; 1813. viii.

——— An Act for further regulating the trials of students and probationers. 1714. vi.

——— Students on entering the Divinity Hall to take with them a certificate from their parish minister, and on leaving the Hall certificates from the professors and from the minister they attended while at college. 1727. xii.

——— An Act and recommendation concerning students—professors enjoined to be careful in requiring testimonials. 1735. vi.

Students. An Act for the better observance of former Acts anent students and probationers. 1736. xvi.

——— An Act consolidating former Acts concerning the study of divinity and licensing probationers. None to be admitted to trials but such as are of good report, and have produced to the professor of divinity, before entering the Hall, either a diploma of M.A., or a certificate that they have gone through a full course of philosophy. Further, they must have given close attendance on the Divinity Hall for four sessions, or have continued to prosecute the study of divinity for the space of six years, and delivered the prescribed discourses, and are of the age of twenty-one years complete. Every student on entering the Hall to produce to the professor, and also to the minister on whom he is to wait during his attendance at the university, a testimonial from the minister of the parish whence he comes; and, on leaving the Hall, to carry with him testimonials from said minister and professor. No presbytery to take a student on trials unless he have resided six months within their bounds. Presbytery to be alone when a student is proposed for trials, and proposal to lie on the table till next ordinary meeting. Presbytery to examine him strictly and privately in regard to his knowledge, piety, ability, and other qualifications necessary. The presbytery, if satisfied, to write circular letters to all the presbyteries within the bounds of the synod two calendar months before the meeting of the synod; and also to acquaint the synod at its next meeting, provided that, where synods meet only once a-year, a student may be proposed six months sooner than in synods which meet twice a-year. The consent of the synod having been obtained, public trials to be taken in the following order:—

1st. Catechetical trials.

2d. A homily.

3d. An exegesis.

4th. An exercise and addition.

5th. A lecture.

6th. A popular sermon.

7th. A trial on chronology and church history, especially the history of the Church of Scotland.

8th. A trial of the student's knowledge of the Greek and Hebrew languages.

The questions appointed by Act x., Ass. 1711, and no other, to be put—Formula to be signed—Act viii., Ass. 1759, anent simony to be read—and student licensed. This Act to be read annually by professors of divinity to their students in the month of January. 1782. viii.

Students. The foregoing Act renewed, with the following alterations and additions:—Students required to study divinity for six sessions, provided that, if a student have given regular attendance during three sessions, his course shall be considered as completed in four sessions; and if he have given regular attendance during two sessions, his course shall be considered completed in five sessions. Every student to deliver his first discourse some time during his second session, at the latest, and his remaining discourses at such periods as may enable him to deliver the whole of them before the end of January of the last session of his course.

The minister who proposes a student to lay his certificates before the next meeting of presbytery, which shall be recorded at full length. No presbytery to take a student on trials unless his residence during the year has been chiefly within their bounds. No student to be transferred from one presbytery to another till after he has finished his private trials. 1813. viii.

——— Enacted that in future every student shall give at least one year of regular attendance at the Divinity Hall, which shall be the first, second, or third year of his course. 1826. viii.

——— Enacted that, previous to the enrolment of any student as a student of divinity, he shall be examined by the presbytery of the bounds in which he resides upon literature, science, and philosophy, particularly Latin and Greek; and that students who give only one year's regular attendance at the Divinity Hall shall, during the currency of the fourth year of their course, be examined by their respective presbyteries on divinity, church history, Greek, and Hebrew. 1827. vii.

——— Every student, on applying to be taken on trials, to produce certificates of having regularly attended the classes of church history and Hebrew during two of the sessions which he claims to be considered as sessions of regular attendance at the Divinity Hall. 1833. ix.

Students. Students from abroad to be examined previous to their enrolment by the presbytery within whose bounds the university at which they have studied is situated. 1835. xv.

——— A critical Hebrew exercise on some portion of the original text of the Old Testament to be prepared and delivered by every student in the course of his attendance at the Divinity Hall. 1836. x.

——— Students of divinity to be examined every year by their presbyteries on the progress made by them in their studies, and carry with them to the professor a certificate to that effect, as also a certificate of moral character from the minister of their parish, before they can be re-enrolled at the Divinity Hall. 1837. viii.

——— Every student, previous to his first enrolment as a student of divinity, to be examined by his presbytery on his knowledge of the Christian religion, as it is exhibited in the catechetical standards of the Church. 1837. ix.

——— No student to be admitted into any Divinity Hall until he produce a certificate of having attended the Latin class in some university for at least one session, and made satisfactory proficiency as a Latin scholar. 1843. xiv.

——— In the peculiar circumstances of the Church, presbyteries permitted to take students who had finished their course at the Divinity Hall, without waiting for the consent of the synod; and also to recommend to synods students who wanted one session to complete their course, provided they had delivered all their discourses. 1845. ix.

——— The foregoing Act restricted. 1846. xix.

——— The foregoing Act rescinded. 1850. viii.

——— Presbyteries enjoined to require from students certificates of attendance on classes of divinity, church history, and Hebrew, taught by professors in communion with the Church. 1845. x.

——— Students before entering the Hall must produce certificates of regular attendance in some university at all the classes required of such as apply for the degree of A.M., which classes must be attended in such order that after

Greek and Latin during the first session, the classes of logic, moral philosophy, and natural philosophy must be attended separately during three successive sessions—mathematics to be studied in a university at least one session before entering the class of natural philosophy. 1845. xviii.

Students. Act consolidating the several Acts of Assembly respecting the study of divinity and the licensing probationers. 1849. xi.

——— Act supplying an omission in the preceding Act in regard to attendance on church history and Hebrew. 1851. viii.

——— No presbytery to examine a student as a candidate for enrolment as a student of divinity, unless he has had his chief residence within their bounds for the previous six months, or produces a satisfactory certificate. 1714. vi.; 1851. viii.

——— Ministers expressly discharged and prohibited from giving countenance or permission to students of divinity to engage in the public ministry of the Word, or to lead the devotions of the congregations of the Church. 1854. xii.

——— All students to give at least two sessions of regular attendance on the Divinity Hall. 1856. xv.

——— Act anent the examination of students by committees of presbytery, appointed annually for that purpose. 1856. xiv.

——— An abstract of all the Acts of the Church in force in regard to the study of divinity, the licensing of students and probationers, transmitted to presbyteries as an overture. 1856. x.

——— Said abstract re-transmitted. 1861. ix.

——— Do. referred to the Committee on the Theological Curriculum. 1862. 14.

——— Do. passed into a standing law of the Church. 1863.

——— A presbytery having refused to take a student on trials, the Assembly found that they were bound to do so, or to assign the causes of their refusal. 1783, ult.

——— An overture anent attendance on the Divinity Hall, transmitted to presbyteries. 1797. ix.

——— Said overture transmitted for four successive years, but finally dropped. 1801. 8.

——— Students claiming the privileges annexed to regular

attendance, required to produce certificates of their having attended all the professors of divinity regularly lecturing in the university at which they studied, whether usually denominated professors of divinity or of church history. 1811. 5.

Students. A presbytery having licensed a student who had not given that attendance at the Divinity Hall required by the law of the Church, the Assembly found that in so doing said presbytery had, in defiance of the laws of the Church, and in contempt of the authority of the General Assembly, been guilty of an unconstitutional act, which merited the severest reprehension; and declared the licence so granted null and void. 1815. 5.

——— Enacted that before any presbytery or synod shall agree to take upon trials any blind student, they shall first consult the General Assembly. 1761. vi.

——— A blind student allowed to be taken on trials in consideration of the very ample testimonials borne to his character and talents. 1815. 5; 1829. 9; 1857. 8.

——— Found that the certificates of a student's regular attendance on the Hall during the currency of the fourth year not having been produced to the presbytery, ought to have been laid before the synod. 1815, ult.

——— A student partially deaf, but able, by the assistance of a common instrument, to bear his part in ordinary conversation without subjecting those who conversed with him to the necessity of raising their voice above the ordinary tone, allowed to be taken on probationary trials, and licensed, if found qualified, in respect of the very ample testimony borne to his intellectual and moral qualifications. 1823. 6.

——— The Assembly affirmed a sentence of a synod refusing to allow a presbytery to take a student on public probationary trials, inasmuch as the presbytery had not subjected said student to the preliminary private trials before proposing him to the synod, as prescribed by the laws of the Church. 1824. 5.

——— The Assembly finding from the report of the visitors of a synod book, that said synod occasionally authorised presbyteries to take students on probationary trials before the commencement of the fourth session of their theological course, enjoined all synods and presbyteries to adhere strictly to the letter of the Acts anent licensing probationers. 1832, ult.

Students. Long delay in the licensing of a student having been occasioned by the serious illness of the presbytery clerk, the Assembly, dispensing with the production of the student's certificates, authorised the presbytery to proceed with his public trials. 1839. 5.

——— A synod having granted leave to a presbytery to take a student on trials for licence before he had completed his theological course and delivered the discourses prescribed by the laws of the Church, the Assembly expressed their strong disapprobation of the great irregularity. 1784. 9. Com., Aug. 13, 1840.

——— Competent for any presbytery to transfer the receiving the public trials of a student, or any part thereof, to another presbytery, but not until the private trials have been completed, and the various preliminary steps taken as prescribed by the laws of the Church. 1813. viii. 6; 1849. x.

——— A presbytery having given a student a transference without taking the prescribed private trials and preliminary steps, the Assembly declared such a proceeding incompetent, and that said presbytery "could make no transference" in the circumstances. 1824. 5.

——— Declared to be expedient that a pastoral superintendent, appointed by the Church, should be established at each of the universities, and a committee appointed to report on the necessary arrangements. 1842. 4.

——— Committee appointed to take overtures on the examination of students into consideration, and report. 1841. 3.

——— Report of said committee. 1843. 12.

——— A presbytery allowed to take on trials for licence, with a view of their going to India, two students who had not passed the synod. 1847. 11.

——— Certain students having petitioned to be exempted from any further attendance at the Divinity Hall than was necessary to complete three regular sessions, the Assembly saw no reason for complying with said petition. 1851. 15.

——— A synod having refused to grant permission to a presbytery to take a student on trials, on the ground that the extract minute of presbytery certifying that the student had passed satisfactorily the prescribed private examination, the Assembly found that said minute had not been produced in the synod through causes for which the student was not responsible, and authorised and directed the presbytery to take him on public trials for licence agreeably to the rules of the Church. 1853. 6.

Styles. Dr Cook recommended to the Assembly a work recently published on the styles of the Church, and suggested that every judicatory should supply itself with a copy. 1838. 1.

Subordination. An Act for preserving the subordination of Church judicatories. 1733. v.

Sufferings. Referred to the Commission concerning the collecting of an account of the sufferings of the late times for religion. 1707. 13.

Superannuation. A committee appointed to consider overtures regarding the formation of a fund in aid of the superannuation of ministers, with instructions to use their endeavours for accomplishing the object of the overture. 1853. 14.

Superannuated. Reference to the Commission concerning Mr James Hart in Shapinshay, anent demitting or getting a helper, he being superannuate. 1703. 9.

Supplementary. Presbyteries recommended to support the scheme of a supplementary orphan fund, for the benefit of the families of deceased ministers, whose widows die within six months after the death of their husbands. 1836. 9.

——— *See* Annual Reports of Committee.

Suspension. Act and sentence of suspension against Mr John Hepburn. 1690. xxvii.

——— Act and sentence of suspension against Mr John Simson. 1728. vi.

——— Certain ministers who had been suspended from acting in a judicial capacity, reponed. 1765. 9.

——— The minister of Crieff suspended *sine die* from the office of the ministry, and strictly prohibited from exercising said office, or any part of it, or residing within the bounds of the presbytery. 1770. 8.

——— A similar case. 1807, ult.; 1826, ult.

——— A minister suspended from the exercise of his ministerial functions until next Assembly, pending a process against him. 1783. 9.

Suspension. The Assembly affirmed the sentences of a presbytery and synod refusing to suspend a minister during the dependence of a process against him. 1785. 6.

——— Declared to be incompetent for a presbytery to suspend a minister without having previously served him with a libel, according to the form of process. 1802. 9; 1827. 7.

——— A minister suspended from the exercise of his judicial functions in a particular case. 1805. 8.

——— A minister having disregarded a sentence of his presbytery suspending him from the exercise of his ministerial functions, the Assembly strictly enjoined him to submit under pain of the severest censures of the Church. 1828, ult.

Suspension and Interdict. A committee appointed to consider a note of suspension and interdict against a presbytery at the instance of a minister under process. 1852. 3.

Sutherland. An Act anent the supply of Sutherland. 1696. xiv.

——— Alteration of the day of the meeting of the Synod of Sutherland. 1836. xvi.

Synod. The synod record, completely filled up and signed both by moderator and clerk, to be laid yearly before the Assembly for revision. 1698. xi.; 1702. iii.

——— Synod clerks enjoined to attend to the foregoing Acts, as they shall be answerable. 1792. vii.; 1835. vii.; 1837. xii.

——— Act containing directions to the visitors of synod books. 1713. iv.

——— Additional directions to the visitors of synod books. 1723. v.

——— Standing order anent the visiting of synod books. 1841. xii.

——— Synod books not submitted to the Assembly to be sent up to the Commission in August. 1837. xii.; 1804. 4; 1810, ult.

——— Visitors of synod books directed to pay special attention to the directions contained in Acts 1713. iv. and 1723. v.; and to draw up their report so as to embrace the different subjects therein introduced, and also the Collections for the Schemes. 1839. 11.

Synod. An Act regulating the meetings of synods in consequence of the derangement caused by the Act of Parliament changing the calendar. 1752. viii.

——— An Act prohibiting synods from disjoining or annexing parishes from one presbytery to another. 1745. v.

——— Every one ordained or admitted as minister of a parish, declared to be, by virtue of such ordination or admission, *ipso facto* a member of the presbytery and synod in whose bounds the parish lies. 1754. v.

——— Synods enjoined to be careful in revising the records of the presbyteries under their inspection, to appoint a competent number of the most fit and experienced ministers for that work, and, if they find nothing censurable, to attest them according to a prescribed form. 1700. ix.

——— Synods enjoined to be very careful in visiting the records of all the presbyteries within their bounds, and in seeing that each presbytery discharge its duties to its members and its parishes, by a strict enforcement of the Acts of Assemblies 1713 and 1723. 1839. xiv.

——— Synods enjoined to ask presbyteries what vacancies there are in their bounds, of how long continuance, and why they have not been supplied? 1759. vii.

——— Complaint against the clerk of the Synod of Galloway dismissed as altogether groundless. 1804. 9.

——— Declared to be incompetent and unconstitutional for a synod to appoint correspondent members to act with a presbytery. 1812. 7.

——— The Assembly finding that in one of the synod books several printed reports and other documents had been pasted on the pages, disapproved of that practice, as tending to suggest doubts of the authenticity of the record, and ordered it to be discontinued in future. 1845. 10.

——— Declared to be incompetent for a synod to order copies of papers not recorded in the minutes of presbytery, upon which alone the synod were entitled to pronounce an opinion. 1836. 8.

——— Declared to be inconsistent with the order of the Church for a synod to send as corresponding members to another synod, elders who exercise the office of the eldership within the bounds of the synod to which they are sent, on the ground that they are already represented in said synod, while the synod by which they are commissioned has no jurisdiction over them. 1836. 10.

Synod. Declared to be the undoubted right of synods to enforce the attendance of their members, but they are recommended to do so with mildness and discretion. 1817. 7.

——— Synods expressly instructed to receive no members from other synods, without regular commissions of correspondence. 1829. 9.

——— Protest taken that members of a synod had a right to sit and vote in the Assembly in review of the proceedings of presbytery within the bounds of said synod in regard to matters which took place subsequently to the meeting of synod. 1830. 8.

——— Dissent and complaint regarding the calling of a *pro re nata* meeting of synod. 1831, ult.

——— A synod having admitted a ruling elder to their roll without a commission, the Assembly unanimously reversed the sentence of the synod, and ordered the name of said elder to be deleted from the roll. Com., 1833, May 29.

——— A synod having rejected the commission of a ruling elder on the ground that it had never been presented to the presbytery, the Assembly reversed the sentence, and found that the commission ought to have been sustained. Com., June 4, 1840.

——— Synods appointed to meet *pro re nata* on the requisition of any three members for the purpose of resuscitating presbyteries. 1843. 11.

Syriac. Candidates for the ministry recommended to study the Oriental languages, especially the Chaldaic and Syriac, so far as they can. 1696. xxii.

T

Taxes. A standing committee appointed to watch over the interests of the clergy respecting the taxes on horses, and other taxes upon their income. 1788. 8.

——— The committee instructed to petition Parliament for an exemption from the tax upon riding-horses, and every other tax to which the clergy are or may be subjected. 1789, ult.

Taxes. The thanks of the Assembly given to Dr Inglis for his judicious and unwearied exertions to obtain exemption for ministers from the house and window tax. 1815. 9.

——— Dr Somers craves extracts to enable him to vindicate his character, which had been attacked on account of the part he had taken in obtaining for the Church an exemption from assessed taxes. 1816. 8.

——— Found to be inexpedient to take any further steps respecting the levying of assessed taxes from the ministers of this Church. 1801. 6; 1808. 6; 1812. 5; 1816. 8.

Teachers. Report concerning vagrant teachers. 1799. xii.

——— *See* THEOLOGICAL.

Teinds. Commission instructed to apply to Parliament for a commission for planting of kirks and the valuation of teinds. 1706. 3.

——— Report of a deputation sent to London to watch the progress of a Bill introduced into Parliament relative to some proposed changes in the Court of Teinds, and the mode of conducting processes for augmenting the stipends of ministers. 1807. 6; 1808. 9.

——— Dr Inglis laid on the table a copy of a new Act of Parliament for regulating and defining the powers of the Court of Teinds in augmenting and modifying stipends, and a full report regarding the parishes where the stipends were small and the teinds exhausted, along with the draught of a Bill for augmenting said stipends. The committee instructed to take such steps as appeared proper for obtaining an equitable mode of striking the fiars of grain, and to watch over the interest of the Church in regard to grass glebes. 1809. 7.

——— A committee appointed to consider the reduction which has taken place of late years in the stipends of those ministers who derive their livings from teinds. 1852. 10.

——— The committee instructed to lay before Government a statement embodying the information which they possessed in regard to the aforesaid matter. 1852. 14.

Tests. Declared to be a grievance and hardship that those of the communion of the Church of Scotland employed in Her Majesty's service in England or Ireland should be obliged to join in communion and conformity with the Church of England, and a memorial sent to Government to that effect. 1715. ix.

Tests. Commission instructed to prosecute the design of said memorial, with relation to the sacramental test imposed upon members of the Church of Scotland when in England or Ireland. 1823. 13.

——— A committee appointed to take the earliest opportunity to obtain redress of said grievance by every legal and constitutional mode which they shall judge to be most effectual. 1790. 7.

——— A motion that the General Assembly should send an address to His Majesty expressive of their high satisfaction with an Act which has lately received the sanction of the Legislature for repealing so much of several Acts as imposed the necessity of receiving the sacrament of the Lord's Supper as a qualification for certain offices and employments, dismissed as unnecessary and at variance with the usual practice. 1828. 3.

Testimonials. *See* CERTIFICATES.

Thanksgiving. Act for a thanksgiving for deliverance from the unnatural Rebellion. 1746. xiv.

——— Act for a thanksgiving for deliverance from a threatened invasion. 1708. vii.

——— An Act for the better observance of thanksgivings and fasts. 1722. iv.

——— Act appointing a national thanksgiving in commemoration of the Revolution in 1688. 1788. x.

Theatre. Presbyteries enjoined to take care that none of the ministers of this Church do upon any occasion attend the theatre. 1757. v.

Theological. Overture and recommendation anent the promoting of theological learning. 1802. xi.; 1826. 9; 1837. 10.

——— An Act anent the appointment and ordination of professors of theology. 1838. xii.

——— A motion against the exaction of fees dismissed as inexpedient and inefficacious for the purpose of improving the status of the professors or the education of the students. 1830. 9.

——— A committee appointed to consult the universities

regarding a preliminary course of education to be required of students before entering the Divinity Hall. 1837, ult.

Theological. An overture on foreign theological degrees withdrawn after discussion. 1854. 6.

——— Committee appointed to consider the status of theological professors. 1862, ult.

——— Committee appointed to consider overtures anent the theological curriculum. 1862. 11.

Theology. Professors of theology recommended that they put none upon theological exercises but such as have passed their course and taken their degrees, and who have sufficient testimonials from the presbyteries where they have their residence. 1706. 12.

Titles. Standing order relative to the feudal titles of new churches. 1842. xv.; 1859. xii. 44.

——— Ecclesiastical Titles Bill, petitions to Parliament against. 1851. 15.

Token. A schoolmaster having repeatedly persisted in sitting at a communion-table after being refused a token by the kirk-session, the Assembly instructed the presbytery to proceed against the schoolmaster according to the rules of the Church. 1837, ult.; 1839. 11.

Toleration. Address to the Queen anent a Bill to prevent the disturbance of those of the Episcopal communion in the exercise of their religious worship, and the use of the Liturgy of the Church of England, expressing "astonishing surprise and deep affliction to hear of such a Bill offered for such a large and almost boundless toleration." 1712. x.

——— Memorial concerning the grievances of the Church from patronage and the Toleration Act. 1715. ix.

Tongue. An Act erecting the Presbytery of Tongue. 1726. iv.

Town-Council. Found that a minority of a town-council may elect a commissioner to the General Assembly when a majority refuse to do so. 1850. 2.

Transference. Presbyteries prohibited from granting a transference to a student from one presbytery to another till after he has completed his private trials. 1713. x.; 1813. viii.; 1849. xi.; 1824. 5.

Translation. An Act for the better regulating translation of ministers, recommending presbyteries not to concur in any translation unless by due comparing of places and all parties concerned, the disproportion betwixt them, and the greater good of the Church be manifestly evident. 1694. vi.

Translation. Enacted that when a sentence of translation has been passed, it shall be obeyed by the minister under pain of suspension. 1695. xii.

——— An Act anent citations in cases of translation ordained that, to prevent rabbling of messengers and horrid profanation of the Lord's Day, the minister himself shall cite the heritors, elders, and others concerned, to compear before the presbytery, if they see cause to defend their interest. 1704. vii.

——— An Act regulating the translation of ministers settled in Highland congregations. 1726. ix.

——— When the minister to be inducted into a parish is a member of another presbytery, a process of translation shall be instituted before that presbytery by presenting to them the call which has been sustained, and a full extract of the proceedings with regard thereto, together with reasons setting forth the expediency of the translation, to which process the parishioners and congregation under his charge are to be made parties by citation from the pulpit. 1856. xii.

——— A commission appointed to sit monthly in Edinburgh for expediting the translation of ministers to the north of the Tay. 1695. 12; 1697. xiv.

——— The Assembly refused to translate Mr Samuel Johnstone, minister at Dundee, to Edinburgh. 1706. 7.

——— Do. Mr John Maitland from Insch to Tongue. 1706. 8.

——— Do. Mr George Anderson from Dunbog to Dysart. 1707. 9.

——— Do. Mr John Witherspoon from Paisley to Dundee. 1762. 8.

——— Do. Mr Thomas Fairbairn from Rothes to Botairie. 1719. 9.

——— Do. Mr James Dick from Carluke to Glasgow. 1720. 9.

——— Do. Mr Archibald Campbell from Kilmonivaig to Kenmore. 1722. 3.

——— Do. Mr Farquhar Bethune from Croy to Kirkmichael. 1725. 10.

Translation. The Assembly refused to translate Mr Patrick Mollison from Walston to Dunsyre. 1794. 5.

——— The Assembly refused to translate Mr M'Naughton from Paisley to St Paul's Church, Edinburgh. 1838. 5.

——— The Commission having passed a sentence translating Mr James Bathgate from Dalgetty to Stirling, he refused to obey it, and offered rather to demit the pastoral office and his licence as a preacher, the Assembly remitted the case to the Commission, with instructions that if Mr Bathgate continued his aversion to go to Stirling, and that the said town insisted to have him there, the Commission should then declare both the charges at Dalgetty and Stirling vacant, and these parishes at liberty to proceed to the settlement of the same respectively, according to the rules of the Church. 1739. 9, ult.

——— A process of translation found to be not applicable in the case of a chapel minister. 1852. 6.

——— Enacted that, in the event of a minister of a chapel of ease in one presbytery being presented to any charge within the bounds of another presbytery, notification shall be given by the latter presbytery to that within which the chapel lies of the different steps to be taken by them in order to his settlement, which communication must be duly acknowledged. 1856. xii.

Trials. The questions and answers in the trials of a presentee appointed to be taken down in writing, that in the event of an appeal they might be transmitted to the superior courts. 1765. 7.

——— In an appeal from the sentence of a presbytery rejecting a presentee as unqualified, the Assembly appointed a committee to examine him, and on their report sustained his trials, and ordered the presbytery to proceed with his settlement. 1823, ult.

——— In a similar case the Assembly affirmed the sentence of the presbytery, and rejected the presentee. Com., June 1, 1831.

Trott. Remitted to the Commission to consider what encouragement should be given to the publishing of Sir Nicolas Trott's book, entitled 'Clair's Linguæ Sanctæ.' 1730, ult.

Tumults. An exhortation appointed to be read from the pulpits within the bounds of the Synod of Galloway, warning them of the sin and danger of taking part in certain tumultuous meetings. 1724, ult.

U

Uist. An Act erecting the Presbytery of Uist. 1742. iv.

Ullapool. A petition from certain parties in the parish of Ullapool anent better church accommodation. Com., August 12, 1835.

Ulster. A letter from the moderator of the Synod of Ulster to be duly acknowledged. 1779. 8.

——— A committee appointed to make inquiries with a view to admitting ministers and licentiates of the Synod of Ulster into ministerial communion with the Church of Scotland. 1816. ix.

——— Committee censured for not discharging the duty intrusted to them. 1817. 8.

——— Overtures for closer union and communion. 1835. 4. 11.

——— Ministers of said synod admitted into ministerial communion. 1836. 9.

——— Deputations sent to visit said synod. 1840. 9; 1841. 11; 1842. 3.

Uncleanness. Ordained that, according to the law and practice of this church, parties guilty of uncleanness shall satisfy the session in that parish whereof the woman was a parishioner at the time the guilt was committed. 1771. vii.

Union of Offices. A declaration and enactments anent the improper union of offices. 1801. 8; 1813. 6; 1814. 7.

——— A motion to the effect that said enactments, not having been transmitted to presbyteries in terms of the Barrier Act, negatived. 1815. 8.

——— A similar motion carried, and an overture transmitted to presbyteries. 1816. v.

——— Said overture passed into a standing law, and presbyteries directed to employ the means competent for them to prevent the same person from holding at the same time a professorship in a university and a parochial charge, which is not situated in the city which is the seat of that university, or in the suburbs thereof. 1817. vi.

Union of Offices. An overture proposing to extend the Act 1817. vi. by further declaring the holding of a principality or professorship in any university incompatible with the holding of a parochial charge in the city which is the seat of the university, or in the suburbs thereof, dismissed as inexpedient. 1825. 6; 1826. 6; 1827. 6.

——— An overture proposing in all cases to exclude a person holding a parochial charge from holding at the same time a principality or a professorship, transmitted to presbyteries. 1842. xxix.; 1847. 6.

Unity. Acts for restoring and preserving the peace of the Church. 1713. vi.; 1714. viii.; 1715. vi.

——— A recommendation to preserve unity. 1735. vii.

Universities. Commissioners from universities to the Assembly to meet annually during the sitting of the Assembly, to consult together and prepare overtures for the advancement of learning and good order in the schools and universities. 1707. vi.

——— An Act concerning the inspection of universities and colleges by the Church. 1711. xiv.

——— An Act for promoting religion and learning in universities and colleges. 1719. xii.

——— The right of electing a representative in the General Assembly from the University of Edinburgh declared to be only in the professors, principal, regents, masters, and others bearing office in the said university—that is to say, the Chancellor, Rector, and Dean of Faculty, if such there be, exclusive of all others. 1723. vi.

——— Acts concerning the forms of commissions from universities. 1723. vii.; 1724. iv.; 1726. viii.; 1770. vii.

——— Declaration as to university tests. 1846. xi.

——— A committee nominated to think of methods for planting the vacancies in the University of St Andrews. 1708. 10, 12.

——— The Commission instructed to apply to Government for the right application of bursaries and mortifications in colleges, particularly at Aberdeen, and for recovery of what thereof is misapplied. 1715. 12.

Universities. The procurator instructed to take the advice of lawyers as to persons who teach academical learning in private, and to proceed according to the advice he gets. 1720. 4.

——— A committee appointed to inquire into the right of election of a representative from the College of Edinburgh to the General Assembly. 1722. 11; 1723. 5; 1735. 11.

——— The Commission instructed to consider a deed of the University of St Andrews, in conferring the degree of D.D. on a person not of the communion of this Church. 1726. 11.

——— Anent the right of the Marischall College of Aberdeen to send a commissioner to the General Assembly. 1730. 15.

——— Anent the qualifications of students presented to the Ramsay Bursaries in Aberdeen. 1735. 6, 11.

——— A student expelled from the University of Edinburgh, and laid under the lesser excommunication, for delivering a discourse in the Divinity Hall to the prejudice of the Christian revelation. 1735. 11.

——— A process relating to the settlement of a professor of divinity in the King's College, Aberdeen. 1736. 5.

——— An overture anent the course of education in the universities, ordered not to be retransmitted. 1801. 8.

——— A right to advise the Town-Council in the appointment of professors claimed by the ministers of Edinburgh, on the ground that it is provided in the Charter of Erection from James VI., that the power of electing professors, as committed to the Town-Council, shall be exercised with the advice of their ministers, "cum avisamento tamen eorum ministrorum." The Lord Ordinary decided that, although the ministers were entitled to advise the Council, they had no right of negative or interdict in their power of presentation. 1805. 7.

——— Petition against a bill for the regulation and visitation of the Universities of Scotland. Com., July 7, 1836.

University. On a representation from the Rector of the University of St Andrews anent certain students of divinity, the Assembly found there were no grounds for interfering with the internal discipline and government of said University. 1848, ult.; 1840. 9.

——— Found that the Principal of the University of Edinburgh, as primarius professor of divinity, was entitled to claim his seat as a member of the Presbytery of Edinburgh if he saw cause, but not imperative on him to do so. 1841, ult.

University. Recommended that the duration of the session in the theological classes at Aberdeen ought to be not less than five months, and that a professorship of biblical criticism should be instituted. Com., Nov. 15, 1837; 1838. 6.

——— The Committee on the Pastoral Superintendence of Students not to be reappointed. 1843, ult.

——— Memorial to Parliament on the subject of university tests. 1844. 12; 1845. 7; 1846. 10; 1851. 15. 16; 1853. 7. 8. 9. 14.

——— Proceeding with reference to the Hebrew Chair in the University of Edinburgh. 1848, ult.; Com., Nov. 17, 1847.

——— Report of Committee on the practical working of the Test Act. 1855, ult.

——— Proceedings connected with the moral philosophy Chair in the University of Edinburgh. 1852. 12. 14; Com., 1852, Oct. 27; 1853. 12. 14.

——— Committee appointed to consider and report on the right of universities to send commissioners to the General Assembly. 1846. 13; 1858, ult.

——— Petition to Parliament against a Bill to regulate the admission of professors to the lay or secular chairs in the universities of Scotland. 1851. 15; 1853. 9. 14.

——— The Presbytery of Aberdeen instructed to communicate with the two universities within their bounds on the subject of theological education, and to suggest to them that they should take steps for lengthening the attendance at the Hall, having regular examinations of the students on alternate days every week throughout the session, and for securing that the prelections of the professors of divinity in Marischall and King's Colleges be on different subjects. 1852, ult.

——— A solemn protest against the recent enactment in regard to university tests. Com., Nov. 16, 1853; 1854. 5. 10; 1855, ult.

——— A memorial relating to the extension of the Scottish Universities. Com., July 14, 1858, and Mar. 2, 1859; 1855, ult.

University. Committee appointed to communicate with the university authorities, with a view to maintaining and increasing the existing means for securing the attendance on ordinances, and exercising pastoral superintendence over the youth of the Church of Scotland attending the universities. 1855, ult.; 1860, ult.; 1861, ult.; 1862. 15.

——— Committee appointed to watch over the progress of the Universities (Scotland) Bill. 1858, ult.

——— Report of University Commissioners laid on the table. 1832. 1; 1833. 2.

——— Committee to watch over a Bill relating to King's and Marischall College, Aberdeen. Com., Aug. 12, 1835.

Utensils. Reference to the Commission anent a decision of the Court of Session, ordaining a kirk-session to pay out of their own pockets a sum laid out by them for purchasing utensils and other necessaries for public worship. 1753. 7.

Utrecht. Commission instructed to write to the professors of divinity in Utrecht and other Universities in the United Provinces, and to call home such ministers abroad as this Church hath a claim to. 1698. 15.

V

Vacant Stipends. Application to Government for the maintenance, out of the vacant stipends, of ministers sent to supply charges in the north. 1694. 15.

——— Petition that vacant stipends might be applied for supporting students having the Gaelic language. 1700. 18.

——— Commission instructed to assist presbyteries in getting vacant stipends applied for pious uses, according to law. 1718. 16.

Vacant Churches. Ministers refusing to obey their appointments to supply vacant pulpits, to be censured or suspended for three months. 1697. viii.

——— Ministers from other presbyteries not to preach in vacant churches without leave of the presbytery of the bounds. 1711. xv.

——— An overture anent the filling up of vacancies dismissed. 1784. 7.

Vacant Churches. Act anent the planting of vacant kirks *tanquam jure devoluto.* 1732. viii.

——— Said Act rescinded. 1734. v.

——— Synods enjoined to inquire at presbyteries what vacancies there are in their bounds, and of how long continuance, and to see that there has been no unnecessary delay in filling them up. 1759. vii.

——— In cases of protracted vacancies occasioned by disputed claim of patronage, presbyteries enjoined to furnish regular supplies of preaching at suitable intervals, to employ licentiates for this purpose, to authorise ministers to dispense the sacraments, and to take proper measures for preserving the interests of the vacant cure. 1820. viii.

——— An Act anent the character and qualifications of persons claiming to vote in the calling of ministers. 1748. iv.

——— Instructions to presbyteries anent the supply of vacant churches. 1843. xvi.; 1844. x.

——— The Assembly affirmed the sentence of a presbytery refusing to allow the assistant to the late minister to supply the pulpit during the vacancy on the days on which the presbytery were not bound to supply it, as being inconsistent with the consuetudinary practice of the Church, and as it might possibly affect the usefulness of the presentee to be nominated by the patron in his future ministry. 1829. 7.

——— In a protracted vacancy in consequence of a litigation, the presbytery proposed to appoint a minister to the pastoral charge pending the process. The Assembly found that it was not expedient in the circumstances to appoint or ordain a minister for the vacant charge. 1836. 9.

Vagrant. Pastoral letter anent vagrant teachers. 1799. xii.; 1799. 8, ult.

——— An Act anent vagrant beggars. 1724. vii.

——— An Act against irregularities committed by vagrant ministers. 1696. xxiii.

——— The conduct of a minister exercising his ministerial functions in a vagrant manner declared to be disorderly and unbecoming, and calculated to weaken the hands of other ministers, and to injure the interests of sound religion. 1818. 9.

Valuation. Aid allowed to a minister in defraying the expenses incurred by him in an appeal respecting the valuation of his parish. 1801. 9.

Vaud. A collection recommended for the support of the suffering ministers in the Canton de Vaud. 1846. 7.

Veto. Act on the calling of ministers, commonly called the Veto Act. 1834. 6; 1835. ix.

——— Said Act rescinded. 1843. ix.

Viaticum. No viaticums to be granted to commissioners from any presbytery of above six members, and not to them unless they live at an hundred miles' distance from Edinburgh, and have a stipend under 800 merks. 1741. 8.

——— £4 sterling allowed to one commissioner from each of ten Highland presbyteries. 1748. 9.

——— No more viaticums to be given until all the debts of the Church were paid. 1764, ult.

Vindication. An Act vindicating the Church of Scotland from the calumny of Thomas Gipps. 1698. v.

Visitations. Instructions to the commissioners for visitations on the south and north sides of the Tay. 1690. xv., xvi., xvii.; 1694. xix.

——— Instructions to the commissioners for visiting the bounds of Angus and Mearns, Aberdeen, Moray, and Ross. 1700. xiii.

——— Instructions to the commissioners for visiting the bounds of Zetland, Orkney, and Caithness. 1700. xiii.

——— Instructions to the commissioners for visiting the Presbytery of Middlebie. 1700. xxiii.

Visitations, Presbyterial. Presbyteries enjoined to be diligent and careful in visiting the several parishes within their bounds. 1700. xxii.; 1706. xvi.

——— The Assembly disapproved of the manner in which a presbytery had conducted their visitation of a parish. 1796. 5.

Visitations, Ministerial. Ministers enjoined to visit all the families in their parish once a-year at a convenient season after due intimation, to take down the names of the several members of each family, distinguishing those who can read, those who are examinable, those who have come into the parish bringing certificates, those who are communicants, those who have Bibles, &c.; to speak privately to the heads of the family, exhorting them to observe family worship, to educate their children, and cause their servants to observe the Sabbath and wait upon ordinances. 1708. x.

Visitations, Ministerial, Schools. An Act and injunction respecting the visitation of schools. 1810. ix.

Visitors. An Act containing directions to the visitors of synod books. 1713. iv.

——— Additional directions to the visitors of synod books. 1723. v.; 1841. xii.

Voluntary. An elder having presided at a meeting at which it was agreed to petition Parliament for a separation of Church and State, and afterwards defended his conduct in the kirk-session and presbytery, the Assembly instructed the presbytery to call said elder before them at their first ordinary meeting, and, if he persisted in his sentiments, to proceed *instanter* to his deposition. 1834. 8.

Vote. Resolution to be observed in all time coming—That when the roll is being called over for the purpose of taking the vote, no member happening to be omitted shall have liberty to vote unless he stand up and claim his vote in his place while the names of the commissioners from his presbytery or synod are being called over; and if the clerk wants to be informed how any person has voted, said person shall be again called upon, and is to stand and speak up his vote. 1748. 7.

——— Declared that by the constant invariable practice of the Assembly, the principal clerk marks the votes while the other clerk calls the roll, and the declaration of the majority by the principal clerk from his marking has been and must be held as decisive, otherwise there could be no end of any dispute, until another method of collecting the votes or dividing the House shall be considered and agreed to. 1771, ult.

——— On a division, the clerk declared a motion carried by a majority of two; but a protest was taken against intimating the finding, on the ground that the votes had not been correctly marked. The Assembly, however, adhered to the state of the vote as declared by the clerk, which was confirmed by two gentlemen who voted on different sides of the question, and who had also marked the votes. 1771. 5, 6, and 7, ult.

Vote. Ordered that in future the agent for the Church shall call the roll; that the sub-clerk shall, immediately after the several members have pronounced their votes, repeat them with an audible voice; and that the principal clerk shall mark the votes, not from the voices of the members, but from that of the sub-clerk. 1781. 5.

——— Unanimously ordered that, whereas it is highly indecent and improper for any person to vote in any cause who has not been present at the deliberations thereon, before the roll begin to be called the doors of the Assembly House shall be shut, and shall not be opened until the judgment of the Assembly be declared. 1789. vi.

——— Enacted that in certain cases when there is more than one motion before the House, the question shall be put, *ay* or *no*, upon each motton, beginning with the last. 1845. vii.

——— Foregoing enactment rescinded. 1846. viii.

——— Enacted that when there is only one amendment to the motion proposed to the House, the vote shall be taken at the close of the debate upon the motion and amendment. 1859. xii. 40.

——— When there is more than one amendment, the vote shall be first taken upon the question which of the amendments shall be put against the motion; and this question shall be decided by one or more votes according as there are two or more amendments submitted to the House. 1859. xii. 41.

——— In a case where there were *three* motions before the House, a fourth motion was made that the Assembly proceed to vote upon the second motion as an amendment against the first, and thereafter the question be put upon the third motion: this fourth motion having been rejected by a great majority, the vote was taken upon the other three simultaneously, the state of the vote being first, second, or third motion. 1819. 6.

——— Resolved that, when the Assembly see fit, the numbers on a division may be ascertained by the members leaving the House by the doors on the right and left of the moderator's chair according as they vote for the first or second motion, the numbers at each door being counted by the mover of one motion and the seconder of the other. 1860. 3.

Vote. In a question as to whether the Commission had exceeded their powers, an objection was taken to those members voting who had been members of the Commission. The Assembly unanimously overruled the objection, and called for the votes of all who were members of the Assembly then present, whether they had been members of the Commission or not. 1813. 8.

——— *See* ELECTION.

Vote, Casting. In the case of an election of two elders to represent a presbytery in the General Assembly, several were proposed, but on a vote being taken it was found that the three highest had each an equal number of votes. The presbytery allowed the moderator to give a casting vote in favour of two out of the three, and the Assembly without a vote affirmed the judgment of the presbytery and sustained the commission. 1850. 3.

——— The settlement of a presentee ordered to be proceeded with by the casting vote of the moderator. Com., Aug. 11, 1831.

——— It having been discovered at a subsequent diet that a false vote had been given in a case which had been decided by a majority of one, the Assembly held that they could not review their decision nor allow the moderator to give his casting vote, found that no decision had been given, prohibited the clerk from giving extracts, and allowed the case to stand over till next Assembly. 1835, ult.

——— Several errors having been committed in taking the vote, members are expressly enjoined to observe the standing orders, particularly with respect to rising up and speaking articulately when giving their votes, that such irregularities may be detected if they occur in future. 1841. 8.

——— Standing order in regard to the mode of taking the vote. 1845. 3.

——— Foresaid order rescinded. 1846. 1.

——— Committee to take into consideration the standing orders anent the mode of putting questions when divisions are called for in the House, with the view of establishing one uniform regulation more precise than the forms hitherto practised. 1819. 7; 1846. 14.

Vote, False. It having been stated to the Assembly that in taking the vote an answer had been given when the name of an absent member was called, a committee was appointed to examine into the circumstances, and consider what means could be adopted to prevent the recurrence of similar irregularities. 1837. 8.

W

Waldenses. The Assembly renew their expression of warm interest in the venerable and scriptural Church of the Waldenses. 1861. 14.

——— Dr Revel, late moderator of the Waldensian Church, introduced to the Assembly. 1862. 11.

Wales. Address to the Prince of Wales on his marriage. 1795. v.

——— Act enjoining prayer for Her Royal Highness the Princess of Wales. 1795. vi.

War. The General Assembly's address to His Majesty on occasion of his declaration of war against the French king. 1756. iv.

——— Warning and admonition to the people of Scotland with reference to the war. Com., March 1, 1798.

——— A day of humiliation and prayer appointed on account of the war in the East. Com., March 1, 1854.

——— Committee appointed to consider the case of the wives and children of soldiers and sailors engaged in the war. Com., March 1, 1854.

——— An address to Her Majesty on the present situation of public affairs, and particularly the war in which the nation is now engaged. 1854. 1.

——— Collections ordered to be made in all churches and chapels on behalf of the wives and families of the soldiers and sailors engaged in the war. 1854, ult.

——— A pastoral admonition on the war. Com., June 5, 1855.

Waterloo. A collection ordered to be made in all the parishes of Scotland for the relief of the sufferers by the glorious and decisive, but sanguinary victory of Waterloo; which collection amounted to the sum of £15,766, 7s. 2½d. 1816. 5.

Weddings. Recommendation against abuses at penny-weddings. 1719. x.

Weem. An Act disjoining certain parishes from the Presbytery of Dunkeld, and forming them into the Presbytery of Weem. 1836. vii.

Wesleyan. A communication from the conference of Wesleyan Methodists laid on the table. Com., Nov. 16, 1842.

Westminster. Committee appointed to consider the subject of the Bicentenary Commemoration of the Assembly of Divines at Westminster. Com., Nov. 16, 1842.

West Indies. On an overture relative to a Presbyterian establishment in the West Indies, the Assembly found that it did not seem prudent to urge the matter in present circumstances. 1824, ult.

Widows. Recommendation anent a *centesima* of ministers' stipends for the relief of ministers' relicts and children in distress. 1698. 15.

——— An overture in favour of widows and orphans of deceased ministers, proposing a contribution of a tenth of ministers' stipends for one year, and other expedients, to make up a common stock for their support and relief, and the erection of a society for managing that stock, referred to the Commission, that they may think on proper ways to make that project useful and effectual. 1717. 11.

——— An Act and recommendation concerning a FUND for maintaining the indigent widows and orphans of ministers. 1718. iv.; 1723. x.; 1733. 9; 1734, ult.; 1735. iv.

——— An overture for providing a yearly annuity to the widows of ministers of this Church transmitted to presbyteries. 1742. 8.

——— Said overture approved of, and application to be made to the King and Parliament to render the same effectual. Professors allowed to accede to the scheme. 1743. 8, 9, 10.

——— Intimation made that the Assembly's plan had received the sanction of both Houses of Parliament and the Royal assent. 1744. 4 and 10.

Widows' Fund. Committee appointed to consider overtures as to cases not provided for by the Acts establishing the Ministers' Widows' Fund. 1835. 9.

——— Report by the committee on a SUPPLEMENTARY ORPHAN FUND approved of. 1836. 9; 1838. 9; 1841. 11; 1844. 12; 1847. 9; 1848. 11.

——— Committee on the Supplementary Fund authorised to commit to the custody of the collector of the Ministers' Widows' Fund, as interim treasurer, the funds which have been, or may yet be, realised by them. 1853. 11.

Wigtown. Certain parishes annexed to the Presbyteries of Stranraer and Wigtown. 1699. 4.

Window Tax. Committee appointed to take the most effectual means for having the ministers of the Church relieved from the tax upon window lights. 1758. 7; 1759, ult.; 1762. 7; 1768. 9; 1791. 9; 1814. 5.

Witchcraft. An overture anent witchcraft or charming transmitted to presbyteries. 1699. iii.

——— Commission instructed to advise presbyteries in regard to cases of witchcraft, sorcery, and charming. 1698. 15; 1707. 4.

——— Address to the Council anent punishing witches. 1699. 10.

Witnesses. Enacted that a person being delator, or informer, does not disqualify him from being a witness. 1707. xi. chap. ii. 10.

——— Declared that a person having been examined as a witness in any part of a process does not disqualify him from being a judge. 1747, ult.

——— A witness who had been objected to on account of a misnomer, allowed to be recited and examined. 1767, ult.

——— Witnesses allowed to be examined *cum nota*. 1784. 8; 1785. 6; 1829. 6; 1831. 7.

——— A kirk-session advised to employ all ecclesiastical means in their power to enforce the attendance of a witness, and, failing these, to consult the procurator. 1783, ult.; 1810. 4; 1811. 6; 1812. 6; 1813. 5.

——— A presbytery authorised to take the deposition of a witness residing in London in any way they might think best. 1813. 8.

Witnesses. A presbytery found to have acted irregularly, in admitting as witnesses persons against whom relevant charges had been made, and offered to be immediately proved. 1815. 9.

——— The evidence of certain witnesses whose names were not attached to the original libel declared inadmissible. Com., May 31, 1836.

——— Presbytery instructed to close the proof for the libellers before entering upon the exculpatory proof. Com., June 1, 1836.

——— Committee appointed to consider and report on the citation of witnesses. 1845. 11.

——— The procurator and agent authorised to select a favourable case, if any such should occur, for having the question tried at the expense of the Church, in regard to the citation of witnesses. 1846. 13; 1848, ult.

——— Anent members of presbytery as witnesses. 1858. 5; 1858. 9.

——— *See* FORM OF PROCESS. 1707. xi.

——— *See* STANDING ORDERS. 1850. xiv.; 1859. xii.

Wodrow. Recommendation to all the members who could conveniently sign for copies of Mr Robert Wodrow, minister at Eastwood, his history of this Church during the late persecution and oppression, now ready for the press, to subscribe for the same presently; and to all the ministers of this Church who have not signed already to do it at their presbyteries; and to deal with such in their bounds as are well disposed to encourage this work, and to send up accounts of what is done to the clerk of Assembly. 1719. 8.

——— Records and MSS. found in the hands of the executors of Mr Robert Wodrow handed over to the agents to be examined. 1739, ult.

——— £30 ordered to be paid for certain volumes of MSS. mentioned in the report of the agents. 1742. 9; 1747, ult.

Worship, Public. An Act prohibiting all innovations in public worship, as dangerous to the Church and contrary to her known principle that nothing is to be admitted in the worship of God but what is prescribed in the Holy Scriptures. 1707. xv.

Worship, Public. An Act concerning people's behaviour during the time of divine worship. 1709. iv.

——— An Act recommending the due observance of the Directory for Public Worship approven by Assembly. 1645. 10; 1705. x.

——— Every congregation at each diet of public worship to have access to the advantage of hearing a portion of the Old and New Testament read, and the service of every Lord's day should include not only a sermon but a lecture on a passage of the Holy Scriptures. 1856. xi.

——— The General Assembly earnestly and solemnly warn all members of the Church against the rash adoption of changes in the order and form of public worship, confirmed by Acts of Assembly and presently practised in this Church; and enjoin all presbyteries, when such innovations are represented as having taken place, to take with all due prudence such course as seems to them most advisable for restoring uniformity within their bounds. 1858, ult.

——— Declared that the practice of preaching the Word of God, or of conducting the other solemn services of the sanctuary, by persons not duly appointed to the office of the ministry, ought not to be countenanced by the courts or ministers of this Church. 1859. 5.

——— Found that it was an innovation upon and contrary to the law and usage of this Church, in the celebration of public worship, to read prayers from a book either in manuscript or printed, and ministers ordered to conform in offering up prayer to the present ordinary practice of the Church. 1859. 7.

Worship, Family. Recommended that ministers and elders take care that the worship of God be performed in the several families, and that none be ruling elders who make not conscience of this important duty. 1694. xiii.

——— Presbyteries earnestly recommended to use their utmost endeavour that the worship of God be set up and performed in all its parts in the families within their bounds. 1711. vii.

——— A pastoral letter to the people of Scotland on the subject of family worship. 1836. xix.

APPENDIX.

I.

List of Royal Commissioners to the General Assembly.

1690.	John Lord Carmichael.
1692.	Earl of Lothian.
1694-1699.	John Lord Carmichael.
1700.	James Viscount Seafield.
1701.	William Earl of Annandale.
1702.	Patrick Earl of Marchmont.
1703.	James Earl of Seafield.
1704.	William Lord Ross.
1705.	William Marquess of Annandale.
1706-1710.	David Earl of Glasgow.
1711.	William Marquess of Annandale.
1712-1714.	John Duke of Athole.
1715-1721.	John Earl of Rothes.
1722.	Hugh Earl of Loudon.
1723.	Charles Earl of Hopeton.
1724.	James Earl of Findlater and Seafield.
1725-1726.	Hugh Earl of Loudon.
1727.	James Earl of Findlater and Seafield.
1728.	Hugh Earl of Loudon.
1729.	David Earl of Buchan.
1730-1731.	Hugh Earl of Loudon.
1732-1738.	William Marquess of Lothian.
1739-1740.	John Earl of Hyndford.

1741-1753. Alexander Earl of Leven.
1754. John Earl of Hopeton.
1755-1763. Charles Lord Cathcart.
1764-1772. John Earl of Glasgow.
1773-1776. Charles Lord Cathcart.
1777-1782. George Earl of Dalhousie.
1783-1795. David Earl of Leven.
1796-1801. David Earl of Leven and Melville.
1802-1816. Francis Lord Napier.
1817-1818. William Earl of Errol.
1819-1824. George Earl of Morton.
1825-1830. James Ochonchar Lord Forbes.
1831-1841. Robert Montgomery Hamilton Lord Belhaven and Stenton.
1842-1846. John Marquess of Bute.
1847-1851. Robert Montgomery Hamilton Lord Belhaven and Stenton.
1852. William David Earl of Mansfield.
1853-1857. Robert Montgomery Hamilton Lord Belhaven and Stenton.
1858-1854. William David Earl of Mansfield.
1860-1863. Robert Montgomery Hamilton Lord Belhaven and Stenton.

II.

Moderators of the General Assembly.

1690. Mr Hugh Kennedy, minister at Edinburgh.
1694. ... John Law, minister at Edinburgh.
1695-6. ... Patrick Simson, minister at Renfrew.
1697. ... William Crichton, minister at Edinburgh.
1698. ... George Meldrum, minister at Edinburgh.
1699. ... George Hamilton, minister at Edinburgh.
1700. ... David Blair, minister at Edinburgh.
1701. ... Thomas Wilkie, minister, Canongate, Edinburgh.
1702. ... David Williamson, minister, West Kirk, Edinburgh.
1703. ... George Meldrum, Professor of Divinity, Edinburgh.
1704. ... Thomas Wilkie, minister, Canongate, Edinburgh.

APPENDIX.

1705. Mr William Carstares, Principal of the College of Edinburgh.
1706. ... William Wishart, minister at South Leith.
1707. ... John Stirling, Principal of the College of Glasgow.
1708. ... William Carstares, Principal of the College of Edinburgh.
1709. ... John Currie, minister at Haddington.
1710. ... William Mitchell, minister at Edinburgh.
1711. ... William Carstares, Principal of the College of Edinburgh.
1712. ... William Hamilton, Professor of Divinity, Edinburgh.
1713. ... William Wishart, minister at South Leith.
1714. ... William Mitchell, minister at Edinburgh.
1715. ... William Carstares, Principal of the College of Edinburgh.
1716. ... William Hamilton, Professor of Divinity, Edinburgh.
1717. ... William Mitchell, minister at Edinburgh.
1718. ... William Wishart, Principal of the College, Edinburgh.
1719. ... James Grierson, minister at Edinburgh.
1720. ... William Hamilton, Professor of Divinity, Edinburgh.
1721. ... Thomas Black, minister at Perth.
1722. ... William Mitchell, minister at Edinburgh.
1723. ... James Smith, minister at Cramond.
1724. ... William Wishart, Principal of the College, Edinburgh.
1725. ... James Alston, minister at Dirleton.
1726. ... William Mitchell, minister at Edinburgh.
1727. ... William Hamilton, Professor of Divinity, Edinburgh.
1728. ... William Wishart, Principal of the College, Edinburgh.
1729. ... James Alston, minister at Dirleton.
1730. ... William Hamilton, Professor of Divinity, Edinburgh.
1731. ... James Smith, minister at Edinburgh.
1732. ... Neil Campbell, Principal of the College, Glasgow.
1733. ... John Gowdie, minister at Edinburgh.
1734. ... James Gordon, minister at Alford.
1735. ... Alexander Anderson, minister at St Andrews.
1736. ... Lauchlin M'Intosh, minister at Errol.
1737. ... Neil Campbell, Principal of the College, Glasgow.
1738. ... James Ramsay, minister at Kelso.
1739. ... James Bannatyne, minister at Edinburgh.
1740. ... George Logan, minister at Edinburgh.
1741. ... James Ramsay, minister at Kelso.
1742. ... Thomas Tullidelph, Principal of St Leonard's College, St Andrews.

1743. Mr Robert Wallace, minister at Edinburgh.
1744. ... John Adams, minister at Dalrymple.
1745. Dr William Wishart, Principal of the College of Edinburgh.
1746. Mr John Lumisden, Professor of Divinity, King's College, Aberdeen.
1747. ... Robert Kinloch, minister at Edinburgh.
1748. ... George Wishart, minister at Edinburgh.*
1749. ... Patrick Cuming, minister at Edinburgh.
1750. ... Robert Paton, minister at Renfrew.
1751. ... John Lumisden, Professor of Divinity, Aberdeen.
1752. Dr Patrick Cuming, minister at Edinburgh.
1753. Mr Alexander Webster, minister at Edinburgh.
1754. ... Robert Hamilton, Professor of Divinity, Edinburgh.
1755. ... George Reid, minister at St Evox.
1756. Dr Patrick Cuming, Professor of Church History, Edinburgh.
1757. Mr William Leechman, Professor of Divinity, Glasgow.
1758. ... Thomas Turnbull, minister at Borthwick.
1759. ... George Kay, minister at Edinburgh.
1760. Dr Robert Hamilton, Professor of Divinity, Edinburgh.
1761. ... John Hyndman, minister at West Kirk, Edinburgh.
1762. ... Robert Trail, Professor of Divinity, Glasgow.
1763. ... William Robertson, Principal, University, Edinburgh.
1764. ... Alexander Gerard, Professor of Divinity, Aberdeen.
1765. ... James Oswald, minister at Methven.
1766. ... John Hamilton, minister at Glasgow.
1767. ... James Murison, Principal, New College, St Andrews.
1768. ... Gilbert Hamilton, minister at Cramond.
1769. ... James M'Knight, minister at Maybole.
1770. ... Alexander Carlyle, minister at Inveresk.
1771. Mr Robert Walker, minister at Edinburgh.
1772. ... Adam Ferguson, minister at Moulin.
1773. Dr John Drysdale, minister at Edinburgh.
1774. ... Robert Henry, minister at Edinburgh.
1775. ... David Shaw, minister at Coylton.
1776. ... John Ker, minister at Forfar.
1777. Mr James Brown, minister at Edinburgh.

* Previous to Mr Wishart's election, he being principal clerk to the General Assembly, it was agreed that, in the event of his being chosen moderator, his office of clerk should not thereby be vacated, but that he should be empowered to depute one, of whom the Assembly approved, to act for him in that office, until the next General Assembly was constituted.

1778. Dr Patrick Grant, minister at Urray.
1779. ... James Gillespie, minister at St Andrews.
1780. ... Hary Spens, minister at Wemyss.
1781. ... William Dalrymple, minister at Ayr.
1782. ... Joseph M'Cormick, minister at Prestonpans.
1783. ... Henry Grieve, minister at Dalkeith.
1784. ... John Drysdale, minister at Edinburgh.*
1785. Sir Harry Moncrieff Wellwood, Bart., West Church, Edinburgh.
1786. Dr Duncan Shaw, minister at Aberdeen.
1787. Mr Robert Liston, minister at Aberdour.
1788. Dr Archibald Davidson, Principal of the College of Glasgow.
1789. ... George Hill, Professor of Divinity, St Andrews.
1790. ... John Walker, minister at Colinton.
1791. ... Robert Small, minister at Dundee.
1792. ... Andrew Hunter, Professor of Divinity, Edinburgh.
1793. ... Thomas Hardy, Professor of Church History, Edinburgh.
1794. ... Robert Arnot, Professor of Divinity, St Andrews.
1795. ... James Meek, minister at Cambuslang.
1796. ... William Greenfield, minister at Edinburgh.
1797. ... John Adamson, minister at St Andrews.
1798. ... William Taylor, minister at Glasgow.
1799. ... William Moodie, minister at Edinburgh.
1800. ... George H. Baird, Principal of the College of Edinburgh.
1801. ... William Ritchie, minister at Kilwinning.
1802. ... James Finlayson, minister at Edinburgh.
1803. ... Gilbert Gerard, Professor of Divinity, Aberdeen.
1804. ... John Inglis, minister at Edinburgh.
1805. ... George Hamilton, minister at Gladsmuir.
1806. ... William Taylor, junior, minister at Glasgow.
1807. ... James Sheriffs, minister at Aberdeen.
1808. ... Andrew Grant, minister at Kilmarnock.
1809. ... Francis Nicoll, minister at Mains and Strathmartin.
1810. ... Hugh Meiklejohn, minister at Abercorn.
1811. ... Alexander Rankin, minister at Glasgow.
1812. ... William Macmorine, minister at Carlaverock.
1813. ... Andrew Brown, minister at Edinburgh.
1814. ... David Ritchie, minister at Edinburgh.

* This year the retiring Moderator proposed two candidates for the chair—viz., Dr John Drysdale and Dr John Macfarlane. Dr Drysdale was elected by a great majority, against which election several members protested as illegal and unconstitutional.

1815. Dr Lewis Gordon, minister at Drainie.
1816. ... John Cook, Professor of Divinity, St Andrews.
1817. ... Gavin Gibb, minister at Glasgow.
1818. ... John Campbell, minister at Edinburgh.
1819. ... Duncan M'Farlane, minister at Drymen.
1820. ... Thomas M'Kight, minister at Edinburgh.
1821. ... Duncan Mearns, Professor of Divinity, Aberdeen.*
1822. ... David Lamont, minister at Kirkpatrick-Durham.
1823. ... Alexander Brunton, Professor of Oriental Languages, Edinburgh.
1824. ... Andrew Duncan, minister at Ratho.
1825. ... George Cook, minister at Laurencekirk.
1826. ... Thomas Taylor, minister at Tibbermore.
1827. ... Robert Haldane, Principal of St Mary's College, St Andrews.
1828. ... Stevenson M'Gill, Professor of Divinity, Glasgow.
1829. ... Patrick Forbes, minister at Old Machar.
1830. ... William Singer, minister at Kirkpatrick-Juxta.
1831. ... James Wallace, minister at Whitekirk.
1832. ... Thomas Chalmers, Professor of Divinity, Edinburgh.
1833. ... John Stirling, minister at Craigie.
1834. ... Patrick M'Farlan, minister at Greenock.
1835. ... William Aird Thomson, minister at Perth.
1836. ... Norman Macleod, minister at Glasgow.
1837. ... Mathew Gardiner, minister at Bothwell.†
1838. ... William Muir, minister at Edinburgh.
1839. ... Henry Duncan, minister at Ruthwell.
1840. ... Angus Makellar, minister at Pencaitland.‡
1841. ... Robert Gordon, minister at Edinburgh.
1842. ... David Welsh, Professor of Church History, Edinburgh.
1843. ... Duncan Macfarlan, Principal of the College of Glasgow.
1844. ... John Lee, Principal of the College of Edinburgh.
1845. ... Alexander Hill, Professor of Divinity, Glasgow.
1846. ... James Paull, minister at Tullynessle.
1847. ... John Paul, minister at Edinburgh.
1848. ... George Buist, Professor of Church History, St Andrews.
1849. ... Alexander L. Simpson, minister at Kirknewton.
1850. ... John Graham, minister at Killearn.
1851. ... John Macleod, minister at Morven.

* Dr George Cook was also proposed as a candidate this and the following year.

† Dr John Lee of Edinburgh was also put in nomination.

‡ Dr Alexander Hill of Dailly was also proposed.

1852. Dr L. W. Forbes, minister at Boharm.
1853. ... J. Barr, minister at Glasgow.
1854. ... James Grant, D.C.L., minister at Edinburgh.
1855. ... Andrew Bell, minister at Linlithgow.
1856. ... John Crombie, minister at Scone.
1857. ... James Robertson, Professor of Church History, Edinburgh.
1858. ... Matthew Leishman, minister at Govan.
1859. ... John Cook, minister at St Andrews.
1860. ... James Maitland, minister at Kells.
1861. ... Colin Smith, minister at Inverary.
1862. ... James Bisset, minister at Bourtie.
1863. ... James Craik, minister at Glasgow.

III.

Principal Clerks of the General Assembly.

1690-1694. Mr John Spalding.
1694-1695. ... Robert Park, advocate.
1695-1701. ... John Bannatyne, minister at Lanark.
1701-1703. ... David Dundas, advocate.
1703-1731. ... John Dundas, advocate.
1731-1746. ... William Grant, advocate.
1746-1778. ... George Wishart, minister at Edinburgh.
1778-1785. ... George Wishart and Dr John Drysdale.
1785-1789. Dr John Drysdale.
1789-1807. Professor Andrew Dalzell.
1807-1828. Mr Andrew Duncan, minister at Ratho.
1828-1859. Dr John Lee.
1859-1862. ... Alexander Lockhart Simpson of Kirknewton.
1862. ... John Cook of Haddington.

IV.

Sub-Clerks of the General Assembly.

1701-1738. Mr Nicol Spence.
1738-1743. ... Nicol Spence and Mr Robert M'Intosh.

1743-1753. Mr Robert M'Intosh and Mr John Baillie.
1753-1754. ... John Baillie and Mr James Edmonston.
1754-1781. ... James Edmonston.
1781-1802. Dr William Gloag.
1802-1808. ... Thomas M'Knight and Dr David Ritchie.
1808-1826. ... Thomas M'Knight.
1826-1828. ... Thomas M'Knight and Dr John Lee.
1828-1859. ... Alexander L. Simpson.
1859-1862. ... John Cook, Haddington.
1862. ... John Tulloch, Principal of St Mary's College, St Andrews.

V.

List of Procurators and Advocates in Ordinary for the Church.

1706-1731. Mr John Dundas of Philipston.
1731-1746. ... William Grant, afterwards Lord Prestongrange.
1746-1778. ... David Dalrymple, afterwards Lord Westhall.
1778-1806. ... William Robertson, afterwards Lord Robertson.
1806-1831. ... John Connell, afterwards Sir John Connell.
1831-1856. ... Robert Bell.
1856. ... Alexander Shank Cook appointed joint procurator with Mr Bell.

VI.

List of Agents for the Church.

1690-1706. Mr John Blair.
1706-1722. ... John Blair and Mr Nicol Spence, joint agents.
1722-1738. ... Nicol Spence.
1738-1743. ... Nicol Spence and Mr Robert M'Intosh, joint agents.
1743-1753. ... Robert M'Intosh and Mr John Baillie, W.S., joint agents.
1753-1754. ... John Baillie and Mr James Edmonston, joint agents.

1754-1781. Mr James Edmonston.
1781-1795. ... George Cairncross.
1795-1809. ... William Murray.
1809-1831. ... William Murray and Mr John Murray.
1831-1855. ... William Young, W.S.
1855. ... John Beatson Bell, W.S.

VII.

Standing Orders of the General Assembly of the Church of Scotland.

Act XII. of Assembly 1859.

Edinburgh, *May* 30, 1859. *Sess. ult.*

The General Assembly called for the Report of the Committee on Standing Orders, and approved of the same; and declare and enact that in future the following shall be observed as the Standing Orders for Regulating the Business of the House:—

I.

As to the Commissions of Parties elected as Members of Assembly.

1. All commissions to members of an ensuing Assembly shall be transmitted, by the parties elected, to the agent for the Church, as soon as conveniently may be after the date of election, and not later than the second Thursday in the month of May in which such Assembly is to meet; and the agent shall, on a day not later than three days previous to the first day on which the Assembly meets, submit all commissions so transmitted to him, to the procurator and clerks of the Assembly, who, along with the agent, shall constitute a standing committee,—of which the agent shall be convener,—for examination of commissions transmitted to the agent as aforesaid; and the said committee shall, by their convener, report to the Assembly, at its first diet, how far the said commissions appear to be regular and according to law and practice, and whether any of the same be, in these respects, defective.

2. Along with commissions in favour of ruling elders, there shall be transmitted to the agent the certificate required by the Act of Assembly 1839, cap. 12, anent the qualification of representative elders.

3. All commissions reported by the agent's committee to be defective, or which, on the report of the said committee, shall be objected to by any party having interest, or by any member of Assembly, shall be remitted by the Assembly to a committee of nine of its members, of whom three shall be a quorum; and the committee of Assembly shall report upon the said commissions to the diet of Assembly held next after the date of the appointment of the said committee.

4. It shall be competent to lodge with the agent for the Church commissions which have not been previously transmitted to him in terms of section 1, *supra*, at any period during the sitting of the Assembly; and such commissions shall be submitted by the agent to the Assembly at their meeting on the day next after the day on which the commissions shall have been so lodged, and shall either be disposed of by the Assembly at once, or be remitted to their Committee on Disputed Commissions, as to the Assembly shall seem proper.

5. The Committee on Disputed Commissions shall, if called upon, or if it shall appear to the committee necessary or expedient so to do, hear the party whose commission is objected to, by himself or by his counsel or agent, in support of his commission; and also any party or parties who may object to such commission.

II.

As to Constituting the Assembly, and the Appointment of, and Procedure before, the Committees for Despatch of Business.

6. The commissioners elected to serve in the Assembly shall convene in the Assembly Hall on the day fixed for the meeting of Assembly, at the usual hour, and after Sermon, according to the present practice,—when, after prayer by the moderator of the last preceding General Assembly, the names of all parties whose commissions have been lodged with the agent previous to the meeting of Assembly shall be read by him to the House.

7. The election of a moderator shall then be made.

8. Her Majesty's commission to the Lord High Commissioner shall then be read and recorded.

9. Her Majesty's letter to the Assembly shall then be read, and a committee shall be appointed to frame an address in answer thereto.

10. The report of the agent's committee upon commissions transmitted to or otherwise lodged with the agent shall then be

called for and read, and shall be disposed of in manner prescribed in section 3, *supra*.

11. The following committees shall then be nominated,—viz., Committee on Disputed Commissions; Committee on Overtures; Committee on Bills; Committee for Arranging the Order of Business; Committee for Classing Returns to Overtures; Committee for Revising the Record of the Commission.

12. When there is a vacancy in any of the offices of the ordinary office-bearers of the Assembly, such steps as to the Assembly may appear proper shall then be taken for supplying the vacancy.

13. The committees appointed in terms of section 11, *supra*, shall meet respectively at the times and places specified in the minute of their appointment; and the Committees on Bills and Overtures shall respectively make a report to the Assembly, at its diet next following the diet when the said committees were appointed, and at such times thereafter as the state of the business brought before them may render expedient, or as the Assembly shall direct.

14. The Committee for Arranging the Business of the Assembly shall report to the Assembly from time to time as the state of the business may render expedient; and the Committee for Revising the Record of the Commission shall report to the Assembly before its close, and as soon as may be after the appointment of the said committee.

15. Overtures from synods or presbyteries shall be presented to the Committee on Overtures by the commissioners from the presbytery, or by the commissioners from some presbytery within the bounds of the synod promoting the overture; and no overture from a synod or presbytery shall be transmitted to the Assembly by the Committee on Overtures, if not so presented to them.

16. Overtures by individual members of the Assembly shall be presented to the Committee on Overtures by the parties promoting such overtures; and no such overture shall be transmitted to the Assembly by the Committee on Overtures unless it shall be so presented to the committee.

17. Applications to the Committee on Bills shall be made by petition, subscribed by a party having an interest in the cause or other matter referred to in the said petition, or by his counsel or duly authorised agent; and in the said petition there shall be specified the cause or other matter sought to be transmitted to the Assembly, and all documents connected therewith also sought to be transmitted.

18. Along with applications for transmission to the Assembly,

of appeals, or of dissents and complaints against the judgments of inferior courts, there shall be produced to the committee an extract of the judgment complained of, and an extract or certified copy of the relative reasons of appeal, or of dissent and complaint, with all documents or copies certified by the clerk of the court whose judgment is appealed against to be correct copies of all documents forming part of the record in the inferior court.

19. In all causes brought up to the Assembly by appeal or otherwise, the record shall be held to consist of the entire minutes of the inferior courts in relation to the cause, and of the evidence, whether parole or documentary, adduced in the same, whether engrossed in the minutes or lodged in the inferior court and kept *in retentis;* and no documents not forming part of the record shall be transmitted by the Committee on Bills to the Assembly, in connection with any cause, with the exception of reasons of appeal, or of dissent and complaint, which shall, in all cases where tendered, be transmitted along with the record.

20. When there shall be more than one appeal in the same cause, or more than one dissent and complaint, or one or more appeals, as well as one or more dissents and complaints, it shall not be necessary to produce, along with the petition to the committee in each appeal, or dissent and complaint, the record in the cause, or a certified copy of the same; but it shall be sufficient to refer to the record, as produced along with the petition relative to any other appeal or dissent and complaint; provided always, that along with every petition to transmit an appeal, or dissent and complaint, there shall be produced an extract of the judgment complained of.

21. Where any cause shall be referred by an inferior court to the General Assembly, the clerk of such inferior court shall, as soon as may be after the reference has been made, transmit to the agent for the Church the record in such cause, or a duly certified extract or copy of the same; and along with every application to the committee to transmit such reference to the Assembly, there shall be produced an extract of the minute of the inferior court containing the reference, and the petition shall refer to the record, or to the extract of the same, as having been transmitted to, and as being in the hands of, the agent for the Church.

22. That in the cases specified in the last preceding section, the agent for the Church shall produce to the committee the record in any cause transmitted to him as aforesaid, and referred to in any application to the committee; and the committee, if they shall agree to transmit the reference to the Assembly, shall transmit, along therewith, the record in the cause.

23. That along with all applications to the committee to transmit to the Assembly original petitions, or other applications to the Assembly in the first instance, there shall be produced to the committee a written copy of such petition or other application, subscribed by the party promoting the same, or by his counsel or agent, and all documents referred to in the said petition, or upon which the petitioner intends to found in support of his application, and which are not already before the House.

III.

Regulations as to Printing.

24. In causes brought before the Assembly by appeal, involving the merits of the cause, the appellants shall print, in the form at present in use, and shall lodge with the agent for the Church, not less than 450 copies of the judgment or deliverance complained of, and relative record, not later than the Monday preceding the day fixed for the meeting of the Assembly; and no such cause shall be entertained by the Assembly, where it shall appear, when the cause is called for discussion, that such prints have not, when the cause is so called, been lodged with the agent for the Church.

25. In causes brought before the Assembly by dissent and complaint, involving the merits of the cause, it shall be optional to the complainers either to comply with the regulations as to printing prescribed by the last preceding section in the case of appeals, or to lodge with the agent for the Church, at the time and in the manner provided with regard to prints in appeals, a complete written copy of the judgment complained of, and relative record.

26. In appeals, or dissents and complaints, upon incidental points not involving the merits of the cause, the appellant or complainer shall print, or furnish written copies, and shall lodge with the agent for the Church, in manner above provided with regard to appeals and dissents and complaints upon the merits, and under a similar sanction, the judgment complained of, and such parts of the relative record as may have a bearing upon the said judgment; provided always, that in the case of such appeals and complaints upon incidental matters, the appellant or complainer shall serve upon the respondent, or his known agent, on the same day on which he shall lodge his print or written copy of the proceedings with the agent for the Church, a similar print or written copy of such proceedings; and it shall be competent

for the respondents, at any time before the hearing of the cause, to print, or furnish a written copy, as the case may be, of such additional portions of the proceedings as they may think fit. In all cases where prints are lodged with the agent for the Church, by either of the parties in a cause, in terms of these regulations, the agent shall be entitled, on application made to him for that purpose, to supply six copies of such prints to the opposite party or parties in the cause, or to his or their duly authorised agents.

27. When an inferior court shall refer a cause to the Assembly, the parties to the said cause shall, at their joint expense, print and lodge with the agent for the Church the minute containing the reference and relative record, at the same time as is provided with regard to the print in the case of appeals; under certification that if any of the parties shall refuse to contribute his share of the expense of such print, before the time when the cause is called for discussion, he shall be considered as having deserted the cause, and shall not be entitled to be heard.

28. Parties promoting original petitions, or other applications to the Assembly in the first instance, shall print and lodge with the agent for the Church, on or before the Monday preceding the day on which the Assembly meets, not less than 450 copies of such petition or other application, and of all documents transmitted along therewith to the Assembly by the Committee on Bills; provided always, that in causes arising out of trials for licence or ordination, or out of matters relating to Church ordinances, or any matter not involving the interests of private parties, brought before the Assembly by reference, or by petition presented to the Assembly by any minister or member of a Church court in the discharge of his public duty as such, it shall be optional to the court making the reference, or to the party or parties insisting in such cause, either to print and lodge with the agent printed copies of the proceedings in the same, in manner already provided with regard to appeals, or to lodge with the agent a written copy of the said proceedings, in manner provided with regard to dissents and complaints.

29. The parties promoting any overtures to the General Assembly shall print and lodge with the agent for the Church, on or before the Monday of the week in which the Assembly meets, not less than 450 copies of such overture; provided always, that in the case of any overtures relating to matters emerging after the meeting of the Assembly, such overtures shall be printed and lodged with the agent at least two days before discussion of the same by the Assembly.

30. The clerk of the Assembly shall preserve two copies of every print lodged with the agent for the Church in manner above provided; one copy of which print, having a copy of the judgment of the Assembly in the cause to which it relates prefixed or annexed thereto, shall be bound up and kept in the records, and the other copy, also having the judgment written thereupon, shall be lodged in the library.

IV.

ORDER OF PLEADING IN CAUSES.

31. In causes brought before the Assembly by appeal, or by dissent and complaint, where there is only one appellant or complainer, or one set of appellants or complainers, concurring in the same reasons of appeal, or of dissent and complaint, and one respondent, or one set of respondents, concurring in the same answers to the reasons of appeal, or of dissent and complaint, the case for the appellant, or complainer, shall be stated by himself or by his counsel, who at the same time shall submit such argument upon the case as he shall think fit; and the party or counsel so stating the appeal or complaint shall be followed by the respondent or his counsel; and at the close of the answer to the opening statement for the appellant, he shall be entitled to be again heard, and the respondent shall also be entitled to be heard in answer to the second speech for the appellant or complainer; and if, in his final answer, the respondent or his counsel shall state any fact, or submit any argument not adverted to in his answer to the opening statement for the appellant, the appellant or complainer shall be entitled to a reply upon the new matter introduced in the final answer for the respondent; but with the exception of this right of reply so limited, in no case shall more than two speeches be allowed to each party at the bar.

32. In such causes as those referred to in the last preceding article, and in which there are more than one appellant or set of appellants, and respondents, insisting on the appeal, or dissent and complaint, or supporting the judgment complained of, on different grounds, and in separate reasons or answers, each appellant, or complainer, shall be entitled to open and state his separate case, and each respondent shall be entitled to make his separate answer, and the debate shall be closed with a reply for the several appellants; provided always, that it shall be competent to the parties, with consent of the House, to make any arrangement for

conducting the debate other than that herein prescribed, which shall have the effect of limiting, farther than is herein done, the number of speeches to be made from the bar.

33. In causes brought before the Assembly by reference from an inferior court, the reference shall be stated to the House by one of the commissioners of the presbytery, or by a commissioner from a presbytery within the bounds of the synod making the reference, in his place as a member of the House, or by some member of such presbytery or synod specially appointed for that purpose; and the Assembly shall thereafter hear the parties in the cause referred, in such order as the shape of the case may seem to require, keeping in view the regulations in the last two preceding articles.

34. It shall be competent for any member of an inferior court whose judgment is brought under review of the Assembly, to appear at the bar in support of the judgment; but where commissioners have been specially appointed by the inferior courts to support their judgment, the Assembly shall not hear any member of such court, other than one of the members so appointed, unless any member not so appointed, and who wishes to be heard, can show a separate and peculiar interest to support the judgment; and it shall, in all such cases, be competent to the Assembly to limit the number of members of an inferior court who shall be heard in support of the judgment under review.

35. Where a judgment of a synod, affirming a judgment of a presbytery, is brought under review of the Assembly, the members of presbytery shall have no *status* as parties at the bar, except in the character of members of the synod; but where a reversal by a synod, of a judgment of a presbytery, is under review, the presbytery may appear and be heard at the bar of the Assembly, as appellants against the judgment, provided always that they comply with the regulations herein contained, regarding causes brought under review of the Assembly by appeal.

36. Where a synod reverses a judgment of a presbytery, on a dissent and complaint, and the presbytery appeal against the reversal, the complainers in the dissent and complaint to the synod may appear, and be heard at the bar of the Assembly, as respondents to the appeal for the presbytery.

37. In causes brought before the Assembly by petition, or other application to the Assembly in the first instance, the party promoting the said application shall be entitled to be heard in support of the same; and the Assembly, if required so to do, shall also hear an answer from any party upon whom they may have

directed such application to be served, or whom they shall consider to be a proper respondent; and the debate at the bar shall be closed with a reply from the party promoting the application.

V.

ORDER OF DEBATE IN THE HOUSE, AND AS TO PUTTING THE QUESTION AND TAKING THE VOTE.

38. It shall be competent to any member of Assembly to make such motion as he shall think fit, upon any matter regularly brought under the consideration of the Assembly; and any member so moving shall state the terms of his motion in writing, to be laid upon the table of the House. It shall not be competent for any member to withdraw a motion which he has once made, or so to vary the terms of his motion as to render the same in substance another motion, without the leave of the Assembly.

39. When a motion so made is seconded, it shall be competent for any member to move an amendment upon the same, of which he shall also state the terms in writing; and when the motion and amendment have been duly made, seconded, and laid upon the table, it shall be competent for any member to be heard in support of one or other of the propositions before the House; and the debate shall be closed with a reply, if he think fit to claim a reply, from the mover of the motion.

40. When there is only one amendment to the motion proposed to the House, the vote shall be taken at the close of the debate, upon the motion and amendment.

41. Where there is more than one amendment, the vote shall be first taken upon the question, which of the amendments shall be put against the motion; and this question shall be decided by one or more votes, according as there are two or more amendments submitted to the House.

42. All motions after the first shall be dealt with as amendments on the first motion, to the effect of being disposed of in manner above provided in article 41.

43. It shall be competent to any member of the House present at the vote to enter upon the minutes a dissent from the judgment or resolution of the House, immediately after the vote; and to lodge thereafter his reasons of dissent, to which any member present at the vote may adhere, either when such dissent is taken, or at the next diet of the Assembly thereafter. But it shall not be

competent to enter a dissent at any diet after that at which the resolution dissented from was passed.

VI.

As to Miscellaneous Business.

44. All applications for constitutions for new churches, and the relative documents, shall, along with the feudal titles of the churches and grounds, be transmitted, one month before the meeting of each Assembly, to the Home Mission Committee, or such other committee as the Assembly may have specially appointed for receiving the same, along with extracts of the approval of the proposed constitutions by the presbyteries of the respective bounds, or of their deliverances upon the proposals; and such committee shall revise the proposed constitutions and examine the titles, and report to the Assembly their opinion as to any alterations that should be made on the proposed constitutions, the said committee giving to all parties who may have appeared before the respective presbyteries, eight days' notice of the day fixed for the consideration of their case, in order that they may attend for their interest,—certifying all parties applying for constitutions for new churches, that if they fail so to transmit for revisal and examination the documents aforesaid, their applications will not be entertained by the Assembly: Provided always, that where the said documents have been transmitted, they must also be thereafter regularly passed to the Assembly through the Committee of Bills, in common form; and all parties who have made compearance in the presbyteries shall be entitled, as at present, to be heard before the Assembly to which the applications are so passed, or any committee to be appointed by them, on their objections to the constitutions for the proposed churches, or to the report of the Home Mission, or other committee specially appointed as aforesaid.

45. Manuscript reports to the Assembly shall be written upon foolscap paper, and so as to admit of being bound up into volumes, and it shall not then be necessary to engross them in the Record.

46. Where several overtures have been transmitted to presbyteries by the Assembly, the return by the presbytery to each overture shall be written upon a separate sheet of foolscap paper.

47. The Standing Orders shall be read over by one of the clerks on the first day of the meeting of every Assembly, if any member shall require that they shall be so read; and any motion for repeal or amendment of any of the Orders shall be brought before

the Assembly in like manner with overtures in regard to other matters; provided always, that it shall be competent to the Assembly, on the motion of any member to that effect, and on cause shown, summarily to dispense with the observance of the Standing Orders, or of any of them, in any particular case.

VII.

Closing of the Assembly.

48. When the business set down for the last Monday of the sitting of the Assembly shall have been disposed of, the Assembly shall be closed by addresses from the Moderator to the Assembly and to his Grace the Commissioner, and by the Commissioner to the Assembly; and with devotional exercises, according to the practice of the Assembly.

VIII.

An Act to remove Doubts respecting the Admission of Ministers to Benefices in that Part of the United Kingdom called Scotland.—(6 & 7 *Vict., cap.* 61.—*17th August* 1843.)

Whereas certain Acts of the Parliament of Scotland, and of the United Kingdom of Great Britain, have declared that the right of collation in regard to the settlement of ministers in the parishes to which they may be presented, belongs to the Church established by law in that part of the United Kingdom called Scotland: And whereas provision has been made by these Statutes for securing to the Church the exclusive right of examining and admitting any person who may be presented to a benefice having cure by the patron of such benefice; and in particular by an Act passed in the Parliament of Scotland in the year one thousand five hundred and sixty-seven, intituled "Admission of Ministers;" of *Laick Patronages*, it is statute and ordained, that the examination and admission of ministers within this realm be only in the power of the Kirk now openlie and publicly professed within the samin, the presentation of laick patronage alwaies reserved to the just and auncient patrones; and by an Act passed in the Parliament of

Scotland in the year one thousand five hundred and ninety-two, intituled "Ratification of the Liberty of the trew Kirk," the government of the Church by presbyteries, synods, and general assemblies was ratified and established, and it was ordained that all presentations to benefices be direct to the particular presbyteries in all time cumming, with full power to give collation thereupon, and to put ordour to all maters and causes ecclesiastical within their boundes according to the discipline of the Kirk; providing the foresaids presbyteries be bound and astricted to receive and admit whatsumever qualified minister presented be His Majesty or laick patrones; and by an Act of the Parliament of Great Britain passed in the tenth year of the reign of Her Majesty Queen Anne, intituled "An Act to restore the Patrones to their ancient Rights of presenting Ministers to the Churches vacant in that Part of Great Britain called Scotland," the right of the Church to receive and admit persons presented to benefices was again recognised and secured; and by an Act of the Parliament of Great Britain passed in the fifth year of the reign of His Majesty King George the First, intituled "An Act for making more effectual the Laws appointing the Oaths for Security of the Government to be taken by Ministers and Preachers in Churches in Scotland, providing that certain Oaths should be taken by Ministers and Preachers of the Church of Scotland, and for preventing Delays in the supplying or filling up of vacant Churches in Scotland," it is also declared and enacted that nothing herein contained shall prejudice or diminish the rights of the Church, as the same now stands by law established, as to the trying of the qualities of any person presented to any church or benefice: And whereas it is expedient to remove any doubt which may exist as to the powers and jurisdiction of the Church as by law established in Scotland in the matter of collation, and as to the right of the Church to decide that no person be settled in any parish or benefice having cure against whom or whose settlement in such parish or benefice there exists any just cause of exception: May it therefore please your Majesty that it may be declared and enacted, and be it declared and enacted by the Queen's most Excellent Majesty, by and with the advice and consent of the Lords Spiritual and Temporal, and Commons, in this present Parliament assembled, and by the authority of the same, That when a presentation to any benefice within that part of the United Kingdom called Scotland by the undoubted patron has been laid before the presbytery of the bounds, it shall and may be lawful for the presbytery, as part and as the commencement of the proceedings in the examination and admission of the person so presented for the cure of that parish, and of the trial of his gifts and qualities, to appoint him. to preach in the church of the said parish at such times as the presbytery may direct, or as may be directed by any regulations of the General Assembly to that effect; and after the presentee shall have preached in the parish church according to the directions of the presbytery, the presbytery, or a committee of their number, shall meet, after due notice, at the said church, and shall intimate that if any one or more parishioners being members of the congregation have any objection to the individual so presented, in respect to his ministerial gifts and qualities, either in general or with reference to that particular parish, or any reason to state against his settlement in that parish, and which objections or reasons do not infer matter of charge against the presentee to be prosecuted and followed out according to the forms and discipline of the Church, the presbytery are ready, either then or at their next meeting, to receive the same in writing, or to write down the same in their minutes in the form and manner which such parishioners may desire.

II. And be it enacted, That the objections or reasons aforesaid shall be fully considered and disposed of by the presbytery by whom they are to be cognosced and determined on judicially, or shall be referred by the presbytery to the superior judicatory of the Church for decision, as the presbytery may see cause, the presentee and all parties having interest being heard in either case on the same; and the presbytery or other judicatory of the Church to whom the said objections or reasons shall be stated or referred as aforesaid shall, in cognoscing and determining on the same judicially, have regard only to such objections and reasons so stated as are personal to the presentee in regard to his ministerial gifts and qualities, either in general or with respect to that particular parish, but shall be entitled to have regard to the whole circumstances and condition of the parish, to the spiritual welfare and edification of the people, and to the character and number of the persons by whom the said objections or reasons shall be preferred; and if the presbytery or other judicatory of the Church shall come to the conclusion, as their judgment on the whole matter, that the said objections or reasons, or any of them, are well founded, and that in respect thereof the individual presented is not a qualified and suitable person for the functions of the ministry in that particular parish, and ought not to be settled in the same, they shall pronounce a deliverance to that effect, and shall set forth and specify in such deliverance the special ground or grounds on which it is founded, and in respect of which they find that the presentee is not qualified for that charge, in which event they shall intimate their deliverance respecting the presentee to the patron, who shall thereupon have power to issue another presentation within the period of six calendar months after the date of such deliverance if no appeal shall be taken to a superior judicatory of the Church, or in the event of an appeal being taken to a superior judicatory of the Church, then within six months after the date of the judgment of the superior judicatory of the Church affirming the deliverance of the inferior judicatory of the Church or dismissing the appeal.

III. And be it enacted, That if the presbytery or other judicatory of the Church, after considering all the objections aforesaid to the presentee, and all the reasons stated against his settlement in that particular parish, shall be satisfied, in the discharge of their functions and in the exercise of their authority and duty as ministers of the gospel and as office-bearers in the Church, that no good objections against the individual or no good reason against his settlement has been stated as aforesaid, or that the objections and reasons stated are not truly founded in any objection personal to the presentee in regard to his ministerial gifts and qualities, either in general or with reference to that particular parish, or arise from causeless prejudices, the said presbytery or other judicatory of the Church shall repel the same, and, subject to the right of appeal as herein-after provided, shall complete the further trials and examination of the presentee, and, if found by them to be qualified for the ministry in that parish, shall admit and receive him into the benefice as by law provided.

IV. And be it enacted, That it shall not be lawful for any presbytery or other judicatory of the Church to reject any presentee upon the ground of any mere dissent or dislike expressed by any part of the congregation of the parish to which he is presented, and which dissent or dislike shall not be founded upon objections or reasons to be fully cognosced, judged of, and determined in the manner aforesaid by the said presbytery or other judicatory of the Church.

V. And be it enacted, That it shall be in the power of the presentee, patron, or objectors to appeal from any deliverance pronounced as aforesaid by the said presbytery acting within its competency as a judicatory of the Church, which appeal shall lie exclusively to the superior judicatories of the Church according to the forms and government of the Church of Scotland as by law established.

VI. And whereas by an Act of the General Assembly of the Church of Scotland, of date twenty-ninth May One thousand eight hundred and thirty-five, it was made an instruction to presbyteries that if at the moderating in a call to a vacant parish the major part of the male heads of families, members of the vacant congregation and in full communion with the Church, shall disapprove of the person in whose favour the call is proposed to be moderated in, such disapproval shall be deemed sufficient ground for the presbytery rejecting such person, and that he shall be rejected accordingly, and certain regulations were passed for carrying the said instructions into effect: And whereas it has been found by final judgment of the Court of Session, affirmed by the House of Lords, that a presbytery, acting in pursuance of said Act of Assembly and regulations, refusing to take trial of the qualifications of a presentee, and rejecting him on the sole ground that a majority of the male heads of families communicants in the said parish have dissented, without any reasons assigned, from his admission as minister, acted illegally and in violation of their duty, and contrary to the provisions of certain statutes of the realm, and particularly the statute of the tenth year of Queen Anne, chapter twelve, intituled "An Act to restore Patrons to their ancient Rights of presenting Ministers to the Churches vacant in that Part of Great Britain called Scotland:" And whereas in some instances a presentee has, in pursuance of the said Act of Assembly and regulations relative thereto, been rejected by a presbytery because of the dissents of male heads of families communicants, and a presentation has thereafter been issued in favour of a second or subsequent presentee, who has been settled in the same benefice, and whose settlement therein and right thereto have not been questioned in any court of law: And whereas it is expedient that such settlement in and right to the benefice should be secured and protected from future challenge on the ground of the incompetency of the rejection of the first or prior presentee; be it enacted, That it shall not be competent to challenge the settlement or right to the benefice of any such second or subsequent presentee, or to maintain any proceedings at law against the presbytery or ministers thereof, or other parties, on account of such rejection, unless such challenge or proceedings shall have been instituted by action raised in a court of law before the first day of May last.

THE END.

CPSIA information can be obtained
at www.ICGtesting.com
Printed in the USA
LVHW100440110522
718424LV00003B/181

9 783375 000899